Captain Iron Mustache

A Novel

William Stuart Gould, M.D.

WMG LTD.
New York

WMG
WMG Ltd. Publishers
288 Lexington Avenue
Suite 6-F
New York, New York
10016
wmg.ltd.publishing@gmail.com

For information about WMG Ltd.'s Speakers Bureau or discounts for bulk purchases, please email: wmg.ltd.publishing@gmail.com

ISBN: 978-0-09912237-1-8 (e-book)
ISBN: 9780991223756 (pbk)
ISBN: 0991223756

ALSO BY BILL GOULD

At Yonah Mountain
In Black Granite
C.O.L.A.
A Heart Wind from the Desert
Raphael's Blanket
Lincoln Friday

To the villagers of Viet Nam:

Finally a bright sun to light your future

Prologue

The Village of My Co
Tien Giang Province
Forty Miles West of Saigon
Democratic Republic of Viet Nam
July, 2012

"ASK THEM WHERE I can find Vu Van Khai. He's the tall one standing next to me in this picture. Tell them it's really important. We don't have much time."

The interpreter turned to the gathering crowd of neatly-clad, elderly Vietnamese. He repeated Weathersby's question. A handsome, diminutive, middle-aged man in pressed Western pants and button-down-shirt stepped forward confidently. Taking the picture with both hands and fetching bifocals from his breast pocket, he studied the image in the peeling, sepia Polaroid. Dozens of younger villagers gathered to peruse the photo over the man's shoulder, though most of them took a quick look then drifted toward the Toyota Century, interested more in the limousine's wide-screen GPS and television than in the foreigner.

The small man spoke briefly, and the interpreter turned back to the graying visitor. "He want to know who you are. I tell him you American. He say..." The little man interrupted, his lips tightening as he wagged an index finger in the Caucasian stranger's face. He tapped the picture hard with the nail of his index finger. *"Ông có biết Đại Úy Rào Weh Da By, không?"*

The interpreter translated perfunctorily. "He want to ask if you know Captain Wehdabee in America."

The American stepped closer, pointed to his own chest, and choked in Vietnamese, "*Tôi là Weathersby*," then in English, "I *am* Captain Weathersby."

The villager turned to the growing crowd. "*Trời đất ơi, Trời đất ơi! Đại Úy Rào.*"

The interpreter laughed nervously. "He say, 'Oh, my God. Oh, my God!' Then he say you 'Captain Iron Mustache, moustache like barb wire.'"

The little man's eyes grew as large as the jackfruit hanging in the hamlet's lush gardens. He dropped the photo onto the reddened earth and yanked up a leg of his trousers. Facing Weathersby, he pointed down to a mangled ankle. He blurted in Vietnamese, "Don't you remember me? I am Huong, *Em* Huong. The night I was in the explosion. You took me to the hospital. Oh, my God, I was scared. Don't you remember? You drove the whole night to Bien Hoa. My grandfather, *Ông* Long, you remember, with the wispy beard and the white turban? He's dead now. I was twelve. You saved my life. Don't you remember?"

"Yes," Weathersby choked, his eyes reddening, "of course I remember. Yes, I remember."

Book I

Chapter 1

The South China Sea
Approaching the Coast of South Viet Nam
4 July 1968

FLYING TIGERS AIRLINE'S International Flight 1949 entered a descent so steep, the negative Gs startled First Lieutenant J.W. Weathersby out of an uneasy sleep. His eyes shot to the window of the Boeing 707 expecting black smoke and glowing shrapnel from a Viet Cong surface to air missile, and then the fatal engine fire that would carry him to his death before he had even landed in the war. But outside the plunging aircraft, there was only a bone-white beach edging Vung Tao. To the north and south of that coastal city stretched an endless ribbon of Viet Nam's azure coast. He peered out at the canted horizon, appreciating for the first time in his life the curvature of the Earth, a remarkable image, though one that did nothing to buffer the acid spurting up into his mouth.

The plane leveled for a moment as the pilot deployed spoilers, bleeding off airspeed so rapidly, the hundred-some passengers were thrown forward as if the driver of a great bus had slammed on the brakes. The nose dropped again and the airliner plunged into a very fast, very long, base leg toward Saigon, screaming across tropical beaches bristling with the red, white, and blue umbrellas of American armchair commandos, the fortunate sons who had been assigned to the resorts along the South China Sea. J.W. imagined the parasols a carefully choreographed patriotic salute to the virgins joining the quarrel.

The jet banked hard right onto final approach, skimming over the brown-water web of the Mekong Delta, dropping through turbulent, murky monsoon cloud layers, eventually emerging below the overcast. It was Weathersby's first clear image of the Eastern world. He became curiously comfortable when the flight engineer opened the valves, sucking aboard the steaming air of Cochin China, scents and odors that culled misted memories of secret trips as a teenager to New York's harsh Chinatown, days truant, a loner sneaking off, drawn by an inexplicable desire to touch the mystic. It was as though, his mother often said, J.W. had trod the Earth a Chinese peasant in a previous life.

He thought back to his last months of college, proclaiming to anyone who would listen that he was ready to die for his country as a soldier in Asia. He knew, though, in his heart, it was more a frantic craving to break from the despondency, failure, and loneliness of his early life that had drawn him into volunteering for combat duty in Viet Nam. Just minutes from war, though, the bravado drifted as far from his heart as he was from the Bronx.

As the Asian landscape grew clearer, his mind darkened, struggling between the pride and excitement of the crusade, and the dread of mortal combat. The two notions vied for thousands of feet during the descent, but with the growl of deploying landing gear, the knot of apprehension, and then of abject dread, clutched bitterly at his gut. It won the battle. Pretending he was coughing, bits of a long forgotten boxed meal over Japan popped into the airsick bag he quickly hid in his lap. It was the first time he had castigated himself for having sent his papers—over and over—to the Pentagon requesting duty in Viet Nam.

What in the lord's name had lured him to take a turn engaging the Communist menace? What menace? He thought he had known what the word meant when the returning soldiers spoke of battle with the godless enemy, but now he thought much harder, wondering if some of his fraternity brothers hadn't been right, that maybe *we* were the menace. The brotherhood had become so bitterly split, at times they brawled in the hallways during study hours, one side screaming madly about genocide, the other shrieking patriotism and courage. J.W. had appointed himself engineer of his faction's train, and as the months flew by toward graduation and active duty, he could not muster the will to jump from it.

The aircraft slowed as it settled on final approach over the alleys and red-mud back roads just south of Saigon. Suddenly, the need to be at the epicenter of history seeped from his heart, and soon also did the urgency to right the political wrongs foisted upon a primitive people so far from his universe. The craving to unearth a new life also faded with each foot the plane dropped closer to the war until all there was left of his valiant dreams was a powerful contraction deep inside him. He fought to hold his bowels.

They were low enough for J.W. to make out scantily-clothed figures milling about, though it wasn't until the plane neared touchdown that he realized the tiny forms were children playing, oblivious to the jet that thundered over their lives. J.W. wanted to ask them how they could be so seemingly indifferent to the fact that they were in Viet Nam. Weren't they frightened to the point that they should be hiding in bunkers all day and all night? How could anyone in his right mind just stand around in a war zone?

With the plane just a thousand feet above the ground, it became evident that these children were living happily, not hidden in protective caves, but outside in the blaring sunshine, running, jumping, and kicking madly at soccer balls. As more and more kids came into view, he was able to make out whole teams taking a break from their matches to wave up at the plane. He could even see some of them smiling at the roaring monster just feet above their heads. Reflecting upon that simple greeting, J.W.'s balled fists relaxed a bit, and for a moment, the joy of the children suppressed his fear. He reasoned that if children were fooling around, there must be pockets of safety. And maybe he would find one of those zones and plant himself there for 365 days. Or maybe he'd dig a hole from which he would not peek for one minute of the year he had so foolishly volunteered away.

But when J.W. gazed back into the aircraft cabin, he could not help but focus on the faces of his fellow travelers, soldiers who already wore combat patches on their shoulders and silver stars on their chests, men returning for second and third tours. As the plane settled closer to touchdown, their jaws clenched more tightly, and J.W. found himself again doubting he would survive his twenty-third year, or that the children romping in the sun would ever see fifteen.

As the 707 taxied to the reception quonset, a harsh, woman's voice issued an order over the intercom for all window shades to be lowered immediately, a mandate J.W. followed until the engines were shut down at the gate. By then, he could not help himself, and lifted his shade a few inches, expecting to see secret aircraft rolling for takeoff, imagining space age supersonic bombers loaded with classified ordinance preparing to ply the Asian skies, tasked to work hand in glove with the ground troops, the grunts, the air and surface arms fighting as teams, dedicated Americans jointly destroying the archaic, though treacherous, army of peasants who refused to acknowledge divine law. J.W. was privy, though, only to the face of a coolie one inch outside the window, a toothless, grinning man atop a ladder, one of two dozen hand-washing the fuselage.

A stewardess touched J.W.'s shoulder and asked quietly, "Would you mind exiting through the rear hatch, Lieutenant? And drop your shade down to keep the cabin cool for the troops going home, if you would." She waited until he neared the door then called out, "Good luck, soldier."

As J.W. started onto the wind-whipped air stairs, he heard her beckon the beaten, sweating men on the serpentine queue at the forward hatch. "Come aboard, gentlemen. Welcome to the Freedom Bird. Thank God you made it."

J.W. ducked back into the plane to witness what he imagined would be one of life's grandest celebrations, but the spent GIs just grunted past her and collapsed into the first empty seats.

J.W.'s companions stood outside the plane in the blistering sun for nearly an hour. Eventually, half-a-dozen olive drab school buses rolled up and the men were herded aboard for the parade from the airport to the 92nd Replacement Battalion. The six vehicles joined a convoy of military police sedans that had rolled perfunctorily to positions at the front and rear of the fleet. The cavalcade crept out of the airport along the semi-paved, mud-soaked, litter-strewn streets of Bien Hoa.

J.W. pondered how the MPs would react if the convoy was attacked. Would they bother to open the windows of their air-conditioned sedans and allow the ferocious heat to wilt their pressed, spit-shined uniforms? Would they fight back with their .45 pistols, or would they just drive off a safe distance, wait out the battle, and return to do the paperwork when the coast was clear?

As the file bumped into the center of Bien Hoa City, J.W. became riveted by the goings-on in the meager Saigon suburb. Peering through the bus's turkey-wire-covered, glassless windows, a defense against the odd grenade being tossed aboard, J.W. cringed as brigades of scooters and divisions of bicycles crisscrossed in front of them, the GI at the wheel of the bus slamming on brakes then gunning the engine when a tiny hole broke in the iron curtain of ramshackle jalopies.

"Holy shit, it's just like Chinatown," he whispered to himself.

In country for less than an hour, and not yet having been wounded, his shoulders relaxed until the bus nosedived into a pothole larger than the aircraft that had carried them there. His hands came up to his face protectively, and a voice sniggered from behind, "Hit the deck—incoming!"

J.W. dropped his arms, pretending to have been wiping his face of the hour's sweat and grime. As they climbed out of the pit, he considered the local architecture, rickety semi-structures fashioned from bits of rotted wood, the tonier homes roofed with rusted, corrugated steel sheets left over from the reign of the French decades before. Back up to street level, he regarded the masses of citizens, every single soul cloaked in threadbare rags. It was *not* Chinatown.

Stopped at the city's only red light, he spied an ancient woman hunkered with a perfectly balanced carrying pole on her shoulder. A nude baby sat in the front basket, a pile of dirty laundry in the rear. The old lady smiled at him, flashing teeth as black as coal.

From behind J.W., a GI mumbled, "Man, that's the rottenest mouth I ever seen."

Another answered, "No, man, blackened teeth is a sign of beauty. They use some kinda mineral or somethin' to get the teeth black and shiny. Takes a few days to get it just right. I read about it."

A third GI could not help himself. "What are you, some kinda fuckin' professor? She needs to brush her teeth—fuckin' period."

J.W. waved at the meager soul squatting at the corner. The ancient lady took the child's hand and moved it in a flutter toward J.W., who now waved with both arms until a voice from behind sneered, "Pinko Lieutenant."

J.W. waited several moments then surreptitiously turned. It was a soldier with silver wings, just like his, albeit tarnished and hanging on his travel uniform by just a thread. More striking than the wings, though, was the pilot's silk Air Medal, stripes of blue and gold crusted with more oak leaf clusters than Weathersby had fingers and toes. J.W. reckoned that decoration represented so many combat hours at the controls of a helicopter, it must be the man's third tour. He snapped his head forward.

The bus jolted to a stop immediately inside the gates of a heavily guarded, sandbagged American base. A spit-shined Military Police Branch major bounded up the stairs. "Welcome, gentlemen, to the 92nd Replacement Battalion. You will spend many days at this oasis awaiting assignment and acclimating to the tropics. Our duty here is to prepare you for your mission, but also to make sure you are treated well. After all, you are America's best. You will have access to the largest PX in Viet Nam, to the clubs, the pizza, and beer halls. These are available to both you new troops, *and* to those soldiers on their way home. A word to the wise—it's best to leave those men alone." He paused, staring into the masses. "Am I understood? And gentlemen," he added as he turned to vault off the bus, "good luck out there."

Again from the mouth of the anti-communist pilot behind J.W. came a hissed, "Many days, clubs, my ass. The guy's full of shit. Fuck me. I'll be back in a fuckin' HUEY flyin' ass and trash by zero dark fuckin' thirty tomorrow morning." As his voice trailed off, he moaned one more, "Fuck me."

After meetings to fill out assignment requests, life insurance forms, and a ten-minute class on how to treat the Vietnamese workers at the 92nd, J.W. found his way to the junior officers' barracks, where he dropped his duffel bag and rolled onto the first empty bunk. As he fell into a stupor, a casualty of seventy-some hours with two or three hours of sleep, and the past two months at Ranger School without any sleep, J.W. heard his name hailed over the PA, but imagined it a hallucination.

A private, daring not enter the officers' billet, came no farther than the quonset door. He shouted at the top of his lungs, "Lieutenant Weathersby, Lieutenant Weathersby, if you're in here, you need to come with me, sir."

J.W. was led to the command shack, where he stood at attention before another major, one whose head remained buried in a manila folder.

"At ease, Lieutenant. Welcome to the 92nd Replacement Battalion." When he looked up from J.W.'s personnel chart, he gasped, "Jesus. What the hell happened to you? What does she look like?"

"Sir?"

"You're all bashed up. Your hands and your face. You got a black eye. Or hadn't you noticed? Are you just getting here, or are you leaving?"

"Oh, the bruising you mean, sir?

"Yes, that's what I mean, Lieutenant."

"That's from Ranger School." J.W. glanced at the major's right shoulder and seeing no Ranger Tab, stiffened his position of attention and announced, "Yes, sir, graduated from Ranger School about a week ago."

"A week? That's got to be some kind of a record. What happened to your thirty-day leave? Who'd *you* make mad?" Without allowing J.W. to answer, the major went on. "Well, you're here now, and we need you. You're going to the First Infantry Division. Be an infantry platoon leader. Good leadership experience. Regular army officer like you needs to prove himself out there commanding men. It's what your career requires. Never gonna be promoted to general without showing what you got. Consider yourself a lucky guy. Chopper leaves zero-six-hundred tomorrow—Pad 36. Good luck."

The major shoved a set of typed orders at J.W. then dropped his head to search for the personnel folder of the next junior officer he would condemn. J.W. cleared his throat and snapped, "Sir, excuse me, but I'm an *armor* officer, *and* a helicopter pilot. I got my wings, sir. Worked hard for them. I'm not infantry. I don't know anything about walking, sir." J.W.'s voice rose, though it was modulated by a dithering tremor. "And I was promised by Armor Branch at the Pentagon that if I got through Ranger School, I'd get back my original assignment to the 11th Cav. That's what they told me, sir."

"Sounds like you need to cool your jets, son. You said you just got out of Ranger School. You're the elite, a commando. You look like an infantry platoon leader. All cut up and tough. Women love that shit, Lieutenant. Cavalry? Tanks and armored personnel carriers? Rocket magnets. And then you spend your whole life soaked in grease, gas, and diesel. No woman I ever met wants to make it with a troop covered in that stuff. It stinks—gets in your pores. You'll never get laid again. Anyway, all that banging around inside a tank makes you impotent. I know you don't want that, Lieutenant. I imagine you'd want your son to be an Airborne Ranger just like you. Chopper, zero-six-hundred. Enjoy the ride. May be the last one for a while. Dismissed."

"But, sir, I'm a pilot! Government spent a hundred-thousand dollars getting me trained up."

"You're not current, Lieutenant. Looks like you haven't flown in months. Viet Nam's not a flight school."

"Sir, that's because I was sent to Ranger School. This is like a nightmare, sir."

"Like I said, zero-six-hundred, Lieutenant. Outta here."

J.W. slithered back into the torpid heat, weaving to his steaming barracks. An infantry lieutenant on the next bunk looked up and laughed, "You look like you just got told you only got six months to live."

"Probably less. I got assigned to the First Infantry Division. I'm armor, not a grunt." J.W. looked at the man's lapel insignia: two polished, brass, crossed muskets. He groaned, "Hey, you're infantry. Where you goin'? A tank unit, I suppose."

"Hell, no, man. Saigon Command. Gonna be the unit hissssstorian. Takin' down and puttin' on paper the goings on in *your* war. May see you out there if I decide to soil my hands and do some field research." He laughed aloud, "And be sure to lemme know when the shootin' stops."

J.W. asked, "What was your major in college? Journalism?"

"Hell, no! Phys. Ed."

J.W. dropped back onto his rack to savor the last serenity he imagined he would enjoy for a very long time, though there was a sudden darkening of the sky. Before he could focus on the window, a thunderous staccato began hammering on the metal roof. He jumped from his rack to run for the bunker at the far end of the quonset. The unit historian shook his head and laughed, "It's just the monsoon, man. Four o'clock every day. Same-o same-o." He pulled a beer out of his duffle bag. "Hey, man, you need to slow down."

J.W. peered through the screened windows, though he saw nothing beyond the sheets of murky water cascading from the roof. The torrent, though, was over in twenty minutes, ending as abruptly as it had begun. With the return of stillness, there were new scents, soaked tropical earth and ozone generated by the spectacular lightning that had charged the rain. As he drifted into a fretful nap, he smiled to himself that the monsoon was just another memory to add to the old lady with the baby.

Before he could dream, the infantry lieutenant shook him awake. "Hey, man, you're Weathersby, aren't you? They just called your name over the PA. They want you at the command shack."

J.W. looked up and smiled, "Thank God. Morons finally figured it out." His shoulders relaxed. He stepped out of the quonset into pitch blackness, the night having burst far more swiftly than in the cypress swamps of Florida during the final days of Ranger School. Though he had spent the weeks soaking day and night in those sloughs, and though the cadres there had assured the students that they were already experiencing the tropics they'd soon see for real, it had been, apparently, but another of their deceptions.

He walked watchfully under street lamps that crawled with moths so grand, so raucous, J.W. thought at first they were bats. Near the command shack, a voice called out of the blackness, "Weathersby, over here."

J.W. froze, searching with squinted eyes beyond the glare of the lights. Despite the barrage of swooping pests, he perceived the apparition of a skinny, withered, nearly bald young soldier hiding in the shadows. J.W. left the path and approached the form. He gasped. For a moment, he refused to believe his eyes. "Hand Job! That you? What the hell are you doing here? I thought they weren't taking cretins yet. Cronkite's right. We *are* losing the war."

Though J.W. expected, from the years they'd shared as fraternity brothers, a smart rejoinder then a grand hug and bales of laughter, all Coulton grunted was, "You haven't changed, have you? No big deal, man, you will. Hope we're both alive to see it."

As J.W.'s eyes further accustomed to the darkness, he was sobered by the dearth of cheer or peace in Coulton's face, and the absence of the puerile smile he remembered from the endless, drunken fraternity parties through which they'd sloshed, arm in arm.

"Look, man," Coulton whispered, "I just got outta the field. Six months in the fuckin' First Infantry Division. The old man liked me, saved his butt once, so he sent me down here. I run the night computer printin' out assignments for new officers comin' into country.

"First Division's losin' all their platoon leaders. Lieutenants are lastin' a week. First Division, 'the Big Red One?' Make that the 'Big Dead One.' Attrition. They're gettin' their clocks cleaned out there, man. Gettin' no help from nobody in the field. No one gives a shit if the infantry dies. Mostly black guys and poor whites. Air Farce won't fly missions for us, helicopters too busy bringing out beer and mail to the senior officers in the field, and we're gettin' eaten alive. The Big Red One sucks the big one. All you got out there are your brothers. Platoon leader's always odd man out. I'm tellin' ya, it sucks."

J.W. opened his mouth to answer, though the words would not come.

Coulton took a breath through clenched teeth, looked left and right then whispered, "I changed your computer card. I'm sending you to the 33rd Mechanized Infantry Brigade. It's not good, but they got some tanks attached and you're armor, and they got helicopters, and you went to flight school. It's the best I could do and stay out of jail. I'm sorry I couldn't get you assigned to Saigon. Like I said, it's the best I could do. Just be at the helipad at zero-six-hundred tomorrow and get on the first 33rd Mech chopper you see. They got a big diamond on the front. Inside's an armored personnel carrier with white wings. Stupidest thing I ever saw. Like the track's going to heaven. Got that? Tell 'em you're new, and you need to get to Normandy Base Camp for assignment right away. That's Normandy Base Camp in My Tho. Make sure they're going to My Tho. Don't forget it. Get out of this place before the major sees you. And don't tell anyone here or in the Mech how this happened. Just don't tell anyone." Coulton looked around again surreptitiously and added, "This area's off limits to enlisted men. I gotta go. See ya, and Weathersby," he paused, "God bless."

Though J.W. called, "Thanks, man," Coulton had already crept off into the void.

⟿ ⟿

That night J.W. made his way to the officers' club and spotted two fresh-faced lieutenants. He was barely able to make out the armor insignia for the dazzle of their enormous West Point rings. They were also headed to the 33rd Mech, though *their* assignments had been carefully formulated by the career section at Armor Branch at the Pentagon. They had been chosen to man tanks, not the flimsy armored personnel carriers most of the Mech's lieutenants commanded. J.W., tight-lipped about his circuitous path to the Mech, laughed that the army was batting three for three in assignments, a world record. The two had also been ordered to present themselves at Helicopter Pad 27 no later than zero-six-hundred hours, and to take the first 33rd Mech chopper to My Tho. The three agreed to meet at 5 A.M. for breakfast at the officers' mess.

J.W., gun shy from his months in commando school, arrived at the pad early to avoid remedial push-ups. He was astonished that, though his two compatriots arrived at six-seventeen, not a soul appeared out of the darkness to torment them. They stood at the edge of the runway as the moon set and a mammoth orange sun took its place. And they stood in the direct sun until noon, when one of his new pals suggested they head back to the O-Club for a bite and a cold one.

J.W., reticent to run into the assignment major, chose to forego lunch and remain out in the glare. It was not, though, until late that afternoon that they boarded a 33rd Mech's D-Model HUEY for the trip to their new base camp. J.W.'s flight training had been on older models, and he crept up on his knees behind the flight crew to scrutinize the new gadgetry. The aircraft commander turned and looked at him, rolled his eyes, and motioned with his thumb to a seat in the rear.

The helicopter sailed south from Saigon into the Mekong Delta, the belly of the ship slapping wild tendrils of unkempt Asian jungle. It dropped precipitously to fly even closer to the ground along the dirt roads of primitive villages, skids nearly smashing into mopeds and taller pedestrians—those over five-two.

At the edge of one hamlet, the ship hurdled a huge tree, sinking again before rocketing into a short climb to slap skids along the jungle top. J.W. probed, furtively and anxiously, the endless hectares of abandoned St. Croix sugar plantation, searching for a trace of the hidden enemy. But at full throttle, a hundred and one or two knots, so near the Earth, the ship quaked like a paint mixer, culling an inexplicable flutter in J.W.'s chest. Above the danger, he sat up straight and smiled.

The pilot looked back at his customers, staring particularly at the cheery Weathersby. He made a quick call to the co-pilot over the intercom. When the man nodded with a grin, the pilot jammed the collective down, allowing the ship to drop suddenly, leveling only when they were at the crests of the teak and mahogany forests. They sprinted in and out of verdant gorges, twisting and jinking, a frenzied, OD halfback. The near-weightlessness of the dive woke the unshaven door gunner, sending him into a fury of sweeping M-60 machine-gun fire, hot brass spitting back over his shoulder, sizzling the passengers' shined boots. The gunner grinned maniacally as red tracers arced in parabolas toward imagined human figures darting in and out of the luxuriant undergrowth, though when the barrel began to smolder and then glow, the gunner tired of his performance. He lifted his torn jungle boots onto the smoking breech, sighed contentedly, leaned back against the nylon webbing of his seat, lit a smoke, and turned to flick ashes toward the three neophytes.

When the helicopter cleared the jungle, the pilot dropped the ship to fly inches above peasants tilling paddies and nearby children fishing with their hands in muddy waterholes. J.W. relaxed in the cool air of the doorless helicopter, gazing down at the weathered Vietnamese who had traveled less in their lives than J.W. had in the past six minutes. A few looked up and beckoned a welcome, waving their stick-like arms, but J.W. glanced at the indifferent pilot and folded his arms across his chest.

After fifteen minutes at war, J.W.'s fatigue overwhelmed him, and as hard as he tried to remain alert for signs of the enemy, his eyes drifted closed, and he fell back into a trance that even the clamor of the helicopter could not disrupt. For the first time in the three or four, he'd lost count, days and nights since leaving his wife, he actually dreamed, but only of the months of Ranger School and the interminable forced marches through the Smoky Mountains and the swamps of Florida's panhandle. Flashes of the starvation, of the forty pounds he had lost in the first forty days of commando training, weaved through the dream. Soon came images of his Ranger buddies, and J.W. pondered their fates, wondering if he would ever see the two men with whom he had shared the endless, painful treks and the deprivation. All they had had for the months of commando training were each other, and he chased after them in his stupor, but neither Branch, the angry Black lieutenant, nor Bearchild, the only Native American officer he had ever met, answered his calls. He finally stopped chasing, accepting he was truly on his own.

Minutes later, the ship's nose pitched up violently into a quick stop, jamming J.W. against his seat belt. He believed the chopper had been hit by enemy fire, though the lurch was just the end of the fast, skimming approach into his new home, a mile-square clearing carved from another deserted St. Croix sugar plantation. The HUEY hover-taxied slowly past barracks, mess halls, a massage parlor, and, finally, a road sign pointing north to Saigon with the majuscule, "40 MILES". A wooden arrow below faced northeast—"L.A.—8,469 MILES" was etched into the wood.

The ship set down beside an unstable quonset hut from which hung a powder blue sign with dark blue lettering.

WELCOME TO NORMANDY BASE CAMP
HOME OF THE 33RD MECHANIZED INFANTRY BRIGADE
THE TRACKS OF DESTINY
SANFORD T. BIERLEIN—COLONEL,
INFANTRY, COMMANDING

Several coolies, indistinguishable from the plane-scrubbers in Saigon, hunkered outside the hut clutching conical straw hats against the helicopter's intense rotor wash. As the three lieutenants stepped from the rear compartment, the laborers popped up and stood deferentially, their hands extended. J.W., supposing they were beggars, reached into his pocket for change, but the coolies stepped forward and took the three newcomers' baggage, depositing it inside the shack. J.W. nodded. These elderly Vietnamese men were apparently trustees, prisoners of war, casualties harvested by one of the units he was soon to lead.

"Consider it is an honor and privilege to have been assigned to so distinguished and venerable a unit as the 33rd Mech." So began Major Douglas Trott as he delivered his welcoming speech inside the hut. "Gentlemen," he spoke perfunctorily, "the Normandy Brigade is a mechanized infantry unit." His arms opened reflexively, stopping and lingering at full spread. "We own hundreds of M-113 armored personal carriers to carry our infantry men safely into battle. We have several hundred trucks and jeeps, a battalion or two of M-48 tanks attached to raise our heavy fire power, and a dozen or so helicopters for command and control. We are named after the brigade's actions on D Day. We were the deciding unit in the war."

Pretending not to be reading from a stack of three by five cards, he went on in staccato. "The 33rd Mech was formed on 28 March 1877, as an infantry brigade with a lot of horses. Not the cavalry, mind you, because our soldiers were willing to get off their saddles and fight like real soldiers. The 33rd was sent off to fight in China, in Mexico, and in the coal strikes out west in the US. In 1921, we traded horses for horsepower." He automatically paused for a laugh that did not come. He frowned and went on. "Then we became a fully mechanized unit and fought brilliantly in World War Two. We distinguished ourselves at the Battle of the Bulge and, as I said, on D Day. Now we are in Viet Nam. When we landed here in 1966, the pundits said mech infantry had no place in the jungle and the mud. They were wrong. We ruled the day from the moment the first M-113 rolled ashore, and now we rule the night. We have added an attack helicopter company. We are as mobile as any fighting force in history. You are lucky to be here. Do not forget that.

"As you all know, our commanding officer is Colonel Sanford T. Bierlein. He is one of the most heroic military men alive. He was the highest decorated junior officer in World War Two. They call Colonel Bierlein 'The Bear,' and the title is well earned. It is full circle for him. He won the Medal of Honor as a platoon leader with the 33rd at the Battle of the Bulge, and that was on top of two silver stars. Now he's back to lead the brigade in Viet Nam. He is very serious about the Normandy, about communists, and about finding the little bastards wherever they are hiding.

Gentlemen, do as you are ordered, stay professional no matter what, and you will have no problem with him. He believes that our mission is to 'root 'em out into the open.' They can't win if we can see them. Remember that dictum, gentlemen."

He let out a tiny sigh, dropped the cards on a table, rubbed his hands together, and went on. "Okay, now down to business. First assignment is Lieutenant Pasternak. Your father a writer or something?"

"No, sir. He's a priest."

"Good. E Company, Second Platoon. You will lead that unit to find, fix, and destroy the enemy. And there's plenty of 'em out there." Before Pasternak could comment, Major Trott's face twisted in surprise. "A priest? What are you talking about?"

"Russian Orthodox Church, sir."

"You're not going to be celebrating a bunch of weird holidays are you?"

"No, sir."

"Good." He turned to the next young officer, snapping, "Lieutenant Alexeeff, First Platoon, G Company. Hey, what the hell is this, the Soviet Army? Your mother a nun?"

"No, sir."

"That's a relief. Funny holidays?"

"No, sir."

"Good, you and Pasternak are taking over for two fine platoon leaders who are at present, shall we say, indisposed at the 69th Evacuation Hospital. Keep your heads down. No heroics. Just fight like you were taught and fight like hell, and everything'll be okay. Questions? No? Good.

"Lieutenant Weathersby, you look all beat up like you've been in a fight. I like that. We need aggressive officers out here. You want to fight the enemy, don't you?"

With the major's comments about working for "The Bear," J.W.'s recently rekindled bravado and excitement quickly ebbed, but he remembered well one of the prime dictums of Ranger School—always pretend you're a soldier. "Yes, sir!"

"That's unfortunate. I'm assigning you to command Headquarters Company. You and your four hundred men will provide security for this base camp. You will ensure that all of the mess halls, barracks, and facilities are in working order, *and* that I get clean eating utensils in the dining facilities. This is an important job.

"I also expect a hot shower every evening, and I don't care how you do it, but I recommend the gasoline-fired immersion heater on the roof of my trailer. The last Headquarters Company CO, the one you're replacing, he's also down in 69th Evac Hospital in Vung Tau, along with Pasternak here and Alexeeff's pals. He's nursing third degree burns about his face and genitals. He was not proficient at lighting the heater on my house. Says here you have a degree in engineering. I trust you will do better.

"You are also in command of the locals, my friend. You speak any Vietnamese?"

"Not yet, sir."

"No problem. You are to learn. It's an easy language. Seventy million of 'em speak it. Can't be that hard. Anyway, you will have two deuce-and-a-halves in My Tho at zero-six-thirty to pick 'em up seven days a week. And I want 'em outta here every night by seventeen-hundred. No Vietnamese after dark, no way, never."

"How many of them are there, sir?"

"Hoards and hoards. Maybe all seventy million."

"What do they do, sir?"

"My, my, aren't we full of questions? Lieutenant, they peel potatoes, fill sand-bags, administer the massage parlor, which the three of you will stay out of, and best of all, you will oversee them as they incinerate the contents of our latrines."

"Yes, sir!"

"Good. Dismissed."

After an exchange of crisp salutes, the three lieutenants made their way outside into the crushing heat. At the sight of the still neatly pressed officers, the hunkering baggage handlers sprang up and loaded the three duffels on their own backs, but a distant whistle blew, and they dropped their freight in place without so much as a fare thee well. They trotted off to join a queue of peasants at the main gate undergoing the evening search for stolen food, pilfered toilet paper, and other contraband.

The Vietnamese workers were herded into narrow, wooden, cattle chutes where GIs superficially searched the men and leered at the females. The peasants who passed muster were tapped on the shoulder with a whittled stick operated by a gnarled American sergeant who sat perched atop a five-foot-high, sawed off telephone pole. With his touch, the workers exited the far end of the chute to climb aboard the cargo bed of one of a pair of U.S. Army Two-and-a-Half-Ton trucks. Paper signs taped to the sides read, "MY THO".

J.W. asked Pasternak what that meant. "I don't know. Maybe it's 'POW' in Vietnamese. I don't know."

So J.W. approached the wizened, stick-wielding sergeant and asked. The man looked down upon Weathersby, saluted weakly, and mumbled, "That's the city they live in, Mee Tuh. A real crap hole if you ask me. Good place to stay out of unless you need to find a whore."

The last contingent herded through the pat-down were members of the crap-burning detail, a gang of fetid, male-only coolies who had apparently found themselves on the boss's shit list. Theirs was to pull from under each and every outhouse the swollen, half-55-gallon drums of yesterday's GI excrement then drag the sloshing barrels into the center of an open area behind the mess hall. There, they were aligned dress right dress and guarded until another contingent of peasants ambled over to add quarts of tainted JP-4 helicopter fuel to the tubs. Eventually, a final gang, armed with tree branches, dawdled over to stir the pudding, preparing it for the czar of the crap tenders. That man inspected the goods and placed his stamp of approval on the black-brown syrup of yesterday's GI waste by ceremoniously dropping a wooden match into the pot. The stick-bearers stepped up and stirred the flambé, fogging the base camp with an unctuous smoke that bore an aroma redolent of the men's room at Yankee Stadium between double-headers.

On his second morning at war, Lieutenant J.W. Weathersby stood with Headquarters Company Mess Sergeant Abraham T. Lincoln, watching as a towering, willowy, Vietnamese man ran about headquarters compound holding aloft a small black pouch, pointing it enquiringly to each GI he passed. Sergeant Lincoln mumbled, "That's *Ông* Khai, lord of the crap burners. What's he got in his hand?"

"Mess Sergeant, why is everyone's first name *Ông*?"

"No, sir. That means 'mister' in their tongue, I believe, sir."

As *Ông* Khai approached the mess hall, J.W recognized the object in the Vietnamese man's hand as a wallet, and he absentmindedly patted his own back pocket, grasping suddenly that the billfold was, indeed, his. He dashed forward and grabbed it out of Khai's hands, hissing, angrily, "Where you'd get that?"

Ông Khai cocked his head in question. Sergeant Lincoln called softly to J.W., "Sir, I don't believe he speaks no American, sir."

Ông Khai stood at near-attention, smiling until he sensed a cooling of J.W.'s indignation, and called to one of the crap burners, entering into an animated discussion. Khai pointed toward a distant, new, pinewood three-holer latrine immediately behind the officers' quarters where J.W. had been assigned a tiny room. *Ông* Khai gently tugged J.W. by the arm, pulling him along to the outhouse. Inside, the other coolie assumed a squatting position above the center hole and made the motion of a wallet popping out of a back pocket onto the floor. He curled his index fingers and thumbs into loops, brought them to his eyes as if looking through binoculars, pointed at himself, and then to the imaginary wallet on the ground. Melodramatically, he mimed picking up the billfold and presenting it to *Ông* Khai, who reassumed center stage and went through the motions of returning it to J.W.

J.W. turned his back to the pair of coolies, trying to decide if the simulated account was true or a fiction conjured to protect the real thief and put one over on the stupid American. Perhaps, J.W. imagined, it was just a ritual of initiation for all new officers, so he cracked, "Ha ha."

But when J.W. glanced toward Sergeant Lincoln, the old non-com gently nodded. "It's okay, sir."

Weathersby's fists loosened, though he opened the wallet and very deliberately counted the funny money, MPCs, military payment certificates, war time cash. He mumbled, "Huh. It's all here. Sergeant Lincoln, I guess the Vietnamese don't use this money. That's why we have to."

"Beggin' yo pardon, sir, I reckon they do. GIs ain't allowed to be in possession of no real greenbacks here in Viet Nam, so all's the money that's filterin' around the country is them MPCs. That's 'bout all any of 'em Veemanese be usin' anymore. They's buyin' hootches and water buffalos with the funny money. What's peculiar is, we pay 'em in Veemanese money, and they get rid of it for MPCs fast as they can."

"Well, I'll be darned," J.W. whispered to himself as he recounted the bills a third time. He jested to Sergeant Lincoln, "So, if the money's all here, none of it was stolen."

Sergeant Lincoln paused to consider the question. He laughed and nodded. "Guess you could say that, sir. *Ông* Khai over here, he's a good man, sir. So's most of the ones he's chosen fo' his detail. Hard workin', just tryin' to make it to tomorrow. That ain't so easy 'round here. They's livin' better workin' for us than ever before in they lives. We feed 'em one hot a day, and snacks, and cool tea, and they get to take home 'nuf pay to care for they family. I wish I had that when I was comin' up. I just wish it, sir. We's good people, sir, we Americans. Don't let a few bad ones over here let you think we ain't the best folks in the world. I been all over the Earth in this man's army, sir, ever since Dubya Dubya Two, and I know that fo' a fact sir."

J.W. reflected on the sergeant's words, smiling softly for having already befriended one of the gems the army had molded from childhood and convinced to stay. He thought back to First Sergeant Cowsen in Ranger School, the tough, no nonsense black Southerner who had come to the army at fifteen or seventeen from a sharecropper's shack. The day he arrived at Basic Training, he was barely able to speak English, save the few words—gee, whoa, and haw—he'd learned to maneuver the family mule. The corner of J.W.'s mouth drooped a bit when he thought back to the abject hatred he and his buddies had held for Cowsen and the other cadres at the Ranger School. At that moment, he wished he'd paid more attention to them.

J.W. pulled a few small MPC bills out of the wallet and held them toward Khai. The lord of the crap burners gently pushed the money back but took J.W.'s hand in both of his and shook it warmly. J.W. wondered if Khai's handshake meant something new was being slipped out of his fatigues.

Sergeant Lincoln's eyes relaxed, and he walked to the mess hall, emerging minutes later struggling to carry a large pot of tea. Several of the coolies ran over to take it from him. "Sir," the sergeant spoke quietly out the side of his mouth, "y'all better take yo's first."

Before J.W. could act, though, *Ông* Khai took the ladle and dipped it in the tea, scooping out a portion from around a huge cube of floating ice. He brought the ladle toward J.W., though Weathersby held up his palm. In the military, particularly in war, a commander did not eat or drink until his men did, so J.W. pushed the ladle toward one of the coolies.

The army of crap burners drank in turn, *Ông* Khai waiting until last. Again he skimmed the ladle, making sure he took tea near the ice, and offered it to J.W. Again, J.W. demurred, conjuring images of cholera and a host of lethal tea-borne maladies, but found the dipper coming closer and closer to his lips no matter how animatedly he protested. When it appeared there was no escape, that J.W. was destined to perish not a hero, but as an infectious disease casualty, Sergeant Lincoln thrust his hand forward. Taking the contaminated dipper, he swallowed a long draw of the cool tea himself. He skimmed it into the pot again and filled a glass, which he offered to J.W.

Weathersby, picturing his two West Point friends already out in the jungle, heads ducking in and out of an M-48 tank turret, took the glass, poured the tea back into the cauldron, and plunged the dipper. Smiling weakly, he sucked down six or seven ounces of the cold tea. "That was delicious, Sergeant Lincoln. Thank you."

The mess sergeant waited until the crap burners drifted toward their appointed rounds before approaching J.W. "Ain't nothin' gonna happen to y'all sir. They may not look like us, but they's clean people. Very clean. And they's moh polite than our troops. You just ain't never been 'round different folk, has you, sir?"

"I don't know Sergeant. Every day for the past two years since I came on active duty, they been warning us this is a guerilla war. Lotta dumb GIs've been killed or poisoned by lettin' their guard down. I heard that these people are all VC, that every one of 'em wants to kill a GI. And now you're sayin' these people are trustworthy. I don't know what to believe."

"Some is trustworthy, some is not," Sergeant Lincoln conceded. "Just you and I don't know which is which. Just like back in the world, sir. But tell you one thing Lieutenant, I be gettin' ready to retire comin' on not so long away. And when I be sittin' on my porch in Natchez, Mississippi, gettin' old, I just wanna' know that I didn't do no bad things to no one who didn't deserve it. So I'll just go on trustin' 'till I be shown different. May sound dumb, but it's what the Lord's instructed me to do. I let Him take care of the rest."

"So, you're sayin' there's no way to tell."

"I'm guessin' y'all need to use yo gut, sir."

At the close of business that afternoon, *Ông* Khai knocked on the door of J.W.'s fusty office in the decaying Headquarters quonset. With him was a tiny man who commenced a prepared speech before J.W. motioned them in. "Luten Weh Da Bi. Mr. Khai, he say, you come my house My Tho eat rice. You come you like. Eat rice."

J.W. asked in return, "Go to your house? Who are you?"

"I inter-peeter Three-Three Mech."

"And you want me to go to your house?"

"Yes, go Mr. Khai house. Eat rice."

"See, you said 'go to *your* house.' You wanna say 'go to *his* house.'"

"No. Go Khai house. Eat rice."

"To My Tho? To eat rice? I don't know about that. We got plenty of chow here. I wouldn't want to take food away from his family." J.W. pursed his lips and sucked in a deep breath. "Lotta VC out there."

J.W. turned to Khai and stared hard into the tall man's black eyes, searching for a hint of his own fate if he made the foolish journey, but *Ông* Khai just smiled and nodded. He spoke to the interpreter, who translated, "He say, 'You no think two time. No VC. For sure no VC. Come my house My Tho.'"

J.W. weighed Sergeant Lincoln's dictum about trusting one's gut. "Nah, can't tonight. I gotta go light the hot water for the boss's shower. Maybe tomorrow. Yeah, tell him maybe tomorrow."

At the major's hootch, a dilapidated, twelve-foot house trailer, J.W. climbed the wooden ladder to a roof-mounted, soot-coated, gasoline-fired water heater fashioned from twisted, corrugated sheet metal, copper pipes, and rusting valves. The contraption had the look of a primitive, 19th Century backyard factory, and it wasn't hard to imagine how this had been the source of his predecessor's ill fortune. J.W. could see down through the burned roof into the shower stall, the floor still under several inches of murky green water.

He discovered the guilty party in a flash—a fuel leak that had left stains of dried gasoline just under the port where one held a match to ignite the small furnace. From the toolbox in his jeep, J.W. chose implements carefully, climbing up and down the ladder, hammering and sawing, patching and bending, until the boiler was twisted back into working order. As the colossal tropical sun began to disappear below the tree line of the St. Croix sugar plantation, J.W. turned the valve to refill the 55-gallon drum with the fresh water his appliance would heat to 103 degrees. That was the number scribbled on a note pinned to the door of J.W.'s office hours before.

Insuring the level of water was well over the business portion of the immersion heater, he dropped a match arrogantly into the ignition port, and with a gentle flame growing, crawled down from the roof, feeling particularly useful and competent, excited over the praise he would soon wrest from his new commanding officer at the end of his very first full day at war.

"See, that's why the army wants officers with engineering degrees," he smiled to himself, laughing derisively at the thought of the military commissioning liberal arts grads to fill leadership positions.

What J.W. had not considered in his reverie, however, was that the laws of physics, and of life's endeavors in general in that star-crossed patch of land, never quite matched up with those of the world in which he had spent his first twenty-three years. Unschooled in the set of indigenous conventions he would master or perish, J.W. stood by the major's quarters for a few minutes, calmly ensuring himself that all was working smoothly. When the exhaust pipe began radiating waves of heat, J.W. mounted his jeep and drove back to the office, rolling very slowly to a stop in front of Headquarters quonset. With the last shimmer of mauve setting over the St. Croix, the earth cooled just a few degrees, setting the tropical air into sufficient motion to rid the camp of the scent of burning crap. It was replaced with the bouquet of the evening's first joints, their effluent wafting in from the perimeter guard towers. When the aroma of steaks and fried onions broiling at the mess hall drifted past headquarters and overpowered the dope, J.W. leaned back in his canvas jeep seat and let the corners of his mouth curve a few degrees north.

Anxious to stride by the first sergeant's desk and mention in passing that the old man would have his goddamn hot shower, J.W. sat up straight, snapped on the parking brake, and hopped out of the jeep. After one step, though, there came a scream so shrill, Weathersby's hand dropped to his holster, though the leather was new and stiff, and tug as he might, he couldn't pull the .45 free. A soldier slid to a dusty stop in front of J.W. He shrieked, "Sir, sir, the CO's house is on fire!"

J.W. was covered in dust when he arrived back at the trailer. A pair of GIs were lackadaisically tossing the occasional helmet half-filled with water on the smoking hootch. The majority of the soldiers who drifted over, though, busied themselves forming klatches by rank and race, lighting up and pointing to various aspects of the heater and then down to an evaluation of the flames licking out of the trailer.

J.W. kicked in the door and, along with the first sergeant who had wandered over, perused the major's personal effects sloshing in several inches of dirty water. The first sergeant pulled a flower-imprinted washcloth from the shower drain and smirked to J.W., "Bet'cha, sir, the old man was so pissed last time, he hopped out of the stall without turning off the spigot. Probably threw his washcloth on the floor, cussin' and carryin' on. I know the man. Served with him a dozen times. Ten to one, the washcloth came in his wife's last care package."

With the spigot open, but the drain stopped up, the fifty-some gallons of water J.W. had pumped into the barrel had emptied into the shower stall then overflowed into the trailer proper, where it pooled in a stagnant slough. The flood had claimed the major's footlocker, and the fire most of what was left of the roof.

"Coulda been worse, sir," the first sergeant mumbled. "Boots are soaked, but a few of his uniforms did okay Not sure what he's gonna say about all that stuff floatin' around, crap that came out of his footlocker. Don't worry, sir, Bet'cha he can take it off on his taxes."

At the officers' club later that evening, the major sat down at J.W.'s table. "Lieutenant Weathersby, I want this to remain a relatively calm conversation. And it will, as long as you can assure me that the damages to my house will be repaired before the close of business tomorrow. A hot rinse in my own little shower stall would be appreciated, Lieutenant. Think you can get that arranged for me? And you might want to get my soaking uniforms and books and boots and pictures out in the sun for a good dry in the morning. What'a you say?"

At the major's hootch late the next afternoon, the crowd of GIs and Vietnamese who had rebuilt the structure and the water heater watched closely as J.W. mounted the roof to drop a match into the ignition port. A gentle orange flame built slowly then grew, and soon tiny bubbles rose from the bottom of the water tank as the liquid warmed. J.W. gave the audience a thumbs up, climbed down, and asked rhetorically, "None of you got any work to do?"

As the crowd dispersed grousing, *Ông* Khai, who had organized the repair detail, and his friend, the little interpreter, approached J.W. The man droned, "Luten Weh Da Bi, Mr. Khai, he say, 'You come my house My Tho eat rice. You come, you like. Eat rice.'"

"No, no. What you want to say is 'Come to *his* house eat rice'. And, nah, I gotta make sure this thing works. If it doesn't, I'm gonna be shot at dawn."

"No, no man My Tho shoot. No VC."

J.W. spoke quietly, "Please tell Mr. Khai I am flattered by his offer, but maybe tomorrow night."

Within minutes of J.W.'s departure, the major's driver rolled up to Weathersby's office and shouted into the quonset that the old man wanted to see the lieutenant, and pretty damn quick. Had J.W. been provided an owner's manual for the shower detail, he would have noted the part that suggested the immersion heater not be left to run until the fuel was exhausted—a ten-minute burn was sufficient. The camp commander had not been interested in a Turkish bath, just a nice warm shower as a reward for twelve years in the army, and for his efforts on this, his second tour in Viet Nam.

"So what you're saying, Specialist," the first sergeant called loudly through the door, "is that the major is still not satisfied. I'll tell the lieutenant as soon as he comes in."

J.W. slipped out the quonset's back door, seeking refuge at the mess hall, apprising Sergeant Lincoln of his predicament, and asking for a place to hole up. The old cook drawled, "Sir, I don't know. Burn down the man's house, flood all his worldly belongin's, then burn the hide right off 'a him? Shoot, maybe y'all better take a little R&R from Normandy tonight. Spend the evening with *Ông* Khai. And anyway, if'n y'all don't go, y'all's missin' a chance to see how these people been livin' for the past thousand years, or some such number."

"You mean it's allowed to go to town?"

"Ain't no law sayin' you can't have dinner with the Veemanese. GIs from the Mech go into My Tho every night. An' if'n you do go, the worse gonna happen to y'all is y'all's gonna git the GIs, or the clap. But you know better than that, sir. I can tell. Far as you goin', I mean regulation-wise, it's your call, sir.

"Now I gotta tell ya, I seen the major hoppin' mad on account 'a dirty fork. No tellin' what he's gonna be like tonight. You may be wantin' to git outta Dodge for a while. But like I said, yo call, sir."

"I know you feel that way Mess Sergeant, but it's gotta be dangerous trustin' a gook."

"Sir, beggin' yo pardon again, but sir, you mightin' not be sayin' that word. I know you wouldn't be sayin' a certain word 'cause I'm Negro. Same thing, sir."

"Sorry, Sergeant. What does it mean? I've heard it a hundred times."

"I'm sure you have. I believe it comes from when we was in Korea, that war. It means country in their tongue, but it come to mean somethin' low. Like not human. That ain't the way you are, sir. I can tell."

"Okay. Thank you, Sergeant. I just learned something. But it's still gonna be hard to trust a local."

"Cain't say yo're wrong, sir. These people be the enemy, so they tell us, but I don't see it myself, sir, not old *Ông* Khai. Yo billfold, sir? Sheeet, in my neck of the woods, y'all'd never put yo eyes on it again if'n you dropped it in the john. No way. Like I said, guess y'all gonna have to use yo gut, sir."

In the city of My Tho at dusk, several miles from the womb of Normandy Base Camp, *Ông* Khai led J.W. through a labyrinth of alleys, past glowering, squatting slum dwellers, extended families hungrily sucking fish-sauce-tainted rice from chipped porcelain bowls. The two men hiked deep into the penury of the provincial town, coming finally to a tangle of paths blocked at the far end by a weathered, long-since-whitewashed stucco structure. J.W. slipped a hand to his holster, unsnapping the flap, pulling the .45 pistol, gently at first then wrenching when the piece did not move. He fingered the butt to insure the clip was seated and tripped the safety to "off." Khai noticed, but said nothing.

At the crumbling former French governmental building, Khai climbed the one step into a large room lit by a single kerosene lantern. He nodded to J.W., bidding him to follow. J.W. tracked behind, though tugged his pistol halfway out of the holster, rehearsing the steps in his mind for jamming a round into the chamber. *Ông* Khai touched J.W.'s arm and whispered, "No VC."

Nonetheless, J.W. peered into the darkened room for communist fighters. On the cold, faded tile floor, though, lay two dozen ragged children broken into three clusters. To the left were diaperless infants on straw mats; in the center of the room lay a dozen toddlers, their bottoms wrapped in scraps of discarded cotton. They stared off at the grimy walls. Seven older children sat in a huddle to the right, each clothed in fragments of third and fourth iteration hand-me-downs. In a far corner, four elderly women stood by a steaming cooking pot. The youngsters eventually turned to stare weakly at the foreign stranger; the four old ladies barely looked up.

By the glint of cooking charcoal, J.W. saw the women nod a distant greeting to *Ông* Khai as he walked up to the primitive wood stove. They demurred to the stalk-like man, who took a ladle fashioned of the thinnest aluminum, filled a few bowls, and carried the watery rice gruel to the older children. While the waifs ate the meal slowly, and a few even pushed their bowls forward for more, most just swallowed a few spoonfuls before lying back on the floor to catch their breath.

When the soupy rice was exhausted, *Ông* Khai led J.W. to a cubicle behind the building where a small pot of steaming vegetables and rice sat on a tiny, rough-hewn wooden table. Khai lit a kerosene lamp, its flickering orange light illuminating a small bed and a shelf crammed with books. *Ông* Khai scraped the food into chipped bowls and handed the fuller to J.W.

As they sat on a rickety picnic bench and ate, J.W. laughed aloud, "I'm here a few days, and I'm already goin' to die of dysentery."

Ông Khai smiled. "You not die, Lieuten. Food boiled hot to be sure. No problem."

J.W.'s jaw dropped. "Wait, wait a minute. You're speaking English? Mr. Khai, I thought…"

"Yes, a little," Khai smiled.

"A little? How come you didn't speak to me in English at Normandy?"

"Ah Lieuten, you see, if speak English, army, they make me interpreter. That not good for family."

"It's gotta be better'n burnin' shit."

"No. army no enough money. Go battle. You see, I finish school become countryside village leader. In three week I am village chief of government Viet Nam."

"I don't understand. You're going to be a village chief? Where? Here?"

"No." Khai shook his head. "Government they send me to countryside Tien Giang Province."

"Then why did you ask me to come here?"

"That question most important. When I go countryside, I ask Army America friend bring food to children. You new boss officer for headquarter. Old boss, he good man. Give beaucoup food for children, but have accident. He go hospital, burn, very burn, then no food to children My Tho unless Army American give."

J.W. probed, "You depend on the 33rd Mech to keep these children fed?"

"Yes. American no food, children no eat."

"Isn't there an agency or something to provide support? The Church? What happens when we leave?"

Khai smiled patiently. "Lieuten now you to Viet Nam. This no America. Every family here, maybe no food. No food for family, no food for o'phan children." His eyes hardened. "You never forget—this Viet Nam."

Before J.W. left that night, *Ông* Khai walked him through the orphanage once again. The old women sat, exhausted, by the fire, wearing expressions as numb as those of the children, most of whom had fallen into near sleep. As before, the women ignored him, and he turned away from them coldly. He started over to a little boy who had popped up off his mat and smiled at J.W, but when Weathersby stood over the child, he recognized what he had thought to be a grin was, instead, a tortured grimace. As J.W. bent forward to touch the boy, he fell back to his mat clutching his bulbous gut. He cried out in a single, high-pitched screech and, with a violent shudder, became silent, quietly fading into unconsciousness.

J.W. trembled, combing through the catalogue of engineering courses, flight school drills, and months of commando training to resuscitate a five-year-old, thirty-pound child whose life ebbed before his eyes. He knelt and stroked the child's face then turned to the ladies, his eyes pleading. One of the women shuffled over, called the others, and sent one to fetch the homemade neighborhood stretcher. Before J.W. could stand, Khai and the ladies had carried the little boy off.

After dinner the following night, Mess Sergeant Lincoln beckoned J.W. to the kitchen, looking left and right surreptitiously before ducking behind a massive refrigerator. "Sir, pardon me fo askin' sir, but is y'all goin' back to the o'fenige tonight, sir?"

"Hadn't planned on it, Sergeant. The place is a bummer. I got nothing to add over there. Maybe some other time. Why?"

Sergeant Lincoln nodded in agreement. "That it is, sir, a bummer." He thought for a moment and added, "Sir, I was just thinkin' y'all might want to bring some of this here leftover liver and milk from the mess hall."

"That's against regs, isn't it, Sergeant? That's like stealing government property, isn't it?"

"Well, sir," Sergeant Lincoln nodded again, "It is, you might say, but the troops ain't gonna eat it, no way. Liver, sheeet. I tells 'em not to put that stuff on the menu, but must be somebody stateside making a bundle on it. Every time I turn around, there's another load of that stuff comin' off the supply trucks. I was just thinking y'all might want to bring them o'fens some food. Old CO was doin' it, but he burned his self on the major's shower, as you know."

J.W. dragged through the doorless portal of the orphanage under the weight of cartons of milk and meat. The most ancient of the woman nodded as she stirred the rice; the other three did not look up, their attention fixed on the piles of tiny sets of rags they were scrubbing by hand.

J.W. asked about the little boy, but no one stopped to answer. *Bà* Chi, the eldest of the women, cubed a small piece of the liver and tossed it disinterestedly into the pot, but when *Ông* Khai handed the enriched gruel to the children, most took one bite and dribbled the meat out of their mouths.

If it had been J.W.'s intention to elicit an animated response in regard to the gift, he would have to wait until the next morning's breakfast, when he passed Major Trott's table. "Giving food away is unlawful disposition of government property," the major accused. "Do you have an explanation? And I've been looking for you for hours. Where the hell have you been?"

J.W., coming to semi-attention, answered quietly, "I've been here, sir. And it's an orphanage, sir. Besides, that meat would have gone to the dogs behind the mess hall if I hadn't given it to the kids."

He shot back, "Lieutenant, how do you know those children got the food?" The major jumped to his feet, flushing, stabbing a finger angrily at J.W.'s chest. "The dogs get meat because they don't rocket this base camp at midnight."

"Won't happen again, sir."

"You're damn straight it won't. And you are not to fraternize with the locals. That means your crap burner friend, too. Is that clear? There's something wrong with that guy. He's a goddamn glad hand. Always gets the job done perfectly. I don't trust him, and I don't like him.

"And once again, it's time to discuss my shower. I may not be allowed to use the enlisted men to light it, but I sure as hell can use you. I'll be damned if this senior major has to light his own shower. Tonight's your last chance. Screw up again, and you'll find yourself on a tank, using your Zippo to light C-4 to cook your C-rations, not my heater. Dismissed, Lieutenant."

Late that afternoon, J.W. pushed through the torn screen door of the legendary 33rd Mech Officer's Club, a decomposing quonset in a corner of a decomposing, two-year-old base camp. At first, he only sipped his beer, glaring through the green-oxidized screened window toward the senior officers' compound, all of two tiny house trailers, little wheeled sheds, one crowned with a heat-scarred gasoline stove that had been assigned to Major Trott, and the other allocated to Colonel Bierlein, who had been inside his billet but once. In a perfect rectangular perimeter surrounding the trailers were white-washed stones, rockery that marked the line enlisted men and junior officers were not to cross without invitation.

Though both quarters had been freshly painted, they were already tainted with circles of moldy olive drab, at the center of which were even darker centers, as if the jungle had targeted them for repossession. "Aiming points," J.W. laughed aloud.

It wasn't until Weathersby was nearly through his beer that he focused more closely at the heater atop the major's quarters and at the wall clock in the club. The deadline for preparing the major's bath was minutes away.

He growled, "I came here to be a troop commander, not a fuckin' butler," and went to the bar for a second brew, his bravado deepening with each gulp.

As he turned toward his table, Lieutenant Pasternak, the platoon leader with whom he had traveled out to Normandy on the helicopter, pulled numbly at the screen door. Unshaven, his hair askew, matted with sweat and road dust, the West Pointer hadn't changed out of the grease-stained fatigues he had worn for two days as a tank platoon leader in the field. He nodded brusquely to J.W. then took a seat by himself in the corner. J.W. smiled and stared to rise, but the muscles in the man's face tensed, and J.W. dropped back onto his bench. Weathersby suddenly thought back to his fraternity pal, Coulton. The faraway look in their eyes was identical, and J.W. shuddered, recalling Coulton's words, that J.W. would come to know what being in Viet Nam meant, and maybe sooner than he had imagined, or wished. How, though, could it have happened so quickly to Pasternak?

For an instant, J.W. thought better of his decision to irritate the major and wind up out on a tank, but after a couple of swigs of a second beer, his perspective began to warp. Two drinks for the officers brooding at the tables around him was but an hors d'oeuvre. For J.W., who had not downed two beers in the same sitting since his early fraternity days, the glow of the liquid courage grew in quantum bounds. "Screw that asshole," he hissed, ordering a third bottle and soon weaving to a seat in the rear of the shack, facing away from the door. He glanced at the wall clock and flipped it the bird, smirking over the six minutes before his handmaiden duties came due.

As J.W.'s finger was retracting, the screen door swung open, banging against the wall. That brought a sudden, threatening silence to the club as Major Trott stepped one foot inside, fists on his hips, searching, eyes darting angrily from corner to corner. His sweat-stained jungle fatigues wafted an awful odor that Weathersby sensed as he turned himself toward the door. The other heads in the club looked up as well at the outpost's commanding officer, whose eyes had locked on his target. He summoned J.W. with a rapid-fire crooking of his index finger.

Trott took another irritated stride toward J.W. but halted and spun around, startled by a deep, resonating explosion that rattled the collection of bottles in front of the solitary drinkers. The major dashed outside, glared at the inert heater above his trailer, and lifted his eyes to search the far sky for flashes and smoke. When the inevitable plume of black rose beyond Normandy Base Camp's berm, he disappeared into the dusk without looking back.

At dawn, Major Trott sent a runner to summon J.W. from reveille formation. Weathersby, nursing a headache, walked sluggishly toward the major's office, turning over in his mind if he could be sentenced to prison, or worse, a combat unit in the field, for failure to heat a very junior senior officer's shower water. He delayed, slowing his gait, walking head bowed, through the unusually soundless camp. His thoughts turned to the possibility of having to restart the clock on his year in Viet Nam after his release from the stockade.

As J.W. neared the headquarters building, the roar of the abject silence stopped him. Along with the dearth of chatter was an absence of diminutive bodies crawling in and out of the latrines and mess halls. It dawned on him there were no local workers in camp. J.W. had read that the French spent much effort converting the Vietnamese to Catholicism, so he reasoned it must be Sunday.

Major Trott greeted J.W. with a lifeless soliloquy. "Lieutenant, I'd like to fry your ass, but I have a situation here, and I can't spare a real officer to take care of matters. So, you're it. Your first order of business on this sunny morning in Viet Nam is to hire replacements for the crap burners. Find a couple dozen gooks and train 'em. And when you get that done, the CO, Bierlein himself, wants a memorial plaque made with all the names on it, and he also wants a commemorative service at the Catholic Church in My Tho. Get it set up for this week, Thursday morning, and he wants to be there himself, so find a place for his chopper to land. And his visit is to be a secret."

"Memorial plaque, commemorative service, sir? What for, sir?"

"The crap burners, the dishwashers, and the baggage boys. They're all dead."

"Dead, sir?"

"Yes, Lieutenant, dead as fuckin' doornails. That's what happens when you hit a fifty-pound VC mine. The lead truck got it on the way back to My Tho last night. These people kill their own. Forty-two this time."

"Was *Ông* Khai killed?"

"Who? Oh, your pal? I don't know, and to tell you the truth, I don't give a shit. All I care about is that one of our drivers and his shotgun were killed. Now, how in the hell am I supposed to write letters to their mothers and tell them they died for nothing, just hauling around peasants?"

Though two trucks drove to My Tho later that morning to gather the surviving workers, they returned in an hour, empty. None of the surviving coolies reported for duty.

"Screw 'em," Major Trott sneered. "We paid them more than they ever dreamed of, and now they abandon us because the war got a little too close? It's not my war; it's theirs. What is *wrong* with these people?"

He ordered J.W. into town to hire a truck-full of new workers. "Tell 'em we're raising the pay to thirty cents a day and three fifteen-minute breaks every ten hours. That'll get 'em back. And talk to them about loyalty. Must mean something, even to them."

J.W.'s first order of business in My Tho, however, was at the orphanage, where he asked the old women about *Ông* Khai, but the ladies mumbled that they had not seen him, and one's eyes reddened. J.W. believed this was his first casualty of the war, and in his heart he knew that he should be very sad, and craft protests of anger and revenge; but he had observed the outward appearance of callousness in his compatriots, those officers who had returned from Viet Nam. Practicing being an authentic soldier, even if his tour was to be passed as a hotel manager, he simply turned away without a word of condolence. These people were so used to loss, he reminded himself, any protest on his part would be seen as weakness.

He went into the scorching streets of My Tho, offering one dollar to the first man who spoke the bare essentials of English, and twenty cents to the kid who found him. Teams of children burst away from J.W. like spokes on a racing bike, little boys rushing through fetid alleys, finally producing a pintsized fellow who was combing his greasy black hair as he slithered up to J.W. The pair marched from house to house unsuccessfully, locating not a single soul willing to work for the Americans. J.W. did not at first understand why most families fled behind threadbare curtains into tiny back rooms as the two appeared at the door.

The quasi-interpreter smiled and repeated at each hut, "He 'fray die America truck. Very numbah ten work American."

As the vaporous South East Asian ambience thickened with the hours, J.W.'s gait slowed. By three, he was approaching unconsciousness. He collapsed onto a rickety stool in front of a local open air restaurant and put his head between his legs. The interpreter took another seat and yelled something toward the proprietor, who rushed over with a pot of boiling tea to rejuvenate the pallid foreigner. A waiter in nothing but a pair of grimy shorts drifted over and stood in front of J.W., staring slack-jawed at the pale apparition. The interpreter jarred the waiter from his reverie, and soon a huge bowl of steaming *phở*, noodle soup, was produced. J.W. sat up a bit to accept the offering, but the interpreter patted the space in front of himself, and there the waiter set it down heavily. The interpreter mumbled something behind his hand to the waiter, who smiled broadly, snatched the bowl off the table, and ran inside to add stringy pork entrails, julienned cow stomach, boiled tendons, *bò viên*—very, very dense Vietnamese meatballs—and lumps of braised fat. With the *phở* back in front of the little Vietnamese man, the waiter pulled a stub of pencil from his shorts to recalculate the bill. That took so long, the interpreter was half-done with his soup before the waiter craned his neck away from J.W. and dropped the slip of tissue paper as near J.W.'s hand as he dared.

J.W., whose color was that of the white porcelain *phở* bowl, did not budge. And he didn't stir when a bony hand with long thin fingers lifted the bill and slapped it with a bang in front of the interpreter. The man looked up, froze, then dropped his spoon and chopsticks, jumped from the stool, and slithered back into his alley.

"Lieuten, why you not tell Khai need help today? You must careful when come My Tho."

As J.W.'s color further blanched at the sight of his dead friend, Khai ordered two fresh bowls of *phở* and sat with J.W. until there had been some absorption of the calories. J.W. pulled his wallet out, but Khai pushed his hand away and left a few cents on the table. He helped J.W. to his feet, and the two walked the dirt paths of town searching for laborers. *Ông* Khai apologized for his absence that morning at the base camp, explaining that he had been quite busy making arrangements for the funerals of the workers who had perished in truck number one.

J.W. was confused and remarked, "I thought we Americans were going to take care of all that."

Khai shook his head. "Lieuten, maybe American soldier help Cat-oh-lick, but most worker Buddhist. Nobody help Buddhist. Cat-oh-lick priest not allow Buddhist people come church for food or be close to God."

J.W. scrunched his face. "*Ông* Khai, Catholic Church'll always help out. They have no politics. It's a church. I'll talk to the priest."

"My friend," *Ông* Khai smiled thinly, "I tell you this. This Viet Nam. This not America. Nothing in Viet Nam as seem."

They trudged silently through the steamy, molding alleys, recording the names of the dead, often invited into paltry shanties to sip weak tea and view the tortured human remains, defeated wives and husbands and children waiting expectantly for J.W. to comment on how well the departed appeared in repose. After the first dozen or so homes, J.W. was no longer shocked to witness within a raw mahogany casket an arm placed haphazardly next to a shoulder, or a right foot sitting at the end of an amputated left thigh.

With a census of the deceased in hand, Khai took J.W. to a local brazier who smilingly agreed to fashion a memorial tablet from melted down, U.S. brass ammunition casings, but only if J.W. would provide the scrap metal.

When Weathersby shrugged and agreed, the brazier added, "This is a very hard project. You must bring much extra metal, double the amount, in case there is a mistake." His smile widened.

Khai wagged his finger no, threatening to go elsewhere for the memorial, but the man threw his arms up in disgust, melodramatically sulking and mumbling, retreating into the slight crease between the two dilapidated buildings that was his foundry.

Khai reengaged him, offering an extra kilo of brass, but the man spit back, "Five kilos, or no plaque."

A moment passed with both camps on the verge of withdrawal, but Khai finally nodded politely, and so did the brazier, and soon tea was served. J.W. opened a pack of Salems in celebration, and the three men relaxed, drawing contentedly on the American cigarettes until *Ông* Khai dug the list of casualties out of his pocket. The craftsman pulled a pair of prehistoric eyeglasses from his leather apron, the lenses nearly opaque with pockmarks left by decades of molten metal showering from his antediluvian furnace.

Contemplating the register of names to be inscribed, he grimaced as he had during the extra-kilos-of-brass controversy and went back into his shop. Khai and Weathersby looked at each other shrugging. The man returned with a pencil, the tip of which he licked with great theater before applying it to the list. He struck off names, offering an angrily muttered explanation for each attack of the graphite.

"This one's a Catholic, and Sanh here, he owes me money that it looks like I'll never get now, will I? And Khanh, the old witch, she told my wife I was drinking *rượu đế* with my friends at our lunch gambling session. Oh, look at this—Thanh, that son of a turtle, he..."

At the orphanage, the old women remained expressionless during the conversation in which *Ông* Khai explained patiently that the small but vital contribution that had come from the coolies' good jobs with the Americans was gone. J.W. assumed that their apparent apathy signaled the women simply did not care. He took a breath to utter a discourteous comment but suddenly remembered the metal box chained to the back seat of his jeep. He ran into the alley and carried in the warm, raw sirloin, tepid milk, and melted cookies. Though the children did not spit out the steak, the old ladies still barely looked at him.

The next morning, *Ông* Khai failed to show up at the Catholic Church to help J.W. make arrangements with the priest for the memorial service. J.W. was miffed, reiterating to himself that no one could be trusted in Viet Nam. He sat in his jeep, smoking, simmering, until an old man came up to him on the street and babbled in French that Khai had had to leave My Tho suddenly. He'd been ordered by the government of South Viet Nam to assume political control of a rice farming village west of Saigon.

J.W. fumbled through his high school Gallic and thought the man related that *Ông* Khai had attempted to scooter out to Normandy Base Camp to say good-by, but had been stopped on the road by an American patrol, searched, and detained for having J.W.'s name scrawled in a child's copy book. Though the American soldiers released him, they refused to let him continue on to Normandy. If J.W. had correctly pieced together the details of the old man's account, he realized he would never see *Ông* Khai again, and that made him ponder again the warnings returnees had passed on about making friends in Viet Nam.

On Thursday, at the Catholic Church in My Tho, J.W. was nudged forward by Colonel Bierlein's aide-de-camp, who urged in a whisper, "Tell the CO you're the one who organized this service. He knows who you are."

But the tall, thin, red-headed Bierlein spun around before J.W. could draw a breath. "You the one who speaks Vietnamese already?" he snapped.

"No, sir. Not very well, sir."

"Good. You tell the priest that at the end of mass I'm going to present the plaque, and that the Regiment's going to provide solatium payments to the families. Can you do that?"

J.W. stumbled through a performance in week-old Vietnamese that included the pointing to and resetting of watches, but when the priest cocked his head,

J.W. uttered several French phrases. The clergyman glared at J.W. and spoke in English. "Lieutenant, I know you are speaking French, but I am Vietnamese. I do not understand a word of that vile language, nor do I wish to. We should speak English, don't you think?"

J.W. turned to Colonel Bierlein and blurted, "He speaks…" but there was a commotion, and the colonel turned away. *Bà* Thai, one of the old ladies from the orphanage, bearing nude infants in both arms, pushed her way through the crowd. She handed one of the infants to Bierlein's personal aide then tugged on the CO's sleeve. She began to howl, though J.W. had no idea what she was saying. A gaggle of beggars outside the gates of the church heard the woman's pleas and recognized that one of their own had made it past the sentinels. Spurred by the woman's increasingly shrill entreaties, the throng of dispossessed snaked through the cathedral's fortified outer gates, through the sanctuary and the priest's private quarters, into the courtyard, and past the American delegation. They descended upon the colonel, pulling at his fatigues and the red hair on his forearms. They beseeched him for everything from food and clothing to a ride in his helicopter.

"What's the one with babies whining about, Lieutenant?"

I think she's saying, "What will we do now? What will we do now?"

Bierlein pulled his arm away gently and bowed embarrassedly to the woman. He turned to the priest and asked, "Father, can you take care of this?"

A nod and a pious smile reassured Bierlein, but as the colonel was whisked away by a security detachment that had to barrel through the growing phalanx of mendicants, the priest clucked indignantly at the woman, shooing her off with the back of his hand.

J.W. was not exactly sure what the cleric had boomed as the woman was escorted from the courtyard, but it sounded like, "This is a Catholic Church. Your orphanage is Buddhist. You know better than to come in here. Now shoo—go away."

Avoiding the major at Normandy Base Camp, J.W. and his jeep driver, Willoby, who had been assigned by the camp commander to keep an eye on him, began supply runs to the orphanage, delivering leftovers three or four times a week, timing their visits to My Tho to coincide with the major's plural amorous adventures with the young Vietnamese women who were provided dispensation from his inviolable curfew parameters. The girls also got jeep rides back to My Tho after midnight with a GI driver, whose buttoned lip Trott secured when the major caught him pleasuring himself while looking at ill-begotten Polaroids of nude GIs. Even better, the major had procured the services of a personal eunuch he could trust with his harem.

Slipping back into base camp before Trott had his fatigue pants buttoned, weeks passed as J.W. and his driver stole into town, delivering food, soap, and toothbrushes to the orphanage; they learned the children's names, the children theirs. *Bà* Thai, the old lady from the memorial service, smiled one night. After a dozen trips, she invited the two GIs to stay for dinner, and as J.W. declined, she dragged him back into the room amidst applause from the other women and the kids.

Some nights at the orphanage, they dined on Sergeant Lincoln's tired hot-dogs, on others, meatloaf, or the kids' favorite, French fries; though no matter the main course, every morsel eventually found itself dipped in strong, low quality *nước mắm*, fish sauce—"Vietnamese ketchup," Willoby dubbed it. J.W. began to use it on a fry or two and developed a taste for the salty, gently fishy liquid. He planned to bring a quart home to the U.S. for his wife, Krista.

During the meals, J.W. tried to ignore the distant explosions, but Willoby kept nagging, "Sir, we need to make tracks. I don't like this shit, sir. Please, sir."

"Willoby, calm down, man. It's dark. We'll go when the shootin's over."

One night, though, the agitation and blue flashes in the eastern sky went on far longer than usual, and it was past midnight when the two crept through the outer defenses of Normandy. J.W. maneuvered through the pea soup fog of spent explosives to slink to his tiny room in the BOQ. He dropped onto his rack, but the rasping of a bulldozer and the clatter of wood and metal kept him awake. He sprang angrily from his rack cursing, wrapped himself in an olive drab towel, and stomped toward the cacophony, intending to chew ass until the engineer battalion agreed to pursue their heavy demolition work at an hour more reasonable than 0200.

The moon that ordinarily silhouetted the mess hall had retreated behind thunder clouds, and J.W. was left to stumble his way toward the ruckus along wood-pallet sidewalks that crisscrossed the mud-soaked camp. He eventually came upon a silent crowd of GIs watching numbly as twisted metal trays, silverware, and shrapnel-pierced cooking pots were heaped by the bull dozer into piles of rubble. J.W. moved toward the machine to order the driver to cease work until daylight, but a lifeless black body in OD skivvies was uncovered by the blade, and the enlisted operator shut the engine down, jumped from his rig, and pushed past Lieutenant Weathersby, ignoring him. The crowd inched forward, carrying J.W. with it, but it wasn't until he was above the corpse that he realized the frozen, pain-contorted face was that of Mess Sergeant Abraham T. Lincoln.

One of the troops spit, "Fuck. Mess sergeant been taken to sleepin' in the kitchen. He's been guardin' his precious scraps for that commie, fuckin' orphanage. Now look. Shit. I hate this fuckin' place!"

At dawn, J.W. ignored the call to an outdoor, cold, C-ration breakfast and spent the hour sifting through the remains of the mess hall, searching for Sergeant Lincoln's personal effects to ship back to Mississippi. At 7 A.M., a band of re-recruited Vietnamese workers, the core of *Ông* Khai's labor force, spied J.W. picking his way through the rubble and came over en masse to lift sheets of splintered plywood and mangled stainless steel shelving.

J.W., as sleep-deprived and depressed as he had been in Ranger School, spun around and screamed, "You knew we were gonna be hit last night, didn't you? Didn't you?" But they just stood soundlessly, smiling.

All J.W. uncovered were shards of shrapnel from the enemy ordinance that had showered for hours onto Normandy, heavy-metal rocket and mortar splinters that he flung wrathfully toward the coolies. He uncovered chunks of jagged steel deep in the detritus. Chinese characters had been embossed into the metal.

J.W. made his way to the still-smoldering gas oven. He was startled by Major Trott's voice. "Where were you hiding last night, Lieutenant? Missed you in the bunker."

"Oh, I saw the whole thing, sir. All that noise and light."

"Back gate guard says you were driving around. What were you doing out there?"

"I was looking for the VC who hit us, sir."

"My ass you were, Lieutenant. You don't lie well, and you sure as hell don't learn well either. I was leaving you alone because Sergeant Lincoln liked you for some reason. He was one of the best the U.S. Army had, and now he's gone because of your pinko friends, and so are you if you disobey my orders again."

The major took a deep breath and spat, "Who the hell do you think you are? You want to take a guess about who's getting the meat you deliver to that so-called orphanage?" J.W.'s lifeless expression enraged Trott. "You don't know, do you? Those people are the enemy. Your enemy, my enemy. They stand for everything our parents fought against. Was your father a soldier, Weathersby?"

"Hell, yes, he was, sir. In the Pacific."

"Then what the hell happened to you? You can't prove the loyalty of the women at that orphanage, can you? That shrapnel in your hand, where the hell do you think it came from?"

"China, sir."

"How did you know that?"

"I took Chinese in college, Sir."

"Why doesn't that surprised me? The Chinese your friends, too? How 'bout the Russians? They tell me one of my jobs is to develop the junior officers under my command, so here goes nothing. How about a little poly sci lesson?" Without waiting for an answer, he barreled on. "We mined the hell out of Hai Phong Harbor in North Viet Nam. Result: the Ruskies can't pull their ships in there anymore. That's where the commies in Hanoi used to be getting weapons for your pals down here in the South.

"So now, your Russian buddies have to send supplies to Hanoi by train through China. The Chinese are smarter than the Russians, and they transfer the Russian ordinance to their own trains at the Russian border because they hate the Russians and won't let them or their trains onto Chinese soil. But the Chinese also hate the Vietnamese, and the Vietnamese hate the Chinese, and the Russians are supposed to like the Vietnamese, so to piss off the Vietnamese *and* the Russians, the Chinese off-load the Russian ordinance halfway down

China. They substitute it with their homemade, second-rate crap, keep the quality Russian ordinance for themselves, and ship the garbage down to Viet Nam.

"What I'm trying to tell you, Weathersby, is that you don't know shit from shinola about this war, and essentially, you've been providing succor to the enemy."

When J.W. looked perplexed, the major shook his head, "That means you've been feeding and strengthening the enemy. Some of our packaged food from the mess hall, the stuff you've been taking to My Tho, has been found in the jungle outside this very berm. Sitting right there next to the Chinese AK-47 shells left behind by the local VC. Your friends at the orphanage sold that food to the VC, or had to give it to them, or gave it to them because they wanted to, and you went right along with the program. Whether you understand it or not, these people are the enemy. We're not here to love them and shower them with our benevolence. We're here to stop communism and to teach anybody who supports a violent communist revolution that we will find you and cut off your head.

"And since they're my enemy, and since the last time I looked, I was the one wearing the gold leaf on my collar, I hold your balls right in my hand. Disobey my direct order again, just once more, and you'll find yourself assigned to the marines on the DMZ, that's the Demilitarized Zone on the border between communist North Viet Nam and free South Viet Nam, in case you didn't know. It's where we've been dying for the past six years to save these people from their chums, the communist bastards."

J.W. stepped back and drew a long breath. "You're calling me a commie for feeding children, sir? You sayin' I'm a traitor for not giving a shit about world politics, sir? Well, ever since I got here, all I've seen is kids with empty bellies and vacant eyes. I've already heard enough wailing mothers and wives. It's madness, sir."

Out of breath and strength, J.W.'s head dropped again, and in the storm of his thoughts, he conceded that in the few weeks he'd been in Viet Nam, he could not vouch for anyone's allegiance. He acknowledged silently that he had disobeyed a direct, legal order, and would soon be on his way, if not to die with the marines on the DMZ, at best, to languish in LBJ, Long Binh Jail, the army's prison for errant GIs, an inferno of a military stockade just a few miles north of Saigon.

Indeed, Major Trott appeared disappointed when J.W. calmed, but the senior officer took another deep, angry breath and snapped, "Your buddy Lieutenant Pasternak, remember him? He got it last night, on patrol right outside the gate. Wasn't in country three fucking weeks. Yeah, pal, you got great friends."

Trott's fists tightened and his fingers blanched waiting for J.W.'s juices to run again. Then, with head bobbing like a boxer taunting his prey, hoping J.W. would take a swing or pull his forty-five, Trott spit on the sandy earth a centimeter in front of J.W.'s boots. But the lieutenant's head drooped even further, and he found himself staring into a murky puddle, drawing only the image of Pasternak's face, wondering how a man could have a priest for a father.

When J.W. finally lifted his face, he whispered to Trott, "You're right, sir. I've been behaving like an asshole."

Chapter 2

For several days, J.W. comported himself a paragon of military propriety, remaining aloof from the Vietnamese workers, even shunning requests for food from the new coolies, who promised to deliver the spoils to the orphanage in J.W.'s stead. But during a memorial service for Sergeant Lincoln and Lieutenant Pasternak that Sunday, J.W. overheard Colonel Bierlein whisper to his personal pilot, "You up for a little schoolyard payback, Tom?"

J.W.'s ears pricked, and he marched up to Bierlein. "Sir, you going to a school? May I go along, sir?"

Though Major Trott's eye's rolled north like a fourteen-year-old's, Bierlein muttered, "I don't see why not. You did a good job on that memorial service. I hear you and Sergeant Lincoln got along well. You've earned a little payback, too."

"Thank you, sir. Sir," J.W. lowered his voice, "could I ask a favor?" When Bierlein did not turn away, J.W. continued. "Sir, I need an hour's stick time to start getting current. Could I fly left seat in your ship, sir? But just for an hour, sir."

Colonel Bierlein pursed his lips. "I heard you were a pilot. Shame that you're stuck on the ground. How long since you've flown?"

"About six months, sir."

"That's a long time, Lieutenant. Cost the government nearly a hundred thousand dollars, or maybe it's a half a million, to train you to fly. Where you been, anyway?"

J.W. stood just a bit taller, "Jump School and Ranger School, sir, and riot duty down at the Pentagon with the 6th Cav."

"That why you're still all cut up? Look at you. Well, about the flying, see, now you're getting into Tom's territory. You need to work that out with him."

J.W. turned and caught the pilot's cold eyes. Though Tom had been haughtily ignoring the conversation, he peeked quickly at the colonel, who was observing the proceedings, scrutinizing just how his personal pilot was going to come to grips with the upstart lieutenant. With all eyes now on Tom, the gifted aviator grimaced and nodded J.W. toward the helicopter. The real co-pilot shot Tom a vexed look, but Tom angrily pointed his thumb at the back seat and bristled off in the direction of the ship.

When Bierlein finished his conversation with Major Trott, he walked with his command sergeant major toward the chopper, and Tom, who had leaned far back in his seat to steal a brief nap, snapped to attention and called out, "Here come da judge!"

In helicopters, the pilot in command sits on the right, as opposed to winged aircraft, in which the senior aviator traditionally occupies the left seat. Arguments have raged for years as to why. In flight school, J.W. had been taught it was because one may never take his right hand off the cyclic stick in a helicopter. If the command pilot was on the left, he would have to reach across his body with his left arm to get to the switches on the panel. However, those instructors with a history of duty in England claimed it was because helicopter etiquette was struck in Britain, where everything is backwards.

Early in flight school, when J.W. called out during class, "Yeah, but English *fixed wing* pilots sit on the left," it cost him an audience with the company commander after class.

But this was Viet Nam, and all the laws of the universe were reversed. J.W. was ordered into the right seat, and the aircraft commander, Tom, strapped in on the left. With Colonel Bierlein and his entourage aboard, and with J.W. desperate to distinguish himself and get transferred out of Normandy Base Camp, he reached up and down cranking throttles, pushing buttons, and flipping switches, initiating the starting sequence as smoothly as if he had been an instructor himself. But without having been invited to take control of the regimental commanding officer's personal helicopter, J.W. reaped for his efforts a hissed command from Tom. "I got the ship. You don't touch another goddamn thing until I tell you to."

Tom remained in control of the helicopter, not uttering a word or even turning to look at J.W. As they cruised north toward the capital, the pilot radioed Saigon Artillery Command for permission to fly west toward the Cambodian border. When they received clearance, there was a hard left turn, a sudden descent, and in seconds, they were sweeping low over sampans, choosing boats with young Vietnamese men aboard, the aircraft slowing to pass at a crawl, nearly capsizing the sampans, taunting the men to shoot at the chopper.

With no takers, Bierlein called over the intercom, "Tom, let's give the lieutenant a turn. Lieutenant, I want you to descend another hundred feet and fly along the banks on the east side of the river. See if we can flush a VC or two out of the bush, see if they're dumb enough to shoot at the colonel's ship."

Seconds later, J.W. took a deep breath and ever so softly dropped the collective, as if lowering a brand new baby into a bassinette, more intent on making a perfect descent than he had been on his final check ride of flight school. But Bierlein's attention was riveted to the scene unfolding on the ground. Over the intercom, J.W. heard the old man laugh sardonically as one miserable soul hopped out of the jungle and fired an AK-47 upward, sweeping green tracers far to the front of the ship. J.W. tensed, and the exceedingly sensitive helicopter jumped nose up.

Tom grabbed the controls away with a malevolent, "I got it!"

J.W. turned to look at Bierlein, who was shaking his head almost sadly, and J.W. understood he had squandered the likelihood he would be plucked from the maddening rear echelon to fly in combat. But Bierlein was not worried about a ten-foot burp of his chopper.

"See," Bierlein mumbled over the intercom, "these are not well-trained soldiers. Someone told the bastard to lead his target, but no one told him by how much. These people have no experience with machines, no feel for speed. Did you know, Lieutenant, that the French, when they invaded this country in the 1860s, opened a bunch of coal mines in the North, but didn't permit the Vietnamese to use shovels? Made them dig with their hands. Even a shovel was more technology than the French were willing to let the Vietnamese learn. Frogs kept them under control that way. Brilliant. And now that's where they are, a century behind. Sad, really. These are good people. But here we are, and here they are…" Colonel Bierlein drew a deep breath and asked, "Well, how do you like 'schoolyard payback,' Lieutenant?"

"Don't understand, sir."

"You will."

The command pilot swung the HUEY wildly back toward the creature, who abruptly apprehended his tactical miscue and dove desperately from bush to bush. The door gunner tightened the blood-red bandanna about his forehead, wiggled his shoulders, wiggled his ass in the seat as if getting comfortable for a good movie, charged his M-60, then grinned back at the colonel like a child seeking permission to take a cookie. Bierlein nodded authorization.

When it was all over, in many seconds more than J.W. believed would have been necessary had not the gunner spewed two belts of ammo in circles around the crawling target, Colonel Bierlein growled, "And give 'im another belt for Sergeant Lincoln—bastards."

Tom growled into the intercom, "You got it," but J.W.'s hands were vibrating so uncontrollably, the pilot admonished, "Get the corncob outta your ass and climb to and maintain one-five-hundred. And that was my kill, boy, not yours."

"Ah, we can give him an assist, Tom," Bierlein laughed over the intercom. "That took a nickel's worth of guts to sit up there on your first hop out of flight school, don't you think? He didn't twitch while we were being fired at." He paused then went on with an animated note in his voice. "Hey, let's go out to the Happy Valley Motel. I need a break. We haven't been there since First Battalion cleaned the place up. Let's take a look around."

J.W. was surprised a major motel chain had come to Viet Nam, and he allowed himself a modicum of excitement and a broad smile over the promise of real American food, an air-conditioned, clean restaurant, and perhaps a flush toilet. The pilot, nowhere near as animated, flew a northerly heading, sending J.W.'s brow into a wrinkled question. That bearing would put them on a course away from Saigon, and J.W. could not imagine a Happy Valley Motel in the countryside. Eventually, Tom gave him back the controls, and J.W. became occupied trying to maintain the stability of the helicopter as his tremors once again made the ship oscillate. To distract himself, he thought of the coming burger, rare, with a slice of American Cheese, a dollop of mayonnaise, razor-thin curls of magenta Bermuda onion, and thinly sliced tomatoes. When Tom asked him to read one of the gauges, J.W. could barely answer, taking several seconds to swallow the buckets of saliva.

With each mile, J.W.'s hands lightened on the controls until he finally guided the helicopter with just his fingertips, the technique that had been drilled into student pilots during the endless months of harsh lessons in flight school. As the colonel's ship cruised over the thick, abandoned rubber plantations of III Corps, the emerald paddies of the world's richest rice fields, J.W. began to understand why emperors and peasants had died fighting over control of Viet Nam for centuries, for millennia. He had never seen food growing in such abundance.

Bierlein eyed a field of dried grass a mile to the west, and he ordered J.W. to orbit about it. "Get down a little closer, Lieutenant; it's okay, I've been here before."

"Wilco, sir. Goin' down."

When the ship was turning lazy circles over the grassland, Bierlein spoke softly into the intercom. "I *have* been here before. My father was, too. It was in the 1600s, a peasant war. Yes, this was the field. If he were here, he'd recognize it. This is really quite remarkable. When we leave Happy Valley, Tom, drop me off in Saigon then go back down to Normandy, to my trailer. I'll give you the key to the safe. Get my father's World War Two diary. He wants me to look in there and find out about this field. Weathersby, give Tom the ship and mark down the coordinates so we can find it again." Colonel Bierlein paused for a final look then snapped into the intercom, "Okay, next stop, Happy Valley."

Twenty miles farther west, at a small Vietnamese settlement surrounded by bright green rice paddies, Tom pointed to a patch of sand and keyed the intercom, instructing J.W. to set up an approach.

"Is this Happy Valley?" J.W. queried.

"Yep. This be the place." J.W. could see neither the motel nor the highway leading to it, for only endless hectares of rice paddy existed this far from Saigon. The small patch of sand toward which J.W. aimed the helicopter was surrounded, not by a swimming pool, cabanas, and tennis courts, but by a tiny army base of a two dozen OD tents and several 105 millimeter Howitzers. A mile of dirt road spread out in two opposite thin spokes from the hub, like a helicopter's main rotor. As they neared the settlement, J.W. could make out grass huts clustered along the red mud that served as Viet Nam's Highway 29.

Tom snapped into his mike, "Steep approach. Maintain at least thirty knots and less than three-hundred feet-per-minute descent. It's hot down there. We're loaded. Pay attention."

J.W. fought to maintain control of the ship as they settled into the night defensive position, the NDP, but the blowing sand disoriented him, and the craft began to roll hard right until Tom stole the controls and bottomed the collective, dropping the ship onto the ground with a vicious thwack. GIs poured from their tents to witness, wide-eyed, the helicopter rebounding from skid to skid. Surely, it would roll onto its side after the next bounce, but Tom pushed this and pulled that until there was a final bang, and the aircraft slammed to a stop ninety degrees from where J.W. had aimed it.

J.W. opened his eyes. Red sand swirled about a sign to his front, inches from the helicopter's canopy:

WELCOME TO HAPPY VALLEY NIGHT DEFENSIVE POSITION
TACTICAL HOME OF THE 33RD MECHANIZED
INFANTRY BRIGADE
THE TRACKS OF DESTINY
SANFORD T. BIERLEIN—COLONEL,
INFANTRY, COMMANDING

From the back of the helicopter Colonel Bierlein snarled, "I thought you told me you'd been to flight school. Where, like Trott says, China? You better stick to translating, Weathersby."

J.W. unbuckled and surveyed the seventy-five-yard diameter loop of sand and mud dotted with cannons, pup tents, and a large command tent at the center. An obscure tree line lay five-hundred meters beyond the razor-edged concertina wire that encircled the 33rd Mech's night defensive position. J.W. stared past the barbed wire into the surrounding village of My Co, eying dozens and dozens of thatched huts arrayed along the dirt highway. At the very edge of the village sat the berm, an eight-foot-high ridge of earth, a medieval town wall sculpted by the U.S. Army Corps of Engineer battalions' bulldozers early in the war. It was the Americans' first attempt at keeping the insurgent Viet Cong out of the villages, to deny them food and recruits. Little thought had been given to the reality that the VC were already inside, for they were the farmers, the village council, and the village chiefs.

The population had dug more gaps in the berm over time than there was berm. By the time J.W. arrived, he was able to gaze freely through the breaks, far into the rice paddies. He stood, enchanted by the asthenic figures in black pajamas and conical hats, the gangs of peasants who threshed rice as far as he could see into the fields. Grey-black, colossally-horned water buffalo hove primeval plows, the massive oxen moving lazily across the muddy plains. Each animal was commanded by a single ten-year-old who snapped at it gently with a skinny stick—the accelerator, and maneuvered the creatures into arrow-straight furrows by yanking on snippets of string looped through punctures burned into the buffalos' nostrils—steering wheels. He shook his head. He was witnessing what he had only read about and studied for years since grade school. He was beholding practices that had given life to the world's ancient societies for untold thousands of years.

J.W. searched for an opening to escape the helicopter crew, its passengers, and the GIs who were ambling back to their tents, grumbling angrily that disaster had been avoided. He walked cautiously toward the thick concertina wire that surrounded the NDP. From the perimeter, he had an unobstructed view of the rustic village of My Co. Dozens and dozens of tiny huts lined the road. He moved closer. The walls of the one-room structures were an amalgam of dried mud, earth stolen from the berm, and rice-stalk stubble; the roof, foot-thick, woven straw. He took a few hesitant steps outside the east gate; merely a gap in the razor wire. He passed two GI guards on folding chairs, both nearly comatose in the withering heat. He loosened his .45 from its holster, edged a few strides along the muddy path, and then a few more until he rounded a curve, now cut off from the NDP. He stopped dead, surrounded front, rear, and on the flanks, by the tenuous hootches, fragile dwellings the peasants of Cochin China had drawn on as shelter for eons. He dared not approach the doorless lodgings just feet away, though when he waved at a little boy, a platoon of nearly-naked children playing about the buffalo and hog pens ran to J.W., pulling fearlessly at his fatigue pants to drag him into one of the huts.

Expecting to be ordered back into the womb of the American base by an angry, shouted order, he listened hard but heard nothing. He sat for a moment in the empty shanty with the kids at his feet; it was musty and dark, the scent unlike anything he'd ever encountered. Frightened, he walked past the children back onto the road. In the brilliance of the sun and crystal blue sky, his shoulders relaxed, and he paced calmly around the bend back toward the NDP. Near the gate, he could see the helicopter crew asleep in and under the ship. The gate guards had not budged, lifeless in the torpid air. He could see into the open flap of the command tent. Colonel Bierlein and the local commander were leaning back, drinking coffee.

The kids took his hands and towed him back around the bend. "Okay, okay, just a few more minutes."

An ancient man with a long, wispy beard had just pulled his ox-cart to a halt in front of a hut. He mopped sweat from his face with a scarf of a once-white cloth then wound the material into a bulbous turban. When it sat on his head just so, he climbed insipidly aboard the rickety wagon to toss overboard piles of straw. J.W. ambled to the tiny dray, smiled broadly, and babbled in English, "Hey, lemme give you a hand there, sir." The man grinned, but as J.W. hopped aboard the pre-Enlightenment vehicle, the old farmer fell to his knees, kowtowing, hands pressed together in prayer, whining in a pleading falsetto. J.W. nodded respectfully to the old farmer, who fell silent but could not arrest the mad tremor of his hands.

Two dozen peasants darted from their shanties, eyes pleading for the huge foreign warrior to spare their elder. J.W. raised his hands into to air, hoping that was how the Vietnamese surrendered. The faces remained taut, so he smiled broadly, and a couple of villagers returned the gesture. He bent forward very slowly to toss the rest of the hay from the cart.

With the wagon empty, he brushed bits of dried grass from the front of his uniform and tugged the .45 free to blow the chaff from it. The weapon wasn't two millimeters out of the holster before a dozen villagers shrieked and sprinted toward their huts. He dropped the pistol back, and the intrepid few who had fled but three steps drew together back at the cart. Several pointed at J.W. then at the pile of straw on the ground. There were gales of laughter, drawing several of the fleeing dozen to peek out of their hootches. A number moved back cautiously. J.W. helped the old man down with one hand and, stabilizing the holster with his other hand, jumped to the ground. The crowd cowered again; the anxious fraction fled for good.

The old man pointed at the sun and took J.W.'s wrist brusquely, pulling him into the hut. A throng of the very young and very old gathered at light speed, crowding the front door and glassless windows cut in the mud walls. The audience gasped as Weathersby removed his helmet and Ray Bans, and became speechless when he lit a perfectly cylindrical, filtered cigarette. The old man put his hand out and J.W. shook it, but the man tsooked, waved no with his other hand, and pointed to the Salems. J.W. smacked his own forehead. The spectators jumped back. J.W. smiled and bowed, and the crowd reassembled. When he placed the pack on the table, an avuncular, bandy-legged peasant in grimy shorts three sizes too large scurried in, bowed, as had J.W., and pulled a smoke free. More ancient men appeared out of the vaporous heat, bustling in one by one, bowing, and slowly emptying the pack of Salems.

A calm descended, and J.W. exhaled to relax in the unexpected coolness. A young woman moved delicately through the throng into the single room. Though her clothing was faded and nearly threadbare, her onyx eyes and flowing, ebony hair captured J.W. His eyes locked on hers. She smiled gently for a moment but averted her glance, as if it was not the first time a man had stared at her.

J.W. recalled the warning given all soldiers bound for Viet Nam—don't discuss politics, keep your hands off the women, and give away a lot of tobacco. He looked away. Quickly, another detail about duty in Asia percolated up through the heat, one delivered by an old warrant officer in flight school. "The Vietnamese don't believe in romantic love. So, don't get your hopes up. There's no such thing as dating, and the only sex is from the prostitutes, and they all got the clap. Word to the wise, rookie pilot, stay away from all of 'em." J.W. couldn't, though, help stealing another glance.

The old man spoke to the woman, "*Cô* Lin, *di...*" "Miss Lin, go and..." but J.W. did not understand the rest of the order barked in heavy, village dialect.

She smiled, obediently fetching from a hiding place in the thatch of the primitive roof a dwarf, rusted tin of sweetened condensed milk, into which she pierced a crescent of tiny holes. From a nook in the hard-mud half-walls, she pulled a small packet of folded, yellowed newspaper, out of which she carefully scooped a few grains of black powder. She picked one of several thick, scratched, French Duralex glasses off the rough-hewn picnic table, tossed the residual tea and leaves on the pounded-earthen floor, then sprinkled in the black powder. She added boiling water from a kettle that hung over a few chunks of glowing charcoal in the corner of the shelter then spooned in nearly half the can of milk, but did not stir.

With two hands, she presented the glass to J.W., obsequiously bowing her head. J.W. sipped, relieved that it was coffee. Stale, perhaps, but it was sweet and creamy. He smiled, searched in his fatigue pockets, and drew out another pack of Salems. They were gone before the coffee was.

The old man with the feathery beard called out to a small child who had watched, wide-eyed, from the door, "*Em* Huong, go and bring..." but that was all J.W. deciphered.

The boy left with dispatch, his tattered sandals flapping sand and dust and pig and chicken droppings as he sprinted to a nearby hootch, the "village restaurant." That structure was, on the surface, no different than the one in which J.W. sat, aside from the battered, sweating, chipped, bullet-riddled, faded red, English language Coca Cola ice chest that held a position of nobility in front of the shanty. Where it had spent its useful life, and how it had arrived on that patch of tired land, was a question no one was able to answer.

Em Huong flew back in minutes, clutching a bowl of charcoal-grilled meat propped upon a mountain of steaming rice, bits of ginger and garlic flecking the grain. The bowl was plopped down in front of the foreign guest. When J.W. smiled uncertainly, his host essentially smacked himself in the head for his boorishness, called out, and was handed a bottle of *nước mắm.* He drenched the fare in the very fishy fish sauce, grabbed a pair of chopsticks off the table, wiped them carelessly on his manure-encrusted, baggy pajama bottoms, and handed them to

J.W. He leaned back, lit one of the Salems, and puffed contentedly as his guest studied the meal.

After a long pause, the gentleman introduced himself in Vietnamese. "I am Long. This is my nephew, *Em* Huong." The boy took a step back and stood in modest satisfaction over the feast he had delivered to the sweat-drenched foreigner. They pointed at the charred meat and then at J.W.'s mouth.

J.W. nodded in thanks and hesitated for a moment as the image of Sergeant Lincoln crossed his consciousness. But he shrugged his shoulders and ate. Inwardly, he took pride in his sophisticated gustatory facility, his aptitude to discern the tired, frozen fowl on which he had been raised from the free-roaming, fresh capon of the Vietnamese countryside. Though there was not all that much meat on the charcoal-roasted bones, it was sweet and flavored with the delicate spices of a mysterious civilization. It was the best meal he'd had in the month since the rooster he had been forced to behead, pluck, and boil in an ammo can during Ranger School.

The old man smiled broadly at the relief on J.W.'s face then spoke again to *Em* Huong, who left at a trot, soon to return with a second helping. J.W. cackled, flapped his arms as if wings, and proclaimed in English, "I love fresh roast chicken!" directing his comments mostly to the young woman. He watched for the slightest flicker of interest, for the most trifling smile, but she ignored him studiously, busying herself at the treadle sewing machine, eyes fixed on the material of the baby's shirt she was mending.

The older men, absorbed by the American cigarettes, and soon by the poorly veiled lack of attention *Cô* Lin was affording the strange guest, spewed a few remarks that shaded her delicate complexion toward the red end of the spectrum. She let her head bob downward, and when J.W. used the pretext that everyone else in the hut was looking at her, he caught her stealing the very briefest glance at him.

J.W. blushed, and the men laughed aloud, but J.W. pointed to the meat and rubbed his stomach. That brought additional howls of laughter from the crowd that had grown so large, the light from the door and glassless windows was nearly totally muted. The young woman stood, turned toward J.W., and straightened the fabric of her blouse as she walked from the hut, unintentionally revealing the most delicate outline of her breasts.

Her exit also sent *Em* Huong dashing off a third time, soon returning, not with charbroiled meat, but toting a string of twitching organisms that had only just gone to their final reward. J.W.'s smile broadened, though insincerely. As opposed to feathers, the creatures were daubed with scabby, dull gray fur. More disquieting, however, were the long, red, scaly tails.

"Same same," *Em* Huong blurted in English, grinning, pointing to the rodents and then to J.W.'s empty second bowl.

Ông Long proffered a third helping, but J.W. patted his stomach, stood, bowed, and walked outside, not sure if he could gain control of his queasiness and avoid a very culturally distasteful physiologic reaction. He stole a glimpse at *Cô* Lin, who stood at an adjacent hut giggling with the girls.

When the neighborhood quieted, J.W. lit his last cigarette, hopped up onto a chord of firewood, and stared at the distant tree line. This was the farthest he had ventured into the war, and he searched for a flicker of movement, perhaps a VC operative scrutinizing the party of dignitaries that had descended upon the village of My Co. What if he actually spied the enemy, he asked himself. Would he run like a buffoon back to the NDP screaming, or would he dispatch the foe himself?

He made a quick decision to take control and fire his .45 pistol then wade through the paddies to finish his quarry, calling over his shoulder for the colonel and his staff to rush into the fields and cover his six. Colonel Bierlein would nod professorially and allow J.W. the kill, taking only an assist for himself, awarding nothing to Tom. With that redemption, he would be accepted into the fraternity of combat in front of the regimental commander, and precariously in the purview of the colonel's Medal of Honor. J.W. would grasp the moment of camaraderie to end his stay at Normandy and find a more consequential way to pass the rest of his year in Asia. With that pretension, he swaggered a few steps out of the village toward the edge of the mysterious forest, but several of the villagers trotted over and tugged him back, gently shaking their heads, no.

On the helicopter back to Normandy Basecamp, Colonel Bierlein mused aloud to his sergeant major, "Top, what would happen if we built a school in My Co? The 33rd Mech provides the labor and material, and the Vietnamese find a teacher. Do you think that would work? We cleaned the place up for their new village chief. Let's say we work with him."

"I don't know," the grizzled World War II sergeant major sniped, "Who's gonna run the project, Colonel? You have an extra officer around to spare on that kinda stuff?"

"Could be an enlisted man. An E-6."

"Colonel, look, I don't have anyone who isn't busy fighting this war. And if you put an EM out there alone, no matter how good he is, none of the government officials gonna pay him any heed. You're also gonna need someone who speaks the language. I don't know, sir. This is a combat unit, not the United Nations, sir. That's a big step."

For a moment, there was abject silence, but from somewhere in the chopper, a phantom voice chirped over the intercom, "Sir, I'd like to give that a try."

Bierlein barked, "Who said that? That you, Tom?"

"No, sir!"

"Sergeant Major?"

"Yeah, right, Colonel."

"It was me, sir, Weathersby, sir. I think can do it, sir. I've already been working with the Vietnamese."

"I know you have. I'm sure you can, but you're a pilot. You know how much the taxpayers forked over for your wings? Million bucks or so. We need to get you trained up and flying again. I can't waste a pilot with guts at Happy Valley, or even at Normandy, anymore. Trott's just going to have to part with you." A laugh belched over the intercom.

Chapter 3

DESPITE MAJOR TROTT'S considered recommendation that J.W. be assigned to fly low and slow over North Viet Nam as a diversionary tactic, Bierlein prevailed and sent J.W. to the Helicopter Company. Eventually, he was given command of a shiny, refurbished D-model HUEY and its crew of three, a co-pilot and two door gunners. Though at first the ship appeared new, and the crew strutted about the airfield, by the end of week two, paint was peeling in sheets from the fuselage, uncovering the patched bullet holes and shrapnel perforations. At the end of the third week, J.W. went to the executive officer and bitched that gauges were popping out of the instrument panel and one of the radios had caught fire.

The captain listened, nodded in sympathy while J.W. went on, then grunted, "Just get on with it, Weathersby."

Three days later, the co-pilot landed hard at Normandy Base Camp on a refueling stop, and soon after takeoff there was an awful bang. J.W. realized his aircraft was taking enemy fire. The crew chief, Thunder Chicken, leaned out of the aircraft and screamed over the intercom, "Holy shit, sir, they just shot off one of the skids."

J.W. turned back to Normandy, where he hovered above the runway at three feet and ordered the crew to jump off. He hovered for another hour, hanging in the air inches off the ground, flying, but going nowhere, waiting for someone to figure out what to do to save the ship and his life. One of the Vietnamese coolies ambled over, watched for moment, pointed at the ground, then tilted his head to the left, closed his eyes, and placed his hands, palms together, against his left cheek. He was ignored, so he ran to the nearby barracks and came back dragging a mattress. He placed it neatly on the ground under the side of the helicopter without the skid. Still, there was no response, so he set out again, this time returning with another mattress and two fuming, pursuing GIs just steps behind.

The order went out for every mattress in Normandy to be purloined and delivered to the airfield. Actually, it took only twelve of the mildewed, ratty pads before J.W. was ordered to let the ship settle. Several GIs pushed on the side without the skid and kept the ship level until the engine and the deadly main rotor ceased spinning.

As the carping from those who had lost their beds grew, Major Trott drove up and agreed to provide a free can of beer to each of the dozen soldiers. As the major reboarded his Jeep, one of J.W.'s crew overheard Trott mumble to the helicopter XO, "Shit, that guy's not worth two six-packs."

When J.W. reported to the Air Cav Company commanding officer that evening, the old man hissed, "Maintenance says the skid wasn't shot off; it fell off. Damaged a long time before you took off today. That's the crap they're sending us—refurbished trash. Got shot to hell here, put on a boat to Seattle, then ferried on an uncovered truck down to Brownsville, Texas. Labor's dirt cheap down there. They spray some paint on it, pretend they're hiding the damage, then some poor schnook just waiting to come back here for his second or third tour gets current flying it back to Seattle. They load it on a ship, leave it out on deck to rot in the salt spray, and a month later, it's back. You can be damn sure the old man ain't ridin' around in no flyin' sarcophagus."

"So, sir, do I get a new ship?"

"Hell, no, you don't. Weathersby, my suggestion is that you make peace with your lord, 'cause that bucket of bolts is yours for the duration."

⁂

By autumn, with the high quotient of attrition to which helicopter pilots were privy, J.W. became one of the senior pilots in the squadron, spending many an afternoon cruising high above the countryside, avoiding the stifling dry season heat. He'd brief his crew that they had been ordered to fly as high as the ship would take them and keep an eye on the war for Colonel Bierlein. At 9,000 feet, J.W. tuned the helicopter's ADF navigation radio to 540 kilohertz,

Armed Forces Radio, and the week's top one hundred. The ship turned endless circles in the sky where the air was cool and didn't smell. The crew bopped around in their armored seats to the steady rock and roll that sustained the tip of America's spear.

After a mission west of Saigon in early October, J.W. looked into the distance and believed he could make out the village of My Co. His first thought was of the lithesome woman with the unforgettable eyes, and he thought about that last glance of him she'd stolen. The haunting image brought the cyclic to the left, and the ship gliding toward the hamlet. When they were within a few miles, he noticed the tents and guns were gone, the regiment having closed up shop to build NDPs ever closer to the Cambodian border.

Over the intercom, he called to the crew that he was taking them to Happy Valley. "I'm springing for burgers and beer."

Thunder Chicken cackled, "Sir, they got imported beer, sir? Because, I need to tell ya, sir, that Beer 33 shit these here Veeeemaneeeses be brewin' ain't what I enjoy."

J.W. was about to answer, but the co-pilot interrupted, "Sir, do you think we should drink and fly? In flight school, they said 'twelve hours between bottle and throttle.'"

"That's right, Lieutenant. We'll have no drinking on this ship. No, sir. Tell you what. You make the approach into Happy Valley. You do a good job, and I'll buy the beer tonight at the O-Club. But it's hot down there, and we're loaded. Maintain thirty knots and less than three-hundred-feet-per-minute on the descent."

J.W. lightened his hands on the controls slowly. "You got it," he called to the co-pilot, but in the heat, the ship plummeted a couple of hundred feet, missed the remnants of Happy Valley Night Defensive Position, snapped the crown from a banana tree, and skidded into a rice paddy nearly a hundred meters from where J.W. had instructed the neophyte touch down. J.W. stuck his head out of his door and surveyed the flank of the helicopter, shaking his head at the veneer of mashed banana that had splattered the length of his ship. "Where the hell did you go to flight school? China?"

The crew slogged through the mud toward a gaggle of laboring peasants, all except Thunder Chicken, who stayed behind, having parlayed a promise to spit-shine the hull into an excuse to avoid walking in the flooded paddies. "Sir, I heard they take a dump in the water to feed the plants. No sir, not for me."

J.W.'s last words to his crew chief were, "Mind the radio, Chick. If the old man calls, tell 'im we're out patrolling the countryside, that we saw some VC and we're goin' in after them. Then just say the words, 'We're givin' 'em a schoolyard lesson.'"

Thunder Chicken, a tough black kid from East St. Louis, was a short, bony figure with a snout that more resembled a chicken's beak than a nose. Incongruously, though, his deep voice reverberated like thunder. As J.W. and the two other crew members left the ship, Thunder Chicken watched from the corner of his eye until his mates were lost in the brush. He threw his cleaning rag to the side and dropped onto a soft patch of moss under the HUEY's tail section. Looking back, it was impossible for J.W. to determine if his crew chief was on his back, wiping banana from the ship's stinger, or sleeping. In the glare of the fiery sun, all J.W. could see to remind him of his crew chief was the decal of Huey Duck under a bolt of lightning pasted to the front of the man's helmet. Thunder Chicken had propped it on top of the tail boom, double-dark visor facing the menacing wood line as if he was their sentinel.

J.W. smiled, recalling the night he had presented Thunder Chicken with an envelope to write to his mother for stickers of roosters and thunder. But all Mother Chick had unearthed at the Five and Dimes of St. Louis were several dozen decals of ducks and lightening, dozens of which wound up pasted to his helmet, his footlocker, his seat in the helicopter, his seat in the mess hall, his seat in the latrine, his M-60 machine gun, his M-16 rifle, the tail section of the chopper, and on the "Jesus nut" atop the ship, the fastener that held the main rotor to the hull of the helicopter.

J.W. smiled again at Thunder Chicken, who sat quietly, peacefully dreaming, his M-16 propped against a skid, the aircraft's mobile radio speaker dangling from the tail rotor. His crew chief was surrounded by an unchanging, ancient, Asian world. The scene was bucolic, and J.W. promised himself he would come out there once a week in the future. It would be good for all of them to experience this nether world, especially Chic, who had but a month or two left in country. J.W. wondered, on the other hand, what the man's life would become once he was back in his ghetto. All the training, all the work, even that which he might learn from peasants, what was it all for?

J.W. led the two other crew members further into the paddies, stopping to smile at the women and take a hand at threshing rice. J.W. looked about for *Cô* Lin as he beat the long stalks of grain, though she was not in sight. The presence of several comely young ladies, though, distracted him, and he happily spent the time practicing his Vietnamese on them.

The three soldiers horsed around in the paddies until a sudden burst of light weapons fire from the area of the parked helicopter rattled the torpid air. The crew chief, Sergeant E-5 Winston (Thunder Chicken) E. James, had been startled out of his nap by what he later swore was a terrorizing vibration of rustling from the jungle. Chic reported that he had sprung from his housekeeping duties under the ship, charged his M-16, and fired at the battalion of soldiers he recognized as dressed in North Vietnamese Army garb.

"Right over there, sir. And I hit one of mutha fuckas, too. I saw him go down and his pals take off. Go look, sir. You'll see. Find the blood, at least."

The co-pilot listened for a bit then walked to a circle of shiny metal near the helicopter. He picked a piece from the ground, gasped, and ran to J.W. "Sir, look at this. It's aluminum. I think they hit the ship."

J.W. scrutinized the fuselage. Other than the peeling OD paint and the hardening veneer of banana, it was pristine. But he noticed a pile of the aluminum shavings on the ground next to a mound of spent M-16 brass, and he looked up. Several holes had been shot into the main rotor. Thunder Chicken looked up as well. "But, sir, I saw 'em, sir. In the woods, sir. I swear it, sir. They must 'a returned fire and hit the ship. But I got one, sir. You gonna give me a kill for that, sir?"

J.W. dispatched the co-pilot and Pecos, the left door-gunner, to sweep the edge of the jungle, but the two scouts scurried back in minutes, shaking their heads. Pecos declared, "No way, sir. Ain't nuthin' out there. No guts, no nuthin'. Brush's too thick. Nobody been out there in years."

The new co-pilot, a shade paler than when they had first arrived in My Co, climbed onto the hull, poked around the holes, and blurted down to J.W., "This thing gonna fly, sir?"

"What the hell do I look like, Werner Von Braun? Only one way to find out. Okay, monkeys, into the ship." J.W. called out the starting sequence, but as the turbine engine came hot, the unbalanced blades began to flap like a pigeon's wings. With hands shuddering, J.W. was barely able to put his finger on the intercom button. The co-pilot, though, grabbed the stick with both hands and warned, "Sir, in flight school they said we should shut down if there were unusual vibrations during the start."

"Thank you, Lieutenant."

J.W. had the crew secure the aircraft then sent them through the paddies into the village. The co-pilot asked if there was a telephone or a radio to call for a rescue plane, or maybe a taxi back to Saigon.

"Yeah, Lieutenant, there's a phone booth at the corner of Water Buffalo Street and Pig Alley. Look, knucklehead, there's never been electricity or running water within twenty miles of this vill. Closest phone's forty klics south. And you seen any cars up here lately? We got a problem."

J.W. gave a traveling egg roll salesman on an ancient Schwinn bicycle a dollar in Military Payment Certificates then made pedaling motions. With that settled, he wrote a letter and printed Moc Hoa, the closest town, in giant letters at the top. He pantomimed that the note must go to an American.

"That's some seventeen miles east of here, young man," the man cackled in Vietnamese, "too far for a dollar." J.W. upped the payoff to three bucks, and the man pedaled off south after giving each of the soldiers a complimentary egg roll.

"That was nice of him to give us a free treat," the co-pilot smiled.

"Yeah, and it was nice of me to give him a week-and-a-half's salary."

Even if the egg roll salesman didn't get to Moc Hoa that afternoon, he would the next morning. Anyway, it would not be long before the search and rescue teams were airborne combing the countryside for the missing half-million dollars of manure-and-banana-crusted technology.

But no one had shown up by the time a red blast of setting sunlight bathed the paddies. The crew was speechless. Even Pecos was moved. "Hey, sir, I don't think I'm ever gonna forget this."

On the other hand, the beauty of the sunset did not mute their vulnerability. If they stayed with the helicopter all night, and the Viet Cong enemy was so minded, the ship would be rocketed and machine-gunned. The aircraft would be destroyed, and they would lose their lives—it was for certain. If they hid in town, though, the VC might be averse to spraying their own home village with lead, and the crew *might* survive the night.

They chose town. The villagers, especially the old ladies, doted over them, plying the four with rice cakes and tea. Late in the evening, when most of the village was asleep, they went to a hut in which a kerosene lantern still flickered. The elderly woman welcomed them and pulled J.W. aside. She wrote the word "Binh" on the edge of a piece of old newspaper and pointed to herself. She made tea and served tiny tropical bananas. When the men leaned back and lit cigarettes, she retreated in a limp to her hammock and napped.

Nearing midnight, with all but the new co-pilot asleep in the obstinate heat, *Cô* Lin, the young woman with the striking onyx eyes, came to old Mrs. Binh's hut. She whispered to the wisp of a woman, not wanting to wake the Americans, but the neophyte co-pilot shook J.W. awake. He looked up at her and smiled. She stared at J.W. slack-jawed when she recognized him, but quickly lowered her eyes. J.W., though, did not miss the edges of the young woman's mouth curl up slightly. Mrs. Binh also flashed the slyest smile. J.W.'s stomach fluttered, and he stared at *Cô* Lin for a moment, wondering if hers did as well.

Cô Lin opened a wooden box on the pounded dirt floor next to the bare wood-plank Vietnamese bed on which Pecos was snoring. She took out a school kid's notebook and pencils then left hurriedly without turning back. J.W. conjectured that she lived there with the old lady, and he looked about the little hut for signs of her soul.

Somewhat awake, J.W. thought he heard a helicopter in the distance. He jumped up and ordered the crew back to the ship as the rotor slap of a pair of HUEYs ground closer. He put five MPC dollars on the table and waved to the old lady, who shuffled to the door to watch them run off.

On the way to the helicopter, Pecos stopped at the village restaurant. He opened the Coca Cola chest and pulled out a couple of beers and a bottle of *rượu đế,* the Vietnamese rice liquor so potent, old-time pilots swore they had used it in lieu of JP-4 to fuel helicopters. He jumped into the hut, dropped five dollars on the single, raw wood picnic table, and ran to catch up. "For later, sir," he assured, "when we get back. The rescue celebration."

As J.W. fired flares toward the helicopters, the ships banked hard, turning away, their crews no doubt convinced they had come under surface-to-air missile attack. They would report the incident, and J.W. guessed the U.S. government would see the use of the new technology as an escalation of the war, and use it as an excuse to nuke Russia or China. Worse, he worried his crew would become the target of heavy American artillery that night.

J.W. sat with his men at the wounded chopper, talking about home, taking tiny swallows from the unlabeled bottle of rice liquor. J.W., exercising his prerogative as commander in chief of the marooned contingent, took for himself the two Vietnamese 33 Beers.

Thunder Chicken shook his head and grumbled, "No, sir. This here *rượu đế* shit taste like gasoline. Lemme hold a can of that of 33 Beer. I be givin' you my share of this shit, sir."

"Nah, Thunder Chick," J.W. laughed. "I know you hate that 33 Beer. You need to leave the suds for me. See, I'm sacrificing myself for my crew."

"Sacrificin', sir?"

"Yes, Thunder Chicken, I'm surrendering my life because I'm concerned about your health. That's my job as your commanding officer. Beer 33's laced with formaldehyde. It's poison. Now *rượu đế*, that is pure rice distillate, my man. Much better for you. A natural product."

"Formaldehyde, sir? Is that bad for you?" The new co-pilot gulped. "I've already drunk a lot of that 33 Beer."

"Yes, formaldehyde, very bad, impotency, Lieutenant. Didn't you pay attention in chemistry?"

When they began to creep back to the village, Thunder Chicken and the co-pilot were sure they saw shadows darting about, so J.W. acceded to their moaning and made plans to remain near the aircraft. They split the guard shifts, two men awake, two hours at a time. J.W. had the two who slept do so away from the ship, feet facing north, on their backs, remaining oriented, even while dreaming—one of the encyclopedia of jungle rules J.W. had internalized in Ranger School. The two men on guard were also away from the ship. J.W. sat awake with Thunder Chicken, watching the crew chief's trigger finger more closely than the wood line.

DISTINGUISHED MERITORIOUS SERVICE WHILE PARTICIPATING IN AERIAL FLIGHT

Such were the words engraved on the citations Weathersby and his crew were awarded for their heroism; though for the four of them, it had been a respite from the war, an in-country R&R of sorts, and even Thunder Chicken had been sad to leave My Co. They had eaten with the villagers, washed with water from their wells, and worked in the hamlet helping repair Mrs. Binh's crumbling mud wall hut. There had been plenty of time for good deeds—the rescue helicopter hadn't shown up until after noon the next day, just as the co-pilot had slipped onto the back of a motor scooter headed toward Moc Hoa. They had flagged it down, and J.W. had forked over more for the ticket than the total value of the tired Vespa. But a moment later, the rescue ship appeared over the horizon, and the co-pilot jumped from the back seat. J.W. howled for a refund. The driver laughed and sped off with a roar that drew the villagers from their hootches.

At the end of the week, an award ceremony was convened at Long Binh Post, near Saigon, to honor the crew. They had become a band of heroes for the brass to parade before the troops, soldiers whose morale had sagged to an all-time low. A few medals were bestowed by the master of ceremonies, General Creighton Abrams, Commander of Troops in Viet Nam, and a luncheon was prepared for the honorees.

It was at the General's table, along with Colonel Bierlein, that J.W. supped on liver with bacon. A lively conversation ensued as the general spoke fondly about having served in the same armor battalion with Colonel Bierlein's twin brother in the deserts of North Africa during the Second World War. "Heroric son of a bitch, that one," Abrams laughed. "Almost as good as you, Sandy. What a family."

When a silence fell over the table, General Abrams turned to J.W. and queried him about his captivity in the enemy village of My Co.

J.W. piped up, "Sir, to be honest, they were good to us. We ate well."

"Better than this, I hope," General Abrams sneered, nodding down at the fare.

"Yes, sir. Sir, to be honest, I'd like to go back out there, back to that hamlet and be an S-5. It's not that I want to turn in my wings, sir, but I think I could do more for you out there than in a HUEY."

"What are you going to with your time? You just can't harvest rice and fix mud huts," General Abrams laughed, but turned to Bierlein before J.W. could answer. "Sandy, can you spare him?"

"You mean spare his life, sir?" Bierlein hissed, softening his comeback with a sly smile.

"So, this isn't the first time you're hearing of his plan?"

"No, sir. But that may be a good place for him. It'll certainly be easier on the regiment's aircraft."

Chapter 4

By the end of October, elements of the 33rd Mechanized Infantry had returned to Tien Giang Province to resurrect Happy Valley Night Defensive Position, now a patch of bare sand in the middle of the village of My Co. Nominally, the base had been abandoned for several months after Colonel Bierlein was satisfied the village had been "pacified," but in truth, the 33rd Mech had been ordered by President Johnson to start secret interdiction missions along the Ho Chi Minh Trail on the other side of the Cambodian border.

During a lull in the war, Bierlein attended a lunch with several other brigade level commanders. The man next to him, the CO of the 526th Engineers, teased, "Sandy, my guys tell me your village of My Co is crawling with VC again. They see them when they fly over. Little bastards don't even try to hide. You want us to rotate through there with our road graders and tidy it up for you?"

Bierlein did not laugh. He sent the 33rd Mech's First Battalion back to Happy Valley NDP the next morning. Twenty minutes after the tanks rumbled into My Co, the colonel's personal helicopter hovered on the road just east of the NDP. J.W. dropped his duffel bag into the red dust and jumped out after it. He was armed with a dusty .45 and a letter signed by Bierlein himself, designating First Lieutenant J.W. Weathersby Mayor of My Co. The document conferred upon him sole permission to enter the hamlet as he saw fit, and to deny entrance to those Americans he didn't consider suitable for the mission of winning the hearts and minds of the peasantry.

The battalion's commanding officer, a brand spanking new lieutenant colonel fresh from the States, recognized the chopper as Bierlein's and sprinted through the gate to meet the ship. When he discovered only J.W., the CO turned to leave. J.W. called out, "Sir, Lieutenant Weathersby reporting. I work for you now, sir."

J.W. presented his credentials, the letter from Colonel Bierlein, with a flourish, and snapped to attention as his new CO perused the grant. The more the man read, though, the tighter his lips stretched, and three-quarters down the page, he took a deep breath and spoke. "In other words, if I am to understand correctly, from now on, Lieutenant J.W. Weathersby tells me where I can and cannot deploy my squadron." He fumed silently for a moment then grumbled, "Go choose an unclaimed bunker and park yourself in it, Lieutenant, until I call Colonel Bierlein and find out who's running this war."

At a remote corner of Happy Valley NDP, as far from the command track as he could live, J.W. dropped his duffel bag into the opening of a small bunker, one left over from the old days. The bag caught part way in the hole, and as he put a foot forward to shove it in all the way, a violent explosion blew the duffel back out, smashing J.W. in the chest and face. He was lifted several feet into the air and landed on his back. That brought two dozen riflemen with charged weapons, all trained on J.W., to the site. His new squadron commander, despite J.W.'s protests, radioed Bierlein's helicopter and insisted it return to dust him off to a hospital, one as distant as possible from his command.

J.W. spent sixteen hours waiting to be treated at the 69th Evac Hospital, and four minutes being seen, leaving him one hour and fifty-sixty minutes short of the eighteen hours of hospitalization required to be awarded a Purple Heart. He was crestfallen, for the Purple Heart meant five or ten free points on the civil service exam he planned to take when he got back to the real world to become a mailman.

He spent a fruitless day-and-a-half searching for his old crew to bum a ride back to Happy Valley, though he eventually abandoned the hunt and boarded a tired, 1950s bus with a very faded "CHICAGO PUBLIC SCHOOLS" barely visible on the sides. It was posh compared to the usual mass transit out in the provinces, and the price reflected it—a dime. That was what the peasants told him, but the driver demanded a quarter *and* a pack of Salems before he allowed J.W. up the rusted steps.

J.W. sat quietly, bumping through the towns of Tien Giang Province, sharing the seat with a woman gripping a bony chicken whose wings and feet were tightly bound. She slept most of the trip with the bird's head facing Weathersby, just close enough for the creature to spend the six-hour ride west pecking at the hair on his arm.

Walking through a gap in the razor wire, he noticed First Squadron's armored command track, tanks, artillery pieces, and radar, every scrap of it, was gone. The technology of the mechanized infantry had been replaced by a maze of pup tents, small general purpose tents, and a single, medium, general purpose headquarters tent, outside of which stood a lieutenant colonel with infantry insignia embroidered on his collar. The colonel, observing J.W. emerging from the bus sans fatigue shirt and helmet, crooked his finger. J.W. reached for his letter before he pulled up in front of the lieutenant colonel. His pocket was empty.

J.W. snapped to attention and reported then rummaged through his pockets once again. "Sir, I am sure my orders were misplaced in the explosion."

"What explosion?" the colonel snarled.

"Sir, the one over by the perimeter, sir." J.W. spun around to point, but the bunker was gone, the patch of earth now home to a single-holer wooden latrine, the only truly solid structure for miles.

"Lieutenant, do you see the bunker ten meters downwind of my personal crapper?"

"Yes, sir."

"Good. You are under house arrest, and that's your house. You will stay in there until I talk to your Colonel Bierlein and authenticate that you belong here. As far as I am concerned, you are AWOL until proven innocent."

J.W. was summoned at dusk for a cold C-ration dinner, and at dawn for a cold C-ration breakfast. When they called him again at 10 A.M., he told the private to inform the CO that he wasn't hungry. That brought the lieutenant colonel himself to the bunker. He announced that the essential elements of the battalion would be departing the NDP at midday.

"You will be returned to the Mech for disciplinary action. Your ride's coming later this afternoon." J.W. stood obediently at attention outside his bunker until the line of helicopters coming to transport the infantry battalion appeared over the rice paddies. Minutes later, amidst the dust and confusion of GIs loading the colonel's crapper and the mess equipment aboard the first set of ships, he slipped off into the village.

He stopped at Mrs. Binh's hut. The ancient lady invited him in by yanking hard at his fatigue jacket, the counter image of a linebacker horse-collaring a diminutive running back. Before J.W. could refuse, and not sure he was physically capable of doing so, the eighty-pound woman stoked the fire to brew a pot of tea. She made him sit at the century-old picnic-table until the tea had steeped. J.W. listened casually for returning helicopters as he sipped the fragrant liquid, but an hour went by without a sound. Eventually, having added three Vietnamese words to his vocabulary, green tea, black tea, and jasmine tea, he took his leave and walked slowly along the dirt paths back toward Happy Valley. All that remained of the infantry, though, was the still-settling dust and the fluttering ream of paper that had fallen from one of the Chinooks.

As he approached the area immediately outside the NDP, things seemed to have changed; the horizon had become more expansive, the light playing on the sand around the tiny outpost sharper. For a moment, J.W. imagined this a sign from God that his life was about to become brighter, but as he looked more closely, he recognized the extra light was the upshot of a dearth of huts bordering the NDP. The typhoon-level winds generated by the transport helicopters earlier that afternoon had blown those hootches to kingdom come.

As J.W. pondered his situation, the day slowly vaporized and the sky dissolved into an amalgam of pastel hues, the brilliance of which he had never imagined. He sipped a steaming hot Pepsi purchased from a seven-year-old and sat under a tree awaiting the vibration of troop-and-junk-laden Chinook helicopters signaling the arrival of a new unit, a replacement for the departed infantry. Surely, someone would arrive before dark to provide security for the night. But the air remained quiet, and J.W. finally accepted that for the first night of his life, he was truly alone.

J.W. sat in a crevice of the berm searching his duffel bag for a can of something to eat, even a tin of C-rations. He found but a plug of Double Bubble, which he chewed until all the sugar had been sucked out; then he swallowed it. He smoked a Salem and watched peacefully as the villagers' evening fires decayed into dark embers. He started toward Happy Valley, but remembered the booby-trapped bunker and steered clear of the eerily empty NDP.

It was when he turned back toward the paddies to find a secluded recess in the dikes to sleep that he spied Mrs. Binh standing at the door of her hut motioning to him. She cackled in Vietnamese with a smile in her voice and, sure he'd soon be dead at the hands of the invisible enemy, he moved cautiously to her shelter. Mrs. Binh took his sleeve and yanked him inside, pushed him down onto the bench at the table, and poured him a glass of green tea. She popped her head through the doorway, peered left and right surreptitiously, turned to J.W., put a finger to her lips, and wrote on the border of an old newspaper the letters, "VC" and her name, as she had on the last trip.

"Thank you *Cô* Binh for the tea," he smiled.

She pinched his arm. "Why do you call me *Cô*? Do you think I'm some pretty, young girl looking for a husband? Foreign man, I am an old married woman. You must call me '*Bà*.'"

"Well, you are very pretty."

She pinched his arm harder, pointed to the four walls, and flashed a thumbs up, as if she believed the fragile mud and straw walls of her hut would shelter J.W. from the war. *Bà* Binh confidently tapped the mahogany plank bed worn silken by the generations. Apparently, that was to be his bed. He worried *Bà* Binh was planning on sleeping on the boards with him, but she crawled into the corner hammock and soon drifted off. Shortly after she began snoring, J.W. rolled off the planks and into the clay bunker dug deep under the wooden bed. At dawn, though convinced he had not slept, J.W. emerged from an awful dream, startled and disoriented. *Bà* Binh was standing directly over the opening with a glass of tea. He ignored the gift and jumped through the portal to aim at the door with the .45 he'd kept charged under the pillow he had made of his duffel bag. *Bà* Binh calmly shook her head no, pushed his weapon down indifferently, handed him the tea, and brought a bowl of water and fragrant Vietnamese soap for him to wash his face.

Slowly it came to him that he had again slept in his clothes and his boots, as he had so many times over the years since he had so proudly attained the title of Distinguished Military Graduate from the ROTC program at Sterling College. While he knew by heart the Cartesian coordinates of the village of My Co, and how desperately far it was from the lush hills surrounding his alma mater, he had no idea in the greater scheme of things where on Earth he had just passed the most dangerous and lonely night of his life, or why.

With the sun barely cresting the jungle canopy a kilometer away, he left the hut and headed cautiously for the earthen berm that surrounded the village, soon joining a dozen old men and children relieving themselves. They laughed as J.W. headed south seeking privacy, but one of the old men toddled to him, gently tugging at his fatigue shirt, pointing farther down the berm, shaking his head "no." J.W. looked toward that area—women were squatting, their backs to the men.

He paced back to *Bà* Binh's, the disquiet in his belly grumbling. He recognized it as his mind's signal that his life was in jeopardy, but when he heard his stomach broadcast a vociferous growl, he understood his uneasiness to be organic, not psychological. His last meal had been a plug of Double Bubble, and the one before that, a rancid tin of C-ration Ham and Lima Beans, Ham and Muthas supplied by the infantry battalion twenty-four hours before.

Turning the corner and entering *Bà* Binh's, his face brightened when he saw the steaming bowl of rice gruel and tiny tropical bananas on the table.

"Lieutenant, had I a shred of meat, I would offer it to you." At least, that was what J.W. thought *Bà* Binh was saying to him in Vietnamese.

After breakfast, J.W. flagged down the traveling egg roll vendor, the same man upon whom he had pinned the lives of his crew eons before, and offered him the usual three dollars for messenger services, this time writing an urgent note to the American forces in the town of Moc Hoa, explaining his disappearance. The egg roll man smiled politely and wheeled off. Within ten minutes, J.W. heard the approach of a single HUEY. He smiled to himself. "The guy's making progress."

The ship did indeed make an approach into Happy Valley, and through the whirling dust and his sense of relief, J.W. recognized Colonel Bierlein's door gunner, then the colonel's sergeant major, and soon, the colonel himself. The three emerged somberly, but J.W. looked past them into the Plexiglas canopy to witness the brushed white of Pilot Tom's grin.

"Lieutenant, I see you're alive. Where have you been?"

"Here in My Co, sir."

"Alone?"

"Yes, sir. *Bà* Binh put me up for the night."

"*Bà* Binh? What is that, a hotel? Get your gear. I'm taking you back to Normandy."

"Sir, excuse me, sir. But I thought I had a job out here, a mission—win the hearts and the minds. That was the deal. You gave me a letter assigning me here. I lost the letter, but you had said okay, sir."

"GIs don't live alone amongst the enemy. It isn't the American way, Weathersby. The Mech's been assigned elsewhere. We can't support you. Get your things."

Bierlein returned to the ship, whose engine had never slowed one percent from maximum power, and J.W. could feel the rotor wash ebb and flow rhythmically as Tom's hand pulsed nervously on the collective. Perhaps it was because Tom was glaring at J.W. so fixedly that the pilot didn't appreciate the darkening of the sky. A pair of massive Chinook helicopters descended toward Happy Valley, the two mammoth, twin-rotor helicopters followed by a tiny observation ship. The Chinooks broke off and entered a hover, creating a typhoon of furiously blowing buffalo, hog, and chicken scat, to say nothing of a fair percentage of the worldly possessions of My Co's populace. Finally, they settled at an altitude of three feet, positioned to belch footlockers and infantry troops from their bellies.

Bierlein's pilot, seeing the approaching cloud of detritus, shot his head out the window to clear the area and caught sight of the small observation helicopter on approach. It was heading directly toward him, nose so high, the pilot could not see Bierlein's ship on the ground. Tom jammed the cyclic forward and wrenched the collective toward the skies. The aircraft burst a foot or two into the air and surged along the sand, more a deuce-and-a-half troop truck than a delicate, half-million-dollar aircraft. The two Chinook pilots, catching site of

Bierlein's chopper coming toward them, peeled off wildly, left and right, just missing the few remaining peasant huts at the periphery of Happy Valley NDP.

The two gigantic aircraft avoided directly striking the flimsy structures, but the one-hundred-twenty mile-per-hour rotor wash did not, and the roofs blew chaotically from several dozen hootches, triggering an exodus of villagers from the disintegrating homes where they had taken refuge from the aerial onslaught. This was the second time in the past eighteen hours they had poured onto the dirt road in panic, though, on this sortie, they were bombarded by the footlockers that tumbled like inert OD bombs out of the still-violently oscillating Chinooks. The wooden crates spattered the dusty road, bursting open to rain reams of military documents over the Vietnamese countryside, whirling sheets of white which papered the rice paddies like so many tiles of linoleum.

The small helicopter that had followed the Chinooks into the village took advantage of the temporary dispersal of the other aircraft to land, off-loading a single passenger, a lieutenant colonel, who surveyed the billow of debris, dust, and straw roofs. He shook his head, ruminating about the restoration and solatium payments his unit was already obliged to provide the citizenry of My Co even before his unit had set foot in My Co.

Bierlein's HUEY did a one-eighty and landed abreast the lieutenant colonel, whose eyes rolled up into his head when he recognized the 33rd Mech's commanding officer's helicopter decal.

Bierlein, still on the ground, crooked his finger for both the lieutenant colonel and Weathersby. J.W., though, missed the call, busy, instead, perusing the damage being presented by a furious assemblage of villagers. The sergeant major hopped angrily from Bierlein's helicopter, barreled into the village through the crowd, and hauled J.W. by the sleeve back to Bierlein's side.

"Weathersby, this is Lieutenant Colonel Ezra Williams, Battalion Commander, First of the Twenty-Seventh. He's going to need some help getting these houses rebuilt," Bierlein smiled. "You interested in staying?"

"Yes, sir. With all due respect though, sir, may I speak to you alone, sir?"

"No. What's on your mind?"

"If I stay, sir, does this mean I'm a light infantry officer from now on? I mean, when they leave, do I become a temporary member of this unit and have to leave with them? I mean become an infantryman, sir, carry an M-16 and all that, sir?"

"No, yes, and no."

Bierlein spun around and jumped aboard his helicopter, leaving J.W. at attention in front of the battalion commander. "Sir, do you remember the order of the questions I asked Colonel Bierlein?"

"No, no, and no, Lieutenant. Put together a list of what we broke; what we owe, and to whom; if anyone got hurt; and how many water buffaloes escaped into the jungle this time. They're always bitching about their water buffaloes. If they're that concerned, they ought to keep them secured in a barn or something. Tie 'em to a stake. Something."

"Tie who, sir?"

"The water buffalo. Bierlein says you speak Vietnamese. I'm impressed. When you're done with the solatium paperwork, put the word out for the people to stay in their huts. Anyone caught outside their hootch is the enemy as far as I'm concerned. You are my ears and eyes in this vill. Make sure I know everything these people are up to."

"Yes, sir, but I trust we can avoid a problem with your Hooks again. They need to be trained not to blow houses off the face of the Earth."

"Lieutenant, you just leave the teaching to me."

J.W. dined on a tin of cold, congealed, C-ration Spaghetti and Meatballs that noon. What bothered him was not the fare, but the fact that he was beginning to like it, and he searched the NDP for another can or two. Despite his best efforts to regain the forty pounds he had lost in Ranger School, every time he looked into his little shaving mirror, he realized he was losing the battle. Nor was he gaining back the energy that had been sapped from him during those months of food and sleep deprivation. Each day, he awoke a bit more tired and depressed than the last, unaware if it was just the being there, the constant, oppressive, dripping heat, the perpetually angry senior officers, or perhaps the exotic bacteria he was convinced were consuming his innards.

But he went on grubbing for more Cs, even accepting another tin of Ham and Limas with a thank you to the mess sergeant. He took a seat in the farthest corner of the NDP and began to open a can, but Colonel Williams bristled over and directed J.W. to a chair behind a little wooden GI table at the west gate of the NDP, just feet into the hamlet. He was to record who and what had been damaged by the helicopters.

J.W. asked to use Private Dinh, the battalion interpreter, but the colonel clucked, "No. Dinh stays here. Bierlein says you can speak Vietnamese. So speak Vietnamese. And remind them just how serious I am about the damn sundown curfew."

J.W. paid *Em* Huong, the twelve-year-old boy who had been the bearer of the string of rice paddy rats months before, a funny-money MPC twenty-five cent bill to gather the villagers whose homes had been damaged. The boy shot off, and in minutes the word of pecuniary promise spread throughout the province of Kien Tuong, provoking the assault of hundreds of villagers upon J.W.'s open-air insurance claims office. Despite his detailed explanation that only those residing in the damaged homes on the periphery of the American base would be compensated, everyone present listed those huts as their own.

J.W. mounted his rickety OD folding chair to address the growing throng in what he believed to be flawless Vietnamese. "Four hundred people living in a dozen, one-room huts? Give me a break, ladies and gentlemen."

There was momentary silence and then a quiet but growing discussion amongst the villagers, until a soft voice from the crowd spoke in very slow, simple, Vietnamese. "Thank you, Lieutenant, for offering to build a house that would hold four hundred people. We have seen pictures of the great houses in which the Americans live, a thousand people sometimes. But we Vietnamese like to live only with our families."

J.W. attempted several clarifications, but the villagers formed klatches, and the tenor of the conversations heated as the minutes passed. He headed for the edge of the hamlet to the hut occupied by *Cô* Thi, a young lady who purportedly spoke English. As he had always done at the entrance of a Vietnamese dwelling, he knocked on the paper-thin sheet metal and bamboo door before lifting and placing it aside to call a greeting. That was local etiquette, and he congratulated himself on having learned the ways of so foreign a culture, and in such a short time. It was, he noted, a bit surprising that the door was shut during the stifling afternoon, but he whispered to himself, "Say hello, wait three seconds, slide the door aside, and stick your head in. You will be hailed with the usual smile and pushed into a seat for tea and tiny tropical bananas. Then you'll have to answer questions about your family—how many children, and if you have more than one wife. And if you don't, do you want a few from the village, and by the way, do you have an extra pack of American cigarettes?"

But instead of the customary bid to enter, there was only grunting from a dark corner, and when he took a step inside, he discovered *Cô* Thi engaged, not in English language study, but in the ancient pursuit of entertaining village elders, on this occasion, *Ông* Oanh, who was gyrating on the wooden plank bed. The old man popped up, recognized the apparition as an American soldier, released a string of tonal expletives, yanked the drawers from around his ankles, and waddled past J.W., holding up his pants with both hands.

Cô Thi faced J.W. and half-covered herself with a brief red blouse, but did so with little fanfare. She smiled seductively and whispered, "GI like *Cô* Thi?"

"Very, very nice, but I need you down by the NDP for a minute."

"You need *Cô* Thi? You money?"

"It's just for a minute. Sorry, no money for this one."

"One minute, one hour, same-same. You no money, you no honey. *Cô* Thi make too many GI happy Saigon. Now come My Co. You look."

She pulled from a cardboard box beside the mahogany-plank bed a thick, red afghan sweater then pushed it toward J.W., allowing her loosely draped blouse to droop forward. She hesitated while J.W. glanced down into the gaping thin silk. His eyes fixed on the still-taut nipples, and *Cô* Thi watched intently as he began to redden. She moved toward him very slowly, brushing her hand against the billfold in his hip pocket.

Cô Thi could not have known that simple act would draw the image of *Ông* Khai and the incident of the missing wallet, the dying orphans, and finally, the dismembered coolies. The vision drove J.W. a step back, his mind clouding sadly as it sought to catalogue what he had witnessed in so few months.

Cô Thi, still holding the sweater, moved slowly forward again. "You look. Very money. Many present from GI Saigon say Thi best girlfriend. GI want marry take Thi America. Buy one-hundred dress give Thi." She held the red sweater closer to J.W., letting the soft material stroke his bare arm. "You like I put on? Next, GI take off? Same-same girlfriend America."

"Very nice, Miss, but I need someone to speak English."

"I talk GI every day. Talk American number one." With that, *Cô* Thi popped her thumb into the air and smiled so innocently, J.W. felt a twinge in his chest.

J.W. stammered, "Good, good, you are very nice, Miss Thi, so maybe you will come with me. Please, we must speak to your people." He turned to leave, crooking his finger politely over his shoulder for her to follow. From behind him there was a loud, angry huff, and he turned to see *Cô* Thi's face harden. She sprang toward J.W. and spit on the dirt floor by his boots.

"I no pig. I no come. I no pig! Why you call me same-same pig?" she bellowed, turning away from J.W. to pull on black silk peasant's pajama bottoms. "If'n you no money, no honey!" she hissed, storming past J.W. through door into the piercing daylight.

J.W. returned empty-handed to the masses, whose numbers had now grown several dozen stronger. Amongst the new arrivals were three villagers he had not before seen, young men in colored shirts far too small for their muscular frames. He also noticed that the fabric was stretched and faded where breasts had once been supported, and he felt quite confused until he realized that these men were dressed in borrowed women's finery. J.W. was also surprised by their light complexions, skin that had not spent long hours in the sun, as had he and the rest of the farmers.

He was about to ask which huts were theirs, but he looked up to see *Cô* Thi marching down the road, scowling, about to join the gathering. She gestured with her head and eyes toward J.W. as she described in vivid, petulant detail, the uncivilized confrontation that had taken place at her hut. The villagers listened intently then turned to J.W. for his side of the story, but as hard as he tried, *Cô* Thi had a rebuttal for every component of the saga. As the eyes of the gathered pierced him more deeply with each dart thrown by *Cô* Thi, J.W. had no choice but to retreat again, this time to the NDP, to besiege the colonel to either cancel the mission or provide him with someone who spoke intelligible Vietnamese.

"Okay," the colonel relented, "but I need to warn you that young Private Dinh may be the battalion interpreter, but he is a virtual prodigy of profanity, and not much else. He has an unsurpassed ability to drag a winning team into the basement." Dinh, the colonel further cautioned, was, at best, a minimally-willing participant in the South Vietnamese government's efforts to stop the communists.

"Is he a sympathizer, sir?" J.W. asked.

"Yep. A sympathizer of his own skin."

The colonel went on to describe how Dinh had come to the South Vietnamese cause via a deuce-and-a-half "recruitment truck" that cruised the streets of Saigon arresting and pressing into involuntary service every single young man over the age of fifteen. But Dinh's prodigious ability to communicate in English with GIs enticed the recruiters in Saigon to place him in an American unit. These Vietnamese conscript evaluators noted that GIs would snap back at Dinh in a lexicon similar to that with which he addressed the American troops. On the other hand, the evaluators did not fathom a single word of English, not even "money" or "fuck," and given that the extent of young Dinh's vocabulary was constructed around these two expressions, the inspectors were hoodwinked into believing that he was far more promising as a linguist than as a rifleman.

They immediately enrolled him in the interpreter school in Saigon. Almost all of the young Vietnamese who graduated were sent to American combat units and soon became close friends and allies of the GIs. "Great guys, most of them," the returnees told J.W. before he left for Viet Nam. Many of the U.S. soldiers had written to their churches and asked the congregations to sponsor the interpreters and their families as immigrants.

Dinh, on the other hand, had been less than stellar at the school in his bid to expand his talents and learn proper English, but given the supremacy of Murphy's Law, which enjoyed especial virulence in Asia, he graduated at the top of his class and was assigned to an American infantry battalion. With the passage of just two days at his first unit, however, the commanding officer put him on a civilian bus, personally paid the fare, and sent him back to Saigon. Thus began a revolving-door career during which he rotated through several more infantry units until he garnered a reputation for cruelty so hideous, colonel after colonel fretted they would be charged with war crimes and tried at the Hague if Dinh was allowed to intermingle with peasants or POWs.

And it wasn't just his demeanor with rustics and captives. Dinh's standard reply to any request for his interpretive skills was countered with a, "Fuck you, GI, I kill you." After getting to know Dinh for an hour or so, even U.S. troops swore that if their colonel didn't rid the command of the private, they would summarily remove the little bastard's bantam family jewels and present them to Ho Chi Minh on a silver platter.

Infantry colonels now feared they would be held accountable for the sexual mutilation of a Vietnamese national at the hands of the soldiers they purportedly controlled, and it became the sole mission of many a battalion to rid itself of the man. So, Dinh continued his odyssey from infantry unit to infantry unit, becoming increasingly embittered by the intensity of the threats of physical violence leveled against him by the stupid Americans.

"Yeah, you take our pint-sized Heinrich Himmler for an hour, Weathersby," the colonel added threateningly, "but I'm not responsible for what happens. You're 33rd Mech. You work outside the gates of the night defensive position I command, so he is hereby assigned to you and *your* unit. Bierlein," he waved his hand dismissively, "not me. Understood?"

J.W. marched back into the village alongside Dinh, who aimed his M-16 into the air, the burst of automatic rounds begetting a nervous silence over all of My Co long before the echo faded.

"First, please tell *Cô* Thi that I think she is very nice. I did not call her a pig. No way. She is very beautiful. Tell her that, please."

Dinh spoke, and smiled seductively. *Cô* Thi grinned back enticingly and spoke in broken English, which Dinh translated as, "She say you call her like pig. You use finger to call her."

"What did she want me to use, the phone?"

"No. Viet Nam people no use finger to call. Call pig with finger."

"Shit! How was I supposed to know that? Who the hell is she, Emily Post all of a sudden?"

Dinh laughed. "What you say? She pissed? Yeah, she beaucoup pissed."

"No, no, no. In America, see that's the way we call friends, and…" J.W. began, but gave up, took a cleansing breath, and went on. "Okay, please tell *Cô* Thi that I am very stupid. I will never do that again. Tell her I am very stupid."

J.W. dropped his head a few degrees and smiled submissively as the translation proceeded. *Cô* Thi considered the apology with twisted lips, but a pouting smile followed, and she whispered loudly, "You come see *Cô* Thi tonight, yes?"

After the yowls of laughter, J.W. had Dinh inform the villagers that the new colonel was a very unhappy man, and that he had ordered all the people to stay in their huts during the hours of darkness. The little private brayed something about nighttime and death. He punctuated his thoughts with a burst of M-16 rounds aimed barely over the heads of his audience.

With his military and diplomatic obligations satisfied, Dinh turned his efforts to dispersing the petitioners. Screaming, cursing, and pushing the women, children, and old men toward the road, he fired his weapon into the air yet again, this time near the ears of the younger men.

But when he shoved ancient *Bà* Binh, Weathersby called to Dinh, "Hey, you little fuck, that's it. Keep your fuckin' hands off her! And stop that goddamn shooting, or I'll kick your slim ass into the next fuckin' time zone. You hear?"

Dinh shouted back, "Dinh get job done. They very stupid fuckers, these ones."

True to his pledge, in seconds only six claimants remained where a hundred had stood just moments before. Dinh, satisfied with his work, swaggered toward the NDP, turning back fifty meters down the road to jab a middle finger in the air. He shrieked at J.W., "You, fuck!"

By sunset, the infantry had erected a mess tent with field stoves, a proper mess line, paper plates, and several cases of C-rations that had been amalgamated in an immense pot. The chef had burned the bottom and sides over the intense fire, but the central blob remained congealed. It was, though, offered proudly by the mess sergeant, who had written "Jambalaya" on a tiny chalk board at the entrance to the mess tent.

Several of the troops grumbled, "Not that shit again!"

But the cooks warned the troops, "Better enjoy it tonight, man, that's the last of the Cs. Cock sucker GIs on the docks in Saigon been givin' the good shit to the local ho's. Out here in the field, man, we ain't gonna be gettin' shit to eat, man. I'm tellin' you the truth, man. Eat up. This is it, baby."

J.W. went to the command tent to report to the colonel on the actions of Private Dinh and to ask about the next morning's breakfast specials, but the CO was briefing his company commanders and platoon leaders for the evening's mission. He motioned with a wave of the back of his hand for J.W. to stand in a corner.

The final statement of the colonel's briefing was the admonition, "If they're out of their hootch in any way, shape, or form, they're VC. They all know that. Lieutenant Weathersby over here's told 'em. Didn't you, Lieutenant?"

J.W. answered with a hearty, "I believe they got the word, sir."

So, the colonel went on, "Three-day pass for every pair of VC ears your troops bring back to me. Two equals three. It's simple arithmetic, gentlemen."

J.W. retired to his bunker and read *For Whom the Bell Tolls* by flashlight but soon fell into the perpetual, uneasy, shallow sleep he had experienced since he'd received his orders for Viet Nam. He dozed until 11 P.M., startled awake by a blast of machine-gun fire from within the hamlet. A minute later, the report of grenades shook his cot and a private appeared at the bunker, ordering him to the command tent for an audience with the colonel.

The commander snapped, "Lieutenant, there's been a shooting in the village. I want you to make contact with our patrol and find out what the hell's going on. I'll give you a Prick-25 radio. You want Dinh?"

"No, sir. Sir, are you saying you want me out there alone?"

"You're the only one who knows the hamlet. I'll tell my patrol to hold fire, that you're on the way. Move out."

J.W. charged his .45, strapped the PRC-25 radio to his back, established radio contact with the patrol leader deep within the village, and started out into the war. As he approached the west gate of the NDP, the gate guards woke, sensing movement behind them. When J.W. heard their weapons being charged, he dropped to the ground alongside the colonel's personal crapper then radioed the headquarters tent to order the sentries at the wire to hold their fire.

J.W. heard the colonel in the background shouting, "Goddamnit, isn't he out there yet? Tell him to get his ass on a stick."

J.W. stopped thirty meters into My Co to urinate before he did so in his pants. Before he was done, he dropped into the prone position when he saw movement near *Bà* Binh's hut. He crawled fifty meters further along the road, saw a small, silver snake with luminescent green eyes coiled inches from his face, sprang to his feet, and sprinted down the road, howling, "Fuckin' VC, fuckin' reptiles, fuckin' army, I hate this place."

Reaching the end of the village, he radioed the patrol and demanded, "Where the fuck are you?"

The platoon leader asked in reply, "Was that you that just flew by? We're fifty meters behind you. We got a dead gook and an old man. He keeps using your name."

J.W. discovered the patrol in tactical position, fanned out on the wet earth surrounding *Cô* Thi's hut. He walked to the door, a burning candle allowing J.W. to see the platoon leader sitting at the table with his .45 trained on an old Vietnamese man. At first, J.W. thought it was same codger upon whom he had provoked coitus interruptus earlier in the day, but, in fact, it was old *Ông* Long, whose prostrate, nude form, sans stained turban, was stretched on the dirt floor in a back corner.

J.W. sensed a metallic scent, and his eyes searched the dim hut. Toward the center, *Cô* Thi lay on the planks of her mahogany bed. Her shirt was unbuttoned, and her eyes were unblinking. A trickle of blood from her open mouth ran along the inside of her arm, pooling in a delicate, upturned palm. Her hand, however, had become full, and drops were oozing through her frozen fingers into the cardboard box on the floor, befouling the neatly folded, red afghan sweater.

J.W. spat, "What the fuck happened, Lieutenant?"

"My men saw a head popping out the roof. They told the gooks to get their heads inside."

"How did they do that?"

"They told' em! That's how. These people know the rules. A head pops out, we dust 'em."

J.W. shined his flashlight on the inside of the thatch roof. "You see a hole, Lieutenant?"

"I don't see shit. I don't need to see shit. My sergeant tells me there's movement amongst the gooks, he warns 'em ten times, they don't listen, so as far as I'm concerned, they're VC. I give 'em the green light. You got an argument with that, take it up with the CO."

"Fuckin' A, I will." He spun around, lurching out of the hootch and past the patrol at a fast walk, the fear of a Viet Cong bullet or an American bullet as far from his mind as the women of San Francisco wearing ribbons in their hair. His pace increased exponentially as the boiling inside him welled, and by the time he approached the barbed wire gate of the Happy Valley NDP, he was running.

He didn't bother to pre-establish contact with the gate guards. All they heard was a shrieking, "I'm comin' through. Put your fuckin' weapons down!" He tugged furiously at the barbed wire gate, ripping a gash in his leg, though any pain he might have sensed was masked by his rage. He was also unaware of the blood running out of his thigh, down his fatigues, and sloshing into his boot.

At the command tent, he yanked the flap open, nearly jumping in front of the colonel, who was standing at an easel marking a large tactical map of the area.

"Sir," J.W. spit, raising his hand in a shoddy salute, "they had no right to fire indiscriminately into a hootch. There was no head popping through any roof. This is bullshit, sir." When there was no returned salute, J.W. brought his arm down violently as if delivering a blast to the enemy's gut, though his elbow hit the colonel's easel, toppling the next day's mission onto the sandy dirt of My Co.

The battalion commander stood for a few seconds without a twitch until he gradually opened his mouth. He sucked in a slow, deep breath, one that would fuel, J.W. knew well, the standard senior-office nuclear explosion.

But all the colonel hissed was, "Eight, nine, ten." He walked around J.W. slowly, picked up the easel, set it back in position, then bent over to lift the map, dusting it off and placing the red and black grease pencils neatly on the easel lip.

There was another breath, one a bit less profound, followed by, "Lieutenant, most of these troops are eighteen or nineteen. They can't spell Viet Nam or find it on a map of the world, let alone make an instant life and death decision ten thousand miles from home in the middle of the night when they've been shot at by children and lost most of their buddies. I'm sorry if there are mistakes. None of us asked to be here, especially those kids. You think they killed a woman on purpose? Do you?"

"No, sir, I suppose not, but…"

"Okay. You got anything else? If not, get the names of the injured parties in the morning, and we'll compensate the families. Get some sleep. I may need you again before sunrise."

J.W. woke at dawn, not to bursts of automatic weapons fire or the koosh of grenades, but to the laughter and bitching of troops returning from patrol. Their vitality was comforting, and though he sought not to concede admiration for the infantrymen, a bit of their intrepid temperament had touched him, and he was proud of having swaggered, not crawled, back into the NDP the night before. He wondered if the grunts at the gate were aware of how consumed with fear he had been out there, alone in the valley, and he pondered if they had quaked as uncontrollably their first time in the darkness.

Breakfast was as presaged—barely warmed, scrambled powdered eggs on stale bread, with a side of boiled, rehydrated carrots, "For those of you cares 'bout yo night vision," the mess sergeant laughed as his customers turned up their noses at the offering.

J.W. sat down across from the CO, quite aware of the frigid stares of the junior officers sitting on the periphery of the mess tent.

"Sir, we need to talk about the killing in the vill last night. I was out of line, I admit, but sir, that woman was a just a whore. She wasn't armed. The old man's a good guy. He's not VC. Maybe we ought to just stay out of the hamlet, patrol only the wood line, sir. That way, whoever wants to fight can fight to their hearts' content. The villagers can stay out of it."

"Lieutenant Weathersby, the villagers are already in this up to their necks. Maybe not the prostitute, and maybe the prostitute. We were sent here to keep the VC out of the villages, to cut off their supply source, hit 'em in the belly where it hurts. We will continue to patrol inside the confines of My Co until I am ordered to desist. Now, I want to meet with the prostitute's next of kin. I want them at the command tent so that I may offer my condolences. I told you last night, I don't want to be here anymore than they want me here, and I'm sure as hell not interested in hurting harmless people, prostitutes or not."

The colonel's voice raised several decibels. "Do you know the definition of hell, young man? Well, I'll tell you. It's where you have to torture the innocent." He calmed himself and added, "I have a mission, and to tell you the truth, from what I've seen of the Viet Cong and North Vietnamese, I've got no problem giving up a third year of my life to stop these bastards. Maybe you haven't seen why we're here yet. Believe me, young Lieutenant, if you last long enough, you will."

The CO took leave of the hushed gathering, as did the officers, who had only picked at the morning meal. J.W. was left to sit conspicuously alone. With their egress, Private Dinh strolled into the officers' mess with an arrogant gait and a loaded tray. He took a seat, his back to J.W.

At *Cô* Thi's hut, a minion of local ladies washed the slender corpse and dressed her in the velvety red sweater and a pair of new, black silk pajama bottoms. Few of the women acknowledged J.W., though one looked up while fixing *Cô* Thi's hair, and J.W. gathered his courage to apologize in Vietnamese. He expected an aboriginal chastisement, perhaps to be stoned, but there was a dearth of anger in the woman's eyes. She nodded without expression, and when her gaze dropped back to her work, J.W. searched *Cô* Thi's face for the agony of the ignominious, random violence that had taken her. It was his first corpse since the workers at My Tho. Since then, he hadn't seen who he'd blown away from inside his cockpit.

He was relieved, for a peaceful mask draped her sharp Asian features. Even in death she exuded a delicacy, and he stared at the gentle curl of her fingers and the stain of blood that had not yet been washed away. He remembered it from the night before; it had been fresh then, just minutes from her having been alive. She had been an alluring woman, so proud and unashamed for having brought warmth to lonely men. Last night the elegance of her hands had been there, and somehow it remained, hours after her soul had fled. J.W. would remember the tarnish of that blood for the rest of his life.

He asked if *Cô* Thi had family in the village. The women looked up as one, metaphorically pointing to themselves with their eyes.

J.W.'s lips tightened, deliberating if that was a tactic to have their names added to a class action suit against the U.S. Army, a transparent jockeying for a slice of the solatium pie. He asked again for a true family member to step forward. This time the women ignored him, took positions around the bed, and spoke in turn to the reposing corpse. J.W. withdrew and headed for Bà Binh's.

As he walked, the infantry commander's helicopter crept up the road at tree top level, slowing over Weathersby. The lieutenant colonel looked down at him and nodded. J.W. saw the man's lips move, and the small chopper flew to *Cô* Thi's hut, hovered as the colonel perused the roof, then whirled up to speed, did a one-eighty, and departed east, toward Saigon.

At *Bà* Binh's, the old woman hobbled out and asked over and over, her voice like a forgotten, creaky gate, "Where you been? Got no time for an old lady? Where you been, where you been, where you been?" She pinched his arm until it reddened, finally dragging him into the hut for a glass of weak tea and tiny bananas. As his eyes adjusted to the darkness, he noticed, hunkered by the fire, a petite, female form, jet-black hair pinned into a bun with a carved ivory comb. When the woman turned toward him, her eyes sparkled, reflecting the embers of the glowing charcoal, though she did not look directly at J.W. She stood and walked to the table. *Bà* Binh spoke. "This is my granddaughter, Nguyen Thi Lin. I believe you have met. She would like to be the teacher in My Co," or that is what he believed the ancient woman had said.

Cô Lin nodded almost imperceptibly, refilled J.W.'s tea glass, and returned to the fire to bank the coals before leaving.

J.W. mumbled to *Bà* Binh, "Yes, we have met. I don't think *Cô* Lin likes me. And, wait a minute, this hamlet doesn't have a school."

Bà Binh cackled, "Not yet, but the new village chief has promised us one." She patted the bed, inviting J.W. to stay for a nap.

He lay wondering if *Cô* Lin would return.

Chapter 5

J.W. AWOKE TO *Bà* Binh chattering at a platoon of children playing outside her hut, admonishing them to be quiet and not disturb her sleeping guest. She waved arms as frail as the bamboo poles on her ancestral alter then tightened the muscles of her ancient face, pulling taut the sagging whorls. The children ignored her.

She turned back to J.W. and complained under her breath, "Kids these days. They don't behave. No respect. When I was a girl, I listened to my elders. Oh, I saw children misbehaving, yes, but it was in the city when my husband and I lived in Lai Khe. I think that was in nineteen-something, maybe eighteen. I don't know, maybe earlier, maybe later."

She shuffled forward arthritically toward her hammock, still mumbling. It took her several tries to lift herself onto the silk, though she continued with her story as she struggled. "When we left My Co, I didn't think I would ever see my mother again. I was only sixteen, or maybe it was eighteen. The city of Lai Khe? Oh, heavens, that was eighty, a hundred, a thousand kilometers from here. Who knows? So far we traveled. I had never been out of My Co before. Even my mother and father had never traveled beyond the village of Thanh Lanh. And that was only three kilometers from here. It's gone now you know." She shrugged her shoulders. "The American airplanes dropped fire on it."

J.W. could not help but think about those numbers, *Bà* Binh's journey of eighty kilometers, maybe fifty miles, and her parents' trek, of a mile-and-a-half from their birthplace. That was in sixty years of life. From what *Bà* Binh went on to say, J.W. learned that the villagers of Kien Tuong Province, and for that matter, the overwhelming number of peasants in both North and

South Viet Nam, had never ventured farther than the local, dusty graveyards in which their ancestors were interred. She nodded almost proudly, "We were busy you know. We were growing food every day of the year. So, every day of the year, there was work to do, only two days off at *Tet*, the New Year celebration, when the moon comes around the twelfth time." She pointed vaguely toward the sky.

"I still don't know why my husband took me that far, to the end of the Earth. How could he have thought it would be better than My Co?"

She stared off again into the thatched weave of her primeval hut, finally mumbling almost dreamily, "My husband, he was much older. Who knows, he was thirty or forty, maybe more. His beard was already gray when we married. He was going to go work for his uncle in the rubber plantations near Lai Khe. The French pigs, they paid ten piasters a day, and he thought that was a fortune. Now an egg roll costs more than that. But the roads in those days, they were covered with mangrove and tamarind. It was like a wedding canopy. And there were clusters of wild orchids hanging from the branches. You could go for miles without seeing the sun." She laughed to herself, her hands waving to the heavens. "It was like riding through a mist of lavender blossoms. And the spirit of our ancestors was with us, everywhere. At least we were safe in those days."

She lifted herself methodically off the hammock. "I'll show you." She pulled a wooden box from beside the crumbling mud stanchion of her bed. She pointed to a second container. "That's my granddaughter's." *Bà* Binh pulled from hers a single pair of black pajamas, far less faded than the ones she wore. There came an ivory comb and a wrinkled envelope, from which she drew a locket of black hair. She stared at it for a moment then mumbled, "My daughter, Lin's mother. She's dead. A mine in the field, right over there." She pointed out the door and waved her finger, pointing nowhere in particular.

"Here it is." On the bottom of the box was a sepia photograph of *Bà* Binh and an oldish man. She was in traditional Vietnamese wedding garb, as was the man, the couple braced at rigid attention.

J.W. took it in both hands. "You are still so beautiful. Maybe even prettier now."

She slapped him on the shoulder. "You should say that to Lin, not to me. What is wrong with you?"

J.W. smiled, reckoning *Bà* Binh's husband must have been born around the time of the American Civil War. J.W. was unable to imagine how much history had gone by in *Bà* Binh's life, nor how eighty-some years in so forsaken a land had failed to dispirit her eyes.

He asked, "*Bà* Binh, do you have other pictures? Do you have one of Lin when she was a little girl?"

"No, that's the only picture in my box. Maybe Lin has one in hers."

"No, I mean where you keep all your things."

She peered at him quizzically. "That is all my things. I'm not you Americans with a full duffel bag of stuff. Who needs all that?"

As if the conversation had drawn the life-force of her ancestors from their graves to her heart, she tottered to a corner, stopping at a hardwood mantle anchored in the dried mud of the hut's front wall. With bony fingers, she arranged the ornamental red tissue and gold Chinese characters pasted to the spindly alter that rested precariously on the shelf. She lit joss sticks poking from the tawny wood of the miniature shrine then waved her hands over the wafting yellowish smoke, the scent of joss drawing J.W. back to the punks he and his pals had burned on summer nights in New York. *Bà* Binh mumbled a prayer to the ancestors, her eyes brushing their faded images in touched sepia photographs on a wicker shelf beside the altar.

J.W. watched the ceremony until the thick, damp breath of the building monsoon drugged him, and he allowed himself to lie back on the mahogany planks, his head resting on a rough-woven bag of rice husks. Though the rain soon plummeted with a ferocity that darkened the village of My Co as if night had fallen, J.W. drifted off to sleep. He dreamed through the deafening deluge but woke with the sudden silence as the rain ceased.

His first sense was that of the nearness of another soul, his mind imagining the angry face of a senior officer coming to arrest him for desertion, perhaps for sleeping on duty. But it was just a dream. In seconds, a gentle rustling roused him again, though as he looked about, all he saw was *Bà* Binh in her hammock, fast asleep.

A soft voice called from outside the hut, and J.W. looked to the door. He squinted to make out the contour of the lower half of a human body, the waist and legs starkly framed by the stunted portal of a door and the glare of the clearing sky. He laughed sarcastically to himself, aware it was simply one of his usual nightmares, but mercifully a speck more benign than usual. Most of his recent dreams were strewn with the images of dismembered bodies, though in this one, there were no faces, no detached crewcut heads circling overhead like predators, spewing threats of dire military punishment.

There was something else different in this dream. It was *far* too vibrant—the cackling of chickens and the foreign scents. He sprang up, startled. The odor of stale sweat, his own, and the musty trace of *Bà* Binh's hut were more authentic than in any dream. He groped for his .45, sure he had left it under the rice bag, though he found nothing. He had entered the village unarmed, perhaps to appease *Cô* Thi's ghost.

J.W., though drugged by both the vapor of the tropical humors and his semi-sleep, realized that he had not been dreaming. The half-form was very real; these were the legs of a tall man who stood outside the doorway of *Bà* Binh's shanty. With movement inside the hut, the figure kowtowed through the miniature opening and unfolded inches from J.W.'s bed. Weathersby lifted his eyes and focused on the austere, etched features of a face that had survived the jungle for years, a countenance free only at night, when the man's pursuers retreated to their forts. J.W. sat up slowly on the hard planks, attempting not to startle the stranger, but another puff of his own stinking sweat wafted into the air, triggering the guest's nostrils to flare and his brow to wrinkle.

Bà Binh lifted herself creakily from the hammock and limped painfully to the smoldering fire in the corner. She mumbled while motioning with the dull tin teapot.

The figure bowed subtly and spoke softly. "Lieuten, it been long time."

Though still in a stupor, J.W.'s eyes accepted the light, making out in detail a gaunt face whose usual smile was gone. He stood. "*Ông* Khai! I'm sorry. I didn't recognize you. I thought it was a dream. You were half a person, just legs, a silhouette in the doorway. I'm sorry. You have lost so much weight! What are you doing here?"

"It very hard in countryside. Every person bad dream here. I come tell you, you must leave village My Co."

J.W. reeled for an instant, nearly falling back onto the hardwood bed. His heart tightened, but he convinced himself it had simply been an error in English, a nuance gone awry, perhaps because Khai had been away from the Americans for so long. He smiled and looked into Khai's eyes, but the Asian face tensed sternly, and J.W. understood that the village chief had said exactly what was in his heart.

It was then that J.W. saw the mutation that had taken place in Khai. A distant sobriety had replaced the warmth in the man's face, and for the first time, J.W. perceived an intimidating hardness. He became frightened by *Ông* Khai's severe features—the jutting cheekbones, the black eyes—and by the pressed blue pants that mocked J.W.'s sweat-soaked fatigues.

Khai, turning away from J.W.'s stare, accepted a glass of tea from *Bà* Binh and stepped outside the hut to sip the pale green liquid. J.W. watched Khai contemplating the fifteenth century settlement, the man's attention fixed on the mile of mud hootches devoid of electricity or toilets—people just moved their bowels behind their houses—or running water; a hamlet of war-maddened villagers, of neighbors who accused neighbors; of families who turned each other over to one side or the other for revenge and reward. Yet, even with the stains of enmity, My Co was still just a smallish, relatively benign tumor on a forgotten arteriole between Saigon and Cambodia, and J.W. reminded himself that he had already passed the most meaningful hours of his combat tour, and perhaps his life, there. He would not allow himself to be shipped back to Normandy to light water heaters and inspect the sanitary status of the major's silverware.

He was about to answer Khai and inform him just how long it had taken him to be reassigned to the village, how much he had already been through, the explosion, the damaged helicopter, and to ask just why he wasn't welcome there, but the battalion commander's aircraft hovered in over the village, and Khai stepped back into the hut, avoiding the prying airborne eyes.

J.W. rolled off the bed. "It's my boss. I gotta go."

As J.W. walked numbly toward the NDP, he asked himself why anyone with a future would give up the relative safety of My Tho to come to the inflamed countryside. Perhaps Khai had fooled him back at Normandy Base Camp—then again, it wasn't likely he had fooled Mess Sergeant Lincoln. But he had, and the answer came to J.W. slowly. Khai had created a personal agenda that demanded he wait quietly, with typical Asian patience, for years if that is what it took, to get what he finally wanted. He would accept his lot as the sovereign of the crap burners, impressing the foreigners with his apparent integrity, biding his time until the American-propped cesspool of a government in Saigon saw fit to ordain him the captain of another hopeless, countryside hamlet.

With that assignment, Khai would be free to leech taxes and kickbacks from the peasants, a scheme that would last as long as he could survive there. And survive he would. All that he had to do was funnel the lion's share of the booty off to the Kien Tuong Province bureaucrats, who would, in turn, forward a percentage to the thugs in Saigon, the men at the highest levels of Vietnamese power, who were becoming fabulously wealthy on the share of what came from the countryside and, especially, what they were squeezing from the Americans.

Khai, himself, would keep just enough hidden in a hole in the ground so that when the American-built house of cards crumbled in a few years, as everyone knew it would, he'd buy his way out of the country and settle comfortably in Cannes.

But why did Khai want J.W. out of the way, gone from My Co? Surely J.W.'s presence would bring some security to My Co, and heaps of American money and matériel, largess Khai could embezzle and sell back to the peasants and, perhaps, even to the Viet Cong. Maybe he was worried that J.W. was yet another body with whom he would be obliged to share the spoils of his fraud, that J.W. was just one of the swine at the trough who had made careers of stealing from the miserable, like the gang of administrators Khai had surely bribed to place him there. Or perhaps Khai feared that J.W. was just one of the Janus-faced Western missionaries who had flocked to China and Viet Nam over the past century, resolute paragons of moral propriety, men fond of turning in corrupt officials during daylight hours but spending the night with prostitutes.

J.W. asked himself where else than from unchecked craving could the nerve have come for this man to tell J.W. to leave, to utter the words that he was not welcome? The village was no more Khai's than J.W.'s. And why should J.W. leave? *Ông* Khai would not stay in My Co for long. During the day, he would make a brave appearance, collecting taxes and extracting graft as had all who had gone before him: the Chinese marionettes of the French property-owners, and more recently, the urban Vietnamese puppets of those Chinese landlords. At night, however, he would repair to one of the larger towns to hide the spoils of his greed. J.W. could barely accept that he had been so easily fooled.

At the NDP, several heavily-armed American soldiers were forming up at the barbed wire gate, listening intently to a lieutenant delivering a patrol order. J.W. overheard the lieutenant brief his troops that the colonel had spied a probable VC in the village, a tall male ducking into a house when the old man's helicopter flew over. The deal was still on—a three-day R&R for each pair of matching ears they brought back to Happy Valley Night Defensive Position.

The soldiers charged their rifles and departed the NDP. Though it was the middle of the afternoon, the troops moved cautiously up the muddy road, weapons pointed toward anything that stirred. J.W. started to search for the colonel, to halt the mission, but he heard yelling up the road and saw the patrol outside *Bà* Binh's. He sprinted out through the gap in the concertina wire, arriving at the old lady's hut in seconds. She was alone, rocking in her hammock rhythmically, poker-faced, shaking her head sadly. A buck sergeant from the patrol sent his fire team deeper along the paths of the hamlet to search huts, reminding them as they fanned out to use bayonets to pierce the floor-to-ceiling, cylindrical, woven-grass rice storage bins, the family's food for the year, and the thatch roofs. "The dinks can be hidin' anywhere."

Several of the GIs had already entered *Bà* Binh's. They were prying the mahogany planks of her bed from the earthen stanchions that served double-duty as the base of the bed and the old lady's bomb shelter. The refuge was pulverized as the men ripped timbers, flinging them across the hut, peering deep into the pit for the colonel's tall enemy soldier. Their quarry, however, had vaporized.

A dozen huts farther into the hamlet, the GIs discovered a pair of early-teens submerged in a water buffalo pen, only their noses sticking above the manure-laced mud. The boys were marched at rifle point, hands bound behind their backs, to an open patch of sand outside the NDP. There they hunkered in the blistering sun, their suits of sludge drying abruptly into brown plaster straightjackets as they awaited the arrival of Private Dinh.

J.W. remained in the background until he recognized one of the boys as *Em* Huong. Weathersby told Dinh to take it easy on Huong, that he was a good kid, but the young interpreter launched the interrogation with a malicious tranquility, plying his trade in a calm, but scornful whisper.

"Why would you two mingle yourselves with the animals, cover yourselves with buffalo piss and shit, do all that, if you didn't have anything to hide?" When there was no answer, Dinh upped the timbre with a sudden burst of screeching rhetoric. "Farmers are stupid cows, but even a farmer doesn't lie in shit. Even a farmer! You are VC. Where is your leader, the man who ran from the helicopter? Is he lying in the shit, too? Where is he?"

He kicked at the boys until washcloth-sized sheets of dry manure flew from their quaking bodies. Still the children remained silent, far too terrified to answer, even if they had understood the questions spit at them in Saigonese dialect, speech as foreign to them as J.W.'s English.

Dinh altered his efforts from lower extremity abuse to knocking the smaller boy, *Em* Huong, in the head with the butt of his M-16. The child rolled into a fetal ball, wet his pants, and began to weep with eyes closed. J.W. was about to enter the conflict when *Cô* Lin stepped forward and wedged herself between Dinh and the boy. J.W. accepted that as the symbolically more powerful intervention.

But Dinh shoved her to the ground and hissed at the GIs, "She VC!"

The American sergeant took *Cô* Lin's arm gently, helped her to her feet, and pointed her back to the crowd.

"That's enough, Dinh," the sergeant grumbled. "We'll turn them over to the ARVN. You can go back to sleep now."

Dinh, throbbing in fury, turned to leave but took a final swipe at *Em* Huong, and during the cursing and threatening that followed, the other young prisoner sprang to his feet and ran into the paddies, his hands till bound behind him. The sergeant pointed toward the sky and nodded to one of his men, who aimed his M-16 and discharged a short burst of automatic fire into the air. The child stopped short, his head and shoulders sagging. He began to turn toward the crowd to walk back, but Dinh took aim and fired, and though missing, the rounds splashed so close, the youngster spun away from the villagers and sprinted off again in a pathetic waddle.

Dinh, screaming epithets, discharged the rest of his magazine. A few of the rounds found their mark. The child hurled face first into the paddy, struggled pitifully for the dike, but slowly stilled under the putrid water.

J.W. whispered, "He's gone."

The villagers stood fixed for several moments, but a spontaneous sway began that resonated with the cadence of the quiet wailing of the women. *Bà* Binh shuffled toward the paddy in which the new corpse surfaced, though several of the villagers pulled her back, tugging at her faded black clothing until she relented and followed them into a cluster of nearby huts.

One of the infantrymen took his own M-16 and slammed Dinh in the head with the butt, though several of his buddies pulled the weapons from both him and Dinh, yelling to the GI, "That piece of shit ain't worth getting court marshaled for, man."

Dinh crawled to his feet, spit at the GI, and swore, "You fuck, I kill you you sleep. Fuck!" Dinh spun for the NDP and the command tent to report the incident and no-doubt threaten the colonel that he would take the matter to the Vietnamese government.

The soldiers led the living prisoner, *Em* Huong, into the NDP, and J.W. took the quiet interval to course along the earthen dikes into the paddies. He stared at the boy's body then at his fingers for a flicker of life. As the corpse settled under the mire of the paddy, J.W. lifted the child from the water and carried him back to the remaining assemblage of benumbed villagers. He set the body down as gently as if placing an infant in a cradle and walked off alone toward the NDP.

An hour later, Colonel Williams had J.W. summoned to the command tent. "Lieutenant, your wish has come true. First of the 27th departs Happy Valley in thirty minutes. The saddest part of this whole affair is that we were here less than twenty-four hours, and we don't get a single Green Stamp for our efforts. And sorry about your prostitute and the kid in the paddies."

"Yeah, and the hootch roofs."

"Yeah?"

"Yes."

"Yes?"

"Yes, sir."

"I'm glad we've got that straightened out. Go and get your gear together. See you in base camp."

Before he left, J.W. asked the colonel what was going to be done with Dinh. Williams reminded him it wasn't the infantry's call, but added that the man who had hit Dinh faced a courts marshal for the assault of a fellow soldier. J.W. tried to explain what had happened, but the colonel contended that the boy was an escaping prisoner who had failed to heed the international warning to stop.

J.W. packed, but instead of joining the line of snaking, beaten infantry awaiting the troop transports to lift them from Happy Valley and insert them into next horror, he hauled the scraps of his existence to *Bà* Binh's, slouching on the remains of her bed, promising the old woman he would fix the structure once the Americans had flown out.

He drifted off to sleep, woken an hour later by the drone of two Chinooks descending into My Co. He stood, avoiding the doorway, peering through a gap in the straw wall as the helicopters approached Happy Valley, skimming in low over the paddies, studiously avoiding flight over or near the few remaining huts.

He laughed sardonically and spoke to *Bà* Binh in English, "Just goes to show even a Chinook pilot can learn."

J.W.'s cheer was ephemeral. Colonel Williams helicopter took off, cruised slowly over the hamlet, but abruptly swung around back toward the NDP. J.W. hissed to himself, "What, forget your keys?"

The colonel's pilot accelerated, planning to touch down before the next pair of Chinooks arrived, but the colonel's four-seater was enveloped in so much sand, the larger ships did not see him. Just as the small craft was about to settle onto the pad, a blast of monsoon-force wind from the CH-47s whirled the small ship nearly on its side. The pilot pulled desperately on the collective to lift the chopper and escape, but the skid caught on a metal post and the aircraft vaulted into a dynamic rollover.

The Chinooks frantically sought to avoid the debris of the disintegrating helicopter and shot furiously to positions left and right, putting them directly over the village. Gone now were the remnants of the roofs that had avoided the full one-hundred-and-twenty-mile-per-hour downwash of the previous day. There they hovered, awaiting further orders, the first of which would certainly be to transport the crew of the destroyed helicopter to a hospital in Saigon, or more likely, deliver the remains to graves registration. The pilots of one of the Hooks leaned out of his cockpit, looked down, and called over the radio to the other ship that he did not see movement in the rolled-over, smoking, still vibrating, little command chopper.

The air of My Co, usually pristine, aside from crystals of Agent Orange floating in from the jungle, now churned with a salad of helicopter parts, straw, the usual lumps of barnyard scat, mud, GI soft caps, and a furiously flapping rooster. A fair portion of this detritus greeted Colonel Williams as he crawled out of the remains of his ship. He ran forward, angrily motioning the Hook pilot to land, and after much discussion, hand waving, and finger pointing, the lead Chinook's crew chief exited the ship and fastened a cable to the toppled main rotor of the small observation aircraft. With the colonel and his pilot aboard the Chinook, the CH-47 lifted into a low hover over the vestiges of the chopper and began a slow levitation. The pilot's charge was to lift the ship and deposit it at Long Binh Post, just north of Saigon, but the Chinook's rotor wash blasted the fuselage of the destroyed helicopter to the north, and the still-steaming, quarter-of-a-million-dollar engine southward.

The colonel's pilot scrambled out of the Chinook, and with the Hook's crew chief assisting, disconnected the cable and reboarded the transport. The Chinook lifted off, leaving the accordioned metal on the ground. The other large ship filled quickly with troops, footlockers, papers, stoves, the colonel's latrine, and sacks of powdered carrots and powdered eggs. J.W. watched, peering through the straw of *Bà* Binh's thatch.

Chapter 6

A FIERY SUN retreated beyond the jungle tree line leaving, J.W. wondering if his was a death wish, to remain alone amongst, if not the enemy, those who would be if they took one minute to consider what he and his compatriots had done to their lives. He walked to the village restaurant where *Ông* Long was sitting, staring off into space. Without hesitating, J.W. tossed a pack of Salems on the table in front of the wispy-bearded elder, an action that drew the old man quickly out of his reverie. J.W. ordered and chugged a cloyingly sweet, Asian brewed Coke Cola, and then a second, but the syrup only worsened his thirst, and he ordered a third, though with that bottle, a critical mass of gas coalesced deep within his gut, cramping his innards to the point that he jumped up, grunted loudly in pain, and leaned over the table, wondering if he was going to explode.

As a concerned *Ông* Long stood and asked if J.W. was okay, Weathersby let out a grand burp, one several seconds in duration and many decibels in vitality. That eased the pain and brought a weak smile to his face. *Ông* Long went back to his cigarette, his third in the few moments since J.W. had arrived, puffing again and again, but garnering no pleasure from the drug. When J.W retook his seat on the picnic bench and opened *For Whom the Bell Tolls*, Long pushed the book down curtly and spoke in a weak, almost pleading tone. J.W., though, deciphered only the words, "*Em* Huong go..."

Lost trying to comprehend, J.W. did not hear the slight crunch outside the restaurant, and was startled a moment later to look up into the very dark eyes of Vu Van Khai. As the man navigated the five-foot-five doorway, J.W. dropped his hand under the table and lifted the .45 a few inches out of its holster, an action that did not go unnoticed by Khai, or by the two other patrons of the tiny eatery. *Ông* Khai smiled stiffly and took a step toward J.W.

J.W. grumbled, "You got me into a heap of trouble today Mr. Khai; and those dumb kids…"

That brought a nervous grin to turbaned *Ông* Long. There was also a smile on the other patron, *Ông* Tinh, Long's brother, who had tried to slide out the door when *Ông* Khai appeared.

Khai, now fully unfolded inside the hut, towered above J.W. and spoke calmly in English. "Lieuten, I am sorry for misunderstand today. I tell you, I no VC. But Lieuten must go from village My Co. VC put price on head. Communist not want you village My Co. Lieuten have much money—build school, market, little hospital. They very worry win heart of people. Already pay kill you. You go. You understand?"

J.W. dropped the pistol back into the holster. *Ông* Khai waited for J.W.'s eyes to flicker in acceptance, and when Weathersby finally dipped his head, Khai sat down beside the glum foreigner.

"Well, right now," J.W. looked up and groaned in English, "the Viet Cong and the NVA don't have to worry a thing about these people's hearts and minds, do they? I am very sorry for what happened today, and last night."

Ông Tinh, unable to contain himself in the presence of two men who were so close to those who controlled the cosmic purse strings, broke into the conversation, speaking to Khai. J.W. understood the man to be griping about the loss of one of his brother's water buffalo, a creature that had been hit by stray fire the night before.

J.W. put up his hand to stop *Ông* Tinh then spoke to Khai, "Tell him, please, that I am very sorry, and that these soldiers don't want to hurt anyone, and that we will pay for the water buffalo. But I want him to understand that our soldiers are very young, mostly draftees, and they don't want to be here, but it was your government that invited us to come." J.W.'s voice hardened as he went on. "In fact, they hate being here, Mr. Khai, and they will fire every fuckin' bullet they can get their hands on at anything, even at a shadow, if they think it's going to turn around and shoot them. These are good men. They just want to go home alive with two arms and two legs and both eyes. As it is, it doesn't look like any of us are going home with normal minds." J.W. paused, trying to calm himself, but his anger peaked, and he jabbed an index finger at the three Vietnamese men as his voice neared a shout. "Kill first or be killed. And every one of them knows it because they've seen it a hundred fuckin' times with their own eyes. This whole place sucks."

The smile had long since dissolved from Khai's lips. He translated J.W.'s invective, and speaking gently in simple Vietnamese, turned to J.W. "I must teach the people of My Co that the Americans have come to save Viet Nam. But the people of My Co do not understand. They are very angry. The boys were foolish to run, but they aren't Viet Cong. They thought the Americans were there to put them in the army. So they hid."

Khai suddenly switched to English. "They should smart, but they children. One dead and one take away. Dead tomorrow. Village My Co people very angry."

J.W. thought seriously for a moment and offered, "Well, maybe I can get *Em* Huong released."

Khai went on in English. "He in hand ARVN, Army Republic Viet Nam soldier, no American army. ARVN torture for sure, and when finish, he disappear. Never see again."

"Well, I have to go up to Saigon tomorrow and turn myself in. Looks like I won't be back, either. I'll ask Colonel Bierlein to see what he can do. He made a commitment to My Co. If they release *Em* Huong, will that make the people happy?"

"Happy, Lieuten? Maybe no so angry. Also, maybe you speak American officer. Last night many water buffalo shoot with machine gun. Infantry soldier say think buffalo Viet Cong." He paused and his face hardened. "Khai hear Lieuten say such young man. Home so far away."

J.W. nodded. "Yep, very far away." His eyes reddened, and he paused, looking away from Khai. Finally, he sighed and added, "I'll get to the bottom of it for you. And, are you going back to where you live tonight?"

"No, Lieuten," Khai went on in English. "Only VC travel road at dark. I sleep here sometime, but change house every night. Where you sleep?"

"*Bà* Binh's, I guess."

"She ask me sleep in house. I go with Lieuten? Is okay?"

J.W. nodded without expression, hoping to give the impression he was fine on his own, though he wondered if Khai saw his shoulders loosen.

Before they left the restaurant, J.W. tossed another pack of Salems on the table for Long and Tinh. Outside the door, *Ông* Khai smiled slightly. "Khai see Lieuten grow mustache. Soon you look mandarin."

J.W. asked, "Do the mandarins have handlebars on their mustaches?" When *Ông* Khai's head cocked, J.W. brought his hands to his lips and whorled his fingers to his upper lip, mimicking a pair of elegantly curled water buffalo horns. As Khai's smile spread, J.W.'s hands moved farther and farther out.

"No, Lieuten. Hairs must point down, never up. Must not offend heaven or emperor."

The two walked the rest of the mile-long hamlet silently. J.W. barely avoided the moon-lit puddles that dotted My Co's road. As his boot approached one of the potholes, *Ông* Khai gently steered him away, whispering, "Please you take care, Lieuten. Beaucoup VC mine in water."

"But, it's only eight o'clock. They haven't come into the village yet tonight, have they?"

"Viet Cong not only in forest. Viet Cong live in house on road. Half villager, maybe eighty of one hundred part, they think communist bring end all problem, foreign greed, thief landlord. Most villager remember war against French. Children and father soldier. That early Viet Cong. Fifteen-year pass. Then name is Viet Minh fighter. Viet Minh give extra bowl rice for kid if count number French troop march by, and how many enemy truck pass in village. Extra bowl rice! You know what that mean to starve people?"

"Were you one of them? A Viet Minh?" J.W. asked cautiously.

"Yes. And father mother brother sister."

"Did you count the trucks or the soldiers?"

"Truck and soldier. You see, Lieuten, Viet Minh not enemy of people. French landlord and China rent collector enemy of people. But Viet Minh change when go Hanoi after French run away—that new story. Then many lie come from China Communist. Mao Zedong promise heaven if all Viet Nam turn to communist. Many good Viet Minh man walk Hanoi, walk, Lieuten, Saigon Hanoi, one thousand kilometer, become communist then walk south again. They fight die." Khai shook his head sadly. "Please you careful puddle My Co road. In Viet Nam nothing what it seem. Most beautiful woman, most quiet lake, everything deathtrap. You must careful.

"The Viet Cong write you every step; they have name Lieuten family from they steal letter. Very clever VC. They in front of eye—you no see. You must leave My Co tomorrow before too late."

At *Bà* Binh's, a single candle glowed through gaps in the straw and mud walls. Seeing the two men, the old lady smiled, satisfied, that she had so easily persuaded the two most powerful men in the village to pay attention to her. *Cô* Lin was hunkered in the corner near the charcoal fire washing her silken hair. The fragrance of the French shampoo commingled with that of the warm water quickened J.W.'s pulse, and he ached for her to sleep there that night, close to him. As the two men walked to the table, *Cô* Lin stood, wrapped a towel around her head, and nodded politely, more to *Ông* Khai than Weathersby. She glanced at her grandmother then walked so slowly past J.W., he sensed her warmth. She glided noiselessly through the door, though the scent of her shampoo lingered. As he involuntarily let a breath escape, both *Bà* Binh and *Ông* Khai shifted their eyes toward him.

From outside, *Cô* Lin called back to *Bà* Binh in very slow, deliberate Vietnamese, "Tomorrow, Grandmother."

Bà Binh motioned in the direction of the one mahogany-planked bed that remained intact, but *Ông* Khai and J.W. straightened what they could of the broken mud piers upon which the planks of the first bed had rested for so many years. J.W. sat on the edge of the boards, flexing his neck left and right to assure himself he could not be seen from outside. *Bà* Binh set glasses of cold, stale tea on the table, refilling them over and over to dispense with the day's leftovers. J.W. placed a crushed pack of Salems on the table near *Ông* Khai.

Bà Binh rolled creakily into her black silk hammock, *Ông* Khai onto the bed nearest the door. J.W., as if a movie director, studied the view from the other bed. He grimaced and shook his head then dropped onto the pounded dirt floor, putting the disintegrated bed between himself and the door. He lay on his back with the charged .45, safety off, tight in his left hand.

As *Bà* Binh swung gently in her hammock, she spoke softly, again recollecting the city of Lai Khe at the turn of the century. "You can get there sometimes, but not when the roads are a sea of mud like during the monsoon. Lieutenant, you must see the *Cáo dài* Temple. I want to see it one last time before I die. Oh, it was a huge house, the biggest on Earth, we Vietnamese say. The *Cáo dài* Temple, oh, my heavens, it was bigger than the whole world." Soon, she mumbled something about her homeland crumbling, there being nothing left of the perfection that was Viet Nam, but her voice soon trailed off and a delicate breathing took its place.

Ông Khai whispered to J.W. in English, "*Cáo dài* Temple destroy Tet Offensive last year. Only ruin now. *Bà* Binh not know, but she right; you should see in old day. Lai Khe beautiful, even today. Maybe you go army there. Much safe than countryside."

J.W. did not answer, for he, too, had fallen off, snoring more resonantly than the ancient men of the surrounding paper-thin huts of My Co.

⇸ ⇷

J.W. woke before dawn, freezing, last evening's tea having expanded his bladder to the point of bursting, though he dared not step from the hootch in the dark. He waited for an hour, until the roosters proclaimed he had survived another night. At the berm, he encountered the usual gathering near *Bà* Binh's, the old men and young boys who watched as he relieved himself, heads bobbing, staring to ascertain if his male member was as different from theirs as was his behavior. He turned away from them, but found himself facing the hunkering women a bit farther south. He saw *Cô* Lin and averted his eyes, as did she.

When he returned to *Bà* Binh's, *Ông* Khai was kick-starting his Vespa motor scooter. Thanking *Bà* Binh again with a slight bow, he took J.W.'s hand in both of his, and J.W. felt the warmth of a subtle tug. "Not many soldier release child. Careful you go Saigon. Khai hope see you again someday. Not forget you."

As the blue-gray smoke of his moped disappeared, J.W. watched for a moment then went inside *Bà* Binh's. He left five funny-money dollars on the table under a banana, a personal solatium payment, to have her bed fixed. It was probably enough to have her entire hootch renovated from dirt floor to mouse-infested thatched roof, and have running water, an indoor toilet, and a radio installed, had any of those contraptions ever been imagined in My Co. He laughed to himself that he might see the maturity of his donation in a magazine forty years hence, flaunting the latest in Vietnamese country living. It would mean, though, that he would have to live through the next few weeks.

He folded his things and shoved them into his duffel bag, though as he left, he whispered to her in English and gave her a bit of a hug, "I might just come back. I like it here, and you're the best."

Chapter 7

J.W. LEFT THE village on the local bus, arriving at Colonel Bierlein's office five hours later minus another five dollars and a carton of Salems. He appealed to Bierlein to have the Mech issue him a jeep, to send a small, permanent civil affairs contingent to the village, and to let him return with them to My Co. While the colonel was mulling over the pros and cons, J.W. added, "And, sir, could you get General Abrams to help me get this kid, *Em* Huong, released?"

J.W. spent the night on the concrete floor of an Officer's Club warehouse, his fatigue shirt rolled as a pillow. He was shaken awake by a private, who handed him the keys to a jeep parked outside. On the back was a badly dented, PRC 46 radio-transmitter. He was ordered to shower and report to General Abrams' office at Pentagon East.

Abrams, the commander of all American troops in Viet Nam, handed J.W. a letter. Under the four blood-red stars heading the document, he cajoled the ARVN commander down the street in Saigon to release *Em* Huong. "What you're doing out there is more important than all the guns in Tien Giang Province. Don't you forget that, son."

J.W. drove the alleys of Saigon, following an ARVN soldier on a Vespa. He had bribed the man with ten MPC dollars to show him where the Army of Viet Nam interrogated, tortured, and executed the fodder shipped in from American units in the countryside. He had to get there quickly, for if Huong was still alive, he would soon be murdered or, worse, shipped on a cattle truck to the south coast of Viet Nam, and onto a slave ship to die in the tiger cages on Con Son Island.

The man agreed, but only to drive past, drop his right arm for a moment, and be allowed to continue on, never letting his eyes shift toward the prison.

J.W. parked in front of the peeling sheet metal gates. He scribbled a note in broken Vietnamese and handed it to a thug at the gate. The soldier pulled at the four inches of arrow-straight hair growing from a mole on his face, glaring until J.W. handed him five dollars. J.W. waited in the scalding sun until noon, when an officer came to the gate and J.W. showed him the letter. There was another officer followed by two pock-marked civilians, and finally a lot of cursing behind the walls. At two, the little boy limped out of the compound and climbed into the new jeep. He was unable to open his mouth, the swelling from his beatings so fresh.

Weathersby spit in the direction of the guard, who started forward and charged his American M-16, but J.W. gave him the finger and sped away. He jammed a round into the chamber of his .45 and left it between his legs, safety off. A mile away, when he was sure they were not being followed, J.W. turned to Huong and touched the child's swollen jaw, remembering the pounding he had taken at the hands of one of the commanders at the Ranger School eons, but only months, before.

Em Huong smiled and took J.W.'s hand. J.W. smiled back, "Kid, lemme tell you something about life. You want something, you ask for it. And you keep asking until you get it."

Huong, whose English vocabulary did not go beyond "same same" and "money," waited silently until J.W. stopped. He looked about to be sure no one was watching before mumbling through clinched teeth about the tortures he had suffered at the hands of the South Vietnamese police. The litany went on until J.W. stopped the jeep in Moc Hoa to buy lunch. The child could not open his mouth wide enough to suck in *phở* noodles, so J.W. drove to the American base and ordered a milk shake, which Huong drew painfully through a straw. He slept for the rest of the trip home, though J.W. shook his shoulder gently as they approached the outskirts of My Co.

When the jeep rolled past the first huts, J.W. straightened in the driver's seat, extinguished his cigarette, and maneuvered around the pot holes as slowly as he could without burning out the clutch. Wearing his linebacker's game face, he stared straight ahead, barely nodding to the villagers. Gasps and shouts erupted from the hootches as word spread, and in seconds, a line of the bewildered snaked along behind the creeping jeep.

Given the reception at the east end of town, and the vibrating conga line of emaciated citizens, J.W. expected shouts of glee and buckets of tears as he pulled up to *Ông* Long's, but the old man pointed sternly to the hut's door and followed Huong inside. The mass of villagers flowing toward the hootch from the east was soon joined with throngs from the west end of town. They chattered noisily, appointing emissaries to enter Mr. Long's, and every few seconds, one of the representatives emerged to brief the crowd, abruptly stopping mid-sentence to duck back in if there was even the slightest change in the register of the angry voices. An old woman pinched J.W.'s cheek and cackled, "This is the most exciting moment ever in My Co," or that was what he heard.

J.W. listened intently, catching a word here and there, but the, "Oh, my Gods," were flying about like chicken feathers after a helicopter landing, and he understood little. He took a tentative step to enter the hut, to witness the spectacle for himself, but *Bà* Binh tottered over, pulled at his fatigue blouse, waved a finger of warning, and growled an unintelligible sentence in irritated Vietnamese. J.W. believed it meant the family needed privacy, so he stepped back. *Bà* Binh let go of his shirt and pushed past to shuffle into the hut. She chastised the team of emissaries with words far more shrill than she had aimed at J.W. She soon emerged to issue her considered opinion. She pointed an arthritic finger at several of the more unruly, jabbering citizens, sending them off in a huff. As the news reports slackened, the masses began a slow dispersion back to the broiling fields.

J.W. evaporated the remainder of the day at *Bà* Binh's, napping off and on. With the cooling of late afternoon, he set out onto the bamboo-lined trails of the hamlet, delving farther into My Co than he ever believed he'd have the nerve to venture. At the nooks and crannies of fifteenth century Asia, he came to curiosities he could never have imagined—the flotsam and jetsam of war, harsh debris reborn as tools to preserve life. The metal banding that strapped artillery shells to pallets had been cut into two-foot lengths, etched by hand, case hardened over charcoal fires, and transformed into saw blades; bits of sharp-edged, ultra-hard exploded 105 Howitzer shrapnel had been fashioned into chisels; the brass canisters of spent artillery rounds were now buckets for a hand-operated contraption that brought water from the lower paddies to the upper plots.

With each nod and smile from the villagers, his self-importance flowered and *Ông* Khai's dictum of caution faded. By dusk, J.W. returned to *Bà* Binh's to sit contentedly in the cool of the thatched hut, silently considering the beams of sun filtering through the hole in the roof over the charcoal fire. As the day mellowed, shafts of light swelled into a ginger glow from the western sky. Nearing seven, when J.W. smoked the next to the last of his Salems, he contemplated the final sliver of the ruby sun as it disappeared from the pastel horizon.

He relished the overpowering smells of exotic spices sizzling in peanut oil, of pickled fish and dried fish, and clouds of starchy steam rising from battered rice pots. The din of spoons rattling on flattened tins of mackerel in tomato sauce, the clunk of emptied red-labeled cans tossed carelessly from doorways to join last night's trash rusting in puddles, all of it afforded a sense of well-being new to him.

In Pavlovian fashion, J.W. began to salivate and pulled from his duffel bag several C-ration selections. He offered the panoply of choices to *Bà* Binh, who curled her nose at the sight of the olive drab cans covered with heavy black letters in a foreign script she wished she'd never laid eyes on. As J.W. pushed one of the tins closer to her face, she shook her head no vehemently, pushed his hand away, and shuffled over to the wicker shelf for a chew of betel nut. He asked with his hand signals if he could place a can of Cs in what was left of the day's cooking fire. She nodded, and he took three steps toward the corner of the hut, tripped on a scrawny chicken, and dropped his eyes seeking forgiveness when *Bà* Binh cackled louder than the bird. In the area called, *nhà bếp*, the kitchen, was a three-foot square of dirt no different than the rest of the single room other than the name, a couple of battered aluminum pots, four porcelain rice bowls, four Duralex glasses, and a few smoldering scraps of charcoal. The straw walls were blackened with soot, as was the thatch surrounding the hole in the roof that served as a chimney.

J.W. left the can in the fire until the odor of burning paint forced *Bà* Binh's nose to curl again. He touched her on the shoulder and left the hut to relax against a jackfruit tree and pick at a tin of lukewarm, but still congealed, Beef Stew. The eerie light of a generous bonfire at the other end of the hamlet caught his eye, and he marveled at the jagged flames and at the Vietnamese, so astute in their manipulation of nature.

He lit his last Salem and looked up through the fresh cigarette smoke, realizing distantly that the glow of the fire that had captivated his attention and imagination just seconds before was suddenly gone, vanished, the light extinguished so abruptly, it was if it had been switched off electronically. A moment later, with the afterglow of the sunset nearly dowsed, he forgot about the bonfire and pondered only his isolation, unable to imagine a life in the world he'd left behind. Barely able to picture his family, he could not fathom that the very same sun abandoning him was peeking over the horizon on the other side of the Earth. There was nothing for him but the settlement of My Co.

The air was cool and the scent of dying charcoal sweet, so J.W. decided to cross the hamlet for a bottle of Coke. It was the first time he had gone out completely alone at night, and though he avoided the puddles, studiously at first, and stayed close to the huts to avoid standing out in profile, he tired of the extra work and traipsed with a touch of bravado down the road, through the potholes, not around them. He had never seen or even heard of a VC in his village. There was no way the enemy could divine that he was on his way to get a soda. He'd pull a cool drink from the ice chest, drop a few cents on the table, and disappear back into the hamlet, to *Bà* Binh's. Yes, there was a war, but it festered miles away in the jungle. He was safe in My Co, trusted, a hero. He had resurrected a child's life. No one had *ever* done that before in the war.

He marched the center of the road, head high, until the loneliness washed over him again. He looked back to *Bà* Binh's, hoping to catch a glimpse of *Cô* Lin. A candle was burning, shadows were moving, and he considered going back to ask *Cô* Lin to walk with him to the restaurant for a Coke. He started back, though the closer he came to bowing through the tiny door, the more he recognized the absurdity of the two of them walking together, the mustachioed, loud, thick foreigner, and the exceedingly petite, genteel, Vietnamese woman. Being seen with *Cô* Lin at night would virtually end the possibility of his usefulness as an instrument of positive change in My Co, of ever being sufficiently respected to bring democracy and modern justice to that ancient village.

Worse, J.W. would eventually leave and surely forget My Co, though Lin would never go anywhere else in her life. Her reputation would be devastated, for no man would touch her, and when the Americans left and the South Vietnamese government was annihilated, Lin would be tainted, a collaborator, tortured, and finally lucky to be decapitated.

He did not know what to do. The loneliness and, he admitted, the need deep inside him, burned hotter with each step, and all he could dream at that moment was of *Cô* Lin's scent, her warm hand touching his, and their arms wrapped around each other, sleeping. Now thirty yards away, he was so blinded by the craving, he skimmed inches from a pair of buffalo in a pen, far closer than he had ever before dared. He was astonished by the breadth of the horns and by the cacophony of grunting and snorting he had instigated. While J.W. passed quickly, and the din of the oxen was fleeting, it set off a gentle, rhythmic refrain of grunts and cackles from the livestock of My Co, voices joined to celebrate, one last time, their precarious survival through another day in Viet Nam.

J.W., even more obsessed to spend that night with *Cô* Lin, was unable to rid his mind of the thought of waking with her nude body covered by his, protected, the two of them sealed by the passion of the most enchanting night of their lives. He relaxed and slowed his pace, allowing himself to draw out the fantasy. He wasn't sure why he was so smitten with her. Was it her gentleness, her face? Why did he feel such a need to shield just her from the struggle, even if it was only for one night?

The single answer he could fathom was that Lin was the haunting image of a young Puerto Rican woman he'd seen as a child. All these years he had not forgotten the girl's ebony eyes, her jet-black hair, and the vision of the violent man who stood over her cursing in English, whipping her from behind with a chain. It was in his Bronx schoolyard, and J.W. had wanted to shield her, to defend her, but he was just a boy. He remembered her name—Lupe.

A few doors down from *Bà* Binh's, he passed *Ông* Nguyen's hut a bit too closely. That startled the old man's buffalo, which was just nodding off in the attached, eight-foot-square sunken vat of mud. It snorted violently, twice, spraying J.W. with a quart of fetid nasal mucous that clung to his fatigues like polyurethane. The bull's grunt was not only sodden, it carried with it a message to the creatures of My Co that there had been yet another breech in the sacred routine of sunset, a violation of village animal etiquette. That infringement irked a mangy canine lying in the doorway of the next hut to spring out and freeze just shy of J.W.'s right leg.

Weathersby, assuming the dog's intentions were to relieve himself, spat, "You piss on my leg, you little shit, and you're casualty number one for the night. Now, fuck off."

In fact, the dog did not urinate on J.W., though he sniffed wetly. When the cur looked up and seemed to smile, J.W. bent forward to scratch its head, but the dog's master, *Ông* Xuan, sprang drunkenly from inside his hut wielding a carbon-encrusted, cast-iron frying pan. The dog's ears peaked, and the jaws spread. Xuan howled angrily in Vietnamese, and the hound peed a few drops then struck, latching onto J.W.'s calf. Weathersby bound off along the path, trying to shake it free as *Ông* Xuan chased behind, weaving left and right into little gardens, crushing vegetable plants. A dozen neighbors streamed onto the paths cursing at him to get off their carrots and turnips. One grabbed the frying pan away from Xuan and clunked the dog on the head so hard, another gaggle of peasants fled to their homes, believing a gun had been fired.

The dog rolled over whelping and screeching, a dissonance that brought an intensified disquiet to the hamlet. Though the mutt soon shuddered and fell to the ground, the animal hubbub in the neighborhood went on for several more minutes, especially while *Ông* Xuan was dragging the carcass behind his hootch. By the time Xuan limped to the front of his hut again, an eerie silence had descended upon the village. Xuan locked J.W.'s eyes, pointed out toward the paddies, and shook his head.

That frightened J.W., but he reasoned there was no way the VC would venture into the hamlet that night, especially with all the day's U.S. Army activity. How could they know if the NDP was occupied, and if it was, the strength of troops left behind? The enemy did not have radio communication with the villagers, and even if they did, they wouldn't dare kick off an operation so close to dusk. He knew from Ranger training that the Viet Cong's modus operandi dictated they wait until long after sunset to infiltrate from the surrounding jungle. So there was still time before the VC, Victor Charley, would steal into town, plenty of opportunity to talk to *Cô* Lin and to invite her for a Coke or even a Ba Me Ba, 33 Beer.

But when J.W. reached *Bà* Binh's hut, it was unlit, and the old lady snored peacefully in her hammock. As J.W.'s eyes adjusted to the dark, it was clear the room was otherwise empty. He went back outside and dawdled a bit in the neighborhood, searching nervously for *Cô* Lin until the evening heat fatigued him, and he gave up. Walking back to the restaurant, he passed *Ông* Long's. His wife popped out to thank J.W. for bringing her grandson home from the impossibly remote city of Saigon. J.W. walked on, stopping at *Ông* Xuan's to watch a fragrant outdoor fire and the slowly roasting silhouette of a skinned dog on the bamboo-pole rotisserie spit. *Ông* Xuan smiled for J.W. to stay and eat, but J.W. bowed, imitating *Ông* Khai, and continued on to the restaurant.

J.W. had become a regular at the village bistro, an institution, he feared, was simply a figment of his perception. It was no more unique than *Bà* Binh's hut in construction and meager square footage, but because the villagers, and J.W. himself, believed it was a public eatery, that was what it was. No matter that it sold nothing other than a bowl of rice, a few ribbons of braised rat, the occasional filet of snake, and a beer or Coke; it was where the local men folk gathered at night to get away from their wives.

From a hundred meters away, J.W. saw the usual warm glow of a kerosene lantern through the holes in the mud and thatch walls. As he drew closer, he appreciated the silhouettes of moving figures and soon heard the growl of men's voices. This was a scene out of the fantastic Asian short stories of Pa Chin and Lu Hsin he had devoured in the beginner's Chinese literature course at Sterling College. As he approached the hut, he sensed a peculiar warmth, thinking of the familiar faces he would soon join. He laughed to himself that he had been there long enough to perceive his friends as neither foreign, nor even Asian. They had become good neighbors, men he thought he would travel across the globe many times in his later years to visit.

At the doorless portal, J.W.'s eyes fixed on four young men he had never before seen. They stared up silently from the primitive wooden table without expression, poker-faced, despite J.W.'s nodded greeting. *Ông* Long, though, shot bolt upright from the corner treadle sewing machine from which he had been listening intently to the men. As J.W. took a step into the hut, Long leapt over to greet him at the doorway, nearly losing his faded white turban trying to block J.W. When *Ông* Long shot his hand forward and took J.W.'s to turn him around and guide him out of the restaurant, Weathersby shook his head in confusion. He wedged himself around the old man back into the room, careful, though, not to come into contact with the man's Mandarin beard, fearful of fracturing even one of the remaining scraggly, brittle, white strands.

J.W., while concerned about the man's whiskers, was, however, a bit perturbed for being given the bum's rush. All J.W. cared about was the cold soda he hoped would take his mind off *Cô* Lin.

Back inside, he stared at the foursome, struck by the presence of male peasants in their mid-twenties, something he had rarely seen in My Co. As he gaped, though, he recognized one of them as the young man he'd noticed in the crowd days before, the petitioner in women's clothing. J.W. was also puzzled by the thick necks and muscular faces held so arrogantly, in such contrast to their faded back pajamas. They appeared more athlete than peasant, and the hardening mien of the man he recognized sent J.W.'s gut into spasm.

Nonetheless, J.W. smiled. "Good evening, gentlemen. I don't think I know you, do I?"

With no change in expression, *Ông* Long began to sweat copiously as he introduced them, the quaver in his hands and legs vibrating the thatch. "Lieutenant, these men are friends."

"Friends?"

"Yes, friends." *Ông* Long grinned mirthlessly.

"Do you gentlemen live here?" No answer and no change in expression.

Ông Long, beads of sweat dripping from under the ragged turban, answered for the strangers again. "No, they don't live here. They were just talking about the new village chief, and how happy we must all be to have him here. And they asked if we were happy that the American soldiers killed so many of the village's water buffalo last night."

"Yes," J.W. answered, "I heard about that. Actually, the new chief told me. The American soldiers thought the buffalo were really Viet Cong. That's why they fired their machine guns."

With that explanation, the strangers' expressions finally changed. One locked his eyes into J.W.'s, boring with such hatred, J.W. took a step back toward the door. Another smirked as if confronted by a lunatic. "Viet Cong. Water buffalo."

"Huh," the third stranger growled with a vociferousness that propelled J.W. two more uncomfortable steps backward toward the door. That was when he felt a rod-like pressure building in the center of his back. An instant later came an angry shove forward. A fifth black-clad stranger, a humorless man wielding a Russian AK-47 assault rifle, had materialized out of the night to block J.W.'s egress. The muzzle soon found its way into the small of Weathersby's neck. It was at that moment J.W. recognized the political affiliation of the "strangers" was, to a large degree, the antithesis of his own.

J.W. took a shallow breath and snapped, "Hey, man, take it easy," but that just brought the rifle to his temple, rotating his head, allowing him to see out of the corner of his eye the least cheerful of the seated strangers nod abruptly toward the door. In an instant, J.W. was propelled into the steaming night, his .45 snatched from its holster as he was shoved across the threshold.

It had all happened so fast, J.W. was not able to process the depth of his dilemma, and he barked at the man with the gun to his neck as he would have at a fraternity brother's prank. "Get that goddamn thing off me, asshole."

Though the Communist soldier understood not a syllable of the demand, the comment resulted in an even harder shove of the weapon. The four men jumped from the table and wrestled J.W. to the ground, tied his hands roughly behind his back, and jammed a nylon U.S. Army sandbag over his head. Weathersby was dragged to his feet and marched toward the berm, the AK-47 rifle barrel still tight to his neck. His last vision of My Co was the Coca-Cola ice chest. He wanted to scream at it, to plead with it for help, but it sat callously observing, stolid only in its duty to do nothing to change the course of the war.

As they crossed over the berm, J.W. discerned the silhouettes of several more black-clad forms armed with AK-47s waiting in a defensive perimeter at the edge of the rice paddies. Realizing their captive was able to see, they tugged a second sandbag roughly over his head and tied this one harshly. J.W. jerked his head angrily and swung his elbows as the pressure built in his throat, though all he gained for his bluster was a rifle butt in the balls and a tightening of the spiky, nylon string binding his wrists.

The lone sound uttered by his captors was a whispered, "*Dễ*!" "That was easy."

They moved in absolute silence into the paddies, but a sound echoed out of the hamlet, and he was pushed down heavily, face first, into a small pond, where he flailed about to lift his head out of the putrid water. A few drops trickled through the bristly woven nylon into his mouth, and he tasted the bitterness of human fertilizer. His thrashing brought him a sandaled foot on his back, one that pushed his face deeper into the mire.

This was a maneuver he had suffered in Ranger School with the rest of his class, the final challenge. They had been captured, each cadet stuffed into a flooded barrel, heads held under water longer and longer with each refused demand for information. They had been drowned slowly, praying they would not die, and longer still until they prayed they would. But that was Ranger School, and while it was at the hands of what he had believed at the time to be a demented corps of cadres, they were soon released, lest the crazed instructors be brought before a courts-martial board for murdering fellow soldiers. It took a few minutes for J.W. to understand that his present subjugators were not bound by those rules.

J.W. held his breath as he searched his ebbing consciousness for the lessons of those painful days in commando training, for the purpose in having survived Ranger School, for the pearl of wisdom that would serve to salvage his life. But nothing came to him except a deepening gray haze and a resignation that his plight was hopeless.

Hours later, now oblivious to the constant shoves and the sound of his own feet sloshing across the Vietnamese countryside, J.W. lost all sense of the miles slogged through paddies and brush. Soon he could not remember if he had been on the march for a day or a month, or if he was really just back in Ranger School, hallucinating that he had travelled to Viet Nam. He was not surprised when flickers of dull light trickled through the web of his sandbag blindfold. He believed the glow to be God's gesture that he had lived to witness another dawn. That triumph, though, brought no relief, for he knew well that with the dawn there would be a few moments of revival then the anguish of alertness.

The light brightened, and the scent of piquant smoke seeped into the sandbag pouch that grated at his face. J.W. fantasized that he was at *Bà* Binh's, the old lady having risen with the dawn to stoke the fire and brew tea, but the dream ended as the tip of a knife sliced into the nylon over his cheek. A second later, a captor pushed something through the rent toward J.W.'s lips. Though J.W. pulled away violently, an enemy soldier steadied J.W.'s head with two hands; another jammed it back through. When J.W. recognized the scent of burning tobacco, he realized the enemy was offering a cigarette, and he inhaled greedily. What he did not realize was that the harshness of Vietnamese tobacco was many times that of the American species, and as the powerful vapor arrived in the deep recesses of his lungs, he lurched forward and broke into a barking cough. There was a round of contemptuous laughter, but after several seconds, the cigarette was poked back through the torn nylon. J.W. sucked less vigorously, holding most of the smoke in his mouth, drawing only modest wisps into his lungs. It was tolerable, even slightly satisfying, but in the end, dizzying.

Before he exhaled the last of it, though, he was pulled to his feet and constrained tightly by the arms of several men. Their thick body odor, while distinctly foreign, triggered a sense of calm in J.W.'s innards, until he felt a rope being wound about his neck. He thought immediately of a book he had hidden in his room as a child, *One Nation*, and of the pictures he had scrutinized night after night, particularly the melancholy image of a southern Negro during the 1920s, sitting atop a horse, noose around his neck, placidly waiting to be lynched.

But he also thought of Branch, his angry, brilliant, driven, PhD candidate Ranger buddy, the only black man he had ever really gotten to know. In J.W.'s mind, he became Branch and then the black man in the book about to be murdered. Soon, the images of the two African men coalesced, and J.W. cursed aloud that Branch would never have allowed an enemy to humiliate him so.

J.W.'s legs weakened, but he caught himself and gathered what courage was left, screaming in English and primitive Vietnamese that he had been a good guy, that he had befriended the villagers, protected and fed them, and had even had *Em* Huong released. The rent in the sandbag allowed J.W. to just make out the astonished expressions on the dark faces of his captors. With that chink in their armor, he swung his elbows out to fight back, cracking one of the men in the jaw with a wild swing. The enemy soldiers backed off for a moment but soon jumped forward to wrestle him to the ground. Though J.W. expected to be pummeled and executed, the men just tugged roughly at the rope around his neck, pulling him back to his feet.

They dragged him forward one step, then a second, and he saw through the hole that they were approaching a thicket of trees, the place where he would be murdered, like the black man in his book, his body left to rot in the jungle, never returned to his wife or his parents. He was to die for crimes he had never committed.

"I am a friend of Viet Nam," he shouted weakly, but that whimpered sentiment was stifled when the rope was tugged, and again, until he stopped talking.

He was soon stumbling forward, towed onto a new sector of his journey. His face dripped with sweat inside the nylon bag, and he whipped his neck from side to side to dislodge the droplets of water as if a soaked dog. The silence of the trek was broken only by the dull crumble of rotted forest detritus; even the crickets and toads were hushed as the band of soldiers and their prey passed through.

He could not understand why it was taking them so long to bring his life to an end, but the trek went on without respite or execution, and J.W. had time to consider the books he had read at Sterling College about the Holocaust, and how the concentration camp inmates, the ones who survived, had savored each breath, refusing to abandon hope. Now, he managed to eke out one celebrated gulp and another, just as he had paid out pushups in Ranger School, thousands and thousands of them over the months. He had learned to do them four at a time, a cadence that made them achievable.

Further along, the earth cooled, and the scent of human waste slowly disappeared. They had entered the true forest, crossing the tree line that J.W. believed had separated him from the war. His shoulders banged into the trunks of rubber trees on the path along which his captors had crept night after night for years, slipping into My Co for supplies and young recruits. Their bodies, so much leaner than J.W.'s, touched nothing.

Flashes of light eventually filtered into the sandbag, and J.W. readied himself for a cigarette, though the radiance intensified, a golden hue rather than orange. There was no smoke. As they marched deeper into the thickening overgrowth, the dawn song of wild birds built, and J.W. thought back to the animals of My Co the night before and how he had laughed at their disharmony. He wished he had taken heed of their veiled warnings.

Even more muted than the fauna was the drone of a distant helicopter, and though J.W. realized the ship was miles off, he was pushed to the ground and held with his face on the jungle floor as the beat of the aircraft approached. He did not recognize the deep pitch of the ship's rotor, one far more sonorous and weighty than a HUEY's, deeper even than a Chinook. He guessed it was a Russian ship, one he had never seen or heard of, one coming to take him to Hanoi to spend the rest of the war as a captive of the North. But the sound of the helicopter continued overhead without a pitch change, and J.W. knew there would be no approach, no landing.

As the booming rotor slap faded, the pressure on his neck relaxed, and he turned his head to the side. He saw through the slit in the bag an erector set in the sky, a Flying Crane, the Sikorski S-64, cruising eastward into the sunrise, away from the Cambodian border, and though miles from them, it was still immense. He thought of the crew, relaxing in the cool air of dawn, smoking, drinking coffee, unaware that one of their own was marching his last steps. J.W. wondered how many prisoners of war he had overflown in his months as a pilot.

When the comforting beat of the mammoth craft dissolved into the countryside, J.W. was pulled to his feet and marched until the heat of the day swelled, and his face poured streams of bitter perspiration. The procession stopped finally amidst the hushed speech of Vietnamese men and the clatter of tin pots and cans. J.W. was pushed to the soil again and tugged head first into a hole along which he was compelled to crawl, yanked from the front by the rope around his neck, legs rammed by a captor driving his boots.

He felt the path a grave, his shoulders cramped so tightly against the gritty walls, the flesh of his arms was being rasped off. The underground heat soon overwhelmed him, soaking his fatigues in an ocean of sweat, converting the clay lining of the tunnel into a lubricating mud. He slid a trace more easily after that, eventually slithering to a node in the warren where he tumbled into a pit. With his shoulders and back free, he sucked in an agitated breath, tasting the musty, stale air hanging motionlessly about him. Despite his near insensibility, he knew he was far below the surface, but became confused by the odor of cooking rice jumbled with the odor of urine, sweat, strong tobacco, and feces.

His hands were untied and a golf ball-sized wad of cold, sticky rice was slapped into his right palm. He shifted it to the left hand and pushed the mass through the slit in the bag to his mouth. A second helping was smacked into his right hand with authority, as if he were an amusement at the Saigon Zoo, but when he tried to shift the wad to his left hand, he was elbowed in the back of the head, and a grumbled warning was issued that he was to eat with his right hand or not eat at all. Derisive laughter filled the earthen prison, and J.W. conceded, though he jammed the lump through the hole angrily. While that brought monkey noises from his kidnappers, it also engendered a sense of renewal in J.W., for the act of shoving the rice through the bag had torn the brittle nylon a millimeter farther, allowing him his first visual image since that of the massive helicopter hours before. As his eyes focused, though, all he could make out was a pair of red-mud-caked boots and jungle fatigues shredded into long strips.

As calories from the rice seeped slowly into J.W.'s blood, his consciousness stirred, and he proclaimed the ability to peer through the slit in the bag his first victory. He forced himself not to raise his head, a ploy to preserve his secret, remembering the dictum in the ancient Chinese philosopher Sun Tzu's *Art of War:* in battle, deception is everything. He wondered if the Vietnamese hated the Chinese so much that they had banned that antique book and were therefore unaware of those tactics. But J.W. thought back to the village of My Co, and then further back to *Ông* Khai, and to the women of the orphanage in My Tho. He allowed that the Vietnamese were the most pragmatic souls in all of

Asia, and he thought sadly that his captors were bound to discover any scheme he might concoct.

J.W. was left untouched in the stale, dirt room, accompanied, he could feel, only by the speechless stirrings of a lone guard. From an adjacent passage he heard soldiers murmuring about recent B-52 bomber strikes. One man choked that after nearly a year-long trek down the Ho Chi Minh trail from Hanoi, his brother had been lost in an American bombing raid. The voice became suddenly louder, and J.W. realized the soldier had come to stand over him.

"Yes," the soldier hissed, "so this is an American? He doesn't seem so powerful now, does he? Look, he is a pilot. He wears wings. Maybe he's the one who shattered my brother."

J.W. heard the crack of metal against his head a millisecond before he felt the pain and perceived the flash of light. A second, lighter impact bashed his jaw, and he rolled onto the floor, wrapping his arms about his face, but there was a scuffle around him punctuated with bitter screaming. There were no further punches.

He heard the angry man being dragged off screaming, "*đụ mẹ, đụ mẹ, đụ mẹ*," "mother fucker, mother fucker, mother fucker!"

J.W. pointed to show his jailers that he had to relieve himself, and there followed agitation and finally the placement of a porcelain bowl in his hand. He used it, and waited for the basin to be taken away, but it remained where he had placed it gingerly on the clay floor. Hours later, it still had not been moved, and the odor choked him until he regurgitated half-digested kernels of barely-cooked rice.

Through the slit in the bag, he watched a kerosene lamp flicker weakly on a coarse wooden table. It illuminated an aboriginal, dust-choked typewriter and sheets of mildewed, wilted paper. He wished, suddenly, that he could type a letter home, to tell his wife and his parents that these were probably his last moments, and that he loved them, and it was his own fault that he would soon be dead. He felt no shame as he accepted responsibility for a massive blunder that would cost him his life. It was what it was, nothing could change it, and in the letter, he'd insist they not blame the Viet Cong, for in truth, he had been dealt with far better in the moments before his death than he had seen captured Viet Cong treated by the ARVN, the allies the Americans had come to die for.

Voices approached him, and he curled into a fetal ball, but there was no battering. A new intonation drew near. It was a northern accent, not unlike that of Mr. Khai. The southerners growled angrily, but the northern man raised his voice, and J.W. sensed a building argument between the two accents. Soon there was yelling and snapped orders. J.W. was pulled to his feet by the rope that had remained coiled around his neck. He was tugged along the tight passageway, uphill this time. He screamed in frustration as more skin was scaved from his arms. "Leave me the fuck alone!" He kicked his legs furiously, and as he had come to expect, was kicked in the head by a man moving up the tunnel in front of him, then jabbed in the balls with a rifle barrel by a soldier pushing him from below. Though he had accepted that he would soon be dead, he calmed, feeling no need to accelerate the process.

After the shoving and cursing, he felt cooler, fresher air, and seconds later heard crickets and the chirp of gecko lizards. He guessed he was in the open and that night had fallen. He was not sure, though, if it was the same night on which he had been captured, or if there had been a dawn and a Flying Crane in between. Perhaps two nights and days had come and gone.

He was again drawn by the neck until a cadence was fixed, and he walked for miles with only sporadic pressure on the rope, a trail horse needing only momentary guidance. Over the hours since his capture, he had tried to count his paces and track how far from My Co he had been extracted, but he could not keep his mind from dwelling on food, and by the first rays of the next sun, he believed he was back in New York City. Certainly, the reek of the urine his captors constantly stopped to produce, as if marking territory, was no worse, or better, than that of the streets of his Bronx neighborhood.

That morning saw no rest. The party of trekkers moved ceaselessly, and J.W. realized he was as far from his people as he had ever been. There were no distant helicopters from which to hide, no American patrols to engage. He thought back to his desire to be alone, away from the U.S. troops, and how his wish had been granted, in spades.

As the heat of the day built, the procession stopped, and J.W. was pushed into a hunker. He was handed a pair of cold rice balls which he consumed greedily with his right hand. He was given water from a canteen, and though it was lukewarm and contaminated with rubbery particles and barley-sized lumps of scratchy matter, he sucked the liquid greedily until the canteen was pried from his lips. A cigarette was offered, and J.W. pulled voraciously on the rotten tobacco, the chemicals in the effluent calming and disorienting him. The respite, though, simply deepened his thirst. When he asked for more water, he was struck in the back with the barrel of an AK-47, and he concluded it would be more comfortable to die of thirst than of a fractured spine. And anyway, he had learned in Ranger School that you can go two or three days without water, even in the desert.

While those had been amongst the most painful days of his life, when the cadres refused to let them drink for nearly forty-eight hours on the hot dunes at the Ranger Jungle Training camp in Florida, he had survived that training, and thirst would not be his undoing. As in Florida, he simply began to shut down his brain, and was soon in a stupor sufficiently deep to blunt his craving for water and even dull the pain in legs from the relentless march.

The scorching air grew thickly humid as the party stopped for a mid-afternoon siesta. J.W. was handed one more ball of rice but ate only half, slipping the balance into his shredded right fatigue pocket. Though the move had been accomplished surreptitiously, a hand jammed into that pocket to remove the contraband. J.W. was not sure what became of his prize, but it was not returned, and he fretted over the loss until the slight cooling of dusk, when the crickets and gecko lizards reemerged to serenade the falling blackness.

Even with the meager decrease in temperature, the sweat continued to pour off him in sheets. When his hands were suddenly again bound behind his back, he became irate, tormented that he was not able to wipe the perspiration from his face. His anger awoke in him a trace of the memory of having been captured in the Prisoner of War Challenge in basic training and then in Ranger School, and the lessons he had been taught about his duty to resist, even under the pressure of torture.

For a moment, he assured himself he would be strong this time, but he soon acknowledged he hadn't yet even considered the first mission of a real soldier when seized—attempt escape immediately, for that was the time, right after capture, in the confusion, that success was most likely. If that failed, J.W. remembered that to try constantly thereafter was the POW's next mission. He feared he was probably as weak as he had been years before in basic training, and even months before during Ranger School. But he also understood it was moot, for it was unlikely he would survive whether he cooperated with his enemy or not.

The buzz of his fatigue soon drowned the discord of the tropic's nocturnal creatures, and he proceeded, one foot after another, in a daze, tugged by the thick rope if he ventured the barest step off the path. In a way, those circumstances were not as alien to him as he first thought, and to some extent he felt a perverse comfort in the familiarity of the lack of freedom and control. As his profound thirst and hunger resurfaced, he wished he was back in Ranger School, where life was simply a bad dream all day, every day. He longed to be thrust into the gator and snake-infested swamps of Florida, where the only terror was the twenty or ten days left until the nightmare terminated, for his orders from the Pentagon said so. He and his compatriots had pissed and moaned around the clock in commando training, but had also laughed constantly at the insanity of being awarded fifty push-ups for wearing wrinkled fatigues after two weeks in the jungle swamps, or for trying to sneak a squashed Mars Bar onto patrol in the hem of tattered pants.

J.W. and his mates had looked forward to being sent to Viet Nam, for the combat returnees assured there was always food and water and *some* sleep; and when he got to Viet Nam he would be safe because he would never be imprudent.

J.W.'s feet now rubbed incessantly on the insides of the soaking wet jungle boots he had not removed for days, the wool socks balled up at the far end, crushing his toes. He asked to stop and take off his boots, and when there was no answer, he appealed again then slowed his pace, dropping into a squat to protest. He was not completely shocked when his entreaty was answered with the crack of gun metal in his back.

During breaks, his hands were untied, but his feet were bound, and he sat accepting occasional balls of cold rice, sometimes flavored with drops of the sharp *nước mắm* he had first tasted as a gift from *Ông* Long many months before. When his captors laughed softly and gently, he gambled that they were beginning to relax, that perhaps they trusted him, and he removed his boots and fixed his socks, wringing out a stream of rancid water. Through the torn mask he saw patches of skin that had worn off his bloated, whitened feet, which had not been free of water for what he supposed were days or perhaps weeks. Salving the throbbing of his feet for those few moments eased his world, though the hunger soon reasserted itself, and he sat in a circle of his mortal enemies, head drooped, the thought of escape less intrusive than the need for a ball of half-cooked rice.

He must have fallen to sleep, for there were no thoughts of food or water, just silence until a smack in the shoulder, the rebinding of his hands, the release of his feet, and a tug of the rope. Though the wool army socks again stockpiled in a soaked wad at his toes, what consciousness left in him was consumed with images of burned powdered eggs and watery mashed carrots.

For hours, no light entered the sandbags, and he banged into tree after tree. Abruptly, though, over a period of ten steps, the humidity of the jungle lifted and muted light trickled through the nylon. With it came a familiar reek, that of human manure, of rice paddies, and soon the scent of burning charcoal. He lifted his head to peer through the rent in the bag. The outline of grouped huts on the far side of a clay berm grew, and he was able to focus in the meager light on a crowd of old men and children gathered on the paddy-side of the berm, hands grasping their genitals. It was dawn.

He was comforted by the thought that perhaps this hamlet was like his own, and if he'd befriended so many in My Co, he would do it again. His imagination brought little old ladies sneaking him tea and bananas, and old men the occasional scrap of paddy rat. And how far could he be from My Co? If it had been three days or even four, all they could have covered was thirty miles, forty at best. He would manage the local dialect. But then he realized they had, no doubt, crossed into Cambodia, where the VC had full, unopposed freedom. He would be forced to march north along the Ho Chi Minh Trail to Hanoi. No one made the trip alive, Vietnamese or American.

The most slender ray of hope, though, stirred as the sun arched higher. The peasants gabbled in Vietnamese, the huts were not on stilts—they had not crossed the border. He believed he knew more about rural South East Asia than any soldier in the Mech, maybe any GI in country, and he conjured plans to persuade the new villagers to slip him scraps of paper and the stub of a pencil. He would secretly record what he'd grasped of the Asian countryside, and parlay that into a place at one of the great universities where he'd become the authority, one of the few Westerners who'd ever survived in the villages of Viet Nam. For a few minutes, he was excited about the notion of a future, and his head lifted. His legs moved with sufficient swiftness to avoid a single tug of the rope. As his party continued toward the gaggle of huts, J.W. looked up again through the rent to see the civilians scurrying from the berm as he and his captors approached.

The familiar scent of wood fires and brewing green tea comforted him as he was pushed into a dark hut. His hands were untied, though the bags were left over his head, and his feet rebound tightly. He heard the flimsy door lashed shut, and he believed he was finally alone. He waited several moments, listening and feeling for the presence of another being before working loose the painful cord about his ankles. Next, he untied the string that held the sandbags in place. Surrounded by utter silence, he took a chance and lifted the sweat-soaked, coarse nylon. It was the first time in days his eyes were unimpeded. He looked about the room, abruptly tasting dread as he focused on the image of a black, silhouetted body propped on a stool in the center of the room. He froze, though when he saw a flicker of movement, he pulled the bag down over his head violently, tying it even more tightly than had the VC.

J.W. sat motionlessly for minutes, waiting for the punch of a rifle butt, but only silence stabbed him. Timorously, he peered through the slit, scrutinizing the figure in the center of the room. He was positive he saw swaying motions, though the apparition did not turn, or even flinch, when J.W. coughed loudly. As his eyes accustomed to the scant light in the sealed hut, he studied the inert figure for many minutes. He grunted loudly and started to come to his feet. When there was no consequence to his taunting, he locked his eyes on the man's head, realizing finally that his sentry was nothing more than a bruised metal pot sitting atop a wooden stool. The rest of the hut was bare.

J.W. ripped the bag from his head again, ferociously rubbing his face, stripping away days of filthy, parched sweat and hardened drool. Hungrily, he sucked in gobs of the clammy, mildewed air. For several seconds, J.W. Weathersby's soul was quiet. He sat back down and leaned against the dried mud wall, took a deep breath, closed his eyes, and rested.

He might have even dozed, but the heat woke him, and he stood, moving a few steps toward the center of the hut, rubbing his eyes. The damaged pot was nearly full of a murky liquid which he drank avariciously before he began to consider the consequences of the exotic illnesses that would soon befall him, of the fevers unfamiliar to Western medicine, and for which there were no cures. But he did not care, for his thirst was in some measure slaked. Foreboding about an assault of alien organisms was useless—apprehension about anything was futile, and he relaxed, accepting that the organisms he had ingested would not have time to burgeon into a fatal infection before the host organism was dead.

After several minutes, the rank liquid J.W. had guzzled thinned his blood to the consistency of 90-weight gear lube, sufficiently runny to support a slow transit within his brain. With the slight clearing of his mind, he tip-toed to the door to investigate the slender rays of light that leaked through the myriad imperfections in the adobe. Beyond the walls, he made out a black-clad figure, a young man, drugged by the heat, eyes nearly closed, squatting several feet from the AK-47 assault rifle he had left leaning against the hut.

As more of the water was absorbed, J.W. remembered that there were numbers and equations lurking deep in his head that could be used to make things happen. He considered how much time he would have between exploding through the stick and straw door, grasping the weapon, and firing it into the sleepy guard. There was no doubt he could manage the feat, and he began to steel himself for the offensive, pushing infinitesimally on the flimsy door to test its might. A small child in a fit of pique could push through it effortlessly. He started adding seconds together: his explosion through the doorway, a fierce football pivot to the right to snatch the weapon, one-point-five seconds to charge it and flip off the safety, one second to aim and fire a round first into the man's chest, the largest target, then pivot again to run and hide. His calculation ended shy of six seconds. He was less than a tenth of a minute from freedom, but also from breaking the covenant, thou shall not kill. After all, the Viet Cong had not made the easy choice to destroy him with a single bullet. But, on the other hand, this was war, and God would understand.

As J.W. steeled himself for his escape, he remembered a cadre at Ranger School who had spoken of how a soldier, at least an American soldier, conducted himself in combat. It was after an ugly assault in the swamps of the jungle school in Florida. The now-seasoned Rangers had overrun the enemy position and were doggedly chasing the fleeing aggressors out into the slough. By that late point in their training, the Ranger cadets had become ruthless in their pursuit of escaping enemy soldiers, GIs, mostly returnees from Viet Nam, who had played the role of assailants, happily carrying out their mission to torment the cadets at every turn. For the Ranger cadets, an attack was an opportunity to get even, to dump the defeated aggressors into the putrid marshes and steal their C-rations. But as the end of their schooling approached, an officer-instructor had gathered the students in mid-attack to make a critical point.

"Rangers, when a man is down, you don't hit him, no matter what. While a battle is raging, you fight to the death. That is your mission, but when it is over, you must understand the distinction between combat and murder."

It was a tenet, the officer went on to explain, he had learned from studying the life of President Harry Truman, and when he met the man himself. It was at the officer's West Point graduation that he boldly approached the former president to ask if he had really taught his men that distinction during World War I. When the great Truman nodded that he had, indeed, ordered his men to stop laughing as they machine-gunned a German patrol caught in the open, the young officer promised Mr. Truman he, too, would teach that lesson to the men he'd someday command.

But, now, months later, J.W. questioned if this was combat, or if the battle was over, and if there was another way to escape and avoid a homicide, the close-range execution of a teenager, an act that would surely burden him for the rest of his life. He looked out through the crack again, seeking the route of egress he would take the moment the guard fell asleep or went to the berm to relieve himself. But as J.W. scrutinized the distant features of the countryside, all of his noble strategy evaporated into the blur of green and brown scorching in the savage sunlight. There was nowhere to run.

At the very corner of the focal field of the crevice in the dried mud wall, he saw movement, and the indistinct shape of another black-clad form. While he could not make out the face, he saw the figure was armed with a holstered, ancient pistol, likely vintage 1920s. Nonetheless, it was a sure sign the man was an officer, perhaps not a ranking official, but not a foot soldier, either. Obviously, there was an entire unit in the area, and J.W.'s escape strategy fizzled, its demise allowing him to become conscious of his hunger. He considered enlarging the hole in the wall to ask for a cold ball of rice, but the guard had come to attention with the arrival of the new man, and J.W. waited by the door, stark still, seeking to decipher their conversation. He understood only that they were not talking about him, and, with relief, he went to the far corner of the cell, placed the bag over his head, and slept.

He woke unknown minutes or hours later to a heat so profound, he began a crawl toward the tin door to demand it be cracked an inch. As if telepathically, the thin sheet of metal slid a few inches to the side, and through the torn nylon, he saw something being slid along the ground into the hut. An instant later, the tin was rammed closed, and he crept to the object, his innards clutching as he realized it was a bowl full of rice covered with a soggy, boiled leaf, a thin green vegetable he had never before seen or imagined. He dared not remove the hood, but crawled back to his corner and began thrusting fistfuls of grub through the tear. He used his right hand.

That much food instantly produced cramps, and he crept painfully to another corner of the hut and moved his bowels in a stream of explosive liquid. Then he crawled to the farthest corner from his toilet and sought sleep, though his eyes opened minutes later to the glaring light of the uncovered doorway. A figure approached him and removed the hood, handing J.W. another plate of food; the rice in this offering sprinkled with bits of what J.W. believed was pork soaked in *nước mắm.*

The soldier was young, handsome, and clean-shaven, rendering J.W. embarrassed by his own loathsome mien. The man asked in slow Vietnamese if J.W. wanted an American cigarette, and J.W.'s hands shot forward beseechingly for the Salem the man proffered. When the soldier took matches from his pocket, J.W. followed the man's hands, recognizing the holster he had seen through the rent in the adobe. It was empty.

With his cigarette burning, J.W. sucked the smoke as far into his lungs as he could, possessively holding the fumes deep within him, treasuring the medicinal effect of the nicotine. As he exhaled, though, a sense of dishonor humbled him as he acknowledged he had given in to his enemy. The battle was already over.

The man told J.W. to relax and sit near the door in the fresh air. With J.W. settled on the ground happily breathing in the delicious, burning Vietnamese afternoon, the Viet Cong officer handed J.W. a second cigarette, but didn't light it.

He asked in the most basic Vietnamese, very slowly and deliberately, "Lieutenant, how long have you been in Viet Nam?"

"Six months. Do you have any more water, please?"

"Certainly. In just a moment. But you speak Vietnamese very well. Where did you learn?"

"In the village of My Co."

"That can't be. You went to the school in America. The DLI language school. Didn't you?"

"No. I learned in My Co, I told you," J.W. answered with a bit of irritation, pleased with himself for baring a spark of soldierly behavior. He flicked the second cigarette onto the pounded earthen floor and looked away.

"Oh, I think you are too good." The man smiled insincerely. "The DLI; what does that mean?"

"I don't know, ah, Defense Language Institute, I think. It's a school to learn to speak Vietnamese, but I was never assigned there."

The man suddenly spoke in English, "That where American train intelligence agent. Yes, Lieutenant?"

J.W. was surprised, but only for a moment, and smiled to himself as he replied in Vietnamese, "Please speak your language more slowly. I don't understand what you are saying. And where is the water you promised?"

The interrogator's eyes tightened in irritation. "I speaking English, and you get water in good time."

J.W. narrowed his eyes to parry the next question. "Tell me," the man continued, calming himself, "You are three-three Mech, and commander Bia-lie. Is true?"

"Sir, I do not understand you. Please speak Vietnamese."

The officer lashed out, "You three-three Mech, no?"

J.W. smiled. "You already know that." He pointed to the patch on his shoulder and snapped, "So why are you asking me?"

"So, you are. It is clear. Good." He called to the guard, who brought a dented U.S. Army canteen into the hut. The interrogator poured a few tablespoons of murky water into the canteen cup and handed it to J.W., who sucked it down hungrily then handed the cup back, his eyes begging for more.

The man smiled again. "You see how easy?"

He poured a tablespoon into the cup and started to hand it back to J.W., but stopped in mid-stride and asked sternly, "Why you live in village My Co? What you do in village?"

"I wanted to build a schoolhouse for the children."

"And what you teach?"

"I don't know. Whatever children are supposed to learn. I'm not on the board of education," J.W. sneered.

The dark eyes of the interrogation officer bore into J.W.'s. Weathersby realized at that moment, if he was obliged to answer questions about drivel for tablespoons of filthy water, when the real interrogation began, he would crumble. First there would be probing questions about the Mech's officers and their weaknesses, both personal and professional, the names of their wives and children, where their families were staying during the year their husbands were gone, and the questions would soon drift toward the tactics in which the officers of the 33rd Mech had been trained, and about the perimeter guards at the local U.S. bases. How many troops were in each bunker, what type of weapons did they have in those bunkers, how many machine guns, how many rounds of ammunition, were there empty bunkers on the perimeters, maybe every third one with a flashlight in it to fool the enemy, and what time did the troops change shifts? How long after they came on duty did they wait to light up joints? What kind of weed were they smoking, and how many were also shooting heroin, and was there alcohol in the bunkers, and were the officers doing the drugs as well?

When all of those questions had been asked, and J.W. played games, the torture would be far more agonizing. He realized it would likely be days before he tasted the rancid water again, if ever.

The intelligence agent spat in English, "When you tell what you teach Viet Nam children, I give water." He paused for a moment then slammed his fist into J.W.'s thigh, growling, "You tell me or die now."

The interrogation he had feared began in earnest, just that quickly, and Weathersby took his fist and punched his own thigh harder than had the Viet Cong officer, and the enemy soldier recoiled at the sound of the whack, no doubt staggered by the violence and lunacy of which his prisoner was capable. J.W. socked himself again, more enraged at his coming weakness than at the VC agent.

J.W.'s fury built as he reminded himself that he had again ignored the very foundation of a POW's survival by having failed to escape hours before. Instead of humanitarianism, he could have burst out of the hut and squeezed off three lethal shots from the AK-47 before the poorly trained, heat-drugged Viet Cong foot soldier at the door knew what had hit him. He could have hidden behind the next hut with twenty-some rounds left to take out each of the VC who ran in confusion toward the firing. With any discipline, he could have disabled an entire light platoon, escape, and been sent home a true hero.

But he had given up his chance and, worse, was about to compound his shame, to provide his enemy with vital tactical information in trade for a sip of fetid water.

As the Vietnamese man took a breath to ask another question, J.W.'s left middle finger shot up, and the interrogator smiled in confusion. "What is that, Lieutenant?"

"That's the finger."

"What is that?"

"It means, 'Hello! I like you a lot.' We use it in America every day. One time in America, an old lady on the highway gave me the finger because I gave her the finger for driving too slow. So, I flipped her off again. We did that for a long time. Just like I'm going to do now."

"Old lady drive car in America?" the interrogator grinned mistrustingly.

J.W. rose without consent and walked to the corner of the hut. He urinated against the wall and went back to his sleeping corner, faced away from the man, and stared into the dried mud. The officer called the guard, who crouched behind J.W. and roughly replaced the hood, cinching it with a snap.

Before he left, the agent stood in the doorway and spoke softly. "We are not done talking, Lieutenant." He emptied the canteen on the ground in a wide circle to ensure not a drop remained.

At dusk, J.W. removed the hood and watched as a new guard came to sit in front of the hut. There was no food or water. Soon he could hear the peasants in the surrounding huts snoring, and he crawled to the corner of the hootch to urinate again, but this time he noticed, in the spare shafts of moon glow, that the patch of wall against which he taken a leak during the afternoon had become soft and crumbled away. He pushed his hand through the moistened mud easily, discovering the adobe to be quite thin and fragile, but as he excitedly pulled additional pieces from the wall, he heard the ropes on the front door being loosened. J.W. threw the hood over his head, dropped his pants, and squatted with his butt toward the door, forcing a tiny drip of malodorous stool onto the pounded earthen floor just as the door opened. The guard grunted disgustedly when he saw the crouched, half-nude figure in the corner.

As the man turned to leave, he began coughing and gagging. He did not hear J.W. moving silently toward him. He didn't see the American lift his forearm, plotting to wrap it about his enemy's neck and strangle him in the deadly choke hold he had learned in Ranger School. But the man was through the door so quickly, J.W. was left in the middle of the floor, frozen, drawers around his ankles, arms suspended in front of him—a statue in a Fellini movie.

He yanked up his pants and sprang back to the wall, pushing his way through in seconds. He crawled into the deliciously steamy night and walked quietly at first, stealthily weaving between water buffalo pens and huts, avoiding the fronts of the tiny structures, desperate not to be discovered by the communist villagers and handed back to his captors.

At a gap in a cluster of huts, he came to a thicket of bamboo where he pushed his way inside, cowered, and let his heart settle. He searched carefully for human forms, and when he saw nothing other than straw walls and thatched roofs, he crawled out of the grove and slithered along the ground, his eyes fixed on a distant, forested patch of land. In the subdued moonlight, he estimated the woods to be a half-mile, the same distance as the jungle that surrounded My Co. If he sprinted across the paddies, it would take perhaps five minutes; his fleeing silhouette would surely be seen, an easy target for an AK-47.

He crept on, coming to a wide path with hootches on both sides. If he took to the semi-road, he could move quickly, but at the same time he would be exposed, and he argued with himself about the alternatives—stealth or speed. His debate endured for less than five seconds. He burst to his feet, galloping faster than he had ever moved in his life, gaining speed, not slowing as he tired, screaming at himself to push harder, to drive on or die.

After half-a-mile, he looked to his flanks and discovered he was passing huts and paddies, many of which had an eerily similar architecture to those in My Co. It gave him succor that he really had become familiar with the Vietnamese countryside, and he believed for those moments that, coupled with his bare knowledge of the language, he might actually survive until sunrise.

With that strength, J.W. continued running along the edge of the road, but soon closed in to straddle the huts and banana trees, seeking to mute his outline as he tired. When he ran past a hut with a battered, red Coca-Cola ice chest sitting glumly by an open front door, he considered waiting in the shadows for a moment and then raiding it for a bottle of something wet. He thought that he had in a sense come full circle, his last vision before being blindfolded that of an indifferent ice chest many villages away.

He contemplated burrowing into a nearby stand of thick bamboo and waiting for morning before setting out again when the VC would melt back into the jungle. At the edge of the village, though, he heard voices, and he left the dirt road to run along the crisscrossing paddy dikes into the tree line, accepting that he would have to move at night until he crossed back into friendly territory.

Rarely stopping to rest, he paralleled the road, pushing himself faster each time his legs cramped, faster each time he couldn't take another stride.

Hours passed, J.W. guessed, but he refused to stop running, crazed by the notion that his captors were on his heels, closing on him. He even kicked across several streams without coming to a full stop, just scooping splashes of water into his mouth as he sloshed through. It was only at the periphery of the provincial town of Moc Hoa, where the Americans kept a battalion-sized infantry unit in reserve, that he allowed his legs to fall into an exhausted stumble.

Chapter 8

In Moc Hoa, he tramped back streets, past hunkered men sucking on pipes oozing dark clouds of sweet, hay-scented effluent. They barely looked up, but even their cursory glances gave rise to jolts of anxiety, for though street creatures, he could see that they were the secret agents of the assassins closing on him. J.W. moved on toward the American base, rehearsing repeatedly a dialogue to account for his absence, but mostly he anticipated being fed well and lionized for his escape. The rest of his war would be spent on the beaches of Vung Tao, a sheltered hero. He would be awarded the Medal of Honor and his children granted automatic appointments to West Point or the Naval Academy. His heart raced, no longer in solicitude, but in excitement over the coming meals and future aggrandizement, in that order.

At the gate of the American infantry unit, J.W. called out loudly, waking the sleeping guard, "Hey, troop, open the gate. This is an emergency."

The soldier growled, "What'd you get hit by, a fuckin' mine or somethin'?" The guard peered more intently as J.W. rattled the barbed wire angrily, but snapped to attention, calling out, "Begging your pardon, sir. I didn't see your rank, sir."

J.W. ignored the apology and demanded the soldier call the officer of the day, a captain, who came to the command shack dripping with sweat, eyes puffy with sleep. Weathersby followed the officer to a guard shack and collapsed onto an OD folding chair.

He barked breathlessly, "Captain, I just escaped from the VC in My Co, miles up the road. I don't know if they followed me, but I ran all the way down here."

The officer squinted and pulled his face away, dodging the odor. "You in this unit, Lieutenant?"

"No, sir."

"Then, how'd you get here? You out with the whores? You look like you got rolled!"

"No, sir. I was captured by the VC, Charley. I just told you. And I want some water—NOW!"

"Don't get snotty with me, Lieutenant, and you sure as hell aren't ordering me to do a damn thing. Just stow it and come along. I need to get to the bottom of this. We've had no alert that an officer'd been captured. Nah, something's not right here."

J.W. was led into the back room and directed to take a seat in a metal chair. The captain yelled at a specialist fourth class to come in and get all the information on paper, "His name, unit, all that stuff. And he's not allowed to leave this room, and neither are you. We got that straight, Specialist?" The man nodded, and the captain added, "Something just ain't right here."

The captain walked from the building muttering to himself. J.W. slumped forward, trying to gather the strength to shoot out of the chair and try the choke hold on the captain. But he could hardly lift his head.

He mumbled to the GI, "Hey, troop, I need some water, and I'm starving. Is there anything to drink around here?"

"Yeah, there is sir, but you heard the man, I can't leave."

"Specialist, let me ask you something," J.W. began, starting softly, but rhythmically increasing his volume and fury. "When it turns out I'm telling the truth, and I was a POW, and I escaped, and I hadn't had a sip of water or anything to eat in I don't know how fuckin' long, and you wouldn't give me any goddamn food, how's that gonna look? How you gonna feel when it turns out I'm telling the truth?"

The soldier thought for a minute. He stood and whispered, "You wait here, sir. Please don't leave the room, sir."

J.W. sat back comfortably, stretching, demanding from himself patience, priming his mind for the gallon of tainted GI water and congealed C-ration Ham and Limas. The SP-4, however, returned in less than a minute without the water or chow.

J.W. jumped up and bellowed, "I told you, I'm fuckin' dying of thirst."

The soldier stood somewhat upright, as close to attention as J.W. had witnessed in Viet Nam. He stammered obsequiously, "Sir, my CO said Colonel Bierlein wants to see you ASAP at headquarters in Saigon. He told me to come back in here and tell you. I'm sorry, sir."

J.W. fumed, "Should I walk over there tonight, or tomorrow morning, troop? Look, I'm thirsty and I'm hungry and I'm tired, and I'm not in the mood for shit from you or your CO. Now get your goddamn captain in here and get me some water and food."

The specialist spun backwards, lurching through the door, but in seconds tottered backwards into the room. The captain sputtered in J.W's face, "Lieutenant, I'm placing you under house arrest for being AWOL. Sit down. Your CO will see you when we free up a vehicle to get you down there. So get your ass on that chair and keep it warm, and that's an order. You don't tell us what you want, we tell you. And don't you screw around with my troops. I trust you understand that."

J.W. nodded and asked, "Hey, sir, you got an extra empty sandbag laying around?" The captain squinted angrily.

As J.W. pondered his options, he tried to count off the number of times he had been placed under arrest since coming to Viet Nam. He thought back to his pre-war life, remembering the day of his brush with the law, a parking ticket the afternoon he had first soloed in an airplane. He'd been so excited, he parked in front of the fraternity house, had two beers with his mates, and fell asleep in an armchair, failing to move his car off the street before sunset. The transgression had cost him a dollar, though he took succor in the fact that he had yet to lose a cent on any of his contemporary legal difficulties.

Though the SP-4 brought J.W. a canteen of lukewarm water, it was not until dawn that a tray showed up from the mess hall half-filled with gobs of runny scrambled eggs, on top of which sat a curled slice of unbuttered white bread. He queried the soldier as to the whereabouts of the powdered carrots, but the man grunted, "Sorry, man, no vegetables. Mess sergeant's saving 'em for our own unit."

At noon, a military police sedan arrived at headquarters shack to whisk J.W. to Colonel Bierlein's headquarters in Saigon. But first, they had a stop to make at LBJ, Long Binh Jail, to deliver two privates between whom J.W. was squashed in the back of the Chevrolet. The men, in hand and leg irons, laughed that they were being transferred alongside a fugitive officer, and spent the trip bitching about the army, bragging openly they had tossed a fragmentation grenade into their platoon leader's tent.

J.W. finally barked at them, "At ease, gentlemen. Just shut up and enjoy the air-conditioning."

One of the prisoners snarled, "Big fuckin' deal, man, LBJ's air-conditioned, too. You'll see."

⟜⟝

At the 33rd Mech Headquarters quonset outside Saigon, J.W. reported to the colonel's office, but the CO was on the phone with grave registrations, listening to a report of the death of one of his platoon leaders, a Lieutenant Alexeeff. Bierlein waved J.W. into the office and motioned him to sit. When he put the phone on its cradle, the old man shook his head sadly. "I hate losing men. Did you know Lieutenant Alexeeff? He came about the same time you did."

"Yes, sir. We came to Normandy on the same chopper back in July."

Colonel Bierlein mumbled, "I only have a few more days here, but I've lost one-hundred-and-six men. One-hundred-and-six men on my watch. That's a lotta gold star mothers. Bothers the hell out of me." The CO sat quietly for a moment then looked straight into J.W.'s eyes. "Okay, where have you been the last few days? Engineer battalion truck convoy went through My Co and said you weren't there. You're not shacking up are you, Lieutenant?"

"No, sir. I was captured, sir, and I escaped, sir," J.W. cracked, sitting at attention.

"Captured by whom, that little old lady in the village?"

"No sir. A unit of VC."

"How do you know they weren't NVA?"

"They spoke with southern accents, sir."

"What'd they say? 'Y'all's captured?"

J.W. did not answer, but his face tightened in anger. The colonel stared into J.W.'s eyes. "You're telling me the truth, aren't you, son?"

"Yes, sir, I am."

"Okay. Lieutenant Weathersby, don't say another word. I want the intelligence officer, the S-2, in here."

J.W. sat alone, nearly comatose, for twenty-minutes until Colonel Bierlein returned to the office followed by a figure that triggered in Weathersby a tiny loss of his bowels. J.W. hoisted himself to attention and delivered a neophyte cub-scout's two-finger salute.

"Lieutenant Weathersby, I'm sure you remember Major Trott. He's recently become my Regimental S-2. All intelligence goes through him. Please tell him your story."

J.W. opened his mouth to begin, but the major intervened coldly. "Take a seat, Lieutenant, and tell us what you were doing in the vill."

"I was living there, sir."

"I know that. What were you doing at the time of your capture?"

"Trying to buy a Coke, sir."

"I see. So they have a local soda fountain?" Trott laughed cynically and turned to Bierlein. The old man's face remained hard as stone.

"No, sir, it's not a damn soda fountain. It's the village restaurant. You can't get much there, but I go there at night and talk..."

"Jesus Christ, answer my goddamn question, Lieutenant." The major stood and took a few steps to calm himself. He went on. "How many beers had you consumed at the time of your so-called apprehension?"

"None, sir. Like I said, I was trying to buy a Coke. I don't drink."

"That's not what I remember from base camp."

"Sir, is this some kind of cross examination? You sound like a lawyer."

"Look, Lieutenant, I'm just gathering the intelligence I need to do my job." He turned to the colonel and appealed with his eyes and his hands. "Sir?"

Bierlein mumbled, "Lighten up Major, and Weathersby, you need to answer his questions."

"Let's try it again. How many beers had you consumed?"

"None! Goddamnit, I told you. I was trying to buy a Coke." J.W.'s eyes reddened, and he hissed, "Look, I'm not answering diddly squat until I get something to drink and eat."

"Weathersby!" Colonel Bierlein exclaimed irritably, but stopped and took a deep breath before asking calmly, "When was the last time you ate, son?"

"Four days ago, sir."

Bierlein continued, "Didn't those bastards feed you?"

"No, sir, they didn't feed me. Well, yes, sir. I got a few balls of cold rice, and that's more than I got from our side."

"Major, excuse us for a second." Trott bristled out of the quonset. J.W. caught Bierlein barely shaking his head and rolling his eyes. He continued. "Lieutenant, I know you're tired and pissed off, but so's Trott. He was out all night interrogating villagers." Bierlein pulled out his wallet. "Here's ten bucks. Have my driver take you to the PX. Buy yourself some soap and a toothbrush then go to the BOQ and take a shower." Bierlein went to the door and yelled, "Top!" The Regimental Sergeant Major popped into the tent, facing J.W. as the colonel went on. "Lieutenant Weathersby hasn't eaten in four days..."

"Or showered either, apparently, sir."

"Thank you, Sergeant Major. Forget the PX. Have the mess sergeant make him a steak quick like. He's earned it."

J.W. tried to hand the ten dollars back to Colonel Bierlein, but the old man shook his head. "Keep it. Go to the PX and get yourself some goodies and stuff after dinner."

Only Major Trott and J.W. were present for the evening session. The S-2 began in a far more pleasant tone than when the morning interrogation had been tabled.

"So, Lieutenant, I hope you're feeling more like cooperating now that we've got your creature comforts taken care of. Let's go back over where we've been. You say you didn't consume any alcohol. Is that your official statement?"

"Yes, sir."

"Well, tell us what happened."

"I got bit by a goddamn dog and went to the village restaurant to get a Coke, and..."

"We know that, and what?"

"And I walked into the restaurant, and *Ông* Long was there, and so were four VC, but I didn't know they were VC, obviously."

"Obviously. So who is this *Ông* Long?"

"He's just a peasant. I don't know. I think he might own the restaurant. He's always hanging around there. He's a harmless old bastard."

"Yeah, just like your meek old ladies in the orphanage in My Tho. We're going to need to arrest him. We'll have Private Dinh do the interrogation, or we can turn him over to the ARVN. Depends on how well he cooperates."

"Sir, are you telling me Dinh works for us now?"

"That's affirm."

"Sir, he's an awful excuse for a human being. And Mr. Long didn't do anything. He's a good man. He just lives there..."

"And domiciles the VC."

"No, sir, you don't understand."

"Lieutenant, you and I have been over this ground before. I'm going to be honest with you. I don't have a hell of a lot of respect for your sense of just why our troops are dying here. I intend to arrest your *Ông* Long and tie him to the front of a fuckin' M-113 and drive his skinny ass through the jungle around My Co, and around again, until he points out his base camp. If he's feeding the VC in his so-called restaurant, he's VC until proven otherwise."

"Sir, he doesn't know about base camps. Why don't you interrogate *Ông* Khai, the new village chief? He's in this up to his neck."

"We did. He's clean as a whistle. He was appointed by President Thieu. Thieu says he's one of the finest men in Viet Nam. Only thing I can find wrong with him is that he thinks you're such hot shit. He was impressed that you had the balls to stay in the village after he warned you to leave. And how you managed to get that kid released—I don't know. Now he wants you back, like a counterpart. He even told President Thieu about you. I will never understand these people."

Bierlein walked into the tent. "Glad to see my troops working together for the common good. Weathersby, I can't believe it, but the G-1 knows about you already. That's division level. They're saying you're a hero, the first GI to escape capture in years. They want you to go back and meet the president, but I gotta figure out somewhere to put you until the pols set up the ceremony at the White House. Can you believe that?

"But we're stuck, as usual. If you leave Viet Nam without combat command experience, your career's in the toilet." Trott burped a snicker which Bierlein ignored and added, "They need a platoon leader in 2nd Battalion, over in E Company. You interested?"

"Is that like fighting, sir?"

"That's what a lot of our combat leaders do."

"Not after six months in country they don't, sir. Options, sir?"

"I'm not going to argue with you. Being a platoon leader sucks. Especially if you've already put in half your tour and have had your butt captured. The alternative is that Mr. Khai wants you back in the village. Not a prime assignment either, but even President Thieu thought it was a nice touch. Then again, if you go back, I want you to keep it in your pants. Stay away from the local ladies. Apparently, your Mr. Khai heard that you had the hots for one of the girls there. President Thieu thought it was funny. I don't."

"Other options, sir?" J.W. asked again.

"Get on with it, Lieutenant."

"May I have some time to think about it, sir?"

"No, Lieutenant."

An image of *Cô* Lin raced through his mind. "I'll take the village, sir."

"Okay, Major, what do you want to do before we send him out there?"

"I want to tie him to the front of an M-113 along with his Mr. Long and catch some VC. That's what I want to do, sir."

Ông Long's wrists and ankles were lashed with telephone wire then attached to the forward section of an armored personnel carrier. J.W. sat on one side of the man, Translator Dinh, newly promoted to buck sergeant, on the other. Before leaving the confines of My Co, the track driver hit the gas hard, accelerating the vehicle with such a leap, *Ông* Long's turban popped off and landed on the road.

The track commander ordered the driver to stop, but Sergeant Dinh snapped, "You no worry. He no need hat where he going."

Nonetheless, the track commander, also a buck sergeant, had the driver come to a complete halt then jumped off the vehicle and retrieved the sweat-stained, muddy turban. He flicked off several chunks of red clay and placed it gently, though somewhat askew, on Long's head, whispering, "Sorry 'bout that, sir."

Ông Long remained stoic, confining his feelings and comments to himself for the jarring two hours of busting brush in the hardwood forest that surrounded My Co. As they poked into areas that had only recently been deserted by the VC, the track on the M-113 dipped suddenly and became stuck. The driver rocked the armored personnel carrier back and forth until it pulled free. The track commander jumped down to check for damage and fell straightaway into a torn-open section of enemy tunnel. He sent his gunner, a tiny man, into the hole. He came out with several pairs of Ho Chi Minh sandals, old rubber tires cut into the footwear that served the entire enemy army. On a second foray, he handed up a VC canteen, an American web belt, and a moldy, black, silk hammock fashioned from an old French parachute. "Check this out, sir. Charlie's still using shit from when they were fightin' the French. I read about this."

"Yeah, well very interesting." The commander ordered his tunnel rat man back into the vehicle. "That's enough, Stillwell. Don't want you any deeper. Who needs it?" He smiled and looked through the booty then turned to J.W. "You like any of this, sir?"

"Nah, it's your track, your men, your stuff."

"How 'bout the hammock, sir? So you can get some rest in the hamlet."

J.W. was about to accept when Sergeant Dinh interrupted. "What 'bout this fuck?" He turned to Mr. Long, pointing at the prisoner's crotch, making a slicing motions with a pocket knife.

Ông Long, though, turban still a few degrees catty wompus, just stared silently into the jungle for the most part, very occasionally uttering in Vietnamese, "I'm not VC. My son is in the South Vietnamese Army."

The track commander waved his hand at the driver, and they set off again. After an hour, Sergeant Dinh spat on Long and turned to J.W. "This pig he warn VC. They gone."

"And so are we," J.W. finally snapped, turning to the track commander to jab an index finger toward the village.

The track commander tapped the driver on the head with a stick and yelled over the engine noise, "Go back," and J.W. untied *Ông* Long. As the vehicle pivoted sharply through the forest, Long pretended to fall off, but instead of coming back aboard, he bolted like a frightened animal and disappeared, loping into the jungle, his muddy turban a perfect target. The gunner on the M-113 raised the barrel of his .50 caliber machine gun toward Long and charged the weapon noisily. The private took a deep breath, preparing to fire, waiting for a nod from his track commander.

The TC, however, moving up the chain of command, searched Lieutenant Weathersby's eyes, saw the terror, and turned to the gunner, pushing the barrel of the cannon down sharply and shaking his head.

"No," he yelled over the engine noise, "he's unarmed. I told you a hundred times, you don't blow away an unarmed man. That's not why we're here. Leave him the fuck alone."

J.W. looked at the sergeant. "Where did you learn that?"

"Church, I guess. I don't know—just plain sense, sir."

J.W. got off in the village, and after conferring with Long's wife, assuring her that the old man was fine when last seen, walked back toward the night defensive position to report to Major Trott. But the S-2 had already received word from the track commander about the fruitless afternoon and was in his helicopter hovering for takeoff. The major didn't look down as the ship skimmed over J.W., making for Saigon and one of the largest U.S. officers' clubs in the world.

The troop of armored personnel carriers that had busted jungle behind Mr. Long's track that afternoon now circled the NDP protectively, facing out, a herd of musk oxen protecting their young. Here, though, the sheltered were the ranking officers in their command tracks at the center of the ring. J.W. considered his alternatives. He could spend the night at *Bà* Binh's and risk the stray .50 caliber machine gun rounds that were sure to fly when the troops became spooked by a rustling pig or chicken, or he could pass the night in the headquarters track with the brass, though the commanders' vehicles, each prickling with a forest of antennas, were perpetual enticements for mortar and rocket attacks. Or, he could choose door number three and drift away from the bull's-eye toward the relatively anonymous track on which he had ridden during the afternoon's search. Anywhere else on Earth, that would have been the least rational choice, clearly the most reckless, and so he took it.

"Sergeant, you got room for a tired and hungry lieutenant?"

The track commander nodded. "What's your pleasure, sir? We are C-ration rich."

"How's the Ham and Lima's today?" J.W. smiled, conceding how far down the inventory of life's pleasures he'd tumbled. He leaned back and listened to a tinny transistor radio hanging from the barrel of the .50. It was tuned to Armed Forces Network—*Sittin' On the Dock of the Bay* had the crew staring into space.

The track commander scooped a tablespoon of C-4 plastique explosive out of the back of a Claymore mine, pressed the blob against the side of the C-ration can, popped a few holes in the lid, and lit the white jelly. It flared with a flame so bright, J.W. thought of the fire that had burned in the village the night he had been captured, the one he had watched in such contentment, leaning against a tree, belly full, calmly smoking his last Salem.

J.W. did not remember when it had dawned on him, perhaps sometime during his sojourn with the VC, that the fire had been a billboard, a primitive, efficient communiqué beckoning enemy soldiers, a primordial all clear signal. The glare of the present fire made him uneasy, but his hunger persevered.

As the Ham and Limas heated, the track commander shook the tin of thickened stew, to warm the contents evenly, then lifted the can, flicking off the rest of the glowing C-4 with his index finger. He opened the lid fully, handed it to J.W., and laughed, "It ain't dinin' on the dock of the bay, but at least we ain't movin'."

He ducked into the track to turn up the volume on the PRC-46 radio-transmitter. He hollered up at the gunner to turn the music down as he deciphered the scratchy voice of his platoon leader.

The track commander emerged, shouting to his crew, "Off your asses, gents. It's on to the metropolis of Moc Hoa." He turned to J.W. and asked politely, "Hey, sir, you comin' along? You can ride with us."

"Nah, I got an ulcer from all that bouncing around this afternoon. I'll be okay here. Thanks." J.W. picked up his duffel bag and the can of Ham and Limas. As he took a step toward the village, he turned back and spoke to the track commander. "You're a good man, Sergeant. You spared an innocent creature's life this afternoon. You didn't have to."

The track commander smiled down. "And you, sir. Gives me hope. Oh, and hey, sir, I almost forgot." He tossed down the hammock. "You take care, sir. Hope I get to work with you again." The sergeant waved a diminutive salute, a gesture of respect J.W. would never forget, but one in the field that could have cost both of them their lives had an enemy sniper been on the other side of the berm.

As the 113s clattered south out of the NDP onto Highway 29, a shower of red mud hurled from the tracks. The armored personnel carriers plowed through deep puddles, grinding past the barbed wire gate of the tiny army base. J.W. watched for a moment then walked through a hole in the western wire toward *Bà* Binh's, wondering if *Cô* Lin would be there. He shuffled along, lost in the pleasant fantasy, believing he had won the firefight against Major Trott. Maybe the little man would look elsewhere for his communist under every rock.

The very moment he passed the hut at which *Ông* Xuan's dog had attacked its final victim, a blast rocked him J.W. so furiously, he found himself on the wet earth, crawling frantically for the mud-filled culvert at the side of the road. He lay there, deafened by the mad firing of M-16s and .50s, and then the screams of a half-dozen of the barely muffled 215 horsepower diesel engines that powered the M-113s.

J.W. peered over the edge of the culvert and saw a barrage of orange flashes followed by puffs of white smoke popping from the rifles and machine guns of the platoon that had come to rest just outside the east gate of the NDP. As he crawled closer, a cloud of greasy, black smoke billowed from the silhouette of a mangled armored personnel carrier. The firing stopped abruptly, and J.W. ran to join the outline of troops pushing through the heat and flames toward the burning track. The front end had been vaporized. Below it sat a vast crater so deep, the crimson mud had given way to a layer of dry, brown earth.

The few men sufficiently crazed to withstand the intense heat pulled a broken, limp, smoldering human form from the twisted commander's hatch. A lone private pushed his way toward the corpse, stared for a few seconds, then barreled out of the circle, leveling his M-16 to fire on full automatic, spraying hootches on both sides of the road. The platoon leader tackled the man, wresting the weapon away and screaming at his men to remount their tracks and form a defensive circle. The private, however, sprang to his feet and pulled the rifle away from the lieutenant. Screaming and sobbing, he fired magazine upon magazine into the hamlet.

J.W. ran to the nearby huts, past wounded animals, bracing himself for the inevitable moaning of the women. He instantly imagined the circle of mourners which would part, revealing their latest sacrifice. But he found only villagers cowering in shallow, subterranean bunkers under hardwood beds, the mahogany planks obscured in shards of exploded pottery and tea cups.

Slowly, as the surviving animals in the pens calmed, the human inhabitants crawled to the surface. J.W. tried to explain to the villagers what had transpired, but *Ông* Long appeared out of nowhere and took him tightly by the arm to a water buffalo pen two huts away. The old man pointed to a gigantic beast which lay on its side, bleeding from tiny bullet wounds in its flank. The creature was wracked by intense tremors as it drowned in the mud. J.W. approached to lift its head, but *Ông* Long pulled him back, whispering, "It's already dead. Let it be. That was all I had, and…"

J.W. raised his hand to end the conversation. "Okay, it's just a water buffalo, *Ông* Long. We'll pay for it. In the morning, we will meet, but now I must go around and see if any of the villagers are hurt." He handed the old man a Salem and walked off along the road, calling out to the elderly who stood at their doors, "Is anyone injured in your house?"

One by one they shook their heads no, so he reversed course and went back to the American unit, glancing out of the corner of his eye at the charred face of the fallen GI, careful not to stare, turning away quickly, lest the GIs take their passion out on the stranger gaping at one of their dead. The briefest glimpse of the corpse's face in the moonlight was enough. J.W. whined, "Fuck me, fuck me, I hate this fuckin' place."

A private covered the body with a poncho, and several of the troops placed it aboard an unscathed track. Some of the platoon set up their perimeter; others stripped the blown vehicle of its radios, guns, and personal effects then tossed in thermite grenades and waited until the charred hull melted in upon itself. The platoon leader directed the remainder of his vehicles to leave Highway 29 and travel through vegetable patches and rice paddies. They rumbled turbulently, parallel to the main road, until J.W.'s image of the tracks disappeared east toward Moc Hoa.

Bà Binh was alone, swinging in her hammock, as J.W. stood in the doorway waiting to be invited in. "Where you been?" she crowed. "Like I said before, you got no time for an old lady?"

"*Bà* Binh, I got captured. Do you know what just happened down by *Ông* Long's house?"

"You mean that your tank hit a mine? Of course, I know." She struggled to lift herself out of the hammock, and J.W. watched her limp toward the smoldering fire in the corner. He used the excuse to search the tiny room for *Cô* Lin.

Bà Binh stared at him for a moment. "Are you feeling well? You haven't been here for a long time. *Cô* Lin said you weren't coming back."

"No? It's only been a few days, and here I am. How is *Cô* Lin?"

"Isn't she pretty? You ought to marry her."

"Very pretty. But I have a wife already."

"Is she Vietnamese? How many children do you have?"

"You know she isn't Vietnamese. But she has long black hair like *Cô* Lin. You know we don't have any children."

"Why not?"

"Too young. And I'm here in Viet Nam, and she's in America."

"Too young? You mean too old. Look at you. You should be a grandfather by now. You're losing time. You could have a wife in America and one here."

J.W. smiled at *Bà* Binh, wishing not to protest too adamantly, but the sick feeling of betraying Krista gnawed at him, and he was relieved nothing had yet happened. *Bà* Binh stared at him, knowingly he feared, as he asked, "By the way, where *is Cô* Lin?"

"I don't know."

"I thought she lives here."

"Sometimes," *Bà* Binh answered, her eyes downcast as she shambled to a corner to prepare a chew of betel nut. The sylph-like creature picked a carefully-chosen brown chip of betel nut from a porcelain saucer, selected a green leaf from a basket, spread it with a thin layer of dazzling, pink, lime paste, placed the betel nut in the center, rolled it all into a ball, and wedged the golf ball-sized lump past her tiny lips.

When the wad was generating smears of pink-black drool from the corners of her mouth, the old lady nodded to the hardwood bed, and J.W. complied, stretching out on the worn planks. He left his .45 in its holster, though it was charged, a round always in the chamber. He let his head fall back, promising himself he would rest but for just for a moment.

He did not really sleep. He rarely had in the months he had survived under the Asian sky. With each grumble of the pigs and water buffalo, J.W. found himself sitting up, hand grasping his weapon, staring through *Bà* Binh's open doorway into the enigmatic night. When the dogs joined the motif with seizures of agitated, shrill barking, J.W. lifted himself off the bed and stole tremulously to the door, hesitating a half-step beyond the sill to peer out into the moonlit hamlet. Looking south a hundred meters, he thought he detected movement in the shadows of the empty NDP, and soon imagined he'd spied four black-clad, armed figures walking north toward *Bà* Binh's end of the village He thought of sprinting out into the paddies, but to where?

So he went back inside and kneeled on the far side of the planks, between the wall and what was left of the bed's mud stanchions. He took his newly issued .45 out of its holster, checked to be sure it was still charged—it wasn't—so he pulled the dust-choked slide back as silently as he could, drove a round into the chamber, and pressed the weapon against his belly under his fatigue jacket. With his meager arsenal aimed at the doorway, he squatted even lower and waited stock-still for half-an-hour. When his knees ached so badly he could no longer hunker, he stretched out prone on the dried mud floor, slithering backward into a corner.

After half-an-hour, the VC had not made their move, so he placed his .45 on the ground to let his arm rest. But as his eyes closed eyes for a second, the dogs of west My Co embarked upon an awesome yapping spell, one so obstreperous, J.W.'s eyes snapped open to witness treacherous shadows passing between the huts near the road. He made a firm decision: if the flicker of a single silhouette crossed in front of *Bà* Binh's, he would aim, fire his pistol, commit homicide without the slightest trepidation, and then run east to Moc Hoa. He would sit at a desk in Saigon or sweep up the general's quarters, boil away time until he was sent back to the world to meet the president. He swore he would never again set eyes on a Vietnamese village, never, as long as he lived.

While he waited, he chastised himself for the insanity of having made an identical mistake twice, by having returned to the village and expecting a different outcome. Why had he again left My Tho and the womb of Normandy Base Camp? And why was he resting his head against the wooden planks and letting his eyes close?

Light in the hut woke him. His eyes opened slowly, imagining at first it was from a flashlight, though he knew no one within thirty miles of the village had ever owned so much as a battery. As his mind cleared, he saw the dawn sun filtering through gaps in the thatch. He was on the floor, on his back, the .45 on the ground next to his hand. A face looked down at him, an attractive vision with a gentle smile and an expression that palliated his dread. Actually, the face was laughing.

"Good morning, *Cô* Lin."

"Lieutenant, why are you on the floor? Is that how you sleep in America? It is much more comfortable on the bed. Really."

Bà Binh shook her head in agreement as she wobbled to the shelf for her early morning slug of betel nut. She stared at J.W., stupefied by the proclivities of her foreign guest. "Does your wife chew betel nut, Lieutenant?" the old lady rasped.

"No, ma'am. We unfortunately don't have that in America. Lot of good things we don't have there." For a moment, J.W.'s chest clenched with the mention of his wife, but it was done, and he looked directly at *Cô* Lin. "Do you chew betel nut, Miss?"

She shook her head and wrinkled her nose. "No. It's awful stuff."

J.W. was captured by the rush of *Bà* Binh's laughter and added, "I knew that already. That's why you have such beautiful teeth."

Bà Binh pretended not to notice *Cô* Lin's self-conscious smile. The ancient woman went to the other corner to rekindle the smoldering fire, but *Cô* Lin rushed over and gently pushed the wisp of a soul away, stirring yesterday's ashes until small orange flames rose, competing with the first rays of the sun. *Bà* Binh placed the teapot over the fire, and soon the three sat silently drinking fresh tea. J.W. glanced at *Cô* Lin for a second longer than he should have, and she slid to the edge of the bench, not looking up at him or at *Bà* Binh.

Bà Binh filled the awkward silence, challenging J.W. with her usual taunt, "Where you been? No time for an old lady? Where you been? Where you been? Where you been? You need a beautiful wife right here in My Co. Buy a few water buffalo and settle down. It isn't unheard of to have two wives, you know."

Cô Lin looked up, subtly shaking her head to hush *Bà* Binh. When the old lady said it again, Lin whispered, "Grandma, please!" Then she caught J.W. staring into her eyes, and the disarming young woman bolted from the hootch. *Bà* Binh went on cackling between sips of tea.

Despite the dawn's serenity, J.W. sensed an uneasiness for which he could not account, and forced himself to cull from memories of the past days the source of his apprehension. It struck him harshly and suddenly that his discomfort grew out of a terrible explosion, though he could not settle in his thoughts if it had been real or just in his troubled dreams. When the image of a burned face formed in his mind's eye, a phantom so real, he sprang wordlessly from the bench at *Bà* Binh's table to tear south along My Co's muddy road, sprinting through the abandoned NDP, each step deepening the image of the charred features of a soul close to him. He stopped running at the scarred, melted mass of jagged aluminum blocking the road.

Outside the village restaurant, children were playing with the spent M-16 shells left by the maddened GI. As he watched the kids throw the shells at each other screaming, "Bang-bang," a motor scooter pulling a dwarf, wheeled cart putted to *Ông* Long's hut. Long dispatched *Em* Huong to gather a squad of villagers, all of whom joined silently to pull the slain water buffalo out of the mud and roll the remains aboard the wagon. The driver presented *Ông* Long with a few piaster notes then struggled to get his scooter moving. J.W. could smell the clutch burning as the vehicle pushed past him at full throttle, making barely three miles per hour.

J.W. went to *Ông* Long. "Sir, we will pay for your water buffalo. I am sorry our soldiers did that, but they were angry that their friend was killed."

"Lieutenant, our son is in the South Vietnamese Army. I have told you that before." *Ông* Long spoke distantly, without expression until he grabbed J.W.'s arm and pulled him into his hut and pointed to a cracked photo of a young man on the shelf near his balsa-wood altar. "Maybe that is why the Viet Cong put a mine in front of my house. I don't know. I just don't know."

J.W. wanted to ask Long why he had run from the track the day before, but the crowd was closing in, and J.W. simply reiterated his promise to pay the man for his loss. The assembly, catching the turn of conversation, broke into klatches to deliberate the value of the dead beast.

One man laughed without humor, warning J.W., his lips twisting sternly, "That animal was worth thirty thousand dong." Because J.W. was silent for a moment, as if in consideration of the demand, the man added, "At least!"

J.W. calculated in his head that he was being dunned for more than three hundred U.S. dollars, many months' pay for ten farmers. Raising his index finger, J.W. admonished, "We will pay what is fair. Maybe eight thousand, but we're not going to be greedy, are we?"

The crowd of kibitzers slowly melded into a single amoebic body of work-and-hunger-assailed peasants, the corpus vibrating with greater and still greater intensity as it washed in heady levels of finance never before bandied about in the chronicle of My Co. J.W. saw the light about him growing dimmer, and he thought for a moment a rare early morning monsoon was building, but it was the masses pushing inward, the tone having shifted from sarcastic remarks to strident demands for a share of the reparations.

He tried to slide out of the throng, but the path of escape behind him closed as well, two dozen old men and women pushing inward, wagging fingers, chattering about lost roofs and dead chickens, and several pleading for the lieutenant to remember the night they'd lost a child to the American patrols.

J.W., increasingly less able to move, began to gather strength, preparing to burst out of this latest prison, a fullback through a line of defenders. Just as he dropped into a semi-squat, bringing his forearms to his waist, priming to explode, a channel opened, and J.W. caught the outline of a tall man in a black field jacket and black jungle hat reaching forward to grasp his arm. The male voice lashed out in English, "You come!"

In the agitation of the milling villagers, J.W. did not recognize the face behind the mirror-finished, Western sunglasses, and imagined he was about to be imprisoned again, this time by a sophisticated, Russian-trained intelligence officer. His eyes searched wildly for a route of egress, but the enraged villagers, Viet Cong, every one of them, J.W. was finally convinced, closed the gap behind the man.

The man's hand jerked him toward the light, and J.W. wondered how long it would be before the rough sandbag was dragged over his head. Instead, the enemy mob parted, allowing J.W. to be drawn toward the road. J.W. peered up into his captor's face. It was *Ông* Khai. The new village chief quickly kick-started his Vespa and pointed to the rear seat.

The two men fishtailed along the water-soaked clay paths toward *Bà* Binh's, J.W. perceiving his hands vibrating at a frequency greater than the shuddering of the decrepit motor bike. It was not until *Bà* Binh served tea that his tremor peaked, and he spilled the tepid fluid into his lap. He laughed to himself that even in that heat, he would have to sit there for some time before his pants dried.

J.W. waited for an apology, a word from *Ông* Khai, a denial that he had had anything to do with J.W.'s capture, a grunt to explain why the sphinxlike Vietnamese man had left the village and not returned for so long, even after telling the very president of Viet Nam he wanted to work with the American lieutenant. With the uncomfortable silence, J.W. threw a pack of Salems on the table and snickered, "I only got a-hundred-and-seventy-eight days left in this hole. I'm over the hump. I can't believe it."

The village chief looked at J.W. questioningly at first then with saddened eyes. *Ông* Khai stood, walked the two short paces to the doorway, and gazed out, finally speaking in English, "I count day until new marketplace and new school build here. There still time for Lieuten help Viet Nam build new village." He turned to J.W. and asked rhetorically, "When Bien Hoa bus come every day, what passenger not stop drink tea in clean, new market we build?"

He beamed at the vision of prosperity in My Co, and it dawned on J.W. that *Ông* Khai wasn't counting days left in Viet Nam, for there was no such thing. He would stay for as long as he could keep himself alive, engaged in a constant, minute-to-minute battle for existence.

Chapter 9

Ông Khai sat down again, his expression hardening, his hands fidgeting with his glass, studiously avoiding even a passing glance at the tea-soaked crotch of J.W.'s fatigues. He looked straight into J.W.'s eyes and mumbled, "I must tell you, Lieuten, mother, five children, wife come live My Co." He pulled a Salem from the pack, accepted J.W.'s light, and puffed absentmindedly. "What children not learn in school, I teach."

"Where do they live now? I didn't know you had a family."

"Live Tuyen Binh. You will see my children. You understand Viet Nam. You know why I bring here. This is future of Viet Nam."

Weathersby was, for an instant, flattered that *Ông* Khai believed J.W. was sufficiently familiar with Vietnamese culture to understand that the presence of his family would lend Khai more credibility than fifty speeches. J.W. reminded himself, however, that this was Viet Nam, and *Ông* Khai was, at the heart of the matter, just a cog in the wheel, likely the least pretentious ripple in the river of extortion that surged toward Saigon. J.W. was surprised that Khai would be willing to sacrifice his own flesh and blood for the pittance of a salary he was promised by the South Vietnamese government, but seldom paid. How could he, one man, withstand the pressure from his superiors to come up with the expected bag of stolen money every two weeks? President Thieu had rooms full of actuaries calculating to the gold earring just how much booty could be squeezed out of a hamlet in Tien Giang Province. It was the way of life in every country within a thousand-mile radius of My Co—authority was a free pass to line one's pockets at the expense of the exhausted poor.

Though J.W.'s father had told him the malady of government corruption was just as virulent at home, right down to the county health inspector and the cop on the corner, J.W. had been schooled to believe government skullduggery was endemic only in the social and political cesspools to which his government sent their sons to die. He had no idea what to believe.

J.W. finally looked up and blurted, "Really? So, when's the family arriving, 1984?"

"Ah, that Mr. Orwell. No, Lieuten." His voice hardened. "For long as Khai alive, Viet Nam never animal farm. That why fight for democracy, no more dictator." He paused to calm himself. "Family here when find proper house. Lieuten and Khai finish tea, go hamlet see if house for living in? You maybe show My Co. I hear Lieuten very know village." The chief picked up his glass roughly, spilling a swig of tea into his own lap. He laughed, "Now look what I do. We wait."

Late in the afternoon, the two men walked slowly along the back paths of My Co, coming upon a tropical world of tiny mud and straw huts and spidery streams. At the edge of the hamlet, a few old, brick buildings, ghosts of the French presence that had tormented My Co for the past century, lay in ruins. Cobalt blue snakes and red-eyed spiders sunned themselves on shards of collapsed roof tile. Under a wide banyan tree, the two men came upon the elderly egg roll salesman, whose eyes opened wide as he recognized J.W. His hand shot forward, palm up, when he saw J.W. go for his wallet, but when only two damp, ten cent paper notes were offered, the man shook his head. *Ông* Khai pushed J.W.'s hand away and paid for the treats himself. The old man drew two *chả giò* pastries from a wicker basket tied by threads to the beaten Schwinn's rusted handlebars. The egg rolls were still warm.

They settled under the banyan tree, and J.W. looked at the bike, laughing gently to himself as he read the English words, "World Roadster", on the little metal tab soldered haphazardly to the frame. He asked the merchant about the cycle, where he got it and for how much. The old man told him it was his father's, and J.W. realized that the man's dad had probably been born in the vicinity of the American Civil War, like *Bà* Binh's husband. He laughed that the bike was probably as old.

The chief waited for J.W. before starting his own *chả giò*. With shreds of shrimp and pork falling into their laps, the troika watched two ebony-horned buffalo snorting and simmering contentedly in a nearby pudding of mud and manure. The chief, the merchant, and the lieutenant, three gentle companions, sat quietly. Shoulder to shoulder, sweating under the same sun, each had a vision, and each struggled desperately not be consumed by the heat and by the war.

The egg roll man studied the clouds. "There is little time left before the rains," he muttered as he loaded his wares. "Are you sure, Lieutenant, there isn't anyone in Moc Hoa I can deliver a message to for you?" he added without expression.

J.W. shook his head gently and said, "Sir, I think, for once, everything is okay."

The little man nodded and pedaled off slowly, weaving to avoid yesterday's puddles.

Beyond a thicket of verdant bamboo, a couple of hundred yards from *Bà* Binh's, stood a handsome, solid, one-room structure. Despite the years since it had been abandoned, the thick, wooden walls remained, and only a few one-foot holes gaped in the red, colonial tile roof. They allowed in a full measure of the gray, humid darkness of the coming monsoon. The banana trees and coconut palms that surrounded the shelter glistened, even in the muted light, with tiny specks of Agent Orange. *Ông* Khai brushed the toxin matter-of-factly from the dying broad leaves, the crystals settling on both men.

Inside, a few battered chairs and splintered wicker remained from the days Phương, the previous village chief, had lived there with his family. The old man had been shot by one side or the other in the early 1960's, and his wife died of something abdominal the following year, the peasants said, but they would shrug and add, "Who really knows?"

Phương's three children moved in with neighbors, though when the oldest was twelve, she stole away in the middle of the night with her siblings, sneaking off on the back of a slicky-boy's scooter, four of them bumping along Highway 29 to the refugee-choked slums of Saigon. Two villagers sold a bit of gold to raise money for a journey to the capital city, an expedition that consumed more miles and days than anyone living in the hamlet had ever before traveled. They combed the slums for the children, finding the ragged little girl on the third day of searching. When they saw her, hair tangled like a raven's nest, clothing in shreds, they tugged at the child, threatening to tie her up and bring her back to My Co whether she liked it or not. She resisted obstinately, swearing she would never leave without her little brothers. When the two villagers told her to fetch the boys, she quieted and nodded in promise then ran off to disappear down a filthy alley. Though the villagers waited in Saigon for two more days, the woman forced to sell her meager wedding ring for food, the little girl never reappeared. No one from My Co ever saw them again.

⟜ ⟝

By local custom, because the home *Ông* Khai was looking at had never been sold or deeded to anyone else, the estate became the property of the village, or in truth, the village council, whose members would sell it to the highest bidder and donate the profits back to themselves in a private, unrecorded exercise. The problem was that there was no proof that Old Phương's children might not come back one day and claim the property, or worse, that an entrepreneurial French landlord might reappear in Saigon, and if the Americans won the war, have bogus papers drawn up and claim ownership. With the war over, he would dispatch a platoon of Chinese henchmen-enforcers to My Co and demand back rent from the present occupants.

Had some fool actually bought the property from the village council, he would have been forced to petition the committee for his money back, or pay the years of uncollected taxes Old Phương's ghost had accrued—all the way back to the days of the French occupation. An appeal for justice would be adjudicated through the village council, which would bear as much fruit as petitioning the lifeless, Agent Orange-poisoned trees that were spreading across the hamlet. All monies purloined by the council instantly vaporized, the men of the ruling body invariably spending the funds on what they sagely claimed was hamlet business. And so, a perfectly good house had stood vacant for years.

Two or three days later, however, the District Governor flew into My Co. His American helicopter, piloted by American officers, and secured by American door gunners, put down in the barren NDP. A brand new American H-Model HUEY arrived behind the governor's ship to offload eight Vietnamese Rangers in burgundy berets. The governor, a fleshy, pock-marked Vietnamese colonel, swaggered into the center of the hamlet, barking orders at the children to go out into the fields and gather the citizens. "Quickly!" the Governor snapped his pudgy fingers. He marched into a random hut unannounced, ordered his men to surround the tiny structure in a defensive ring, then sent a kid off to summon J.W. He lit a Salem and called for tea.

When the villagers dribbled back from the paddies, he had them hunker opposite him in a half-circle facing the sun, formally introducing *Ông* Khai as the new and indisputable principal of their hamlet, adding that he was awarding Village Chief Khai the Phương' old family house. There was a bit of grumbling, until he hissed that the structure, in fact, belonged to the government of Viet Nam, as the province administration had studied the matter carefully and declared it abandoned property.

"It follows," he went on superciliously, as if completing a mathematic proof in graduate school, "that there will be no payment to the village council for the property."

The grumbling, though, hushed as the governor's armed subordinates walked menacingly amongst the squinting, sweating citizens, glowering at anyone whose lips curled down even a millimeter. With the matter settled, the governor bowed slightly to J.W., accepted the pack of Salems Weathersby proffered, and boarded his private chopper back to the sanctuary of Moc Hoa.

Two days later, a couple of ox carts labored into My Co hauling *Ông* Khai's worldly possessions. An hour later, two motor scooters and a cyclo arrived carrying the family, eight of them.

J.W. saw less and less of *Bà* Binh as he began to share the cool evenings with *Ông* Khai, drawn by the tales of ancient Vietnamese heroes Khai recounted to his children. The five brothers and sisters sat enraptured on their teak beds as he recited the saga of *Ông* Thach Sanh, a woodsman of forgotten times, whose moral purity saved a suffering princess, and thus the ancient kingdom that eventually became Viet Nam.

As the nights passed, more and more of the neighbors sent their children to *Ông* Khai's house for the stories and, also, for the bowl of cold rice Khai handed each youngster. He made a production of sprinkling the grain with a few drops of *nước mắm* and a pinch of sesame seeds he kept in a tiny paper sack deep within the inner pockets of his black field jacket. On the nights he read to the gathering, the children refused to leave before he told their favorite story, the one about a little boy in the Mekong Delta whose father let him herd the family buffalo to high pasture during the springtime floods. Their eyes grew as large as those of the oxen when *Ông* Khai yowled that the boy was nearly swept away as he crossed a rushing stream behind the buffalo. The children begged Khai to tell it over and over, but eventually he sent them home when the nightly explosions crept closer to My Co's berm.

At the end of most evenings, *Ông* Khai's wife limped into the house to chant the children a bedtime verse from the most famous of all Vietnamese chronicles, *The Tale of Kieu*. As *Bà* Khai rose from her stool beside the sleeping children, her black silk pants outlined a withered left leg, and each time J.W. detected the stick-like limb, he looked away quickly, though a sense of lingering uneasiness gnawed at him. He sat quietly, remembering his little sister wheeled away to a polio ward in New York. It was 1948, and his gentle father cried that day, and harder when the doctors told him his daughter would never walk again.

J W., though only three at the time, was convinced he remembered his father's tears, and had always been terribly depressed by polio's lingering stain—shriveled arms and legs, the distinctive limp. J.W. wondered if *Bà* Khai's father had cried the day he learned his daughter had been cursed.

As the nights wore on, J.W.'s Vietnamese improved to the point that he was able to tell his audience about the western world, of rushing to the office, of becoming stuck in elevators, and about shoveling snow. While the men listened politely, Khai seemed more interested in how J.W. had come to be in Viet Nam. J.W.

explained that he had been an ROTC graduate, an officer in the United States Army by dint of having completed four years of military training as a student in the Reserve Officer's Training Corps. The chief asked if that meant he had been to college. When J.W. nodded yes, Khai asked, "That Sorbonne, maybe Cambridge, Oxford?"

"How do you know about those schools? They're so far away."

For a moment Khai was still, reflecting on times long past. Finally, he took a sip of cool tea and answered. "You see, Lieutenant, my father was doctor. He go medical school China, Shang Hai. But when Japan come, he escape France, finish train. *He* teach me English, French, but very bad now."

J.W. took a deep breath and spoke quietly. "No, sir, your English is excellent. Amazing, in fact. And it is getting better by the day. You should be very proud. Did you ever live in France?"

Khai laughed. "Never leave Viet Nam. You first man I talk in English. But study every night a little."

J.W.'s shook his head. "You really are amazing, my friend."

Khai waved his hand to deflect the compliment. He quickly asked about J.W.'s early years, probing, querying J.W. about his education in the United States. J.W. described his academic career as an undergraduate, though the chief and the others allowed that they hadn't heard of Sterling College. Nor had they an inkling about college linebackers, or even American football, or drunken fraternity parties that had cost J.W. the hope of ever being permitted onto the grounds of Oxford, Cambridge, or the Sorbonne.

Ông Khai's eyes clouded almost imperceptibly in the light of the dying fire as he thought aloud, "Sorbonne my father university. He also go Britain with friends for Christmas and summer. Very different than Viet Nam, and he love his country more than any man, but he also very miss England, maybe more than miss France. Many evening we sit. He teach me English, teach me England democracy."

J.W. asked, "What did he miss? It's an awful place, I hear—cold and wet. And I hear the people are also very cold and wet."

"No, Lieuten, British very good to father. They treat father with respect, dignity you might say. He invite to people house talk politic, government. No one scared police come take away. Free to speak mind. King esteemed, but no man in England, not king himself come you house no have warrant take away arrest for speak peacefully. That he miss and talk until he die."

Some nights, after the stories, *Cô* Lin came to listen to the very old men speak of My Co from the Twenties, through the war years, into the Fifties and the partition of Viet Nam into the North and South. She sat unobtrusively on the outskirts of the gathering, as far from J.W. as she could and still hear. She was so intent upon the banter, it was almost as though she was taking mental notes for a book. The men recounted being forced to join the Japanese-led, anti-French youth clubs during World War Two. No matter the opening subject, though, the conversation always drifted back to the debts they still owed the French landlords from the colonial days, and how the Gallic property-owners had paid the Saigon Army and Chinese mercenaries to drive out to My Co and execute *Ông* Lam, and *Ông* Chung, and *Ông* Quang, all in front of their wives and children because they couldn't pay their rent. They spoke of their own brothers and sisters, who had gone out each year in greater and greater numbers to join the Viet Minh back in the 50s, the predecessor of the Viet Cong, to avenge those killings. *Ông* Long grunted that, once again, most of the hamlet's teenagers were dead, their Viet Cong units decimated to the point that the few still alive were out in the hinterlands, reduced to serving as guides and laborers for North Vietnamese main force units.

"Except my son." Long piped up. He's in the South Vietnamese Army. I wish he wasn't."

J.W. asked, "How did that happen?"

Long shook his head, "He was the best student, so we sent him to Saigon to apply to go to high school there, but the South Vietnamese Army drove by in a truck and picked him up off the street. They held a gun to his head and ordered him to get in the back of the vehicle where a lot of teens sat on the floor under the barrel of an M-16 that the Americans had given the South Vietnamese guards. Next thing we heard, he was in basic training. He told us that if he went AWOL, the army would come here and make me take his place, so he did what they told him to. He is a good son."

Late each evening, a lone 707, the Freedom Bird, passed overhead, and J.W. thought about the men aboard. He often became angry that dozens of armchair commandos, REMFS, "rear echelon mother fuckers," who had sunned themselves on the beaches of Vung Tau for a year, were aboard. But he also thought about the 11Bs, the infantrymen, eighteen and nineteen-year-olds who had plied the noxious jungles and paddies for that same year. Some nights he envied every man aboard that plane. On others, J.W. gloated that so many had missed touching the enchanting fabric of Vietnamese life. But as he drifted off to sleep, his last thoughts were always fuzzy images of taking the first steps to board that plane.

⟶ ⟵

One steaming early December evening, J.W. waited impatiently until the stories and kibitzing came to an end. He gathered his nerve to ask *Cô* Lin, "Miss, are you going back to *Bà* Binh's?"

"Yes," she spoke very softly.

"May I walk with you?"

Her face reddened and she turned slightly toward the old men whom she knew were watching. She shook her head very subtly no then turned and walked off toward her grandmother's. J.W. concentrated on her lithe form in the black silk pajamas until she left the road to enter a cluster of huts not directly on a line joining *Ông* Khai's and *Bà* Binh's. He guessed she knew a path along which the dogs and water buffalo were a bit less brutal. He waited a few moments, excused himself with a silent nod, and left to walk behind *Ông* Khai's house as if he were heading toward *Bà* Binh's. But he cut back through the thickets of bamboo that ringed the village separating the rice paddies from the tiny shanties. Eventually, he stumbled into a clutch of hootches in a section of My Co he had not visited.

He looked back and saw Khai's house, certain he was near the point *Cô* Lin had left the road. He stopped and listened intently for a human whisper, for a sign that she was there, but the dogs had captured his scent and howled angrily until several old men woke and peered out of their huts. One, a man so prehistoric he could not straighten his arthritic neck to look up, came out wielding a heavy wooden club. He swung it wildly as he neared J.W, who pulled his head away from the undulating truncheon, though not far enough to avoid the thick reek of *rượu đế*. The man stunk so, J.W. imagined he must have downed a liter of the rot gut rice spirits.

J.W. retreated into the bamboo and waited motionlessly. When the dogs quieted and the old man limped back into his shack, Weathersby turned toward the paddies, looking for a concealed path out of that section of town. Even *Cô* Lin wasn't worth having his brains beaten out.

Instead of empty rice fields stretching to the wood line, his attention was drawn to silhouettes crossing the paddies toward him. He crouched deeper in the stand of bamboo, splintering twigs and reawakening the dogs, sending them into an even more furious wail. Soon the pigs and the chickens and the water buffalo joined, the cacophony dropping the black shapes prone onto the paddy beds.

When the dissonance of the barnyard creatures lulled, the sinister shapes lifted off the earth and moved closer, entering the hamlet just feet from J.W.'s thicket. He counted six figures, four of whom brandished AK-47 assault rifles with bayonets affixed, daggers they poked menacingly into the darkness with each deliberate, barefoot step, a fire team stabbing at the night as if they had been trained to expect the enemy to emerge from another dimension just millimeters in front of their eyes. An exceedingly tall man in a dark jacket walked at the center of the column. He was armed only with a 9 millimeter handgun holstered on a frayed French pistol belt.

J.W. recognized the man's gait. He pursed his lips to spit, and whispered to himself, "I fuckin' knew it!" But he forced himself to consider the logistics, and realized he had just left *Ông* Khai's home. There was no possible way Khai could have sprinted across a half-mile of muddy rice paddy, joined an enemy patrol, and then surreptitiously tip-toed back the same half-mile into My Co, all within six minutes. Perhaps the familiar bearing was simply that of those few men of Viet Nam who had grown over six feet in stature. When the towering soldier passed J.W.'s thicket, Weathersby saw the gaunt, ill face of a creature who had survived, but just barely, below ground for many years.

There was also a petite, unarmed woman in black silk pajamas walking silently near the tail of the column. J.W. ground his teeth "Mutha fucker!" So *Cô* Lin had detoured into the paddies to lead the Viet Cong to the hamlet. When the woman, though, was close enough to distinguish her features, they were nowhere as sculpted as *Cô* Lin's.

His face dropped into the sand to allow his neck to rest, but his generous nose struck a brittle twig, which cracked noisily. Realizing his cover had been compromised, and that it would only be seconds before the Viet Cong patrol fired madly into the bamboo grove, J.W. shot his hand to his holster to snatch the .45. He decided to shoot as many of the bastards as he could, milking the seven-round magazine, making every bullet matter. He would spring out of the thicket and run for his life back down to Moc Hoa, where he would be arrested, again, returned to Colonel Bierlein, again, undergo interrogation by Major Trott, again, and finally be offered command of a tank platoon or an opportunity to return to My Co, again. But he would use his head and not his heart, and refuse to ever again set foot in that Stygian corner of the Earth.

Just as the .45 slipped out of its holster, the dogs and pigs and chickens and cows and water buffalo and geese and ducks and goats and a lone cat began screaming in such passion, his faux pas passed into the darkness, undetected.

The trailing rifleman sniggered derisively, "A dog's fart," a sentiment that brought laughter to the other soldiers, except for the pistol-armed man in the center, who hissed for quiet.

Sucking gulps of fetid air, J.W.'s eyes followed the column as the soldiers took up positions, weapons at the ready. They surrounded a hut less than ten feet from him. The man with the pistol entered the mud-walled shelter, the woman followed closely, obediently. As the livestock calmed once again, J.W. heard the whispers of a woman's voice, then a man's, and the woman's again, but he gasped when he could not be sure the female voices came from the same person.

A moment later, he was sure it was two. A sour taste of fear and disgust coated his mouth as he became aware that his wish to be very close to *Cô* Lin had come true.

J.W. listened as the male voice asked in a Northern Vietnamese accent, "The American running dog, he is in My Co now?" There was a pause, and the man's voice rose slightly, asking again, "Is he here?"

Cô Lin answered, "I have not seen him for some time."

"This village chief appointed by the pigs in Saigon. Is *he* here?"

"He lives here."

"Do the farmers listen to him?"

"They have to. He is always making speeches. Our comrades listen, but they ignore him. Yes, they ignore him. What are we going to do to him?"

"I will make my report and wait for the decision of *my* comrades. Do the farmers listen to the American pig soldier?"

"He doesn't say anything except, 'Don't worry, the American government will pay for it.'"

"What do our people say?"

"How much?"

"Where does the money go when he pays them?"

"He hasn't paid anyone yet."

"If he does, that money must be used to buy rice to feed my regiment. You must convince the farmers that the money is rightfully under the control of the revolutionary government."

Cô Lin lowered her voice and commented politely, "Comrade, if the farmers believe that money is going to the feed North Vietnamese soldiers, they are going to disappear it, and you will never see a single piaster of…"

The man's voice cut sharply into *Cô* Lin's lecture. "Stop speaking and listen to me closely, Comrade Lin. If you and your compatriots do not understand the role of your Northern brothers in the Vietnamese people's great struggle against the imperialist running dogs, perhaps a political meeting of the villagers is in order. We will demonstrate the sacrifice your Northern comrades are making for you."

"Comrade," *Cô* Lin said, raising her voice very slightly, "I am not arguing with you. I am just telling you how these people think. They are Southerners. They don't know a thing about our comrades from the North. All they know is how hard *they* work for their rice and how little they have left after taxes, and how much a water buffalo costs, and they spend sleepless nights wondering how they're going to survive without one. So, if they get a little bit of money, maybe saving a few *dong* toward a buffalo, they're not going to part with it very easily. They have to live."

He countered instantly, "You are a teacher. It is your responsibility to explain them that the sooner we drive out these foreign bastards, the sooner they will stop losing their water buffalo. You must convince them their lives will become a paradise when the capitalist swine are dead. They must be educated." The man was silent for a moment but suddenly slammed his fist on the table and spat, "There will be a village-wide political education meeting tomorrow night. Arrange it."

J.W. was not sure he had understood much of the conversation, except the part about a meeting the next night. He hugged the ground, sweating profusely, formulating plans to inform Colonel Bierlein of this opportunity to capture a North Vietnamese regimental officer. That would be good for a Bronze, maybe even a Silver, Star, and Bierlein would parade him around to General Abrams and the whole intelligence machine in Saigon. It would buy him a decent respite from the war and the village, one he might parlay into a few months, after which, he would be a short-timer with far too few days left in Viet Nam to be ordered back to My Co or to a tank platoon. There would be no choice but to grant him an early DEROS, "Date Eligible to Return from Over Seas," and the promised audience with President Nixon, who would ask him what he wanted most in life. He would request the man use the awesome power of the presidency to grant J.W. admission to Harvard Medical School, maybe Cornell Law, perhaps even the Sorbonne.

J.W.'s dream of impending achievement faded as he noticed a small form slinking toward his thicket. In the moonlight, he saw a tail erect in the night air, and, at the other end, a nose skimming the earth, tracking his scent. J.W. rolled to his right, toward the flank of the bamboo coppice, proud of his Ranger training, of his ability to move with stealth and cunning. He inched onto an open patch of sand, all the time slithering toward the berm, his silhouette hidden from the enemy patrol by the thick hedge.

Reaching the mound of earth, he edged to the top on his stomach then rolled down the far side into a dry paddy. From behind, there was a whoosh, a growl, and a sudden biting pain in his shoulder. The dog had followed J.W. over and leapt upon him. Weathersby jumped to his feet and tore at the creature, pulling it free, only to have it lock on his wrist. J.W. raised his arm and slammed the mutt against the berm. It let go, though yelped so piercingly, the armed soldiers dove as one to the ground, forming a defensive ring around their regimental political officer. The man crouched beside his men, eyes searching left and right before whispering them forward.

Protected by the regenerated animal roar that was reaching a crescendo, J.W. could not remain in the open and had no choice but to steal back over the berm and return to his thicket. An enemy scout was dispatched to the edge of the hamlet to reconnoiter their rear. He passed the bamboo grove just feet from Weathersby's shivering hands. At the berm's crest, the lookout eyed an ancient man relieving himself, turned to his commander, and shouted, "Just some old fart pissing."

The regimental officer was irate at the breech in security and hissed for his party to depart My Co. They moved toward the paddies slowly, once again poking bayonets to their front and flanks, probing the emptiness between the hamlet and the expanse of distant jungle. As the trailing elements tip-toed past the bamboo thicket, J.W. aimed his weapon at the officer's chest then selected his second and third targets.

As one of the black-clad men stopped abruptly and turned to stare into the bamboo, J.W. whispered to himself, "Fuck 'em." He reaimed and coldly designated a new set of lives to snuff. He turned his head slightly, chose an exit point on the far side of the hedge, and calculated the exact pivot he'd execute to join the spider's web of paths he knew well. When he entered the village proper, under cover of the closely placed hootches, he would slip into an empty buffalo pen, or a hut vibrating with the drunken snoring of an old man. He reckoned that by the time the lead soldiers had run back around the bamboo barrier, discovered the casualties, and taken up defensive positions to reform their leadership structure, he would have had enough time to rig a second ambush.

He realized, in these few seconds, likely his last, that he was no more noble than any of the young American draftees with whom he had been so angry, men from ghettos and trailer parks compelled to shoot at the slightest flicker or die.

A moment later, he heard a double hiss from the regimental political officer, and the lead elements picked up the pace slightly. J.W. allowed himself a slight breath. He lowered the .45 an inch. When the soldiers at the rear had fully passed J.W.'s position, and all were accounted for, he relaxed his taut muscles, took a proper lungful of air, and lay back down until his body stopped shuddering.

But there was crunching behind *Cô* Lin's hut, and J.W. feared he had miscounted the soldiers. He allowed his head to turn a few degrees—it was but a villager with a long white beard and turban ducking in to talk with *Cô* Lin. From inside the hut there were murmurs, and soon *Cô* Lin stepped out and yelled in a whisper to the political officer, "A large American patrol has entered the village at the east end. You have time to escape, but you must hurry."

The political officer barked in a harsh whisper, and the troops fell in around him, their eyes searching every inch of the darkness. He slapped the back of his wrist very quietly, and the squad of enemy soldiers dropped to their bellies, slithering as if reptiles across the humid terrain. Three hundred meters into the paddies, they stood and ran madly, instantly melding into the jungle. J.W. crawled out of his lair.

He stopped as he passed the door and stole a look inside. *Cô* Lin's sat at a table, writing by the dim glow of a kerosene lamp. She looked up, startled. He searched her face, wanting so badly to feel her warmth again, and he began a step inside, but as her eyes locked his, a sense of numbness blanketed him. He turned and walked away. Nothing in Viet Nam was as it seemed.

He felt he should return to *Ông* Khai's, to tell him of the encounter, but as he peered into the darkness for the American patrol, sure that they would be ignorant of the presence of a GI in the hamlet, he decided to make contact and leave with them when their mission was over that night. As he neared the east end of the village, he detected none of the usual symptoms of a large patrol: no boots crunching the earth; no orders being shouted; no grumbling or cursing, and not a single cigarette lit the night. There was no American patrol in My Co.

J.W. slept fitfully in a corner of the Khais' house, a seven-foot by four-foot area demarcated with a line of roof tile shards. The children were admonished not to venture beyond the magic lines that circumscribed their guest's territory—except by invitation. J.W., though, woke several times during the night with the toddler sleeping next to him, the sweet scent of the child calming his worry. He spent some time wondering if there would ever be a child of his own to snuggle, perhaps one who would return to My Co with him half-a-century later, a child by then a doctor, who would extend to these people recompense for the acts of kindness that had preserved his life.

When a neighbor's dog began barking wildly just before dawn, J.W. vaulted from the wooden planks, chambered a round in his .45, and crept along the floor to the doorway. He stuck an eye against one of the many holes in the sheet of tin that served as a door and did a full perimeter check. There was no movement and, suddenly, no animal din. J.W. began to raise himself to his feet, fearing the family would see him crawling about their home in his skivvies, carrying a loaded, cocked, semi-automatic pistol. Halfway up from his squat, he paused to peer through another, larger hole, spying a mangy mass twitching in the dirt just feet from the door. It was the neighbor's surly mutt. Saliva drooled from its sagging mouth, and it whimpered weakly, its head lifting and falling back to the ground. It made feeble lunging, biting movements toward a coiled, vibrating mass inches from its nose. In the glimmer of the new sun, J.W. saw a reflection of electric blue on the helix. It was a krait, the most poisonous of all serpents in Asia.

He considered opening the door to shoot the snake *and* the dog, for no creature survived blue krait envenomation, but he paused for a moment of contemplation: the shot would startle the entire village, especially the half-dozen Viet Cong soldiers who had spent the night at home on R&R with their wives, and a handful of ARVN, Army of Viet Nam soldiers from the Saigon regime, home on leave as well. The hamlet would erupt in chaos, with bodies dashing from hut to hut, figures escaping across the paddies to the wood line, others down the road on motor scooters. J.W. had at the tip of his trigger finger the makings of a catastrophic mini civil war in the settlement to which he had been dispatched to create a measure of security and peace.

He thought even harder. If he did spot the enemy and fired at them, he and Khai's family would be decimated in an instant, the reedy walls sprayed with automatic weapons fire from both sides. On the other hand, if he didn't fire at the VC, everyone in town would know, and it would leak to the American command in hours that one of their soldiers in the field was a bloody coward. He'd be charged with dereliction of duty, and that would be the end of his heroic welcome back to the States and his audience with President Nixon.

His mind drifted back to the immediate problem—the snake. The chances of J.W. hitting it with a .45 pistol were essentially nonexistent, especially considering he had not been able to hit an eight-foot square paper target at twenty feet on the pistol range back in basic training—and he was the best shot in his platoon. Tying up the loose ends in his mind, he concluded that with the report of his pistol, the serpent would head off into the hinterlands; the neighbors would rush to the scene and see no snake, but note the carcass of the dog. J.W. would be charged with shooting an innocent mutt, just the most recent episode of J.W.'s apparent penchant for animal cruelty. Surely, everyone remembered the incident with *Ông* Xuan's dog and the frying pan, and it wouldn't be very many hours before the previous evening's battle with the cur on the berm would be public knowledge. Someone would conclude that if Lieutenant Weathersby remained in the village, all the local hounds would be deceased by the end of the month.

Soon, the rodents would take over, for dogs were the mousers in My Co. In fact, if a dog didn't consume a sufficient number of rats to control its hunger, it would starve, for who in My Co had extra food to waste on an incompetent predator? J.W. looked out at the dog again. It was barely twitching. J.W. mumbled aloud, "Little shit's trotting down to doggy hades as we speak. Leave it alone."

While still bent forward, peering through the thatch, J.W. sensed someone approaching from behind. It was *Ông* Khai. As he lit a fire, he asked over his shoulder, "Lieuten say to who leave alone?"

J.W., still on one knee, turned to answer Khai, searching for the words in Vietnamese to describe what had happened, but there was movement outside, and Weathersby turned back to watch. The dog's owner had come to lift the lifeless creature and carry it off. As he bent forward, though, he paused spotting J.W. hiding behind the door, pistol in hand.

When Khai finally understood, he opened the door, though there was nothing left to see. He sucked in a deep breath and invited J.W. to the table for tea and a bowl of last evening's rice.

As they sat over breakfast, J.W. considered telling the chief of the Viet Cong political meeting planned for that evening. But, he knew if he warned *Ông* Khai, the village chief would send his wife and the children back to Tuyen Binh on the scooter. With experienced enemy intelligence agents ranging from kids of six to decrepit men of eighty-eight operating in all corners of the hamlet, the Viet Cong knew every move every villager thought about making before they made it, even those of the new chief. If they got wind of the family's departure, the VC would intercept them before the family had driven a mile from the hamlet. They would be held for ransom, or worse.

Then again, if he didn't tell Khai, and the family stayed in My Co that evening, the kids might be dragged before the meeting, tortured, and murdered. It happened every night in the countryside. It was one of the VC's favorite attention getters.

But more likely, the VC would gather the opinion leaders, make their spiel, and be gone. They had studied Khai's storytelling schedule and knew he went to sleep at ten each night. Surely, they understood that if they assassinated him, the South Vietnamese government would inform the Americans. Bierlein would be finally forced to concur with his commander colleagues that the notion of winning the hearts and minds of these ungrateful peasants was simply liberal folly.

That would lead to American airstrikes, and when nothing was left, the 33rd Mech would grind in and work the debris into the mud. My Co would cease to exist, and the VC would lose a major source of rice and recruits. It would also mean the torture and death of many of My Co's Viet Cong families. Wives and children of the insurgents, and dozens of innocent, neutral clans who had been fingered as insurgents by personal enemies, would be sacrificed. It was one of the South Vietnamese government's favorite attention getters.

As the sun's early rays crept through holes in the old tile roof, J.W. heard the rest of the family stirring, and he watched as the kids came to the table. *Bà* Khai ladled out bowls of rice gruel dusted with minced green onions and slivers of roast goose, *Ông* Khai's favorite breakfast. She placed the first bowl before J.W., then one for her husband, then for the kids, and finally for herself.

J.W. was so preoccupied, he did not look up to thank Mrs. Khai. When he realized his faux pas, he nearly jumped off the bench and apologized. He groveled on nervously about his rudeness until the family spied him askance. He finally muttered to himself that the chief had been through this a dozen times. He knew what he was doing, and J.W. needed to keep his nose out of local business. He tried to smile.

Ông Khai stared at J.W. for a moment. "Is everything okay, Lieuten? You seem unhappy. My family so flatter you stay with us. Children really like Lieuten."

"No, no," J.W. snapped almost before the man had finished his sentence. "I'm fine. Just have to drive up to Saigon and go to a meeting with the Colonel. I'll be back in a day or so. Wish I didn't have to, but the boss ordered me down there. Got no choice."

J.W., though, went on ruminating, seeking to convince himself that in the many weeks since the chief and his family had arrived, surely there had been other political meetings, and *Ông* Khai had not been molested by the Viet Cong. He mulled over his reasoning continually, satisfying himself each time, as if repetition could make the lie true. Yes, the chief and his family would be just fine, he finally nodded.

After a final glass of tea and a cigarette, J.W. excused himself from the Khais' table and mounted his Jeep. As he rolled away from the house, he spotted the chief's children capturing luminescent green beetles, domesticating the latest troupe of pets, tying them to leashes fashioned from bits of thread the boys had pilfered from the local seamstress.

"Hey, Bao Ngoc," J.W. yelled to the chief's eleven-year-old daughter, "tell your father to take the night off. No stories. You kids understand? All of you should go to bed early tonight. Really. Let your father have the night off."

She smiled warmly, calling out, "Good bye, Lieutenant. Please come back soon."

J.W. motored off waving, smiling cheerlessly, down Highway 29.

At the American base in Moc Hoa, J.W. stopped to stock up on food for the trip. He drove through the concertina wire, past the same guard shack to which he had crawled the night he'd escaped from the VC. He ignored the salute of the GI at the gate, drove to the mess hall, introduced himself, and asked for breakfast. The mess sergeant plopped a refrigerated slab of last night's meatloaf on J.W.'s tray, two slices of hard-crusted white bread, and a runny egg.

The sergeant curled a lip and grumbled, "Don't like it, *Sir*? Give it back here." He grabbed at the meat with his fingers, but J.W. pulled his tray back, threw the fodder into a scruffy sandwich, and glowered until the privates began drifting over. He bristled, about-faced, and marched from the building.

A few kilometers east of Moc Hoa, as J.W. shoveled the last crust into his mouth, he came to a column of white-clad, elderly Vietnamese on the highway. They were struggling through the mud, weaving around sodden potholes, carrying a very small, raw wood casket. The bitter wailing reached him before he saw the hardened frowns of the mourners. He pulled off the road and cut the engine until they passed. An old man trailing the column thanked him with a nod.

J.W. asked, "Was this a child, sir?"

"Yes. Her name was Linh. Eleven years old." The man nodded again respectfully and continued with the procession, smiling faintly a final time.

J.W. bellowed, "FUCK ME," as loud as his lungs could expel the fetid air. The grieving peasants flinched, and a painful silence draped the procession. J.W. mumbled an apology as he turned the jeep around and started back to My Co.

He sped through Moc Hoa, heading west as fast as he could drive until perceiving a plume of crimson mud lifting off the highway far to his front, the footprint of a motor bike racing east. When the two vehicles were a hundred meters apart, the scooter driver started to wave wildly, and as they closed, J.W. recognized the black field jacket.

"Lieuten, I so happy to see you. I tell you I been search for you for one hour. We find out VC come to village tonight for meeting. Better you didn't come back a few days. It seem so funny. You tell Bao Ngoc go to bed early tonight. You have a dream VC come?"

"Shit, I have that dream every night," J.W. snorted. "Let's put your scooter in the back of the jeep, and I'll take you to My Co. We can load up the family and drive to Tuyen Binh before dark."

Cô Lin was walking along the berm near *Bà* Binh's hut. She averted her eyes when she saw the jeep pull back into town. *Ông* Khai noticed J.W. watching her, but other than the chief's nearly imperceptibly tightened lips, he remained outwardly indifferent.

J.W. continued to watch *Cô* Lin as she ducked into *Bà* Binh's. The old lady walked lamely out of her hut toward the road, cackling aloud in his direction, waving him over. "You hardly ever come around anymore," she chattered, adding, "but you can't sleep here tonight. No, you can't."

For fun, J.W. said, "I don't understand. You just told me I never come around anymore." And then he took the most brazen step he had since arriving in Viet Nam. He giggled, "I miss you! I like sleeping with you."

The old lady blushed, her dark complexion reddening deeply. J.W. saw her about to smile as she slapped his shoulder, but she gathered herself and declared, "I told you. You just go away today. Come some other time. I'm busy tonight."

"Ah, you have another boyfriend," J.W. laughed.

"Oh, my God, no! You just go away! Go to Saigon," she barked with a frightened look. "Go away." With that command, she gave him a shove and turned back to her hut, creaking through the five-foot-five door, the sill a foot over the top of her head.

J.W. loaded *Ông* Khai's family aboard the jeep as the sun stretched far to the west, embarking on its brisk plunge below the horizon. He honked the horn for the chief to join them. *Bà* Khai limped from the house and squeezed herself into the front seat. "*Ông* Khai is not coming. He wants to stay here. He won't listen."

"I'll go talk with him," J.W. grumbled impatiently, leaving the jeep.

"There is no sense in trying to tell him to leave. He wants to stay. He is always like this."

By the time J.W. had untangled himself from the children's arms and legs in the jeep and entered the house, Khai was gone.

J.W. drove the family west until the jeep reached a high point on the road. He mounted the PRC-46 antenna and tried to radio the 33rd Mech's headquarters, but strikingly dark monsoon clouds were sprinting toward them, rendering the atmosphere far too unstable to carry the forty-mile connection. Somehow, J.W. remembered a frequency at the base in Moc Hoa, and after being redirected through a dozen units, he was eventually patched, via an operator in Moc Hoa, to Mech headquarters. Bierlein himself took the radio at the other end. J.W. advised the colonel through the relayman of the tactical opportunity in My Co, and that he had left the hamlet with certain "special women and children," to deliver them to Tuyen Binh before the enemy invaded. "But," J.W. emphasized, "tell my CO that friendly local, I say again, local honcho remaining behind. If they come, use caution."

Bierlein's reply was direct and simple; the relay operator delivered it forcefully, "Your six said to, and I'm quoting, 'get your ass back there and get set up for some schoolyard amusement.' He said you'd know what that meant."

J.W. asked the radio operator to ask Bierlein if he had time to drop the family off. After a delay, the radio operator in Moc Hoa called J.W. and broadcast the colonel's reply. "He said, and I'm quoting, 'Tell him I'm giving him a direct order to get back to the village immediately and be out there to direct our troops.'"

J.W. turned to the chief's wife. "*Bà* Khai, I need to go back to My Co. How much farther is it to Tuyen Binh?"

"Half-an-hour."

"It'll be dark by the time I get back. Do you know anyone in this village you could stay with till morning?"

"No."

"How about the next village?"

"No."

"Okay, hold the children tight. This is going to be a fast trip."

He pushed on, more conflicted each moment, struggling to settle to whom he owed his allegiance. Was it to this innocent family, or to his commanding officer, who had issued the most reasonable order he had ever received in Viet Nam? Colonel Bierlein had been sent from America to engage and destroy a soulless enemy who tortured and raped as standard operating procedure. The Vietnamese communists had followed nearly to the letter the tactics of China's lionized Chairman Mao Tse Tung, the most prolific murderer of all time, a demagogue who had overseen the death of sixty-some million human beings, not demonized Jews or Gypsies, but his very own people, all in the name of the sanctity of the human spirit.

J.W. had been entrusted to serve Bierlein as an officer, not a shallow assignment, which meant he was to follow the legal orders he had sworn with up-lifted right hand to obey. He had volunteered to stop the communist take-over of South Viet Nam, even if it cost him his life. He knew that when he signed on for ROTC, and especially when he pushed for combat duty several times before the Pentagon finally approved his request. The decision was not a theological conundrum. Enlisted men and officers had followed such difficult orders since the beginning of time. Even packs of animals had leaders to whom they remained loyal. Brutish hyenas, ferocious lions, the fastest geese, all of them obeyed leaders; it was how nature insured survival. J.W. accepted that. Bierlein's command was a legal order. His only issue, as he continued west, was how he'd manufactured such a dilemma.

As they tore along the potholed roadway, the overloaded jeep slammed into colossal ruts so viciously, the children began to cry. J.W. slowed down, though only because of the violent shimmy in the front end and the suddenly impossible steering. He was having trouble keeping the vehicle on the road. Veering left and right made the children sob harder, and with each mile, the problem worsened. At the next village, J.W. hired a pair of scooters to take the family the rest of the trip. It cost him five dollars.

He started back for My Co with the radio switched off, morphing into the hear no evil monkey, but he surrendered a few miles down the road. The instant the PRC-46 warmed up, the radio crackled with the impatient voice of Bierlein's pilot demanding J.W. answer.

J.W., suddenly the speak no evil monkey, sped even faster until he was just a few miles north of My Co, where he finally answered, swearing he had heard the pilot calling on the helicopter's powerful radio, and had tried to answer, clearly a victim of the dented, outdated Prick-46 the Mech had assigned him.

"Just drive down two miles east of the vill," Tom snapped, "and turn your headlights on for an LZ when I tell you. And stand by for further orders."

J.W. radioed back, "Vehicle is inop."

The pilot answered, "Well, get some of your local pals to push it down there. I expect lights in fifteen minutes. Out."

J.W. coerced the jeep to thirty miles per hour, and though it rattled his teeth unrelentingly, it wasn't until the left front wheel tore off and the axle dug into the mud, and J.W.'s mouth was thrown into the steering post, snapping off a fragment of one of his incisors, that he finally understood he was, once again, flirting with a sojourn at LBJ, Long Binh Jail.

The vehicle came to rest in a culvert, on its side. J.W. had been pitched into the front garden of a Vietnamese hut, face first, which pushed the fractured incisor through his lower lip. From his vantage point on the deck, peering through the cabbage leaves, he had the opportunity to survey the remnants of the jeep for which he would no doubt have to pay.

J.W.'s major challenge at that moment, however, was what to do with the PRC-46 radio bolted to the back of the vehicle. If he destroyed the transceiver, that would be another few thousand he'd owe; though if he left it with the jeep, it would be captured by the VC; and so would he if he didn't get down the road back to My Co, where he was probably going to be captured or killed, perhaps by his own commanding officer.

He pried the tool box from under the mangled front seat back and found a rusted crescent wrench to disconnect the radio. Stashing flashlights and the microphone in his pockets, he heaved the forty-pound, metal-boxed radio onto his shoulder and waddled toward My Co at a jog. He slowed quickly to a fast walk, then a walk, and then a crawl, chastising himself all the way for not having doused the jeep in gasoline and torched it. Either way, he was going to pay for it, but now, if it was taken by the enemy, he would be the subject of a courts-martial for aiding the enemy.

He finally left the radio at the north end of My Co, hidden in a culvert which he covered with straw from a water buffalo pen. He ran the rest of the way to the east end of the hamlet, greeted by the rotor slap of a heavy chopper. He positioned his flashlights as if they were jeep headlights, waited until he could see the dark silhouette of the HUEY, then turned the lights on.

Colonel Bierlein's helicopter's landing beacons switched on at the last second as the rotor blast blew the flashlights to kingdom come—more missing equipment to be accounted for. The regimental sergeant major popped from the ship before the skids brushed the earth.

He ordered, "Take me to the village, Lieutenant. We need to set up a command post. Wait a minute. Where the hell's the jeep, sir?"

"Inop, like I said, Sergeant Major." The man ran back to the ship to let Bierlein know there was no ground transportation, and after a string of expletives exploded from the aircraft, there was a moment of quiet followed by a roar as thunderous as the turbine engine. The old man, though, did not emerge.

J.W. and the sergeant major hiked west into the village as the helicopter departed, relieving a bit of J.W.'s anxiety, but the ship soon came about and flew inches above their heads at fifteen or twenty knots, the usual ruse to draw fire from the enemy, who, J.W. had informed the highest levels of command, had surely infiltrated My Co.

J.W. realized he was witnessing the latest iteration of schoolyard payback—the evening edition. The premise of the coming performance became partially clear to J.W. when he figured out that if a single VC hopped out of a hut and fired at the chopper, the report of the weapon and the muzzle flash would serve as an aiming point for troops on the ground, though, at the moment, that boiled down to J.W. and the sergeant major, who, like J.W., was armed with only a .45.

Weathersby was reasonably sure Bierlein was willing to sacrifice an underperforming first lieutenant, but he couldn't quite grasp the old man forfeiting a very senior command sergeant major. He wondered what he was missing. And seconds later, the answer erupted as tanks and armored personnel carriers charged down the main village dirt road, grinding in from the east, closing on the NDP at thirty miles per hour. A second platoon of armor, in a burst of deafening clanking, churned in from the flanking paddies. It was as if they had materialized from the ether, but it was all part of Colonel Bierlein's grand tactical plan. He had had his pilot determine from which direction the storm winds were blowing then ordered the tank attack into that air current to hide the din until the last moment. He had even ordered they roll painfully slowly into position to mute the seismic waves that preceded an armor attack.

It was genius, masking the clatter of many hundreds of tons of rolling machinery, but Colonel Bierlein had not factored in that he was still in Viet Nam. As the main road contingent of tanks switched on their searchlights, all they saw in their fields of fire were two "friendlies," J.W. and the sergeant major, both waving their arms frantically, trying to stop the charge. The tank drivers, blinded by the abrupt mutation from pitch tropical darkness to the overwhelming brightness of the xenon searchlights, jammed their tracks off the road, away from the course that would have crushed two of their compatriots. The escape route, however, sent them slamming through flimsy animal sheds, gardens, and several straw huts before they could brake to a halt.

Pigs, chickens, water buffalo, and incensed villagers peeled from what had been their ancestral homes onto the road, where J.W. and the sergeant major shooed them away, searching for the tank company commander, to chew his ass in the colonel's name and make him do it all over again until he got it right. The chaos was familiar, in fact identical to the training exercises at home, just another boring drill to which he had been subjected over and over. He laughed that he could just hear it: the company commander would chastise the offending platoon leaders, who would berate the platoon sergeants, who would reprimand the tank commanders, who would call down to the drivers and laugh, "Hey, Jimmy, that was okay, man, but let's next time see if you knock off a pig, not just a fuckin' chicken."

But it struck J.W. harshly that this wasn't Fort Knox any more, and these kids weren't back from Viet Nam, finally safe, waiting to go home. These were angry, scared conscripts from the projects, kids exposing their lives, and he pondered how many would die that night to satisfy the greed of the gray-haired, corrupt, impotent, old men who dominated Washington. At least for this night, though, he swore he would not allow any one of those troopers to be harmed by his actions.

As he turned to call one of the tank commanders, to tell him to move his unit out of the line of anti-tank fire, J.W.'s face was sprayed with blood. He did not know if he had been hit and froze, but saw the sergeant major crash to the ground, grabbing frantically at his shoulder. Before J.W. could stop the bleeding, the door gunners from the command helicopter dove from the aircraft, pushed J.W. aside, and pulled the sergeant major aboard. With the ship taking off in a jumble of sand and poultry, J.W. sprinted to the lead tank and yelled up to the track commander, "Lights off. Follow me!" He dashed along the main road through My Co, fist pumping the air over his head as he screamed for the column to stick to him and avoid the planted areas.

At that moment, rocket propelled grenades, RPGs, began to sail in from the paddies. The tanks rolled back onto the main road, sprinting west, to regroup and turn their guns on the VC. But from a hundred meters up the road came a sudden, deep rumbling and the silhouette of five more tanks emerging from the dust. They were bearing down, head to head, on the first column.

The opposing lead tank commanders switched on their one million candle-power, xenon searchlights. Both men were instantly blinded. A second later, white-light fire balls began exploding in the sky. J.W. looked up to see Puff the Magic Dragon, one of the 1930s, reclaimed Air Force DC-3's, dropping flares. Each illuminated a square mile, turning the midnight countryside into high noon for sixty seconds. The plane then rolled north over the paddies, firing its six-thousand-round-per-minute Gatling guns at the black figures illuminated by the flares.

J.W.'s vision was disabled by the flood of intense lights. He jumped off the road at *Bà* Binh's to escape the two columns of tanks, two-hundred-and-fifty tons facing two-hundred-and-fifty tons, closing at forty miles per hour. There were also foot soldiers, waves of them, weaving up the road, flanking the armor. When he spotted several shadows moving between the huts, he moved toward them, .45 charged. He passed *Bà* Binh's and looked in quickly. A lantern cast a weak light on the ancient soul and then *Cô* Lin, who sat next to her grandmother breathing heavily. He stared at *Cô* Lin for a few seconds, and though she did not avert her eyes, J.W. did not venture farther in. Before he left the hovel to re-establish contact with the Americans, he barked at the two women to get into the bunker under the bed; neither stirred. He shook his head angrily and ran back to the road.

From the edges of the village behind *Bà* Binh's house, several American armored personnel carriers pivoted and swept through the gaps in the berm to disgorge squads of infantrymen, groups of two and three forming to enter the huts. J.W. turned back to see one patrol duck into *Bà* Binh's. From inside, a man shouted, "Hey, you two, come here!"

J.W. started back to the hut.

Several of the patrol members, hearing villagers unambiguously admit guilt by causing a GI to yell at them, pushed J.W. aside roughly and ran inside. Another fire team dropped to the ground and took up defensive positions around the hut. Behind J.W., a second infantry patrol advanced through the area cautiously, two GIs bringing up the rear, their M-16's aimed at the neck of a tall man who marched along silently, hands tied behind his back.

But J.W.'s attention was now riveted on *Cô* Lin, her hands also bound. She had been marched out of *Bà* Binh's and shoved along with a rifle to her head, forced to join the other figure. In the light of a fresh flare from Puff, J.W. recognized the black field jacket.

The American squad with its two hostages joined several other patrols on the road, where prisoners were being pooled, blindfolded, and herded to the center of a circle formed by tanks and armored personnel carriers. Major Trott appeared out of the mist and smoke. He pulled J.W. aside. "You know any of these people?"

"Yes, sir. You just managed to capture the village chief. You remember Mr. Khai? He used to work for you burning shit. Sir, he's the one the president of Viet Nam adores, the tall guy in the black field jacket over there being pushed around with the M-16, sir."

"Platoon leader said he was carrying a 9 millimeter."

"Wouldn't you if you were village chief? He didn't use it or pull it out, did he?"

Major Trott turned to the platoon leader and hissed, "Let him go. The Lieutenant here says he's one of us. Take the rest of them into separate bunkers in the NDP. Don't let them sit down. Don't let them talk, and keep them blindfolded."

"Sir," J.W. interrupted, pointing toward *Cô* Lin, "the young lady is okay. She's a school teacher. I'll vouch for her."

"Ah, the teacher. She the one you're porking, Lieutenant?"

"No sir, I have not touched her."

"That squad over there says she was out of breath and sweating and trying to escape from the rear of the hootch. Why?"

J.W. started to fabricate an answer, but the major cut him off.

"Why did she try to escape?"

"Sir, she was probably out of breath running home to protect her grandmother. I don't know. And you can't get out of the rear of her hootch, or any hootch. They don't have back doors. They're just small rooms. She's a good lady. She lives there, and she's helped me quite a bit. She's *not* VC."

Major Trott pushed a sheaf of curl-edged papers into J.W.'s face. "Then how come she had these on her? What are they, lesson plans? What do they say, Lieutenant? Sergeant Dinh says they're troop movement orders. He says your name is on them." Trott spit on the ground angrily, just missing J.W.'s boots. "No, no. You can have the chief, but this one's mine."

Trott turned away from J.W. and bobbed his head toward the platoon leader to take the prisoners into the abandoned NDP. As they were marched off, J.W. watched *Cô* Lin guided toward his old bunker. He faced Trott to plead his justification for releasing the woman, but the major was on the radio with the latest Americans to arrive, a flight of helicopters carrying officers and noncoms from regimental headquarters, higher ranking military officers from III Corps, and four Caucasian men, unshaven, long haired, who jumped from an unmarked, gray helicopter and bristled toward the village. The brass from III Corps slowed and allowed them to pass.

The civilians took up positions with fists on hips, surveying the village under the light of an airborne flare. Their beards were scraggly, though the white shirts and chinos were crisp. The pilots who disembarked to service the helicopter confused J.W., for he not seen unmarked gray flight suits before.

Major Trott sprinted up and reported to the civilians, remaining braced at attention as if greeting the Joint Chiefs of Staff. Two uniformed captains joined one of the beards and dispersed into the NDP. The civilian who ducked into J.W.'s old bunker carried an army TA-312 Field Telephone under his arm. It was the device soldiers manually cranked to generate electric power to send a sharp ring tone to the next phone, sometimes as far as 22 miles down the line.

J.W. followed slowly, heading as obliquely as he could for his old bunker, finally standing at the mouth of the dugout listening to a woman's tremulous voice weeping in fractured English, "I'm doe know, I'm doe know, I'm doe know."

J.W. climbed down into the bunker. The blindfold lying at her feet, *Cô* Lin stood in the glare of several flashlights pointed at her closed eyes. Wires led from the field telephone to her great toes. One of captains turned toward J.W. and asked, "Who the fuck are *you*?"

"I live here. And what the fuck are you doing to her? She's a school teacher."

"Yeah, and I'm fuckin' Ho Chi Minh. She had troop movement papers in her hands when we nabbed her." The beard spit, "You have no business in here. Take off, Lieutenant." He turned away from J.W., cranked the generator on the telephone for three seconds, and demanded, "You VC?"

Cô Lin's body stiffened and vibrated in resonance to the agonizing electrical current. A tear escaped her, but they soon came in torrents as she wept uncontrollably, "I'm doe know, I'm doe know."

The beard cranked for a full five seconds this time, and she shrieked, "I'm doe know, I'm doe know!"

The captain laughed, "She doesn't even know if she's VC. We got a winner here. Must be an elementary school teacher."

J.W. snapped, "She's trying to tell you she doesn't understand English. That's the way they say it. She doesn't understand a word of English. Leave her alone."

The beard turned toward J.W. and removed a .38 from a holster hidden under the cuff of his chinos. "Lieutenant, I told you to fuck off. You will disappear from the face of the Earth if you're not out of here in about two seconds flat. And even if you leave, I will come back to this shithole and blow your fuckin' brains out if you don't forget pronto what you've seen here. It's not a threat pal—it's a promise."

J.W. crawled up the earthen stairs and left to search for help. He found Major Trott in the bunker next door, sitting quietly in the rear, eyes averted from the proceedings, this theater featuring a young male with the telephone wires hooked by alligator clips, one to his left big toe and the other to his scrotum.

"Sir, I need to speak to you." J.W. whispered. Trott looked up and followed J.W. into the night air. "Sir, I know you don't like me, but sir, they are torturing an innocent woman in my bunker, sir. You have got to intervene. This is not what you want, sir."

Trott was silent for several seconds then pulled J.W. by the fatigue jacket away from the bunker. "No, it is not, but I have no control over these bastards. They come from levels of power you can't imagine. You're right. I don't like you. But I respect your commitment, Weathersby. You got a serious set of nuts on you, I'll say that, living out here, coming back after all you went through. You're going to be somebody someday. So be smart. Keep your trap shut and live through the night. This is bigger than the regiment. Write a book about it when you get out."

J.W. turned away and ducked back into his own bunker. The first thing that caught his attention was *Cô* Lin's blouse on the dirt floor, buttons sprayed over the ground. Then he saw her frayed bra, which now lay next to the blindfold at her feet. He looked up slowly and saw alligator clips on her tiny nipples. The beard cranked and cranked until *Cô* Lin fell to the ground vomiting.

The interrogation staff shook their heads disgustedly and left the bunker, passing J.W. roughly, offering, "You want her, she's yours, Lieutenant."

J.W. placed the blouse over *Cô* Lin, but she looked up into his eyes with a glacial stare that he had never before seen in a living creature, and he ran from the bunker to *Bà* Binh's, took the old woman by a stick-like arm, and dragged her into the NDP. Several other women, sufficiently furious to be undaunted by the presence of the soldiers, followed and climbed into J.W.'s bunker. He left them and ran out of the Happy Valley to find Khai.

The chief had returned to his house and was at the table sitting motionlessly in the shadows cast by a candle. J.W. watched for a moment then sat down and offered him a cigarette.

"*Ông* Khai, I'm sorry for the soldiers. They're really not bad kids. They're so scared. They don't want to be here anymore than you want them here."

"Lieuten, it is the way it has to be. They just do what they told. I understand. American boy come here help. This same World War Two. This what you government must do—send men here finish communist."

"No, sir. Nobody in America wants this. This is not what Americans do. The soldiers are good men. They're doing their best. They hate it here. I'm sorry to say that, *Ông* Khai. I love your country, but these men dream of only one thing—going home. That's all they have to keep their minds from exploding. But those men with the beards, and the high officers, they are out of control. They are the worst of America. I never met a single American like those bastards in my whole life. They are not America. I swear to you they are not my America."

Khai thought for a moment and answered. "That what our war do to America soldier and Viet Nam people. But you never forget. Maybe that why you here—you and soldier friend never let happen again."

He paused and took a long drag of the Salem. "Lieuten, in three day Christmas. People in My Co no understand. They Buddhist, but I Cat-oh-lick, and my family invite you come Tuyen Binh for holiday. We hire local boy guard jeep."

At that moment, J.W. remembered that he had not had a chance to tell Khai what had happened hours before. "*Ông* Khai, ah, about your family. Now, they're fine, don't worry, but I had to send them on a couple of cyclos the rest of the way to Tuyen Binh. And I don't have the jeep anymore. I had to leave it up the road because the wheel fell off."

"Wheel fall off?" He laughed, but caught himself and shook his head. "You leave outside village? VC, they take anything, fix. I give credit for that. But you burn with termite grenade, for sure."

J.W. stifled a laugh over the thought of termites eating through the jeep. "Well, I didn't burn it. I didn't have a thermite grenade, and there wasn't enough time. Maybe we should go up there now and check on it." He paused for a moment. "Nah, wait, wait. They can't move a jeep with a wheel missing. You know how much that thing weighs? They're not that good."

"No, they not that good. But Lieuten say wheel just fall off?" He looked away, but J.W. saw the edges of his mouth curl up. When he looked back, his face was tightly neutral. "Yes, tomorrow. First thing after soldier sweep road for mine, we look for jeep."

"Yeah, good idea, but I do have to go up the road and get the radio. I left it in a ditch at the edge of town."

"You leave radio on road, Lieuten?" His face hardened, and he thought before answering. "Yes, must get radio tonight. It easy carry off." Khai asked nervously again. "You jeep? Wheel fall off?" He shook his head, and his lips tightened to stifle a smile. "But we wait American soldier leave."

J.W. excused himself and went back to the NDP. The prisoners deemed worthy of further questioning were tied to the rails of an armored personnel carrier, while a few others lucky enough to have been reckoned impotent were sent off to stumble home. J.W. walked to the prison track and scrutinized the five detainees. He recognized four old men and a middle-aged woman, *Bà* Binh's younger sister.

J.W. ran to one of the helicopters as Major Trott boarded. "Sir," J.W. called out. The major turned and stepped back out. "Sir, these aren't the people I saw here last night. They were young. A bunch of men, five or six of them and one young woman. These are just villagers."

"Yeah, villagers who can't explain why they were out of their houses during the sweep. And age has nothing to do with it. Age is venerated here. At the minimum, these are potential political leaders. And anyway, this one's out of my hands, like I said." J.W. sucked in a deep breath to speak, but Trott continued, "And out of Colonel Bierlein's, and out of everybody else you know. I don't trust your judgment, Lieutenant. You must have gone to one of those left wing bullshit colleges, but I don't want to see you murdered, either. Like I said, leave it alone."

The sundry gray and OD helicopters came to a hover, each awaiting the command to depart for Saigon, their beacons and nav lights flicking off as single ships took their turn to leap north east into the night. When the armor rolled slowly out of My Co, J.W. noticed several track commanders, eyes to the heavens, lips moving, no doubt thanking God for having their crews intact, alive, unmaimed, even if it was just for one more night.

J.W. went back to *Ông* Khai's. The two lit cigarettes and walked along the road, heads down, searching for the radio until *Ông* Khai put his arm up to stop J.W. then pulled him into a thicket of bamboo. He pointed into the darkness at a cluster of motionless, black lumps lying in the mud-filled culverts. The two men watched wide-eyed as the sinister mounds unfolded to retreat across the paddies toward the tree line. A figure in the middle of the detachment waddled as if burdened, J.W. was sure, by a hefty bag of rice.

After five minutes, *Ông* Khai motioned for J.W. to follow, and they stalked along the edge of the road until J.W. stopped at the spot he remembered leaving the radio. He thought he found the straw under which the transmitter had been hidden, so he searched the culvert a hundred meters to the west, and added another hundred to be sure. His chest gripped more and more painfully as he turned to comb the road a couple of hundred meters in the other direction.

He walked to the chief at the end of his expedition and shrugged. "I'm a dead man. The VC got the radio."

"No worry, Lieuten, one tank probably find, maybe run over. Push into mud. VC not use; not have wire, electric. Not worry so much."

"Yeah, they can't use it, but that thing cost a lot. Maybe a million dollars. Do you have a million dollars? I don't have a million dollars. As it is, I'm going to have to pay for the jeep. Fuck me, Mr. Khai."

Khai laughed for a second but realized J.W. was quite serious and asked, "Army make you pay car ruin in war?"

"Well, when you're hauling women and children around in an army vehicle against direct orders, and you manage to destroy that same army vehicle, sometimes the government doesn't like that. But we can come back and check again in the morning."

"Lieuten, not worry so much. You alive. Could be more big problem.

At dawn, J.W. knocked on the bamboo pole of *Bà* Binh's door sill. She slid the tin sheet aside tremulously and limped slowly to J.W, but didn't invite him in. He asked quietly, "Is *Cô* Lin okay? I am sorry for the soldiers."

"She is okay, but she must rest." *Bà* Binh turned her ancient eyes to the sky and stared at the tawny sunrise. She did not wait for J.W. to leave before going back inside and sliding the tin back over the portal with a bang.

He walked to the edge of town, poking at the mud in the culvert with a bamboo stick, but uncovered only a blown out flip-flop, a scrap metal collector's mother lode of rusting, empty mackerel cans, and a femur. He gasped at the discovery but realized, when he lifted it out of the mud, that it was far too hefty to be that of a human. He continued up the road, jabbing occasionally in the red clay, walking around one bend after another, hoping to capture a glimpse of the jeep, but when he had paced a couple hundred meters west, he stood alone, unarmed, out of uniform on a desolate road in South East Asia, flanked by a kilometer of open rice fields, and endless stretches of empty road to his front and rear. He had found neither the jeep nor the radio, both gone, despite *Ông* Khai's lie that everything was going to be okay.

Bronx-born First Lieutenant J.W. Weathersby was thirteen kilometers from the nearest American, thirteen thousand kilometers from home and, at best, thirteen hours away from facing courts-martial for the destruction of government property and provision of government assets to the enemy—first, rotting food, and now a shoddy jeep and a feeble radio. He sat down on a log by the side of the road, lit a Salem, and accepted that he had done nothing in Viet Nam except make poor decisions, piss off foreign dogs and superiors and, worst of all, abdicate his duty to fight. He sat with his head hung.

From the east, a motor scooter came toward him shattering his reverie. It slid to a halt, but J.W. sat with his back toward the driver, watching a lone air force tanker drop clouds of defoliating crystals over the jungle half-a-mile away. He saw the gray mist of poison catch the wind and drift toward My Co, not a single molecule of it landing on its intended jungle target.

Ông Khai touched J.W. on the shoulder. "Lieuten, we go before poison come. I think not good for body. We go look for car."

J.W. was silent as they scootered west, coming to the wreckage just two hundred meters farther up the road, right around the next curve. It appeared untouched, except there were no wires from the radio control box by the driver's seat to the radio mount and, worse, there was no antenna. J.W. racked his mind to remember if he had taken the aerial with him, but *Ông* Khai nodded. "Lieuten smart take out battery."

"I didn't take the battery out."

"Look." He pointed to the empty battery rack.

J.W. started to climb onto the wreckage, but the chief grabbed him by the arm and pulled him away, screaming, "NO! NO! They come here! Not touch!"

Khai had jumped forward and yanked at J.W. so hard, Weathersby fell backwards, slamming onto the ground. His head struck a rock, and he saw a bright flash. A second later, he jumped to his feet, fists locked, glaring at Khai until his mind cleared sufficiently to grasp his own blunder.

J.W. stood deflated. How many times had he been warned in Ranger School to avoid anything the Viet Cong might have touched? The instructors had cautioned that left-behind Chinese AK-47 rifles with full magazines were surely booby trapped, not so that they'd explode when first picked up, but customized so that the first American to fire his captured prize got a brain full of splintered gun breach.

Beware, the cadres counseled their nascent commandos, of colorful, hand-painted propaganda posters tied by the VC with nearly invisible fish line to captured Bouncing Betties. The GI who snatched the artwork also tugged the filament, launching the mine several feet into the air. Designed to detonate at waist level, the booby trap easily wiped out an entire squad.

They told the students of the nearly lifeless, gagged, nude, American soldier tied to a tree in the middle of the jungle. The enemy had lashed one end of a string to his genitals, choking them purple, and the other end to a swinging rock. What nineteen-year-old private coming upon his missing compatriot wouldn't run to cut the rope? But what nineteen-year-old private ever had a teacher, a minister, or a coach able to imagine a so-called human rigging that rock to a captured 155-millimeter artillery round hanging in a tree above the gathered, thirty-man platoon?

J.W. knew the horror stories by heart, yet in the crucial moment, it had fallen to an untrained, provincial village chief to save his life.

J.W. took a seat behind *Ông* Khai on the motor bike. They bobbed slowly back into My Co, where J.W. donned his filthy uniform from the night before, armed himself, and left with *Ông* Khai for Tuyen Binh on the back of the scooter.

⊰ ⊱

At the 526th Combat Engineer Brigade's headquarters in Tuyen Binh, J.W. presented himself to the S-4, the logistical officer, to report the loss of the jeep and radio. The major asked if he had eaten, offered him a meal in the officer's mess, and sat with him, taking down the particulars of the incident. He read back the statement. "Is this correct, Lieutenant?"

J.W. muttered, "I'm afraid so, sir."

The major nodded professorially, stood, and smiled, "I should place you under arrest for the misuse of government property, for transporting unauthorized civilians in a government vehicle, for failure to secure government matériel, and for not reporting this loss to your commanding officer in a timely fashion, when these problems could have been obviated.

"But, on the other hand, Lieutenant, it could have happened to any one of us, don't you think? Truth is, we should all be living in villages along with these people, building schools and marketplaces. If we were, the war would be over in a week. And guess who would have won, and for a lot cheaper? Okay, let's go down there, pull your vehicle into maintenance, and see if we can't get you mobile again."

J.W. and the major rode in a wheeled recovery vehicle—an olive drab tow truck. The driver and his helper hooked the jeep and pulled it onto the road, threw the severed front wheel into the back seat, and drove west, stopping less than a kilometer outside Tuyen Binh to realign the tow cable. J.W. walked off the road to relieve himself, though the major stayed behind.

As he buttoned his fly, J.W. turned back toward the road. The tow truck driver was grunting as he pried at the grill with a crowbar, and the major walked over to lend a hand. The other crew member manned the controls of the winch, but as the jeep lifted, the bumper came loose, allowing the vehicle to drop several feet to the ground. As it bounced, a fire ball exploded from the engine compartment, coating the major and the tow truck driver with flaming orange gasoline. The control operator was blasted off his perch, landing on the ground near J.W.

Weathersby ran around the man toward the vehicle, though the intense heat stopped him fifteen feet away. He stepped further back when some of the burning motor oil spattered onto the tow truck itself, igniting the paint and creating a viscous, flaming admixture that dripped onto the wheels. Several tires caught fire and exploded. The stench confirmed J.W. had entered hell.

The other crew member ran up to J.W. and screamed, "Sir, we can't help. We need to get the fuck outta here. I've seen 'em go up before." He grabbed J.W. by the sleeve and pulled him along the road, shoving him into a culvert a millisecond before the shock wave of the second explosion, the tow truck's gas tanks igniting, passed over them. The report was so thunderous, it carried for miles, attracting a column of 526th Engineers armored vehicles from Tuyen Binh. An hour later, when the remains of the S-4 and the driver cooled sufficiently to be scraped into body bags, J.W. accompanied the tracks back to their base.

He was ordered to report to the Cav's brigade commander and walked slowly, hunched, eyes glued to the red sludge of Tien Giang Province as he made his way toward the air-conditioned headquarters quonset. The colonel barely looked up from an open file on his desk, returning J.W.'s salute with a Brownie wag of the fingers.

"From the beginning, Lieutenant. Let's hear it."

Weathersby, at a Viet Nam fashion of attention, started quietly. "Sir, my vehicle lost its axle on the road last night."

"What were you doing on the road last night?"

"I was on the road last night, sir, hurrying back to my village on the orders of Colonel Bierlein." The colonel did not interrupt, so J.W. went on. "See, sir, two nights ago, I overheard the VC saying they were coming to the village to hold a political meeting. I drove out of My Co on the road toward Tuyen Binh so I could get the radio high enough on that hill east of here to contact Colonel Bierlein. He ordered me back to the village immediately to organize an ambush. I was just trying to get there, sir, when the wheel fell off my jeep."

The colonel put up his hand to stop J.W. "You overheard the VC? Okay. What was my S-4 doing there?"

"I came up here late this morning to get some help and met with the major. He went with the recovery vehicle. Charley must 'a wired a booby trap to the frame. The jeep bounced, there was an explosion, a fire, and they got it. End of shitty story, sir."

"What's your assignment?" the colonel asked.

"S-5. 33rd Mech. I live in My Co. It's a little village fifteen miles east of here."

"You live there? Since when do our soldiers live in Viet Cong villages?"

"Since October or November, sir. I can't remember."

"Shit. I need more information." The colonel slammed the file shut and bellowed, "Sergeant Major." A gray-haired, rock-jawed E-9 with a combat patch from World War II on his left shoulder appeared in the doorway

"Yes, sir."

"Find Lieutenant Weathersby a bunk in Headquarters Battalion. Lieutenant, you're going to write up a statement on what happened. I want detail. Attention to detail. This whole thing isn't good. And stay put by your rack. That's an order."

"So, I'm under arrest again, sir. Is that it?"

"I never placed you under arrest before. I've never even seen you before. What are you talking about, Lieutenant?"

"Nothing, sir."

"Sergeant Major, we need to make arrangements for the S-4's remains and the driver's, and then contact the 33rd Mech for me. I want to talk with their '6'. Then I gotta find a new S-4. Goddamnit, this whole thing has potential. Top, we got work to do."

J.W. wrote for two hours, creating a statement that would preclude the need for further investigation of the destruction of two human beings, one large recovery vehicle, one jeep, one dented radio, several hectares of farm land, and a few military careers. Most of the statement obfuscated his role in the matter, but by early afternoon, he understood that this time, he would not dodge the bullet, regardless of the contortions of logic he was able to spew from his mouth, or his pencil.

At three o'clock, a sergeant came to J.W.'s hootch and advised, "Sir, there was some tall gook at the gate looking for you. The guy had a pistol and some drug-like substance they found inside his black field jacket. They think it's marijuana seeds. The MPs arrested him. Old man wants to know if you know him."

"Apparently, I can't leave here to tell the Colonel that I do know him, and that he's on our side. He's the government-appointed village chief of the hamlet I live in. He's authorized by the provincial governor to carry a weapon, number one, so have your colonel call the governor. He'll straighten it out. And, number two, the 'drugs' are sesame seeds. Tell your CO that's food, not something to get high on. And, also, please tell the village chief he might as well go back to the village by himself. I have a feeling I'm going to be here for a while."

The sergeant left but returned quickly. He bellowed, "Colonel wants to see you, sir. Follow me."

The brigade commander was more relaxed, offering J.W. a seat. "Lieutenant, I spoke with your unit. I hear you're doing a bang up job down there. I didn't know there were people with guts enough to live like that amongst the people. Good for you. You're free to go."

The colonel rose and took J.W.'s hand. "Keep up the good work." Still grasping J.W.'s hand tightly, he pulled Weathersby closer. "I do have one last question for you, Lieutenant. Do you happen to know which of your squadrons took our four-holer?"

"Sir?"

"A Chinook with a big, winged M-113 stenciled on the front came in here a couple of days ago and hovered around for a while kicking up dust, so we couldn't see what it was doing until it dropped a line and a man. They hooked the whole damn latrine. As if we weren't going to notice a four-hole shitter flying away from here east toward Normandy Base Camp. These things don't come cheap, Lieutenant. I want it back. Tell your CO I know he has it."

"Was anyone in it, sir?"

"I'm not kidding, Lieutenant, you tell him I want it back."

J.W. left Tuyen Binh on the rear of *Ông* Khai's Vespa. When they stopped for a smoke, J.W. asked if he had been treated well by the infantry.

"They just doing job. Khai understand."

Chapter 10

J.W. SPENT THE next several days at Long Binh Post, the 33rd Mech's new headquarters, twenty miles north of Saigon. The concentration of American brass in the capital had become so burdensome, their sedans clogged the roads, and the highest generals had to beg for a table at the better French restaurants. So, the command shuffled many brigade headquarters away from the flagpole. The move irritated full colonels, who suffered as a class from "Flag Fever," the frantic pursuit of a first star. In Saigon, a dashing colonel easily became drinking buddies with generals from the West Point class two or three before him—out in the field, that same colonel became a liability, for no matter how professionally the man commanded his brigade, enough went wrong each day in his unit to insure one or two of the myriad incidents made it to the briefing room at the White House.

It took that many days to fill out property loss forms and answer Major Trott's questions about the paltry results of the botched night mission in My Co. J.W. went to visit the regimental executive officer. He talked the man into another jeep, a less-beaten PRC 46 radio with a long-range antenna, and a 4X4 trailer, all elements he swore would make possible the gathering of quality tactical intelligence. He collected six cartons of Salems, six cartons of C-rations, and a cardboard box full of books labeled, "*The Classics—Donated by The Ladies' Auxiliary of Charlottesville.*"

The regimental personnel officer also had business with J.W. The S-1 looked up from his desk, opened a drawer, flipped a tiny box at J.W., and cautioned, "You don't wear these until 0001 hours on 26 Dec 68." Through the cellophane window, J.W. saw a pair of still-varnished, silver captain's bars, "railroad tracks," and he realized it had been nearly eighteen months from the day upon which he had been commissioned an officer and gentleman in the United States Army. His back arched a bit straighter, and his head lifted a few degrees, though he knew well it was just an automatic upgrade in those turbulent times of rapid turnover in the combat arms. The promotion was simply to fill the vacuum left by the wounded and dead.

"Congratulations," the S-1 added dispassionately. "Maybe you can have your pal in the village pin them on you."

⇴ ⬳

Though every male in his extended family had served in the United States Army since the first refugees landed at Ellis Island from Eastern Europe in 1911, J.W. was the first officer. Whether a perfunctory advancement or the result of heroic deeds, for J.W., the promotion had a special meaning. He stopped his new jeep on the road back to My Co at the outskirts of Long Binh, tarrying under the colossal, bright red and white checkerboard water tank, the checkpoint air traffic control used to organize approaching flights. He lit a fresh Salem and allowed himself a few minutes to rest and reflect on what he had seen in his twenty-three years. He thought of the hundreds of times he had flown over the water tank on approaches into Long Binh, and then of the pilots and crews who had not made it back to see the legendary marker one last time. As the smoke curled up about his face, he relaxed and leaned farther back, doing absolutely nothing for ten minutes. He sighed, sat up, and pulled at the cardboard flaps of the box the ladies of Charlottesville, Virginia, had donated for his reading pleasure.

The selection sitting on the top was *Moby Dick*. "Wouldn't you know it," he mumbled to himself, remembering the novel from high school, the horrifying narrative of good and evil that Herman Melville had never been able to sell in his lifetime. He recollected Mr. Celeste, his senior English teacher, lecturing that Melville had died penniless, and that it wasn't until fifty years later the work was finally published and recognized as a literary masterpiece.

What had it all meant? Millions and millions of kids had read *Moby Dick*; millions and more millions of dollars had flown into the hands of those who had embezzled Melville's sweat and spun it into largess for themselves. And here

After the next cup, the two left for the 526th. At the headquarters quonset. J.W. relayed Bierlein's condolences over the loss of the soldiers retrieving the jeep, and gave the colonel an update on the investigation over the loss of the man's jumbo latrine.

The colonel nodded and turned away. "What the hell do I tell their mothers? Their kids died over a worthless jeep? That'll help 'em get over it." The man turned back. "Well, the show must go on, doesn't it? About that four-holer, Lieutenant?"

J.W. spoke slowly. "Sir, I think those Chinooks were reassigned to other units. They're supposed to change the unit decals, but what with the war and all, sir. I'm sure I can get ahold of a list of who got those ships, sir." J.W. went on, not pausing for a breath. "And, sir, by the way, does the Cav happen to have a hundred sheets of high-grade, corrugated roofing metal lying around that you don't need? We're going to put up a market in My Co, bring prosperity to the place. Shorten the war, sir. Win this damn thing."

The colonel listened patiently, but only for a moment. "Yeah, well, how come *your* CO had the latrine returned this morning? Sandy was in the room next to me at West Point." The colonel turned to the window, his stare a world and a generation away. "He's been waiting nearly thirty years to get back at me. Lucky it was just a latrine."

"Yes, sir."

The colonel shook his head and spoke softly, "You can have a few sheets. You're doing good work, but don't fall in love with our supply shop, Lieutenant."

J.W. managed the hundred sheets, but it cost him his pair of captured Ho Chi Minh sandals, the primitive flip-flops created from used truck tires, the only footwear issued to the better-equipped North Vietnamese soldiers. They were far too small for J.W., or any other G.I., but they were authentic, and the only item of value he possessed. He offered the supply sergeant *For Whom the Bell Tolls* in trade for twenty sacks of concrete, but the sergeant asked, "For who what, Lieutenant?" and J.W. left Tuyen Binh with a trailer weighed down to the axel with tin, but no concrete.

As they pulled into My Co, J.W. spoke seriously to *Ông* Khai, "You know what, it would have been too much weight for the trailer anyway if we'd gotten the cement."

J.W. was not sure if *Ông* Khai nodded.

Chapter 11

THE NEXT AFTERNOON, *Ông* Khai showed up with a few three-foot by three-foot sheets of brilliant watercolor posters depicting staunch, steel-jawed Vietnamese communist freedom fighters firing AK-47 rifles, shooting at and downing American helicopters and F-105 Thunderchiefs. He smiled at J.W. as he handed over the posters. "Lieutenant, how many bag cement this bring from supply sergeant Tuyen Binh?"

"*Ông* Khai, we need to be careful. The colonel warned me to stay out of there. We don't want to push too hard. We're going to need a new approach, but I have an idea. When do you need the cement?"

Ông Khai thought for a moment. "First, must make clean land outside Happy Valley NDP. Dirt My Co same as rock. That four day many people dig. Next roof. That four day. Next bring old piece broken tile from village. Maybe two day. Then mix old tile with cement make floor. So, Khai say two week."

J.W. grinned and rubbed his palms together. "Yeah, and we'll get the 526th Engineers' grader driver to do it. Guy comes by every day. We'll trade him one propaganda poster for twenty minutes of his time. It'll work. I guarantee it."

"Lieutenant, you think twenty minute?" Khai asked, his voice betraying skepticism.

"That's all it'll take. You'll see. I know about this stuff. I used to do construction, summer jobs. The guy comes through on his way back to Tuyen Binh on his grader late in the afternoon, yes? Always waves at the kids. Looks like a nice guy. We give him a propaganda poster, and he gives us twenty minutes of his time. Everybody wins. Let me talk to him."

They drank tea for a half-an-hour until the deep rumble of an unmuffled diesel engine shook the table. J.W. placed himself in the road, waving nonchalantly at the driver. The grader rolled to a halt in front of J.W. "Specialist, how ya doin'?" The driver eyed J.W. suspiciously and then the chief curiously. "Must be getting' short. I've seen you on this road for, I don't know. Seems like two years."

"You been here that long, sir?" He looked left, and right, and behind, then called down from his high platform, "You okay, sir? I mean I heard you been livin' here all by yourself, I mean alone with the gooks."

"No, it's okay. Usually got an infantry battalion watchin' over me." The driver's eyes squinted warily, but J.W. broadened his smile. "Can I ask you for a favor?"

There was a pause as the man stared at Khai's hands, though when the chief folded his arms in front of his chest, the GI turned back to J.W. "What can I do for you, sir?"

J.W. sensed the compelling ethos unfolding in front of him. Thirty seconds before, neither the low-ranking GI nor the near-captain had ever spoken a single word to each other, yet the two men knew by the tenets of military courtesy they would engage politely, and whatever the problem was, work together to solve it. J.W. wondered if he'd miss that someday.

"Specialist, thanks for stopping. We need to get this small patch of land cleared. You have the skills—we don't. It'll only take a second, and we have a special something for you."

"And what's that, sir?"

J.W. handed a propaganda poster to the driver. "What is this, sir? It's got gook writin' on it. I can't read that shit."

"I can't either. And you don't need to read it. It's a genuine communist poster captured from Charley just last night. We got it in an ambush. This thing's worth beau-coup bucks back in the real world."

"How much do you think?"

"Specialist, I can't say to the penny, but a couple 'a hundred to the war protestors. It's the real thing. Look at the coloring. This is a piece of history, and you were part of the chronicle. It's a good deal. Everybody wins. What 'a you say?

Twenty minutes of your time. You get the poster, you help the war effort, and you get to stay out of Tuyen Binh for a few extra minutes."

"Okay, sir," the soldier nodded, "I'll give ya some time, but I need to get back up there before too late. Every once in a while, old man checks to see if I'm keepin' the maintenance up on the machine. It's okay, that's usually only when the colonel's scheduled to come 'round the next day. I'll get it done for you, sir."

Khai ran to the land just outside the western gate of the NDP and dropped shards of red roofing shale at the four corners of the plot. The GI worked slowly for seven or eight minutes, clearing a strip of land twenty yards long and three yards wide—there were that many stumps poking through the rock-like earth. The engine steamed a bit, and the driver leaned forward to investigate. He stopped the rig and got off just as a relatively benign explosion juddered the neighborhood. The large bore hydraulic hose that controlled the grading vane burst, gushing oil like a new well. The blade, in the down position at the moment of the rupture, dug into the earth.

J.W. was not sure if it was the enraged bellowing of the oil-soaked driver or the violence of the mechanical failure that sent the spectators sprinting home and diving into their under-bed bunkers. J.W. and Khai were now alone with the specialist, who kicked dirt at his rig.

J.W. offered, "Hey, I'm sorry. I guess we'll do the rest by hand."

"Well, now, sir, how am I gonna get this thing back up there before dark sir? You need to give me a hand, sir."

"Of course, I will, but it's getting late. Why don't you stay the night. I'll drive you up in the morning."

"No way, sir. I ain't staying out here in Indian country for no night. No way, sir. I don't wanna, pardon my French, sir, fuckin' die."

"Just wait here, Specialist. Lemme check on something."

J.W. drove up to *Cô* Chun's, the new prostitute who'd filled the vacuum when *Cô* Thi's life was taken. Chun hemmed and hawed about entertaining the driver, grousing about the tainting of her assets should she consort with a foreigner, but when J.W. offered to pay a premium, she agreed to a secret visit.

When J.W. told him of the plan, the driver was wordless for a moment then pulled J.W. aside, away from Khai. "Sir, I don't know." He dithered a bit before whispering, "You bein' an officer and all, I guess I can tell you. See, sir, I ain't got that much experience, if you know what I mean. I mean I was kind of a church boy at home in South Dakota, sir. Parents were pretty tough on me."

"Specialist Shore, you don't worry one little bit. *Cô* Chun'll teach you everything you need to know. A man's got to take the step someday. What's wrong with today?"

The next morning, Shore promised to come back soon, maybe that night, to check on the grader.

When J.W. and the chief arrived in Tuyen Binh to drop off the driver at the engineer battalion, they explained to the commanding officer that they were standing there on the road when the grader came through My Co, and that they had witnessed the spontaneous explosion of the hose with their own eyes. J.W. turned to Khai, who nodded gravely. They told him that Specialist Shore had begged for a ride up to Tuyen Binh just minutes after the breakdown, but J.W. ordered the man remain in the village, the early evening road far too treacherous.

J.W. offered to have a contingent of villagers stand guard over the vehicle until the new hose arrived. That pleased the major until Weathersby told him there was, naturally, a fee for such labor. Asking the men to leave their important work to sit in the beastly sun hour after hour smack in the middle of an enemy village was not a volunteer position. The major's lips pursed as he went into the S-4's office and came out with $50 for the deputation of a platoon of villagers to sit around, smoke, drink tea, and shoo kids away from the machine.

J.W. retreated to his jeep and sat there for a few minutes, waiting for Khai, who had taken a cyclo to check on his house. He smoked a Salem and thought about the power these funds would bring Khai in the village, though he fretted over simply dropping the money in the chief's hands. There was still a question as to whether the chief could survive without siphoning off a portion of any funds that came into his hands.

J.W. imagined, even if the chief didn't skim for himself, a portion of the money would go through the old men of the village council to *Cô* Chun. It would be Khai's best bet to secure the council's cooperation in running the village. Either way, it was good American taxpayer money after bad, and J.W. lifted his hips to slip the envelope into his back pocket. He'd dole it out himself; it was the only prudent alternative. But he also contemplated the face Khai would lose if the young American overruled his older counterpart on which projects were best for the hamlet's future.

When *Ông* Khai returned to the jeep, J.W. handed the money over. Khai nodded subtly and gently placed the envelope inside the black field jacket. J.W. started the jeep and smiled, mentioning casually that they might as well visit the supply sergeant. "Why waste the trip up here? Do you have the time?"

Khai smiled warmly.

Supply Master Sergeant Paul Bloom was already aware that Specialist Shore, the grader operator, had been recompensed for his earth-moving activities with an authentic enemy artifact. "Shore told me you need cement. You got any of them posters you gave him? I'm sure we can arrange a mutually good deal. What 'a you say, sir?"

J.W. returned the next morning with four posters, the paint barely dry, the chief and J.W. having spent several hours the evening before creating the phony murals with the help of two artistic twelve-year-olds. Nearly 30 bags of concrete were stuffed into every crevice of the jeep and trailer, and half-a-dozen tied to the hood, as if returning from a deer hunting trip. Three miles out of My Co, a tire blew, and J.W. discovered that the spare he had never examined was gashed so deeply on the inside face, it blew up the instant they lowered the jack. *Ông* Khai walked into town and conscripted a column of unhappy villagers to plod out to the jeep and hand-carry the booty for the rest of the journey home. J.W. took a tire from the trailer, fit it to the jeep, loaded the trailer onto the jeep, and limped into the hamlet.

He radioed that night for a spare and laughed at the thought of receiving it before he was aboard the Freedom Bird. At nine the next morning, a 33rd Mech helicopter dashed in and hovered over the NDP at ten feet as the crew chief dropped a spare wheel out of the cargo hatch. The tire landed hard, bounced up nearly as high as the chopper, and on its next touchdown transferred some of the up-and-down energy into a little forward motion, then more and more, each bounce adding two or three miles per hour. Eventually, it trundled through the west gate of the NDP into the village, through a garden, over a chicken, and into a livestock pen, coming to rest against the head of a water buffalo. The animal sprang up out of its mire, splintered the wooden stanchions, and galloped into the paddies.

J.W., however, was not watching, for the crew chief also dropped a brown paper bag. It was J.W.'s mail, nearly forty letters. As he sorted through the stack, he came to some dated three months earlier and others not addressed to him. The final crash was a carton of books, donated this time by the ladies of Cedar Rapids, Iowa: *Idylls of the King*; *Moby Dick*, again; *The Short Stories of Fyodor Dostoevsky; The Short Stories of Franz Kafka;* and *For Whom the Bell Tolls*, again.

He opened the most recent letter, the thinnest of the pile. It was from Krista, but already three weeks old. There was talk back at the 6th Cav that many of the officers returning from Viet Nam were to be sent to Alaska, to prepare for war with the Soviet Union. She mentioned that the rumors were Alaska was an unaccompanied tour and many of the officers' wives were furious. "J.W." she wrote, "that means when Alaska is over, we'll be married four years, but only spent three weeks together. Can they really do that?"

J.W.'s chest tightened, but his attention was stolen by old *Bà* Dao, who flew out of her hut screaming that the chicken, which lay cackling its last, was the only thing she owned in this world.

Against the rotor blast of the departing HUEY, she gathered up the failing bird and tore into the NDP at a crooked run, ignoring the signs in Vietnamese that warned of summary execution for anyone who entered without authorization. She was headed for the tail rotor of the helicopter waving a limp chicken, so J.W. jumped up, threw the letters to the side, and rushed to stop her. The paper bag was blown into the air around the ship then brutally sucked back down through the main rotor.

J.W. grabbed the toothpick of a woman, who scratched madly at him with one hand and waved the chicken in his face with the other until, in a final breath, the creature swiped at J.W.'s eyes, scratching his cornea. With the ship gathering air speed for takeoff, the lieutenant let go of her, turned away, and scrubbed at the eye with his fist. She tottered around to face him, reached up, and tweaked his cheek vengefully. "That bird was a prize, worth three hundred American dollars, at least. That thing was better than that stupid water buffalo of Long's, that you gave him five hundred dollars for. I know all about it. I heard. A water buffalo doesn't lay eggs, does it? You can eat eggs, but you have to wait ten or fifteen years to eat a water buffalo. No, no, American monster devil soldier, sweating like a pig, with the mustache pointing in the wrong direction, you must pay for my prize chicken—three hundred American dollars—at least."

J.W. covered one eye and looked down at the old lady. He spoke disinterestedly. "Madame, your claim will be addressed by the powerful government of the United States. President Elect Nixon will write you a letter explaining how much the chicken was worth. He is a wonderful man. You will not be disappointed."

The coils of her wrinkled face relaxed, she bowed slightly, and tugged his cheek again, almost fondly, but with sufficient muscle to draw him through the gate to her home, where she invited him in for tea and tropical bananas.

Inside *Bà* Dao's hut, J.W. beckoned what appeared to be at least a great-grandson and offered the boy five cents in MPC to carry the box of books, shy the ones he had not read, up to *Cô* Chun. J.W. learned that she was able to read and write English, at least well enough to have scribbled a note to the latest commander, explaining that she had revamped her business model to accommodate a more racially assorted clientele. She drew a heart under her signature and added a PS. "You come. You sample *Cô* Chun. You send American GI for sure. *Cô* Chun number one!!!!"

J.W.'s offering was a miscalculation. Miss Chun assumed J.W. was trying to secure her favors through barter, and sent the books and a written message back via the child: "*Cô* Chun speak fife dollah—same same all GI. No happy rate for live in My Co mustache lieuten."

⥼ ⥽

Ông Khai spent the next morning sending out word that all females under the age of forty were to gather beside the abandoned grader when the sun was directly overhead. The women arrived in pairs and threes toting baskets and carrying poles, and soon a work party of fifty ladies in conical hats hunkered in a small circle. *Ông* Khai mounted a pile of sandbags. He proclaimed the gathering to be one of the most weighty events in the history of the chosen hamlet of

My Co, and suggested the market would bring a new, rich world to My Co. He straightened a bit and announced that those women who labored the hardest would be invited to attend the grand opening. There were a few jaded yawns until the chief added that a traditional Chinese opera company from Saigon had been engaged to mark the occasion.

"Let me ask, when was the last time anyone of you had a chance to wear your other set of clothes, the white silk *áo dài*? He looked around, and those women not napping stared back at him blankly. "Well, that could be the day you will. Just think of it. In the first row will be the dignitaries, behind them the Council of Elders, next to them, the menfolk, and on the sides and behind the theater, that's where the good workers will watch. Think of it. You will watch a *Chinese opera*. You will hear the performers, maybe even see them from so close, so close, in fact, you will think they are singing to *you*." He pointed toward the ladies with a sweeping index finger. "The acrobats, the musicians, the *pipas*, the drums. The ancestors will be shrouded in the good fortune you have brought to My Co. Their spirits will sing along with the actors. Yes, ladies, the ancestors will smile upon you. And you will look so beautiful."

He stood for a moment staring down at the gathering then clambered off his stage to set off for a meadow on the other side of the hamlet. The women rose slowly, stretched, and followed Khai lethargically through the back paths of the village, finally coming upon a former French-style home that had long since crumbled. The residue of that once-handsome structure was now a hillock of rubble, the wooden remnants powdered by rot. The red tile roof had crashed into a heap of worthless shards that had gone untouched for a decade.

Ông Khai picked a few pieces of red tile off the ground and placed them in one of the women's baskets. That lady, however, did not move a muscle. He picked a few more shards from the ground and laid them in another basket, but that did not motivate the band either.

He scrambled up a mound of broken tiles and delivered Part II of his labor opus. "Well, I am sure we can arrange for some of you to stand inside the market at the grand opening. You will be honored guests, so close to the opera performers."

At that, the women began a slow, apathetic gathering of the little red tile scraps. J.W. had parked his jeep on the closest road. The women eventually toted their loads to the trailer. When it was half-full, J.W. drove to the market site, where another crew of women off-loaded the trailer and separated the shards into piles by size.

The gathering and transport continued for an hour. Khai called for a break, and J.W. joined the ladies to talk them up. It wasn't thirty seconds before a wave of giggling erupted, and he was offered the hand of one of the women in marriage. It was, of course, on the condition that he move to My Co, for his bride had to remain in daily contact with her family, friends, and ancestors. This was not a totally abhorrent fantasy, and he smiled warmly until they shoved the chosen forward. The bride-to-be was the homeliest of the crew, of the village, and perhaps of all South East Asia. And she knew why she had been offered, and why everyone was laughing, and why she was the only one with red eyes. J.W. smiled courteously, and *Ông* Khai reminded the women that the lieutenant already had a very pretty wife, one as comely as the presented fiancée. J.W. bowed respectfully, took the hand of the young woman, and kissed it gently in European fashion. The women oo'd and ah'd and then became quiet. J.W. seized the calm to smile at the woman, bow slightly, and escape in his jeep.

He sat in the shade for fifteen minutes until two pistol shots rang out from the area in which the chief and women were working. He charged his .45 and ran through the fields to the site, but instead of the usual death wail, the women were hunkered, chanting angrily, "Snakes and spiders, no way, no way. Snakes and spiders, no way."

J.W. noted that *Ông* Khai had retaken his position on the mound and was once again addressing the young women of My Co. At his feet was a dead blue krait. The chief was laughing. "One small blue snake, a few carmine-eyed spiders. They're harmless. The snake's dead. The spiders heard the gun and ran away. Everything's okay. You know, I've been thinking about it. We can get all of you *into* the market for the opening. Inside. Maybe even seats. You will be so close."

The women looked to their flanks, and when one of the more mature ladies rose, the rest came to their feet. A slow-paced drudge resumed, and the chief nodded happily to J.W., who eyed the pile of rubble, home to the deadliest serpents and pests on Earth. He tiptoed back to his jeep.

By late afternoon, several yards of tile had been transferred to the market site. The ladies, though, ceased their toil once again, this time to petition the chief, not tenderly, to construct a roof to shelter them from the relentless sun.

The women dropped back onto their haunches, and J.W. realized he was witnessing a revolution of sorts. Khai took the stage and promised economic development in which the women were to be major players, the new entrepreneurial class of Cochin China, but only if they invested of themselves.

J.W. sat outside the NDP in the jeep, enjoying a fresh Salem from his new carton, staring at the insignificant patch of land that had for eons been just rice paddy. He wondered how it had so suddenly become a site of social upheaval. Though women had been quite prominent in the political and social history of Viet Nam, for these particular isolated peasants to revolt over work conditions was more than uncommon. The war was transforming traditional society in Viet Nam, and all over the world. He pondered anxiously what other unintended consequences the market would bring to My Co.

Khai left the women, walked to the jeep wearily, sat with J.W., and lit a Salem. A minute later he mumbled, "I just can't deal with them anymore today. I feel sorry for the communists if they win the war." *Ông* Khai was quiet for a moment then shook his head. "Lieutenant, I going home for dinner. Lieutenant come?"

Because J.W. saw *Cô* Lin walking slowly toward the market site, he declined the invitation and stepped out of the vehicle to speak to her. Before the chief left, he turned back to J.W. and warned in English, "Lieuten, be careful."

J.W. had not seen *Cô* Lin since the night of her capture and was not sure she would speak with him. He knew that she knew that he had seen her breasts, and he wondered how he would have felt if she had witnessed his torture, his genitals yanked out and violated. She noticed the jeep and stopped but turned away and continued, approaching the pile of tin and cement. She glanced back, not at J.W., but at the pile of shale the women had amassed. Her head bobbed as if counting. A minute later, she turned toward him. Her eyes were dark, piercing and fetching, and they stayed on him. He screwed up the courage to approach her.

"Miss Lin, are you okay?"

"Yes. How are you?

He started to apologize for what had happened but lost his nerve. Though he stood before her silently, she looked up at him and smiled very gently. "Thank you. The people of My Co are not stupid. They are happy you are here." Though he was never sure, for it was so soft, he believed that she had touched his hand. But she fled a second later, and it would be some time before he saw the beautiful Asian woman again.

Chapter 12

COINCIDENT WITH THE sluggish progress of the market was a lack of attention to the grader. It sat motionless, day after day, as the 526th Engineers re-supply convoys rumbled through My Co. Each morning at ten, like clockwork, the trucks rolled from the warehouses around Saigon, up Route 29, and through the abandoned NDP, making for the engineer base in Tuyen Binh. As the soldiers threw fistfuls of candy from truck windows, throngs of children spilled from their hootches in Pavlovian fashion, dodging gasoline tankers and reefers, scrambling madly for a piece of Tootsie Roll.

No one ever stopped to examine the grader, which was now so thick with red grime and rust, it was hard to tell which was which. Though still the emblem of America's largess and potential, in J.W.'s eyes, the only utility left in the sixteen tons of machinery lie in the droplets of hydraulic oil dribbling from the rubber fronds of the torn hose. The older children came once a day and gathered the oil-soaked sand below the hose, waited until dusk, then lit the mixture with precious specks of glowing carbon donated by the local charcoal man. As they danced around the smudgy flames, mobs of younger kids descended on the makeshift amphitheater, dragging neon green pet beetles, to play marbles with little round stones. When the champion knocked his last opponent's pebbles out of circles drawn in the sand, he'd gather the final challenger's bugs, drop them into a tiny woven basket, and strut about until someone challenged him to a twig contest. Here, the ten-year-olds snapped toothpick-sized pieces of tree stem into a circle, aiming to cover an opponent's twig.

One little boy, *Em* Lan, had become village champion of the evening games, mostly because he had been tossed out of school for fighting and stealing and lying. He spent most of his waking hours in a corner of the schoolyard, snapping sticks a hundred times, a thousand times, drilling himself, his fingers as adept as a child prodigy's on the concert piano. For most of the school day, he made himself readily visible from the open-air classroom, rubbing his freedom in the faces of his chums.

When J.W. walked up to Lan and asked if he had learned his lesson, and if he was ready to go to the teacher and promise to mend his ways, Lan looked up from his pebbles, smiled, and thumped J.W. in the balls.

With little to do in the village, J.W. made occasional trips west the dozen miles to Tuyen Binh for a GI meal and to hear English spoken. He stopped in to see the supply sergeant, bringing with him stacks of three-by-six-inch slips of tissue paper on which the Viet Cong had printed peculiar slogans directed toward the American troops. A few read, "GI, throw down your weapon and present this pass to the revolutionary fighters of Viet Nam. You will be given free and safe passage to your home"; "Viet Nam people are fighting for independence same American people do in revolution with British"; and "The American man Benjamin Franklin said in America revolution, 'success 10 percent inspiration and 90 percent perspiration.'"

Actually, J.W. believed the last maxim was articulated by Thomas Edison, and he took one of the leaflets and wrote a polite, in case he was wrong, correction. He left the amended handbill on a pole in the paddies, and though the paper was gone the next morning, a week later, there was still no response.

The 526th Engineers' supply mastermind, Sergeant Bloom, was quite pleased with the offering, and admitted there was more than simple cultural curiosity involved in his new-found collector status. "When I DEROS, sir, I'm gonna peddle this shit to the antiwar hippies back in the real world. They got money. Yeah, every fuckin' one of 'em's got an old man that's loaded. That's how they're stayin' out of the army. You're lookin' at the next Mr. Macy's."

J.W. asked if he was willing to take money from antiwar activists. The sergeant laughed, "Shit, sir, their money's as green as anybody's, ain't it?"

J.W. also queried the status of the requisition for a new hose to get the grader back on the road. Sergeant Bloom looked away and mumbled that Specialist Shore, the driver, had had his ass chewed for unauthorized use of military equipment and been reassigned, as were most troublesome combat engineers, to the mine sweeping detail.

"Sir," Sergeant Bloom heaved, turning toward J.W., "I don't know how to tell you this, but Shore got blown away his second morning out. Now, no one gives a shit about that goddamn grader. But I'll get on it for you, sir. We can't just leave the thing out there in Bum Fuck, Egypt, forever. It just ain't right. His memory and all."

As J.W. left Sergeant Bloom, he knew the grader would rot in place, destined to become another American-financed, windblown pile of iron oxide. After a few more steps, he gasped when it clouted him that Specialist Fourth Class Stanley Shore wasn't coming back; he wasn't in Bangkok, on a real R&R, trying out what *Cô* Chun had taught him. J.W.'s shoulders drooped halfway down his body. Nearly comatose, he was becoming convinced again that everything he had touched in his months at war had turned to shit.

A team of diesel mechanics arrived the next morning on a deuce-and-a-half. Sergeant Bloom followed in his personal jeep. They repaired the grader, and J.W. asked, "Hey, Sergeant Bloom, think you could flight test the thing by skimming a couple of yards here and few feet there?"

It cost J.W. a South Vietnamese dog tag, one J.W. had found after a fierce battle outside the village. He convinced Bloom it was from a dead VC. A second faux commie dog tag secured an OD tarp, which J.W. and *Ông* Khai draped over the untouched bags of cement.

⟿ ⟾

Ông Khai invited J.W. to Tuyen Binh for Christmas. Khai also managed to get word to Sergeant Bloom that the lieutenant was coming, and that the Khai family requested the pleasure of his company as well. *Ông* Khai wrote in the invitation that J.W. was to be promoted to captain on Christmas Day, and, "Perhaps, sir, you would do the honors of pinning the bars on our esteemed friend."

Ông Khai was unaware that various American surnames connoted religious preference, nor was he cognizant that a good many Americans were not even Catholic, and that some did not celebrate Christmas at all. Nonetheless, the morning of the 25th of December, 1968, witnessed the improbable gathering of disparate cultures at the three-hundred-square-foot, brick shanty occupied by Khai's extended family. With the first prayers to the Lord Jesus, Sergeant Bloom whispered to J.W., "Sir, I don't mean to be disrespectful or nothin', but I'm Jewish. Would you mind if I just sat here and smiled?"

"Sergeant," he whispered back, "so am I. How 'bout we both just smile? Like at home, huh?"

"Ah, sir, this here's gonna get complicated in a minute."

"Why's that?"

"See, sir, when Mr. Khai here told me you was gettin' promoted, I told the S-1, that's the brigade personnel officer, sir."

"I know that, Sergeant Bloom."

"And he's comin' over with the brigade historian and a photographer. They want your friend to pin on the bars, not me. And that's as it should be, don't you think, sir?"

J.W. did not have time to answer, for the guests arrived at that very moment, a bash of jeep clatter drawing Khai and his family away from their Vietnamese rendition of "God Rest Ye Merry Gentlemen." The American contingent poured through the tin entryway to fill the tiny hovel with their bloated, sweating Caucasian bodies. There was suddenly so much indoor commotion, J.W. couldn't move past a single man to get to the S-1. He had wanted to conference with the unit historian, the photographer, the S-1, and the two interpreters, to set ground rules for the celebration.

Ông Khai stood rigidly for seconds, bobbing his head, counting the number of curious strangers engulfing his home. With the census taken, he drew a green bottle from the wicker basket at the foot of his bed, carved the cork from the cock-eyed neck with a pocket knife, then poured a quarter glass of cloudy rice wine for each of his male guests.

Sergeant Bloom proposed a toast, "To the defeat of the commies, and the promotion of Lieutenant Weathersby. Oh, and Mr. Khai, would you mind if I took the empty wine bottle when we're done? I really like the way that neck there kind 'a twists around. I'm collecting the fine art from your country. If there's a charge, I'm glad to pay for it."

When the S-1 nominated *Ông* Khai to do the honors of promoting Lieutenant Weathersby, the chief demurred several times, but finally smiled warmly at J.W. and pinned the new captain's bars to the lapels of his friend's wrinkled, dusty jungle fatigues. Khai stood square-jawed, shaking J.W.'s hand, staring into the horizon as several rolls of film memorialized the occasion.

The guests partook of the tough, emaciated Christmas goose for which Khai had spent a month's salary, and ate several bowls of locally grown rice and locally grown vegetables. All, aside from J.W., joined in politely refusing even a dash or two of the locally brewed *nước mắm*. The chief offered locally grown tobacco, though J.W. was the only American who took the hand-rolled cigarette. He became nauseous after two puffs of the coarse-cut leaf, but guessed his queasiness was more from the reminder the odor culled of his capture than from the smoke itself. Finally, locally grown peanuts were offered at the end of the meal, with locally grown coffee sweetened with locally grown sugar. The coffee was lightened with Borden Sweetened Condensed Milk from New York City.

J.W. left the hut for a moment to get a breath of air and was standing by the jeep when a radio message directed to his call sign came through from headquarters in Long Binh. "Arrange X-mas party for vill. Twelve hundred hours, two-six Delta-Echo-Charlie, six-eight. Your six to supply chow. Delta-Charlie honchos to accompany six."

J.W., still reeling from the poisonous tobacco, nodded to himself and made a mental note to draw up plans for a village feast. At first, he did not appreciate the event was less than a day away, and when it finally dawned on him the Delta-Echo-Charlie stood for December, and Delta-Charlie for Washington DC, he tried to drag *Ông* Khai aside and enlist his help, but the guests were making their good-byes, and Khai spent the next half-hour thanking his visitors for attending his paltry celebration.

When the Americans left, J.W. tried again to corral the chief, but *Bà* Khai limped out of the kitchen, a three-foot by three-foot bricked-in, windowless corner of the tiny house where she had spent the day chopping, peeling, and cooking. She gave her husband a rigid stare, and *Ông* Khai gathered the dishes and took them outside to the semi-well for washing. J.W. stepped forward to help, but the family, even the toddlers, pulled him back into the hut to drink tea.

J.W. realized that he had not seen *Bà* Khai at all during the celebration. Her only link with the outside world had been to hand plates piled with rice and vegetables and goose to her children, who carried them silently to the table then retreated into the steaming closet. The kids, all five of them, spent the rest of the time in the kitchen fetching and cleaning, listening carefully for their father's voice, for a whisper that something was needed.

At dusk, the family sat in the small main room listening to the chief spin yarns of a happier time in his land and of the sacrifice of Christ. He reached into the pocket of his field jacket, and J.W. thought he was going to pull out the sesame seeds. Instead, he produced a sachet of red silk, which he handed to J.W. with two hands and the soft words, "From my family to yours."

J.W. opened the pouch, exposing two filaments of 999 gold braised into a tiny, fragile crucifix, more of the precious metal contained in the offering than the chief could have bought with his government salary for a month, maybe two. The children's eyes widened as J.W.'s face flushed, and he touched his fatigue pockets for the gift that wasn't there.

He stumbled through a sentence in Vietnamese. "My family thanks yours, and I will do all I can to help build the hamlet of My Co."

Ông Khai added, "Captain, when the market is completed, we will build a dispensary. Someday, someday, maybe you'll become a doctor and return to serve the people of My Co."

Chapter 13

AT FIVE-THIRTY IN the morning on the 26th of December, 1968, the peasants of J.W.'s village were preparing to shuffle into the paddies. They sprinkled *nước mắm* on cold rice-balls and wrapped them in pieces of old cloth. It was an ordinary day, except for the voice of Vu Van Khai calling through his megaphone from the rear seat in J.W.'s jeep. The two men drove the main road of My Co several times to announce the coming Christmas party. Along with the invitation was the promise of *chả giò*, peanuts, water buffalo milk ice cream, and cigarettes. In truth, though, J.W. had no idea what the colonel was bringing. They made a final sweep through the hamlet, prodding citizens to bring tables and chairs to the nascent marketplace. With the arrival of several one-foot-high wooden stools, a two-foot-high picnic bench, and a single wicker table, J.W. and the chief sat back and waited for the masses to gather. A few souls drifted down the road, mostly old men holding out their hands for J.W.'s Salems. By 10 A.M., the sun blistered so, the early guests retreated deep into the hamlet.

In mid-afternoon, hours late, J.W. heard the faint rumble of a half-dozen HUEYs. His stomach twisted in knots, for not a single guest had shown up to greet the colonel and his entourage. He and *Ông* Khai drove through the village once again, imploring the citizens to abandon whatever they were doing and rush down to the marketplace to sample the delicacies promised by the Americans.

By the time Colonel Bierlein, several generals, and two U.S. dignitaries, the latter in sweat-soaked, unmarked khaki uniforms, arrived in the airborne convoy, but twenty villagers had materialized, all new mothers with infants held tightly in their arms. J.W. could see in the women's eyes an uneasiness as they hunkered, holding conical hats over their babies' faces against the mighty rotor wash of the landing helicopters.

"Wait a minute," one of them popped up abruptly and shouted, "who gives things away for free? Ladies, ask yourselves, what does the foreign devil want? Must be something. Nobody gives anything away for free. I've heard of this before. They will make us trade our children for food. And if we don't take the food, they'll take the babies anyway."

In the torrent from the HUEYs, several conical straw hats were wrested from the ladies' hands, shredding as they blew into the paddies. The political concierge rose to her feet. "See, it's an omen. Now we don't have hats anymore, what's next?" Half of the women sprang up and ran along the paths of My Co as if pursued by baby-eating Asian tigers.

J.W. greeted the dignitaries with an apology that there were not more partygoers, but droned on that the people were toiling for that night's meal out in the paddies. One of the American civilians walked to the edge of the hamlet and glared into the fields. He called over his shoulder, "I don't see anyone out there, Captain. Where are they?"

"Sir, there are fields beyond the trees. Maybe they're out there."

"Maybe?" a brigadier general interrupted. "You don't know where your people are?"

J.W. turned and searched the general's eyes for a hint of a smile, an inkling of holiday spirit, a twinkle over the joke he had just spoken, but the man steadfastly maintained his vexed stare at the dust-covered junior officer.

"Sir, the people here are very poor. They either work or die." J.W. turned to the chief. "*Ông* Khai, do you think more people are coming to the party?"

Ông Khai stood in respectful silence for a moment then answered softly in Vietnamese, "Captain, let's drive through village again. Maybe some of the farmers were in their fields first time through." He waited until the interpreters in the entourage had turned away before whispering clandestinely to J.W., "It'll buy us some time."

But My Co was a single, one-mile road, and the two arrived back at the gathering empty-handed six minutes later. J.W. jumped out of the jeep to debrief

Colonel Bierlein, "Sir, how dumb of me to forget. It's Wednesday, market day. Everybody's gone off on the bus to Moc Hoa."

J.W. waited to be thrashed over his declaration that the villagers suddenly up and leave every Wednesday for a market, two thousand peasants squashed into one rickety, long-retired, surplus American school bus. But when no one bothered to dispute his claim, he added, "I'm sorry there isn't anywhere to sit in the shade, gentlemen, but if you would follow me, I'll show you around the village. We can stop by *Bà* Binh's house and say hello. She's a great old lady."

There was much conversation amongst the Americans, particularly the civilians, who mumbled veiled enquiries about the level of security in My Co, but J.W. intervened and announced almost superciliously, "The village is secure by day; not to worry, gentlemen, I live here, and I can assure you I am not suicidal." Bierlein rolled his eyes, but offered no aside.

Eleven American dignitaries and three interpreters tramped the paths of My Co. They stopped to gaze out at the fields in which subsistence crops had been cultivated by one civilization or another since a thousand years before Jesus trod the sands of Judea.

Old men and children stood at the doorways of their mud and straw huts, posing genially and nodding to the Americans, who repaid with flat smiles, the large men's eyes darting left and right. Then came dogs and pigs springing from huts to dart forward and backward, nipping at the intruders' legs. That brought farmers descending helter skelter on the entourage, chasing animals in circles. The commotion caught the attention of several water buffalo, who snorted and kicked in the mud of their wooden enclosures, struggling to lift out of the mire and maul the collection of bizarrely-scented visitors.

At *Bà* Binh's, J.W. knocked on the door sill, dipped down, and entered. The old lady was asleep on her hammock. She had taken off her black pajama bottoms to cool off, and when startled awake, the ancient woman forgot she was only partially clothed. She sprang from the bed and ran next door to hide. As she coursed through the visitors like a midget half-back, she yelled a sentence in Vietnamese which one of the interpreters laughingly deciphered as, "She say, 'Oh my God. This worst and final terrible dream of life!'"

Bà Dao, the neighbor lady, provided *Bà* Binh with black silk pajama bottoms and spoke softly as she guided her friend out of the hut. Mrs. Binh emerged muttering the Vietnamese equivalent of, "Jees, Lieutenant, why didn't you tell me you were bringing guests?"

She yanked J.W. in for tea and nodded over her shoulder for the others to follow. No one budged, so she limped back outside and pulled them in one by one, some by their earlobes, until the single room was overflowing with the aroma of Caucasian perspiration. *Bà* Binh turned up her nose and grunted, "It stinks in here."

The two civilians were invited to sit at the rough-hewn table, and the brigadier general reached around to the back of the crowd and pinched J.W.'s arm, pushing him forward to sit with them. "Captain," the general added from behind, "I'm sure you recognize the distinguished gentlemen with whom you are sitting. Please introduce them to this lovely lady."

In fact, J.W. had no idea who they were, but whispered to Mrs. Binh, hoping the interpreters would not hear. "*Bà* Binh, these are big men in America. They say 'hello'."

"They're big all right. Each one of them is the size of two Vietnamese," she snipped, scrutinizing them up and down. "My God, they look like water buffalo, and they smell worse."

"I don't know their names, but they asked me to thank you for the delicious tea."

She beamed, chortled, and ran through the door, returning with a cluster of diminutive tropical bananas, passing them out with two hands to each of her anonymous, but legendary, guests. As their eyes accustomed to the dark, the American dignitaries spotted the oily, crystalline glaze of Agent Orange on the fruit and placed the produce back on the table, wiping hands uneasily on pants and shirts. There was an eerie silence until several chickens snuck under the table and pecked at the hair on the men's legs. They pushed away from the table, and Mrs. Binh took a broom to poke at the birds, whacking them until they ran through the crowd, squirting guano on spit-shined boots.

J.W. was unaware that *Ông* Khai had drifted away until the chief knocked at the bamboo portal. He stood tensely and spoke in Vietnamese. "Please tell our guests that the Christmas party will start when they are ready."

The retinue stood and bowed very deeply to *Bà* Binh. Her gasp froze the fetid air of her hut. She had been all smiles, but as her head rose, the smile became a terrible frown. She took a step backward, her hand behind her, feeling for the door. The men looked at each other, shrugged their shoulders, and bowed again, this time into a near-kowtow. Her mien hardened, the expression of anger deepening with each retreating step.

J.W. had seen that intensity of rage in a Vietnamese face only once, on a recent night the men had gathered to spin yarns at *Ông* Khai's after story hour. That evening, *Ông* Ming had smuggled under his tunic, past his wife, a large bottle brimming with *rượu đế*. Khai supplied the glasses. As on most nights, the subject of the 1940s eventually percolated through the banter to surface as the main topic of conversation. There were the routine grumbles about the French, but that was the first time the Japanese occupation of Viet Nam had been breached. Initially, the comments referred to the Asian invaders as *cái thằng chó đẻ*, the sons of bitches, but after the bottle had made its second round, the men began to recount their own stories of World War Two. With each downed shot, their faces twisted in deeper wrath, until the bitterness became so passionate, J.W. looked behind him, fearing he'd have to retreat.

Ông Ming, barely averting his eyes from J.W.'s, hissed, "The foreign bastard Japanese officers took over our houses, and they bowed down so far mocking us, their heads nearly touched the ground. They laughed and laughed, but when they stopped grinning, they sent their soldiers into My Co to rape as many women as they could find. They fucked each woman on her own bed, in front of her children and husband. When they couldn't get it up anymore, they kicked us out of our houses and slept on our beds. In the morning, first thing, they farted in our faces then screamed something in Japanese. We tried to understand, but we didn't know what they were saying, so they beat us until we figured out the officers wanted us to heat water so they could wash. In one day, they used up all our charcoal for the year."

The bottle made another round, and *Ông* Dai took up the story line. "They ate our rice for breakfast, damn near all we had left. All in one sitting. Then they farted again, bowed down even lower, and sent the privates out to round up the women who had escaped the night before. These ones, one man raped her and another strangled her at the same time."

The glasses were drained and Dai took a breath to start again, but *Ông* Long jeered a *cái thằng chó đẻ* and Dao deferred to him. "He's right," Long growled as he pulled nervously at the frayed tail of his turban. "The women who begged for mercy or fought back the night before, they brought them before the senior officer. They had no clothes on. We dared not look at them. Maybe we wanted to, but no man in My Co would dirty our women like that.

"But the officer dirtied them, all right. He looked up and down. If he flicked his finger, that one was taken outside. They raped her, hacked her breasts off, and threw them into the pig pen. *Then* they cut her head off.

"Your friend, *Bà* Binh, she was the prettiest of the village women. The bastards used and used her, every one of them. They fucked her sister and laughed while they murdered her. Threw her whole body into the pigs.

"When there were no women left, the officers bowed deeply again and settled in for lunch. They forced us to slaughter the pigs that ate the breasts and made us eat that meat in front of them. I haven't eaten a shred of pork since. Now we didn't have rice or livestock. That was the end of our food for the dry season.

"They slept for a while then whipped us and sent everybody into the paddies to smash the dikes our ancestors built. They wanted to make sure there would be no rice crop that year, so we would be too weak to fight back against them."

The men spit violently. One very old soul sat up straight. *Ông* Long looked at him and announced with a slur, "Let Thieu, here, talk. He's the smartest of all of us." Thieu shook his head modestly, but Long waved the back of his hand and mumbled, "Go on. You are the smartest of all of us."

The ancient soul began in a voice so frail, it was hard to hear him. "I was a teacher in those days, over in Saigon."

Long countered, "No, you weren't a teacher, you were a *professor*, at a *college*. The only reason you came home to My Co was to care for your old parents. You were a respectful son."

The men mumbled in agreement, and Thieu began again. "See, by 1944 the Japanese knew the war was lost. They weren't going to capture all of Asia like they had planned. They weren't going to get our hardwood and rubber and coal. That's what they wanted from us, resources, so they could take it home and make it into war machines to conquer the world. But by now, they knew the French were coming back, and they knew they would be punished for how they had tortured the French dogs at the beginning of the War.

"But they were stuck here. The Japanese government didn't even send ships or money to bring them home. They had nowhere to go. So, the officers kept on beating the lower ranks, screaming at them that the Chinese and Vietnamese, and the rest of the Asians, were not human, just low animals no better than pigs and dogs. They made them repeat that over and over during the beatings then sent them out to kill some more of us to make sure the lesson stuck. Maybe they figured they could intimidate the Vietnamese into an army to fight the returning French. I don't know. But they killed so many of us by famine the next year; some say half a million, some say two million, what does it matter? We were useless, starved, and when the French sailed back into Viet Nam, they took over again without a problem.

"My university in Saigon was Catholic. The visiting priests from Europe said we must learn to forgive the Japanese, that they weren't Christian, yet, and didn't know what they were doing. It's the Christian way, the priests said, to forgive your enemy. Well, it's not my way." He paused to take a breath. "Am I talking too much?"

A chorus rang out. "No, no, you go on. You tell the Captain." All eyes locked on Weathersby.

"Captain, you should listen to this. Maybe you will understand why we don't want you here." He thought for a moment. "Do you know why you are here?"

"Yes, to protect you from the communists."

"Ah, so you *don't* know." His voice grew louder. "Maybe you will die here, and you don't even know why. Please listen to me and these men. We have lived through it."

He paused again, taking a sip of the liquor. "Captain, you must understand what I'm saying. In the early 50s, the French were back worse than before. They looked the same as you, well, maybe not as fat, but the face was the same, the big red nose. They made us pay back-rent on land for all the years during the war.

They said it was the law because they owned the land. But how can they own our land? It was our land by any set of rules on this Earth. We told them they were crazy, and they went away. We thought we were finally rid of them. But they kept on stealing the rubber and the coal and the hardwood, selling it for a fortune overseas. Nothing changed.

"Next thing you know, a bunch of Chinese devils from Saigon drive up to My Co in an old bus. The French were too scared to come and demand the money, so they hired the Chinese and gave them guns. If you didn't pay, they killed one of your children in front of you and the whole neighborhood. Everyone had to watch. See, it was better to kill a child. If they killed an adult, that was one less hand to work the fields and earn rent for next year. I forgot to tell you, the government in Saigon supported them because they got a cut of the rent, and the Chinese pigs also collected taxes at the same time.

"What could we do? We're Buddhist. We believe in fate. And, also, we weren't allowed to own guns. Any man caught with a gun was executed on the spot.

"So, we let them murder us. It went on and on until the North sent people down from Hanoi to tell us our religion was like a drug, opium, they called it. They told us to wake up from the nightmare and fight back. So, we sent our young men up to Hanoi on foot, more than a thousand kilometers each way, to learn how to organize an army and fight for our freedom, to rid ourselves of the white bastards. Would your soldiers walk that far?

"No, sir."

"And neither will the ARVN that your government pays to fight us. I should say your mother and father pay in their taxes so that their son can come here and be killed. No, the local government soldiers won't walk one meter because they are fighting for nothing. They ask why they should die so their families can go on being cheated by the politician-robbers and the foreigners.

"Anyway, the men we sent to the North came back changed. They told us the only way to stop our families from being murdered was to start killing the invaders. Some of us believed them, some didn't. We who joined were taught Marxist Communism. It was against our thinking at first, to let the government own everything, but it was our only salvation, or so they told us. You have heard of the Viet Minh?"

"A little." J.W. looked at Khai, whose eyes had hardened along with those of the old men.

"That was the beginning of the local fighters. But there were also farmers who just wanted to be left alone. They wouldn't join, even though they were happy, because, now, the Chinese goons were too scared to come to Viet Minh villages. These farmers just wanted to reap the benefits of the Viet Minh, but not do any of the risky work. So, the Viet Minh came and convinced them to join. Same tactics, murder a few families, and the word gets out. Political power grows out of the barrel of an assault rifle. The Chinese man Mao said that."

He rested for a bit, took a stiffer swig of the *rượu đế*, drew in a meager breath, and looked to his comrades in the flickering light of the smudgy kerosene lantern. The men waved their hands at him to continue.

"Well, Ho Chi Minh kicked the French out of the north half of Viet Nam in 1954, but in the truce, the French and the puppet government in Saigon got to stay in power here in the South. We wanted the North to help us kick them out, too, but they had their own problems organizing a whole new country, and they couldn't send war supplies. So the Viet Minh down here disbanded for the most part. Well, until a few years later when the pigs in Saigon had our own soldiers killing children in front of us when we couldn't pay our taxes. This time, our peasant army was called the Viet Cong—it is short for 'The Communist Party of Viet Nam.'

"We were going have to do it all again, but we didn't care. At first, it went well. The French stayed in the cities, but they still tried to squeeze the last drop of blood out of us. Now, our own South Vietnamese Army troops murdered us with fancy guns from your America when they came to collect the rent and taxes. It made it look like the bastards in Saigon were a sovereign government, that they were respected by the Americans, which is the most important country of all, isn't it?" The men sniggered. "So now they could do in the eyes of the world what governments do—enforce property laws and collect taxes.

"The corrupt government in Saigon was losing bad, so they asked your people to do more than just send guns. They wanted you to come and help our government. They said it was to stop communism. Your President Kennedy wanted to stop the communists, but this war wasn't about stopping communism; it was about us fighting to stop the French and our government swine from murdering us for taxes.

"When the American soldiers arrived, Hanoi was finally strong enough to send down troops, so your government sent more troops, so Ho Chi Minh sent more troops. He swore he would not die until he rid the country of the foreign devils. It will happen, but he is very old, like me, and maybe it will be after our time. Who knows, who cares, but it will happen, you can be sure.

"Now it's your President Nixon who has taken over. We will see if he has the courage to leave. I think he is a very weak man. We shall see.

"And here you sit, Captain. Perhaps you will live, perhaps you will not. But I hope, at least, you now know why."

J.W. was silent. He handed out cigarettes, though some of the men refused. He took a deep breath and asked, "Mr. Thieu, aren't you afraid to talk so openly?"

"Are you going to turn me in?"

"Of course not."

"You are a kind man, Captain. All the people say that, but you are still an invader, and the good in your heart will not protect you. The wounds are too deep."

As *Bà* Binh's back hit the mud wall, she went slack and dropped to her knees, finally spreading her arms in surrender. She would either die at the hands of the foreign monsters in her meager home that afternoon, or at the hands of the Viet Cong tyrants that night for having offered tea to the enemy. As her face lost all expression and color, the men rushed from the hut, speechless. Khai and J.W. helped her into her hammock then left for the party.

A general caught J.W.'s arm just feet from the hut. He snarled under his breath, "What the fuck was that, Captain?"

"Last time foreign officers sat in her hut, they raped her and murdered her sister. Fed her to the pigs. That good enough, sir?"

"Then why the hell did you drag us to see a crazy old lady?"

At the NDP, a crowd of thirty villagers, all young mothers, milled around two tables covered with plates of cookies—the Vietnamese didn't eat sweets; half-pint containers of whole milk—the Vietnamese didn't drink milk, and even if they did, they would never have been able to pry open the tops; and cups of yellow and purple Kool Aid. Six-ounce Duralex glasses were spaced every foot along the table and filled with various brands of filter cigarettes, though Vietnamese women in the villages rarely smoked. Khai had paid an old man two cigarettes to keep the kids from raiding the tables while the foreigners were at *Bà* Binh's.

The highest-ranking general turned obsequiously to the eldest of the perfectly coiffed American civilian dignitaries and grunted, "Senator, they'll stand here all day until you start. Very polite people, sir."

The man took a cookie off a paper plate and handed it to an eighteen-month-old baby held in the arms of a haggard, cachectic, peasant woman. As the child pulled the biscuit toward its mouth, the mother spun around, snatched it out of the toddler's hand, and jammed it into her own mouth. The senator's jaw dropped and his face became a deep crimson. His hand shot forward to pull the cookie from the mother's mouth, but she snapped her head back, snatched another cookie off the table, and with the baby in a death grip, ran headlong into the village, losing a flip-flop but not stopping to retrieve it.

The senator's shoulders drooped in defeat. "I will never forget that as long as I live." Shaking his head, he stood quietly for a few seconds then bolted for the parked choppers. He waved his index finger in a circle above his head for the snoozing pilot to crank up.

J.W. tried to sidle up to the man and explain that mother's milk was the only source of food that she could count on during the war, and that she needed calories, no matter how they came, to produce it, and that Vietnamese children didn't eat cakes and sweets anyway. But the hiss of the engines coming hot drowned his speech, and the rush of the staff to join the official nearly knocked J.W. to the ground. The ships lifted off in seconds, and while the senator did acknowledge J.W., it was with a distant, transparent stare.

That evening J.W. sat with *Ông* Khai and asked why the people had stayed away. The chief was solemn. "Captain, these people Buddhist. Most never know Christmas or even our Jesus. They know to plant rice, raise animal, only enough stay alive one more day. Maybe if they have food enough for one week, it is best week of life.

"They believe in ghost, spirit in kitchen, spirit in thatch roof, spirit in buffalo pen. Most never go to next village, especially women. Who been all way to Saigon come back tell great tale of dragon ghost surround great stinking city. That scare people too much, so people ask, 'Who want to leave safety of wonderful, modern My Co hamlet?' And I must also tell you Viet Cong soldier in My Co pass word, people who go to party have house burn down tonight. That what these people believe."

Though J.W. kept his eyes peeled for bonfires, not a single photon of light left the hamlet that night. The few villagers who had come to the party were so poor and hungry, they did not have homes or belongings to torch. In the final analysis, they were simply unworthy of Viet Cong bullying. These were young widows who slept from hut to hut, as they were tolerated. The luckiest, usually the prettier ones, were permitted to tie rotting grass mats to four sticks and camp in the front garden and create a twenty-four-square-foot lean-to. And there they lived, usually a very young mom and her two or three children, the remnants of a family fathered by a deceased Viet Cong or the antithesis, an Army of the Republic of Viet Nam soldier. There the vestige of that lineage survived under the bare carapace for weeks or even months.

In the old days, a year or two before, the wretched sent the oldest child into the woods to gather a clump of bananas or a jackfruit. But since the American airplanes had started spraying the "crystal fog," most of the fruit trees had become barren.

Chapter 14

The new year, according to the news reports in the U.S., was to be even less politically promising for the land of the Viets than the one just concluded. Nonetheless, a flurry of construction commenced at the market. Sergeant Bloom provided construction goods on credit, maintaining a methodical tally of the material granted and its value in communist booty. Next to, "nails - #12 / 5 lbs.," was the commentary, "posters, communist, 2 ea., color," and "lumber, 2X4 / 50 bd. ft., - bottle, wine, light green in color, uneven glass, 1 ea."

Ông Khai enlisted several of the older men to engineer a market roof from the 526th Engineers' largess. J.W. began the proceedings by demonstrating to the elders how one nailed several 2x4s together into lattice-work triangles for the suspension of a corrugated metal crown. The ancient men watched politely, a few even smiled, though when J.W. was done, they calmly pulled the awkward frames apart, tossed away the nails, and set about notching the lumber at the ends and mid-portions, fitting the pieces together as if a giant set of Lincoln Logs. Their tools were homemade blades of ill-cast steel and leftover war matériel lashed to mahogany handles. Some of the artifacts, though, had been passed from father to first-born son over the generations, and the men cradled them as if treasures. After several hours, the carpenters of My Co came to their feet, stretched, and stood back, nodding.

Ông Long was appointed to oversee the raising of the roof. He directed an army of women to dig six deep pits in the rock-hard earth surrounding the proposed market floor. Then the men stepped forward and, using locally-woven hemp rope, easily lifted tall poles of thick mahogany, maneuvering the fat ends into the holes. J.W. suggested concrete be poured into the cavities to stabilize the poles, but the men chattered back at him about not wasting precious cement.

The women reappeared to pour water into the holes and layer dirt and stones around the base of the logs. Another contingent appeared with heavy sticks and pounded the muck tight. Long took a couple of the nails and tapped them high into each log, one in the front and one ninety degrees away. He took a piece a string, tied a rock to the bottom, and had the men push the pole until the string ran down the very center of the log. The women broke into teams and took turns pounding madly. By the time J.W. finished his cigarette, the shaft was lodged plumb.

When *Ông* Long gave the collection of poles a final nod, he turned and wandered off without a word—the men left first then the women. J.W. stood alone. He shrugged and drifted toward *Bà* Binh's for a nap.

Casually, he asked the old lady, "Have you seen *Cô* Lin recently? She never talks to me anymore. I am sorry for the Americans. I really am sorry."

Bà Binh chuckled an answer, but J.W. did not understand and was too embarrassed to persist.

Late in the afternoon, he returned to find the roof magically in place and scores of women spreading rocks and large pieces of shards where Vu Van Khai had declared the floor was to be poured. The chief smiled and lit a Salem, speaking quietly of his plans for laying the concrete, sagely predicting that the grandest undertaking in the history of My Co would be accomplished within the next few days. "For sure, Captain, for sure."

The two men stood, enjoying the waning minutes of daylight before walking slowly back to Khai's house. *Bà* Khai had prepared a meal of rice, boiled leaves, and meat from a C-ration selection J.W. had contributed. Though the children curled their noses at the lumps of years, if not decades, old beef, *Ông* Khai picked at one particularly fatty chunk of meat with his chopsticks and thanked J.W. for the delicious treat.

⟿ ⟾

Each morning for the next week, J.W. arose early and waited for *Ông* Khai to outline the plans for the day, to look into the sky and dreamily paint the next rung in the grand construction opus, though the only mists of the future came from the steam coming off the coffee they sipped for an hour. There was never a mention of the market, for there were more pressing matters overshadowing the future of My Co.

Khai had been informed by a man on a motor scooter, a ranking provincial official, that the province chief had chosen two policemen to secure My Co from the Viet Cong. The man assured Khai that the two were totally committed to the ideals of the South Vietnamese cause, touting them as caring law enforcement officers who had proven their honesty and incorruptibility.

The men arrived the next morning, a cloud of red dust enveloping the Vespa scooter on which they screeched into town. An hour later, they called a wildcat strike, demanding a police station be constructed across the road from the market. They marked out in the dirt just where each of their desks would sit. They also decreed that they would be provided with private assistants, young women from the hamlet, who would fetch tea and *chả giò*.

Ông Long, recognized as *the* exclusive carpenter in My Co, was summoned. He arrived proudly, a woven grass bag of primordial tools slung over his shoulder. The chief asked J.W. to go along as security with a platoon of women to a section of town patrolled by a pack of mange-infected dogs. There, the ladies gathered three dozen wooden pallets upon which American munitions had been shipped to Viet Nam.

When they returned, J.W. asked *Ông* Khai, "Where'd you get these?"

"American truck. Fall off. I have more. And I have special box fall this morning. Tonight Lieuten and Khai open."

For the balance of the day, *Ông* Long worked silently on the police station with no breaks. *Em* Huong brought him tea, cigarettes, and a bevy of archaic tools. The new constabulary watched from the shade of the roofed market, though retired to the village restaurant for a meal and a couple of beers at noon, again during the mid-afternoon siesta, and for a final visit at dusk. The quiet left *Ông* Khai and J.W. time to investigate the box that had jiggled free from the 526th Engineers' truck convoy that morning.

Actually, it had been *Em* Huong who had found it. He often sat secreted in a bamboo thicket at the far end of town, waiting motionlessly early each morning as the procession of 5-ton cargo trucks headed to the 526th's headquarters in Tuyen

Binh passed through My Co. The gigantic pothole that reappeared daily was of Huong's doing, and just before dawn each morning, he dug it a trifle deeper and wider, generating an obstacle that caused the uncaringly-rigged trucks to bounce wildly. It was also a subterranean locker in which the droppings remained until the convoy was far out of town. He had dragged that morning's parcel into the bamboo, covered it with dead leaves, and darted back into My Co for *Ông* Khai and the chief's scooter.

Khai rolled the wooden crate out of his house, carefully protecting the surface that had been damaged by the fall from the truck. He gently pried free the shipping planks, saving the wood, which was potentially more precious than the contents. With the last strip of banding and pine peeled away, there sat in My Co a two-foot by two-foot by two-foot apparatus concealed beneath a neatly sewn black nylon cover. He called out to J.W., who had drifted off to stare across the road at *Cô* Lin. She had seen him first, and when J.W. felt her presence, their eyes met for a trice longer than ever before, but she turned away quickly and disappeared into her cousin's hootch.

"Captain, what is GE-S-TET-NAH?"

"A what?"

"GEH-TA-NAH. What is that?"

J.W. turned distractedly back to Mr. Khai, who was touching the golden letters embossed on the nylon. He came over to stand above the chief's shoulder. He laughed, "GESTETNER 260", mouthing the printed logo. "Wow! *Ông* Khai, why don't you pull off the cover. I think *Em* Huong found us a mimeograph machine." J.W. used the English word, and Khai screwed his face in question. "It makes copies of things you write. Copies, copies."

The chief's expression remained unchanged.

"The same sheet of paper over and over." J.W. tapped his left index finger on his forehead, closed his eyes, and raised his head to the heavens, concentrating as if faced with an Einsteinian conundrum. He shook his head, bent forward, and pulled the cover free. The burnished, gold-painted machine drew the breath from both men.

J.W. hissed, "Shit, this thing's got more movable parts than a HUEY. Have you ever seen one of these before, Mr. Khai?"

Khai, though, had not heard J.W., too busy tapping knobs and dials with his screwdriver.

J.W. sidled to the machine. He took two sheets of the newspaper that had been used as packing, placed one in the intake port of the copier, motioned turning the crank then pretended to pull the second sheet from the other side of the machine. Khai smiled and nodded knowingly.

J.W. laughed, "This thing's worth a thousand bucks. *This* is how you're going to move My Co into the Twentieth Century. Information, *Ông* Khai. It's the wave of the future."

"Captain," he asked, eyes glowing, "maybe you make copy this. Please show how to work." Khai handed J.W. a sheet of paper from his village census book.

"Ah, see, we can't do that yet. We need a bunch of things—paper and ink and stencils and a stylus. Still, this is the hottest thing in My Co since sliced bread. Do you know what you've found? Just don't tell anyone where you got it."

"When we get things? I go tomorrow. You go?" Khai laughed, his excitement building.

"Okay, we can get some supplies, but what about the market, *Ông* Khai?" J.W. asked, his voice with a bit of an edge.

"Captain, please no worry. There much time. Finish before long. And where we go get bunch of thing for machine?"

J.W.'s first thought was a quick ride up to see Sergeant Bloom, but even Bloom could not countenance the outright theft of a mimeograph machine. "We can try Saigon. How about it? Shoot, I'll buy the stuff myself. How much could it be?"

Chapter 15

Ông Khai roused J.W. before the roosters woke. As the first shafts of light crept over the eastern paddies, the two men unhitched the trailer and threw paper sacks with a change of clothes, a toothbrush, and a razor into the rear seat.

At noon, they reached Saigon. At the main gate of the American compound, they sat through negotiations with the private on guard duty, his sergeant, the platoon leader, the company commander, and eventually the battalion XO. When the barrier lifted, they drove past movie theaters, massage parlors, and PXs, coming finally to a building with a traditional Chinese edifice and a hand-painted sign in red letters proclaiming the grand opening of the China Enjoyable Food Wine House.

J.W. offered, "Let's eat here. My treat."

They parked along the already-moldy, unpainted, cinderblock side. J.W. removed the distributor cap from the engine, placed it in his paper sack overnight luggage, and carried the filthy bag into the restaurant to the stares of both diners and the tuxedoed Chinese maître-d'. His nostrils flared and his eyes squinted at the scent and sight of the grime-and-road-dust coated mendicants. He directed them with nose raised toward the men's room.

As they stepped up to the pastel blue sinks, J.W. assessed the temperature of the crystal-clear water with two fingers. The chief momentarily blinked at the mud-free stream and then at the throttle-like faucet handle. J.W. eyed it as well, remembering seeing one at the Waldorf Astoria in New York the night he and Krista spent their last hours together. *Ông* Khai surreptitiously scrutinized Weathersby's manipulation of the lever and was soon testing his own flow with two fingers. J.W. pushed on the wall-mounted soap dispenser. By the time the first drops of viscous green detergent hit his palm, *Ông* Khai's hands were already lathered. At the electric hand dryers, J.W. and the chief finished neck and neck.

It was already 4 P.M., far too late to conduct business, so they drove at a leisurely pace around the capital, enjoying the fume-filtered sunset over the Saigon River. A military police sedan pulled up behind them. The two patrolmen stared suspiciously before the driver rolled his window down, grimaced at the blast of exhaust-tainted sizzling air that swept into the vehicle, and called out, "Hey, troop, come 'ere."

When the MP saw it was an officer, he slapped the hand of his mate, who dropped his cigarette and crushed it on the floor of the patrol car.

J.W. walked to the sedan. "What can I do for you, Sergeant?"

"Just checkin', sir. You know you can't be having gooks in your vehicle unless they're military."

"He's a village chief," J.W. answered politely, smiling at the REMF, the rear-echelon-mother-fucker, pale-faced military cop. "A veritable Vietnamese luminary. And don't call him a gook."

"Sorry, sir, I'll need to see some papers."

J.W. reached into his pocket to produce the well-worn letter from General Abrams, but a wisp of smoke from the cannabis wafted out the window of the air-conditioned patrol cruiser. "Sergeant, I want to see your military ID. I'm placing you and your pal under arrest for the use of an illegal drug. Step out of the car, both of you."

J.W. had to jump back when the cop dropped the sedan into drive and peeled out. As J.W. screamed for them to stop, he pretended, using his finger, for he had no pen, to record the medallion number on the back of General Abrams' letter.

J.W. laughed, but *Ông* Khai's face was tense as they drove into Cho Lon, the teeming Chinese district of Saigon. They stopped at a hotel *Ông* Khai promised was very inexpensive. He was right. They were assigned to a room with three other Vietnamese men and a very dark man, who immediately informed them he was a prince from the island of Mindanao, the most southerly tip of the Philippines. He growled for hours about the downturn in business in his home city of Zamboanga, and how expensive it had become traveling Asia to hawk life insurance to Philippine expatriates. He fell asleep protesting his lot in life then spent the night snoring powerfully, in resonance with the hacking of a tubercular guest who shared the room.

Through the rice paper-thin walls, J.W. listened to the voices of men speaking in whispers, sure he heard them plotting to seize him right under the noses of the American high command. Their occasional drunken laughter and the constant howling of curs in the street added to the cacophonous night, and at 3 A.M., *Ông* Khai lifted his head and asked J.W., "Are you still awake, Captain? I am sorry for the uncomfortable hotel."

In the heart of Saigon, on Tu Do Street, they found the black market stalls. J.W. bought stencils, ink, paper, and even an instruction book, but for a different brand of mimeograph machine. Though it was in German, the chief studied it page by page, nodding as he understood the pictures. They ate at a street restaurant. *Ông* Khai chose chopsticks for J.W. from a stack in a tin can on the table, dipping the ends in his cup of lukewarm tea before handing them over. The chief ordered noodles and roast goose for both of them.

J.W. beamed. "This is the most delicious meal I have ever had. Better than the Chinese restaurant in Long Binh. You know what, *Ông* Khai, I'm kinda beginning to like it here in Viet Nam."

When the waiter came to clear the table, J.W. asked him to wrap up the leftovers, "For my dog at home," but the waiter rolled his eyes, wiped the chopsticks on his grimy pants, placed both sets back in the tin can, and walked off with the scraps from both bowls, dropping them into a pot of barely simmering stock.

J.W. stopped for a moment at a jewelry shop, "Cheap Charlie's," as they wheeled through Bien Hoa on their way back to My Co. He chose a pair of tiny gold earrings. "These are for my wife," he proclaimed boldly to the chief, though Khai's nod back was as shallow as J.W.'s lie.

On the road, J.W. stopped in My Tho to see the supply sergeant at the 33rd Mech's logistics quonset. He requisitioned a compact, five-hundred watt Honda generator, like the ones he had seen in the black-market shops of Saigon. He concocted a story for the supply sergeant that he needed it to fill out intelligence reports at night, but J.W. really dreamed it would someday power the television that had fallen off the Engineers' trucks a few weeks before. He planned with the chief to build a heavy wooden case at the budding market in which they would lock and chain the TV during the day, but at night tune it to American Westerns playing on the GI stations. The evening entertainment at the market would bring even more prosperity to the village, and J.W. could imagine a day when My Co would grow, after the war, into a destination, with a hotel or two sprouting on the grounds of the NDP.

J.W. also liberated, when the supply sergeant walked out, a spool of wire. In the latrine, he unscrewed two sixty-watt light bulbs and wrapped them in his dirty fatigues from the day before. He threw the bundle nonchalantly into the back of the jeep, but when he tossed in two six-packs of 33 Beer that were sitting forlornly on the steps of the NCO club, one of the light bulbs was crushed.

On the five-hour, forty-mile journey back to My Co, J.W. noticed the temperature gauge begin a slow, but relentless, climb, creeping into the red miles after they had bumped through Moc Hoa. At first, he passed it off as a result of the increasing wrath of the afternoon sun, whose rays blistered the countryside more furiously as winter wore on. But the needle was soon pinned at the far end of the red, and the scent of very hot metal blew into the vehicle.

J.W. pushed on, driving even faster, but *Ông* Khai convinced him to stop and investigate. The radiator was bone dry. While J.W. spit on the ground and cursed his luck, *Ông* Khai took J.W.'s steel helmet and walked off to search for a stream. As the chief entered the wooded area, three 526th Engineers' helicopters passed over, skimming the ground. One of the gunners spotted the chief, and the ships turned on him, the crew excitedly charging their machine guns. J.W. waved them off, pointing to the chief and then to himself, gesticulating and screaming, "He's with me, goddamnit."

Two of the ships tipped left and right to let J.W. know they had seen him and understood, but the third made a run directly at Khai, though veered at the last second, turned hard right, and fired an endless burst of M-60 machine gun fire at the feet of a herd of terrified water buffalo. The animals sprinted madly into the paddies—one tumbled head first into a well.

The three aircraft rejoined and sped north toward Tuyen Binh. *Ông* Khai came out of hiding and filled the radiator. After several trips back and forth fetching stream water, they restarted west toward My Co, but in five miles, the radiator ran dry again. The chief made his way to a rivulet that was more sand than water, and they spent an hour filtering the sludge through J.W.'s tee shirt. They limped into My Co at dusk.

Bà Khai ran to her husband, eyes reddened, tears glistening on her cheeks. As she drew a deep breath to speak, *Ông* Khai's face hardened and drained of all color. He turned away from her and looked about, passionately counting his children. *Bà* Khai's lips now tightened with rage, and she coughed between each word, explaining that three American helicopters had overflown the village hours before, dropping tear gas grenades and shooting at cattle. Only one water buffalo was dead, but they had destroyed the cement cache at the marketplace with machine gun fire then hovered over the open bags, blowing the cement into an atomic cloud.

She sobbed she'd actually seen the door gunners' faces. "They were laughing."

The chief quietly explained the raid to J.W., who furiously started off for Tuyen Binh, ignoring the chief's calls to wait until morning. Khai needn't have worried. The jeep was out of water in minutes, and J.W. had to ask the villagers to push him the half-mile back into My Co. He worked on the vehicle in the darkness, apologizing to the chief that the Gestetner mimeograph machine would have to sit fallow for another day. An hour later, with just the dying embers of his GI flashlight to guide him, he found the leak, just a loose petcock, and readied the jeep for the trip to Tuyen Binh at sunrise.

The engineer brigade's commanding officer listened politely and sent J.W. to see the S-3, the division operations officer, who sent J.W. to see the helicopter company CO, who denied that his ships had been operating in the area the previous day. "Sir, I saw them with my own eyes. You might notice, sir, the wings embroidered on my fatigues."

"Pilot or not, you're wrong, Captain. But I'll tell you what I'm going to do to help. We'll get you some cement. We'll even fly it down there. How's that? I mean, if they were my ships, you have to admit that they stopped shooting at your friend the very second they realized who he was. That was decent of them, don't you think? They're really a pretty good bunch of guys."

"Sir, I'm sure they're just the best great," J.W. mocked, "but they're twenty-two, and they're half-a-world away from home, and they went through a hell of a lot to get their wings, and," J.W. paused, "they're twenty-two, sir."

"And how old are you, old man?"

"About to turn twenty-four, sir."

Two mornings later, several 526th Engineers choppers hovered over the market site and dumped several dozen bags of concrete next to the police station across the road from the market. The bags burst open, but Vu Van Khai mobilized the hamlet's womenfolk, by driving hurriedly between huts, announcing on his megaphone that the moment had come to pour the floor. A slow-moving conga line of grumbling young women snaked its way to the jobsite. Several dozen ladies swept the blowing cement into piles, others loaded reed baskets with bits of red tile, and the larger women, those over five feet, dug a bow-shaped hole in the cast-iron earth to mix the concrete.

Khai motored up the road, one hand on the scooter handlebars, the other holding his megaphone. The batteries went dead just a hundred yards from the market, and J.W. had to run to his bunker and pull the new batteries from his flashlight. It took forever to organize the streams of villagers who closed on the market carting water in bottles, old ammo cans, and wash basins. Even *Ông* Dinh Dau, the village idiot, brought half a glass of water. *Ông* Khai thanked him with his subtle bow and added the water to the slurry. By dusk, the site had a soupy, forty-foot by thirty-foot, four-inch-thick, mortar-proof deck.

With the darkness, J.W. walked alone to the embryonic market. He stopped in the bare moonlight to smoke a Salem and consider the future of the structure and of his own life. This was the first time he had ever experienced what had been simply an image, a fantasy in a man's brain, actually mature into a tangible entity. It dawned on him that all of history's endeavors—automobiles, jet planes, the wheel, every book, radio, the Pyramids, every atrocity in every battle in every war, every single accomplishment, positive or destructive—grew out of a single notion, a few immeasurably weak electrical impulses weaving through some fallible human's vision. He paused to consider that sobering notion but soon laughed at his philosophical interlude as he stole around to the northeast corner, looked around, and placed his left palm and fingers deep into the soft concrete.

Chapter 16

THE MARKET WAS now a floor and a roof, and that was where the work ceased. Provincial Governor Nguyen flew in on his personal American helicopter with his new personal American pilot, an American Army major. The ship blew the roof off a hootch that had just been rebuilt. Nguyen, his face and belly a gradation or two fuller than during the last visit, sent a child to summon Khai.

J.W. pretended not to listen as the governor spoke. "The bastard Americans have decided to let these bumpkins vote. Drop everything and teach them about democracy, but not too much. The election is this Thursday. I don't care who they elect to be Village Chief, just make sure it's you."

The man spun around, snarled at J.W., brushed past him, and hopped aboard his ship. Another roof succumbed.

Ông Khai stood motionless, staring at the cloud of refractive crystals settling back onto the hamlet amid the flurry of straw. He turned to J.W. "An election by Thursday? How do we do that in three days? My school showed us how to teach democracy, but not overnight."

J.W. screwed up his face. "*Ông* Khai, just make it a simple vote, two or three names. And you stand up in front of them and say, 'Ladies and gentlemen, please put a mark next to the name you think will do the best job to help My Co.'"

"Captain, they can't read. We need to assign a little picture to each man, a water buffalo, a chicken, or maybe a house. But still, they've never heard of such a thing. We need to get the old men of the council together and teach them how to teach the people how to use a pencil."

That night, the skeleton of the new market transformed into My Co's Faneuil Hall. Khai stood before the men who squatted on the still damp concrete, most of them ignoring the benches and chairs. "Esteemed elders of My Co, we will have an election in three days. Each man will say who *he* wants to help My Co in these trying times. There will be five men on the ballot. Three of those men will be chosen to make the rules for My Co."

Ông Sanh called out, "And what does 'ballot' mean? You Northerners, I can't understand a word you say. Sounds like you have six *chả giò* in your mouth."

He laughed pompously until *Ông* Long snapped, "Sanh, you buffalo's behind, a ballot is a piece of paper with the names of the good men of My Co on it. And let the man talk."

Sanh called back, "I'm a good man, and I don't want my name on anything. It's just a way for the bastards to steal more tax from me."

Khai raised his hand unobtrusively, and when the grousing ceased, he dissected the process in terms so simple, even J.W. was able to follow the Vietnamese. Some of the men nodded when he asked if they understood, but *Ông* Dao stood and spoke slowly. "So, you say if we elect Long, here, for instance, and he says the government can't collect taxes anymore, we can tell the collectors to go to hell? I like that."

"Not exactly. Some rules will be made here, some in Saigon."

A withered voice called from the back, "So, we don't make the rules then."

"You will make some," Khai added with a smile. "You will tell the governor and the president what you think is right and wrong, and they will have to listen to you. If more than half the people want it one way, it doesn't matter what the people in Saigon want."

Another gentleman called out from his hunker. "I already make some of the rules. In my house, I am the master. No one tells me how to run the family. In the province, there is the governor. He is the master of everyone in his house, and his house is the province. I do not tell him what to do in the province, and he doesn't tell me what to do in my house. And the emperor in Hue is the master in his house, which is all the world, and no one tells him anything. And why? It's because he is not one of us, even if he looks like a man. He is from heaven, and that's where he gets his power. A good emperor lets a little of his power leak down through the governor to me. Now, you're saying we can tell the governor *and* the emperor how to run their house? Next thing you know, my kids'll be voting and making rules for me. That's not what Confucius taught us. You can't have harmony unless everyone under you obeys and doesn't ask questions. That is the only way life can be organized, the only way there can be an ordered society. If we challenge that scheme, the first thing Heaven will do is stop the rain, and we will all starve. There's no need to change things."

There were more grumbles, all praising the traditional wisdom of the last speaker, so Khai looked at his watch and nodded as if in agreement. "Gentlemen, it is late. You are very smart men. You are good Vietnamese men, good Confucian scholars. You are smarter than the farmers in the villages around here. We will talk again in the morning. No matter, the governor has decreed that we must have an election on Thursday. Please think about who *you* think has the most sense."

J.W. walked home with *Ông* Khai. He laughed cynically, "Yeah, emperor, son of Heaven and all that, but the village council isn't all that excited about sharing graft with their exalted governor, are they? System's not so foolproof."

Khai stopped and thought for a second. "Captain, I must speak in Vietnamese." He went on slowly. "The answer to your question is yes and no. Captain. You see, in Viet Nam for many thousands of years, the spirit of the kitchen, the spirit of the buffalo pen, and the ancestors determine a man's life fortune. It has nothing to do with what he wants, or how hard he works. There is no such thing as a man's *right* to take a share—a man doesn't have *rights*. There is no such thing. He has a *fate* which comes from heaven. It cannot be changed. And if you become greedy and take more than what you know very well fate gave you, you will be punished by your superiors, perhaps in the here and now, but surely after you die. Your family, and everyone else, will know that you are a terrible ancestor. That means shame and poverty for your lineage. What could be worse?"

J.W. smiled thinly. "But you can always say the 'spirits' made me do it. You had no control."

"No, Captain. Every man knows when he is defying his place in the design. If you become the governor of the province, it is because fate smiled and put you there, and along with the smile comes tribute money from district chiefs, and they get their tribute from the village councils. It goes on and on. It isn't wrong that they take money. It is heaven's will. That is what these people believe. Every man's superior must remain in control so that harmony is maintained. As long as he uses the graft to maintain harmony, all is well.

"The day to day happenings are the sole decision of capricious spirits. And no one has been able to figure out how they work, so the only thing you can do is worship them and hope for the best. On the other hand, there has to be some way to control the spirits. That is why we had an emperor whose authority came from even higher than the ghosts. It is not that much different from our Christianity. God and the devil, good and bad, the constant struggle. It goes on and on. Think of our Jesus, Captain. Even *he* is not strong enough to control evil. That is why there are jails, and also why we seek grace."

He looked into J.W.'s eyes. "You want to ask if I take graft."

"Well, I guess I really didn't understand, and..."

"No, Captain, I do not. You see, that is the old Viet Nam. That thinking is why we are in a civil war, why my country is burning. I believe in work, a future that you can earn. I also believe no man is better than the next, that is until he doesn't control his greed, or, worse, harms the innocent. Then he must be stopped. I am sorry to say there are times when I cannot make myself turn the other cheek. It is what my father taught me. He learned it in Europe. I am sure he is right, even if he and I are not perfect Christians. So, if I steal from these people, I am dishonoring him. That much ancestor worship still burns inside me."

The next morning, Khai was up with the sun, talking to the villagers. J.W. tagged along for a few hours, but he understood nothing of the conversations, and it seemed his only function was to provide Salems for the old men. When the smokes were depleted, he drifted off to spend the sweltering afternoon with *Bà* Binh, to rest on the hardwood bed and read his classics. *Cô* Lin did not appear, and he finally screwed up his courage and took from his pocket the earrings he had brought to the hamlet, placing the tiny silk box on the austere table.

Bà Binh rose from her hammock and exclaimed, "They're beautiful. Ah, they are for *Cô* Lin! It's too bad she isn't here now. Sometimes she teaches in another village. It is very far away. That is because My Co has no schoolhouse. Why don't you build one here?"

J.W. was frightened by the transparency of his stratagem and laughed, "No, no, they're for you."

The old lady screwed up her face. "Well, I think you should give them to *Cô* Lin. They would look much better on her. Take them off the table and put them in your pocket. Go on, do as I say."

At *Ông* Khai's that evening, several of the village's not-yet-drafted, early teenagers, were gathered around the mimeograph machine studying the wheels and gears, making assembly suggestions to the chief. Khai looked up at J.W. and nodded in excitement as he placed a stencil on the inked drum and smoothed away the air bubbles. It was as he had deduced from the German language instruction pamphlet back in Saigon. He placed a ream of mildewed paper in the feeder and asked the captain to perform the first crank. J.W. turned so enthusiastically, three sheets pulled through and jammed deep within the machine's bowels. *Ông* Khai studied the feeder tray, opened a panel, reached in, cleared the clammy shreds, reset the parameters, and directed J.W. to step up once again.

J.W. wound the crank a few degrees and very gently. "Harder, Captain!"

A single sheet sucked through, though the gurgles and spitting worried J.W., and he stopped, the page again lost again in the depths. A little boy in wisps of clothing made a cranking motion, the other boys yelled their concurrence, and Khai nodded. A faintly printed sheet of limp paper crept out the back end and slumped to the ground. The children fluttered around it in circles, dancing and laughing. *Em* Huong lifted it reverently from the ground and handed it to *Ông* Khai. He studied the print. J.W. looked over his shoulder and saw several of the older villagers' names; next to each was a star, a rice plant, a water buffalo, or a two-wheeled ox cart.

Khai waved his finger at Huong, who turned the crank and produced a few more ballots, each one darker and crisper than the last. J.W. took one, printed his name on the bottom, drew a round face with a handlebar mustache, and handed it back to *Ông* Khai. The children howled, but *Ông* Khai was curiously silent and serious. As the chief's demeanor hardened, the kids swallowed their giggles, until one called out in Vietnamese, "I'm going to vote for *Đại Úy Rào*."

J.W. asked *Ông* Khai what that meant, and Khai spoke, tempering his answer with an uncomfortable smile, "It means Captain Iron Mustache."

J.W. turned in embarrassment for having cost the chief face. He saw *Cô* Lin looking on from a distance, and his chest tightened, but he turned back to Khai, apologized, and spun the crank until the chief lifted his palm. Khai wrapped the ballots in a scrap of cloth, as if a swaddling an infant, and carried them carefully into his house.

J.W. took the respite to walk over to *Cô* Lin, who, while she did not take a step toward him, also did not take her usual few steps backwards. His hand jammed reflexively into the pocket that held the red silk jewelry box. He cared not who saw. He pushed the box forward and spoke softly, "For you."

She opened it and gasped, her eyes sparkling with a glint he hadn't seen in them before, but her spine straightened, and she spoke resolutely. "I cannot. I am too ugly. I am not worthy of such a thing. You must take them back."

J.W. laughed for a moment and turned to walk off, leaving the gift in her hands. "No," J.W. called back over his shoulder, "it is I who is not worthy to present them to you."

J.W. returned to *Ông* Khai's house to sit with the chief and his wife, both of whom were resting outside with glasses of cool tea. *Bà* Khai poured J.W. one and looked out toward *Bà* Binh's, saw *Cô* Lin watching J.W., and motioned her over. She came but drank only a sip then excused herself, saying that she had to go help her grandmother. J.W. offered *Ông* Khai a Salem, and together they watched *Cô* Lin walk delicately toward *Bà* Binh's hut. When she was out of earshot, Khai became very serious and whispered his warning again: "You must be cautious, Captain. In Viet Nam, nothing what it seem."

The election took place on Thursday at the market site. The men showed up in their Sunday best, kibitzing for an hour before moving en masse, pushing and shoving to get to the voting table first. *Ông* Khai, though, had to slog from house to house to convince the women that they were included in the process. It took endless cajoling and finally pleading, and in the end, only a handful of the ladies appeared, and those who did refused to look at the ballot. Having not been given the class on how to use a pencil, they shut their eyes tightly and pointed in the general direction of the paper. The election officials Khai had paid a kilo of rice to maintain order placed a mark next to the picture that seemed closest to where the women had aimed index fingers.

Despite the threats from the VC to level My Co before sunset if even a single villager dared vote, that night only a few families were erased from the face of the Earth by Viet Cong mortar rounds. The last of the shells buried itself deep in the mud at the front of the market, steaming and hissing menacingly for a few minutes until it cooled and was designated a dud, to be dealt with the next day. When all was quiet at midnight, the hamlet asleep, the device detonated, clearing a perfect hole for the new flagpole.

The next morning, after Khai massaged the council members with another kilo or two of rice, the ballot count got underway. By late afternoon, the three-hundred papers were counted. He was declared winner. After several speeches desperately straining to explain what "winner" meant, Khai mused to J.W that it was probably because he had gone from house to house promising prosperity, while the other candidates had tramped out into the fields each day from dawn to dusk, working desperately to find enough grain to bring to their families for dinner.

The other two men, who were to be his council, squatted next to him that evening as Khai stood on a mound of dirt outside the market and delivered another speech, this one thanking the people for their confidence. The majority of the villagers either stared blankly or shrugged. He turned to welcome the arrival of a company of Provincial Regional Force-Popular Force, the RF/PF, "Rough Puffs," Vietnamese citizen-soldiers sent by the provincial governor to secure My Co on Election Day. He did not mention that the troops had not arrived until the morning after the sowing of the first seeds of democracy, long after the smoke from the Viet Cong mortar attack had drifted out toward the browning forest.

Ông Khai, nevertheless, touted the spirit and bravery of the early adolescents, the soldiers of the district army who had been granted uniforms and outdated U.S. rifles. Khai promised the villagers that soon those very troops would be stationed permanently in My Co to protect them. It was a powerful concept:

armed local men, trained by the all-powerful American Army, serving in their own provinces and districts, protecting peasants from the maddened old men holed up in Hanoi, a thousand miles to the north.

The RF/PF, though, moved slowly through Kien Tuong Province toward their assigned villages, the less than three cents a day they were granted obliging them to drag wives and children along through the countryside, scrounging food, uniforms, pots and pans, and even furniture from the destitute peasants. They hauled all of it along on benign troop movements, and occasionally into battle, eventually settling into assigned hamlets, their officers bribing the local elders for patches of unwanted land to pitch the tiny military tents in which they would live until the end of the war.

J.W. asked Mr. Khai how they could live on so little. The chief rubbed his fingers together and spoke in English to avoid the nosy old men poking around them. "Captain, general in Saigon and politic man take what American give. Soldier here soon die, so no need money.

"RF/PF. American say come live to My Co. Will love village, fight until die. But no one at home village to guard mother. They never see ancestor grave again. Maybe way in America to protect stranger mother but not his mother."

When the RF/PF's meager food rations ran out, the displaced men often turned to the villagers for supplies, whether the villagers were willing providers or not. And if the citizens of the hamlets under Rough Puff influence did provide stores, willingly or not, the communist Viet Cong visited those very civilians in the middle of the night, suggesting that support of South Vietnamese government troops, of any ilk, was contrary to their longevity. To punctuate their message, the Viet Cong went first to the families that had been *forced* to provide supplies, tore them from their hardwood sleeping pallets, dragged them out the front door of their mud and woven-weed hovels, slammed them to the ground with the butts of AK-47s then riddled a family member or two with bullets from the other end of their guns. J.W. often wondered if his anti-war, fraternity brothers at Sterling College, the ones who had plastered the frat house walls with portraits of Ho Chi Minh, ever read his letters.

⟝⟞

With the raising of the flagpole two days later, life drifted back to normal in My Co. The forty-foot, creosoted telephone pole, that would be become the highest point in the history of the hamlet, had rolled from a 526th Engineers' eighteen-wheeler the day before. *Em* Huong, in his warren, was so excited, he jumped out of the bamboo as the pole rotated off the truck. The driver, however, jammed the brakes, and Huong was caught in the open. One of the passengers saw him, smiled, and threw a Hershey Bar. Huong pasted a false smile on his face and bowed several times to the man.

He started back into hamlet, resigned that he had lost the prize, but the soldiers in a following truck yelled at the driver, "Fuck that piece of wooden shit. Fuck it. Move the fuck on!"

Huong sprinted into the hamlet and corralled *Ông* Khai, telling him that there was a "fuck" on the road, and that they needed a rope to drag the fuck back. Khai towed the pole back into My Co behind his mini bike, one surface of the shaft ground flat.

That afternoon, the village elders gathered about the hole at the market left by the VC mortar round. They tied several hemp ropes to the top and began the haul and heave. When the post neared vertical, J.W. beamed, and the men returned genuine smiles. It had been worth coming to Viet Nam.

Em Huong gave J.W. a thumbs up and yelled, "Fuck!" as he pointed to the pole.

They say that in the sciences, fully fifty percent of what one learns in college is obsolete within five years of graduation. While it wasn't quite five since J.W. had walked with his class, the laws of physics he was about to revisit were not amongst those that had been superseded. The men of the hamlet, however, had apparently slept through the course on force vectors, for though the pole was quite erect, it was not yet perfectly perpendicular to the sands of My Co. Considering it to be close enough, several of the men could no longer contain their delight over the phallic talisman, and they laughed heartily, pointing animatedly to their own genitals, several with both hands. Consumed with the fantasy of ever again achieving an erection, several more let go, and J.W. dashed forward, grabbed three unmanned ropes, and pulled wildly, managing to pivot the shaft until it stopped rotating, finally locking on its flattened surface. There it teetered for a second, and J.W. breathed in relief, but the pole promptly skidded out of the hole and fell to the earth, whacking him a glancing blow on the head. When the half-ton stick took its final bounce, it cracked along its length.

J.W. danced in pain, cursing in English, blaring at the old men who were still smiling at him, and now, seemingly to placate the mad foreigner, pointing at his genitalia and then at the pole upon which little eddies of red dust were settling.

The blow must have shaken from J.W. his cultural intellect, for he knew better, or should have, by this point in his sojourn in My Co, to think these men would harm him by causing him to lose face. That much respect J.W. Weathersby had culled from the villagers for the *cajones* he'd shown to live alone amongst them.

In fact, these decent men were smiling as an acknowledgement of embarrassment and error, not in satisfaction or humor. That particular form of Asian practice, to smile gently when embarrassed, and to laugh when mortified, was a fine point he had forgotten a half-year after coming to the village.

For having blown his stack in public, J.W. did lose face, and several of the men drifted away from the barbaric spectacle of the foreign devil stomping around like a wounded ox. J.W., becoming even more furious at the elders for abandoning him without so much as a crack at an apology, raised a perfect bird and stormed toward *Bà* Binh's. He tried to nap, but he couldn't keep his eyes closed and soon doubled back to the market to ask for forgiveness from the chief, the only one left on the job site. He bade *Ông* Khai apologize to the men for his conduct. Though the chief obliged with a dispassionate nod, it meant he would soon become umbilically involved in the incident. That was certain to cost him face—and J.W. even deeper humiliation for involving a dear friend. The chief was forced, as a last resort, to call a moratorium on the construction work, lest the market be forever tainted.

And that was just as well, for J.W. was scheduled to fly away on R&R, rest and relaxation, the next day. He left Viet Nam for Hawaii, to spend a week on Waikiki Beach with his wife. *Cô* Lin was standing at the door of *Bà* Binh's when he arrived to say good-by, and as he approached, he was excited, and guilty, to see the earrings he had presented her reflecting in the fierce sun. She went into the hut and prepared tea. J.W. stood there for a moment, convincing himself it was better that nothing had happened between them.

Chapter 17

J.W. RETURNED FROM R&R a week-and-a-half later, shaking more violently than did the HUEY as the aircraft began its descent into the village, back into the war zone, where he was scheduled to spend four more months. The ten days away from My Co, seven in Honolulu and three in Saigon, had spoiled him. His first night in Hawaii, he got up several times, not to use the toilet, but just to flush it and watch the water swirl. Yet, it wasn't so much the lack of creature comforts in the Vietnamese countryside that tore at him; it was returning to a daily life that made no sense or progress, just an existence in which there remained much time to forfeit his life.

As the ship settled into My Co, it sucked a scraggy rooster through the main rotor. J.W.'s shoulders drooped when he caught the stick-like figures of *Bà* Huong and *Bà* Vu flying out of their hootches to confront the chopper, brooms thrashing. With the burst of sand and grated chicken gushing into the helicopter, J.W.'s head dropped, longing already for a toilet and a source of clean water to wash himself of the next months.

But he also realized that his personal desires and needs made not a fig's difference anywhere on Earth, and most particularly not in the hamlet of My Co. He laughed cynically that if he were killed, not a single soul in the village, or anywhere else, would run about screaming and shaking brooms menacingly at the killers. He was more expendable than the local poultry, and the flood of depression that blanketed him was so intense, it dwarfed what he had suffered during his capture months before. As he jumped off the hovering ship, all hope was lugged from his heart.

He dragged his things into the abandoned NDP, removed the sandbags blocking the entrance to his underground bunker, shook the dust from his cot, and lay down for a nap. Though he promised himself he would rest for just a bit then go back into the hamlet and catch up, his respite from the village proper lasted through the evening, the next day, and into the next night, despite the children playing and calling to him from outside his self-imposed cell. *Ông* Khai stopped by on the second evening to welcome him back, but J.W. pretended he was asleep.

After two-and-a-half days, with his stash of C-rations and cigarettes nearly exhausted, J.W. emerged from the bunker and walked perfunctorily into the village for a closer look at the market. In the hiatus, little had been accomplished. The chief and several old men were patching the roof where a mortar round had pierced the metal.

Ông Khai scrambled down the ladder and ran to J.W. to shake hands and zealously draw blueprints in the sand for the next step in the construction. He pulled the tarp back to expose gallons of red and yellow paint, the colors of the Vietnamese flag that Sergeant Bloom had delivered to coat the pallet wood of both the market and the tiny police station. He pulled J.W. by the sleeve to a grand pile of new pallets in a field across from the market.

He smiled excitedly, "This will be the site of the village schoolhouse. We have hired a teacher. You will be very happy with the choice."

J.W. gulped. So *Ông* Khai had hired *Cô* Lin simply to please him. Had his attention to *Cô* Lin been that apparent? He blushed as *Ông* Khai invited J.W. to a nearby hut to discuss the new school.

"Captain, I would like introduce *Ông* Tay, our new teacher."

An old man with a wiry white beard looked up from an antique tome, exhaled a sharp snort, and let his eyes settle back down on the page with such exaggeration, J.W.'s eyes were drawn to the book. The page was covered in Chinese characters.

Ông Khai bowed very slightly and nodded reassuringly to J.W. The chief lifted his upturned palm toward Weathersby, who stuttered, "Oh, yeah, ah, we welcome you to My Co. It is an honor to meet you, sir."

When the gnarled creature looked up impatiently, Khai stood straight and spoke in very slow, basic Vietnamese to insure J.W.'s comprehension. "It was the province council and governor, *himself*, who appointed *Ông* Tay. He has many years' experience as a scholar, *and* he has the official Kien Tuong Province stamp on his license."

When J.W. did not comment, Khai went on. "*Cô* Lin is a good teacher, but she charges too much to tutor our children. What she does with money is another question. We plan to educate the children of My Co for a very small amount of money. And, by the way, she does not have the red seal from the provincial government on her teaching papers."

With that, Professor Tay stood and snapped together the heels of his flip flops as he presented his credential, a ratty slip of rice paper upon which were typed a few official looking paragraphs in Vietnamese. At the bottom was a silver-dollar-sized, vermilion imprint, the ancient mark certifying government, and by extension, heavenly, authority in Asia.

"And Professor Tay speaks French!" *Ông* Khai added with a bit of an audible flourish.

After another click of the heels, *Ông* Tay asked, "*Monsieur, parlez-vous Français?*"

J.W. shook his head negatively. "No, but I've learned to speak a little Vietnamese."

Ông Tay turned away, eyes rolling, a puff of studied Parisian air hissing through his lips. He busied himself unpacking well-worn paper bags stuffed with French-titled books. J.W. pondered the value French might have in the new Viet Nam. It was a dead language aside from France, a small portion of Canada, Haiti, and a few destitute African countries. As it was, few of My Co's farmers spoke their own language on anything more than the most fundamental level. Perhaps a handful could read.

J.W. wondered why anyone would want to speak French, the language of the imperialists who had decimated the fabric of Vietnamese society. This man had been tainted by the French invaders; he was a turncoat, a *collaborateur*, lucky his life had been spared in the post-war spasm of violent retribution against the European colonialists in the 50s.

There was little doubt the man would treat the villagers with a condescension deeper even than the French administrators who had ruled the country for over a hundred years. On the other hand, he would happily teach for a month or two, accepting the salary the provincial government paid. And then it would start—under-the-table tuition to keep kids in his school. It was a time-honored scheme for separating the peasants from the little they possessed.

Ông Tay would address the populace using important sounding words, perhaps throwing in a bit of French, all of it calculated to bully the villagers into believing that a third-grade education, for that was the highest level the old man had attained, would equip their kids to become doctors and successful businessmen, allowing escape from My Co.

The villagers would, eventually, not be able to come up with the ever-increasing tuition, and their anger would build, especially when they realized that the American propped and financed South Vietnamese government's promise of universal opportunity was as hollow as the Viet Cong's promise of a socialist utopia.

Then what? J.W. would have no choice but to save face in front of the villagers and go to the provincial governor to demand money for collective tuition, threatening the political loss of My Co if the government didn't pony up funds to fulfill their pledge to educate all the kids.

The governor, having been confronted by a twenty-three-year-old foreign devil junior officer, would file a formal complaint with the president of Viet Nam, who would manipulate and pervert the process to gain face and power by using the incident as an excuse for contacting President Richard Nixon, who would order the State Department to make it right, a euphemism for shipping over even more monetary reparations.

There would follow a demand for J.W.'s commanding officer to issue a formal apology on behalf of his errant underling. The loose-cannon captain would be disciplined for having lost control of the peasants he had been dispatched to manage, and for fomenting an international episode. And this would end badly, as had the overwhelming majority of emergent situations in which J.W. had found himself embroiled since joining the army.

The new teacher ignored J.W. and continued pulling books from paper bags, a dozen titled in Vietnamese, and finally a few in Chinese, which the old man made sure to place on the top of the pile. The latter of these works sparked an ember in J.W. He spoke gently with the old man, "Sir, I see you read Chinese! You must be a grand scholar." J.W. searched his mind, digging into its deepest recesses, scratching to cull forth the few words of Chinese he had learned in a primer course at Sterling College. He had found himself explaining a "D" in that class to his father. "Hey, Pop, it was during football season." But there must be, he told himself, one or two phrases still lurking in the interstices at the bottom of his brain.

He closed his eyes and dug through the muddle until there surfaced two Mandarin expressions: "Sir, would you rather drink wine or beer?" and "Do you look forward to eating mandarin duck this evening?"

J.W. lifted a children's book from the Chinese pile, opened it, and pretended to read, running his finger up and down the pages, mumbling the words for man, big, very, and China, the only pictographs he remembered.

Ông Tay looked up from his housekeeping duties in disbelief, eyes as round as the official governmental seal on his formal papers. "Yes. I like wine, *and* duck, yes, duck. Do you have duck here?" He paused for a moment and stared at J.W. "But how do you speak Chinese? It is not possible."

"Revered sir," J.W. went on, but in Vietnamese, having totally exhausted his Mandarin, "I am not very smart. I speak a little, but my reading is not very good. Perhaps you would be my professor. Only the brightest scholars read Chinese well."

Ông Tay took J.W. by the sleeve, sat him down at the crude table and put a kettle on the fire. They spoke mostly in Vietnamese, though J.W. occasionally peppered his answers with a "yes," "no," or "good" in Chinese. Late in the afternoon, the three men sat smoking J.W.'s Salems and drinking *Ông* Khai's coffee, and then, as the daylight faded, they retired to the chief's house and drank the chief's wine. Khai bought a duck from one of the villagers; Mrs. Khai roasted it. She cut the scrawny bird into two dozen pieces and placed a few shreds on each of several plates piled high with noodles. Each time Tay gobbled down the last piece on the plate, she appeared with another platter, smiling coyly, until six tiny glasses of wine later the old man was tittering.

The chief leaned back and smoked comfortably as Tay stripped the last bone of the last scrap clean. Khai smiled to himself. and J.W. nodded. The two had crafted a pipeline of construction goods for the school and, in but a single afternoon, a happy teacher.

It was unclear to J.W., though, why all work on the market had suddenly ceased and the schoolhouse became a priority. It was too late in the year to begin a semester, for the next planting was scheduled to commence within a month, and the children would be needed in the paddies, not in a sweltering classroom. Nonetheless, the school was completed in three weeks, and all the benches filled for the short-course in chanted grammar and arithmetic.

During the first weeks of class, there was an optimism in My Co that J.W. had not seen before. Parents and students walked, heads high, along the sandy paths of the hamlet soon after dawn to hand-deliver to *Ông* Tay the grand hope of their lives. But it was not long before *Ông* Tay was invited to address the village council and explain why tuition had suddenly doubled. He took a paper from his tattered leather briefcase and presented it with a flourish to *Ông* Khai. The old man had scootered up to Tuyen Binh and, over the heads of Khai and the My Co village council, convinced the province chief, his brother's son-in-law, to provide a paper allowing him to raise the rates. Unspoken was the fact that a portion of the tuition would bounce back to the very province leaders who approved the hike.

The moment Khai left the meeting to wake the pair of policemen to break up a fight between two kids over a garter snake, *Ông* Tay looked out the window to make sure Khai was out of earshot, and slid a few MPC to both junior councilmen. He smiled unctuously, "It's just a few piasters to help defray your expenses. I know how overworked you men are." The motion carried two-to-one.

Cô Lin, aware of the appearance of the old man before the ruling body of My Co, presented herself within the hour to *Ông* Khai and the council, J.W.'s earrings twinkling. She was wearing the more fashionable and clinging of her two blouses. She petitioned to become the new teacher on the grounds that Tay was raising the rates he had promised not to, and anyway, he hadn't been past third grade. Miss Lin presented the certificate that proved she had gone through ten years of schooling then sat down and bowed her head.

My Co's first elected officials were aware that the more left-leaning of the hamlet's populace had boycotted *Ông* Tay's, and that was lost tuition, a portion of which they had long since appropriated for themselves. With facial contortions and hand wringing of Biblical proportion, they came to their pronouncement—there would be two teachers. The councilmen charged J.W. with the mission of providing material and labor to erect a wooden partition at mid-school. There was more discussion when he demanded he be allowed to use nails. He won that vote two to one. There would be a ceremony to cut an entrance in the rear to match the one in the front, and in doing so, sanctify the back room. The twenty-foot-by-forty-foot schoolroom would hence become two, twenty-by-twenty, very distinct institutions—the only multi-roomed structure within a radius of twelve miles.

The body of lawmakers decreed that *Cô* Lin and *Ông* Tay arrive and leave school at different times to avoid meeting. They postponed, however, the decision as to who would take the more prestigious front room, the one with the door facing the village road. Lobbying continued over the next two days, and mysteriously, the governor popped into My Co on his HUEY and left a note for *Ông* Khai granting Professor Tay the prime frontage real estate.

Three days later, *Ông* Khai and J.W. stopped by the building. The chief walked quietly into *Ông* Tay's class, J.W. into *Cô* Lin's. The two schoolrooms, hailing the élite guests, recited their lessons more and more vociferously than the contralateral assemblage. *Cô* Lin looked to J.W. and then away, raising her hands to the class as if a maestro conducting the Saigon Symphony Orchestra.

Two nights later, the VC rained upon My Co a barrage of mortars that splintered the schoolhouse. The kerosene lantern *Cô* Lin used to prepare lesson plans at her desk burst into flames, igniting the churning splinters. A funnel cloud of flame illuminated My Co's night, but darkened its future

Chapter 18

BY EARLY MAY, J.W. accepted that it would not be his to see the market completed. On certain days, he almost wished he had never begun to color in his short-timer's calendar, the figure of a nude woman whose body had been divided into 365 tiny, numbered squares. It might have been better to just let the time empty at its own pace, less excruciating than massaging the calendar each night before bed, filling in another minuscule piece, round and round her belly, slowly spiraling in on the last square neatly circumscribed in the very center of her crotch.

With eight weeks and change to go, he embarked on a period of tallying the minutes until he could fill in that day's bit of the woman's belly. When he got to her inner thighs, he started reckoning the seconds as well. At times, he lay listlessly on his mildewing cot in the mornings, some days napping for hours after the villagers were already hard at their toil seeking to prolong their lives for just another turn of the Earth. He castigated himself for his frailty, for his weakness, sentiments that only dragged him further into despair, a never-ending spiral of dysfunction that made time crawl even more slowly.

As the remaining weeks vaporized, J.W. spent more and more of his time alone, an isolation that begat an even deeper fester. The notion that he had squandered a year of his life, that he had done nothing but shirk his duty as a real soldier, grew from an ember into a snarling flame. It was crystal clear his efforts and those of Khai had been for naught. The hamlet was no different today than the moment he'd arrived, except for the dozen or so dead villagers now credited to his watch.

He wondered if the exertions of the highly respected senior officers had had any consequence. They fed men into the grinder—that's what hardboiled combat commanders did. It was a war. A nation sacrifices its best young people for the greater good. Even J.W. still sufficiently believed in the righteousness of America—his country right or wrong—to stand when speaking to a superior officer. There were still sufficient numbers of believers at home to consecrate the badge of honor warriors harvested for their sacrifice. The commanders would go home to bright futures. Some would parley a glitzy war record into a fast track promotion to general; some would massage it into a seat in congress or the senate, and, in due course, junkets to the third world as the next war boiled, their presence bringing nothing but anguish to everything they touched.

The clouds of self-doubt and futility churned through his waking hours, and then weaved themselves into his dreams. Each day, he stayed on his cot until later and later in the morning. After a few days, it became too hard to leave his bunker to eat.

Despite the constant tropical sun exposure, and though he was superficially tanned, when he shaved at the shard of remaining mirror, he could see the stark, boney outline of his face, and the pallor. He had never remembered feeling so enervated and beaten.

Each morning as his eyes opened, he forced himself to think positively about witnessing the completion of the market before it was time to leave My Co, but as the dawn light filtered into his bunker, waves of sadness rolled over him, and his mind became mired in hopelessness and deepening anger. He lay in bed, unable to tease from the morass of helplessness just who to target for his failure.

Once or twice, the fog lifted for a few moments, and he concluded that he had accomplished what he could, and his reward was that the villagers had given him far more than he had provided them. They did not care if the Great Mr. J.W. Weathersby was fulfilled, nor, in fact, if *they* were fulfilled. They had never heard or thought of a notion as frivolous as self-fulfillment—theirs was to dodge the night's snares and then the uncertain growing seasons that lie ahead.

The best he could do was console himself with the thought that even Jesus, as Khai had reminded him, was unable to curb the suffering and cruelty that continued to cloud human existence. He forced himself to say aloud, over and over, that he had had nothing but fortune in his life, that, as an American, he was heir to a future that guaranteed a job, a roof, and food—forever. He was as blessed as any man in history. Not one of those miracles would likely come to pass for the villagers of My Co, or for the overwhelming majority of beings crawling the Earth.

It was in the midst of such chaotic contemplation that the chief shook J.W. awake at 8:30 A.M. "Captain, I have just received word that the opera company has agreed to come to My Co. They will be here in ten days. We must finish the market. There is no time to waste. I would like to invite your commanding officer and all the important men of the command in Saigon. We want everyone to come. We will create an invitation and you can take it to them. This will be a special day. No one in My Co or Saigon will ever forget it. But we must keep it a secret that the dignitaries are coming."

Though J.W. knew not a single officer over the rank of lieutenant would accept, he dutifully created a guest list of American dignitaries housed at Pentagon East, presented it to *Ông* Khai, and by dawn the next morning, the chief came to J.W. bleary eyed, presenting a collection of delicate, hand-engraved, personal invitations. The new captain persuaded *Ông* Khai to accompany him to Saigon to deliver them personally, and they left for the capital early the next morning.

On the road, they had so often traveled together, the chief was quieter than usual, and J.W. finally asked, "Are you upset with me, *Ông* Khai? You seem so unhappy."

"Oh, no, Captain, I am thinking about my father. What would he say if no one comes to the market opening, like the Christmas party? He's been gone many years, but I know he's watching. All my ancestors are. I owe them everything I have now, and I have so much. Like meeting you. It's changed me, you know."

"I am flattered, *Ông* Khai. I will never forget you. Do you remember when you told me about Oxford and Cambridge and the Sorbonne? And about becoming a doctor? I have to tell you that I am not very smart, and I did so poorly in college that at first I laughed at the idea of going back to school. But I have written to my wife and asked her for the addresses of those universities. The one thing I can promise is to return here someday, to do something positive. And I will come back and see you. I give you my word."

They were silent for miles, until J.W. pulled into the base at Moc Hoa for a snack. He stopped in front of the mess hall, asked the chief to guard the jeep, and stealthily emerged seconds later, his fatigue pockets bulging with three Tasty Cake cakes. J.W. gobbled his and was licking his fingers by the time *Ông* Khai had struggled through the cellophane wrapper. He nibbled, mostly when J.W. was turned toward him, but when the jeep dropped into a pothole, the cake flew out of his hands into a muddy rut. He carped that he'd scarcely gotten a single bite. J.W. smiled, took another from his breast pocket, and pulled the wrapper apart. Handing it to Khai, he beamed, "I was gonna save this one for later, but it's not fair to make you wait."

In Saigon, *Ông* Khai was not permitted onto the manicured grounds of Pentagon East. He commented from outside the gates that he had never seen grass so green or cut so perfectly, nor had he ever dreamed a building that large and tall could be air-conditioned. "Silver glass, Captain? I've never seen this before."

J.W. shrugged. "It's the world's biggest mirror. Supposed to keep the heat away from the pansy asses inside, I guess.

Khai shook his head. "Captain, it's not that hot here. In Hanoi, during the summer, when I was growing up, the heat was unbearable. It was painful. You didn't move during the noon hour. The French did, though. They walked around outside sweating like animals. Wherever they stopped, there was a little puddle by their shoes. Actually, the weather in Saigon is quite pleasant, don't you think?"

J.W. dropped *Ông* Khai outside the gate and motored along the paved, arched driveway to stop at the tallest of the bone-white high-rises. He left thirty invitations with the Spec-5s and sergeants who sat in outer offices, men in starched, pressed jungle fatigues, their mission, to insulate the colonels and generals from the riff raff wandering in from the war.

Then it was on to the 33rd Mech's headquarters up in Long Binh. J.W. left an invitation at Colonel Sacker's office, the man who had assumed Colonel Bierlein's command. Bierlein's old sergeant major heard J.W.'s voice and popped his head out of an office. J.W. had not seen him since the night the man had been shot in the shoulder.

"Hey, sir, good to see ya."

"Sergeant Major, I'll be darned. How's that shoulder?"

"Shoulder's doing great. Just a scratch. Thanks for asking."

"I was worried about ya."

"Nah." He waved his hand. "Shit, sir, I didn't know you were still in country."

J.W.'s face hardened. "That night sucked cock, Sergeant Major."

"Fuckin' A it did, sir." He paused and when he went on, his voice was soft. "You still out in My Co, sir?"

"Maybe for the rest of my life."

"You know, sir, you did a damn good job out there. Escaping those bastards and all, and then goin' right back. Making do out of nothing. Colonel used to talk about you all the time."

Chapter 19

A DOZEN RED and yellow hand-painted signs were created to welcome the expected dignitaries, but they remained hidden behind Khai's house until the morning of the market opening, lest the VC get wind and plan a daylight suicide attack. The local women raked and re-raked the half-acre of sand surrounding the market until the land transcended the caliber of a sand trap at Westchester Hills Golf Club on tournament day.

The girls chattered amongst themselves, postulating the sum and substance of the guest list. One asked if Captain Weathersby's wife was coming, but another young woman snickered, "No way. She's mad that he fell in love with *Cô* Lin."

With the grounds manicured, the women hung sheets of filched OD canvas along the sides of the market to enclose the structure, and then around the far sides and rear of the structure, creating a backstage and private dressing rooms for the opera company. This closing off of the market to the public was a modification encouraged by *Ông* Tay, who insisted it was the European way, though J.W. caught him selling tickets to the old ladies and Dinh Dao, the village idiot.

As the women rushed about dusting and washing, *Ông* Khai sent everyone home to dress in their finest. An unusual quiet descended on the hamlet. The chief stood alone, staring at his endeavor, fingers twitching nervously as if he were in the early stages of Parkinson's Disease. He kept glancing up and down the road for vehicles he longed would bring the luminaries he secretly knew would never arrive.

Then, at 1245 hours, several olive drab helicopters swooped into the NDP to deposit the American guests, amongst them Colonel Sacker, J.W.'s new commanding officer, and nine civilian and military leaders. Fifteen minutes later, a caravan of Vietnamese jeeps arrived from the north. One carried the province chief. In the back seat, squashed between two of his body guards, was *Ông* Khai's mother. Khai counted thirty-six influential visitors. He and J.W. handed out cans of lukewarm beer to each guest. The American officers pretended to sip from the cans. The province chief finished the first and snapped his fingers at *Ông* Khai's mother for a second.

They sat in the sun in front of the market as several guests were called forward to deliver unprepared speeches. At 1400 hours, the performers bumped into town, six stuffed into a rusted 1948 Peugeot, and five more on the top of a Lilliputian bus swollen with props and costumes. As the company of performers repaired to the enclosed market dragging piles of costumes, the province chief weaved to the podium for an hour's oration celebrating the commitment *Ông* Khai and the people of My Co had made to improve their lot. He thanked Captain Weathersby and expressed his amazement that a foreigner had been able to learn the names and order of Nguyen Dynasty emperors, and even a few lines from the *Tale of Kieu*. Facing blank stares, he went on to deliver a slurred lecture explaining that *Kieu* was to the Vietnamese a saga of moral propriety as important as George Washington telling the truth about the cherry tree, or Abraham Lincoln running miles to return a penny to a patron.

While the chief's eyes swam with ecstasy, with the pride of having distributed such essential knowledge to J.W., the Vietnamese dignitaries, on the other hand, were dozing in the blistering heat, and the province chief turned his oratory back to the subject at hand.

"A school, a market, a police station. These were only dreams six months ago, citizens of My Co," he exhorted. "These are the fruits of democracy. Raise your hand if anybody here has ever voted before in an election." J.W. raised his hand. The provincial governor took a deep breath, and went on. "You see, citizens of My Co, in America they vote."

Colonel Sacker, shot an irate look toward J.W., only the second time the colonel had eyed him. The initial glance had been an hour before, when the sergeant major first introduced them, and the CO mumbled, "My pilot has a package for you. Sergeant Major had us fly all the way down to the docks in Saigon to get it."

With the return of the governor to his seat, a second can of Budweiser was placed in front of each visitor. This time, the military men did not open theirs, but the village elders weaved in and out of the American military guests asking with bowed heads, "Excuse me, very large, sweating foreign devil, if you aren't going to be drinking that beer, would you mind sending it my way? And how about a few of those cigarettes?" As the crowd was finally invited out of the sun into the theater, J.W. paid a kid ten cents to collect the unopened cans and cigarettes and dump them into his bunker.

The opera company had erected panels of pastel scenery, and the performers were dressed in glistening, jewel-bedecked costumes, a composite, like their language and culture, of ancient Chinese operatic apparel jumbled with the formal dress of the aboriginal Cham people, who had for the millennia populated the southern reaches of the land now known as Viet Nam. The troupe sang their operatic compositions in the falsetto of the Han, as the present-day Chinese referred to themselves, but danced with the gentle hand movements of the dazzling women of Cambodia and Siam, whose cultures were, themselves, influenced profoundly by their proximity to India.

The denizens of South Viet Nam, at the ethnic crossroads of the Indian and Chinese civilizations, were so very different than the population of the Chinese-like, overly serious, stiff inhabitants of North Viet Nam. The friendly villagers of My Co were open and tranquil compared to their distant cousins a thousand miles to the north, and they swooned that day. It was for many for the first time they had ever heard live music, and they were drugged by the melodies that had grown out of the melding of the societies of Asia. For an hour, they were permitted to ignore that they had been abandoned by the gods, content to stand quietly and relish the artistry of the players they had drawn to My Co with their sweat.

The Western guests applauded politely at the conclusion of the festivities inside the sweltering market, escaping quickly into the relative cool of the bright sun and blistering sands surrounding the fête. There were rounds of handshakes between the American and Vietnamese dignitaries, a flurry of bowing, and a swarming toward the helicopters and jeeps. J.W. ran up to Colonel Sacker and asked, through the door of the regimental commander's aircraft, about the package they'd picked up in Saigon. As Tom began the engine ignition sequence, the colonel fished around in the back of the ship to find a wooden crate, which he pushed forward with his foot. J.W. reached up and grabbed for the parcel as Tom yanked the collective, bringing the helicopter up to a high hover right before jamming the cyclic forward for a nose-low, sprinting take off.

J.W. carried the box to his bunker and propped it on top of the two-foot-thick layer of ground-level sandbags that served as his roof. He dropped into the trench, retrieved two of the warm beers, and was preparing to put a third in his pocket when *Ông* Khai came by to invite him for dinner with the opera troupe at the market. J.W. collected the cans of beer and carried them to the gathering. He offered one to *Cô* Lin, who had also been invited, but she turned red and whispered a refusal. J.W., emboldened by having downed several of the brews on the way to the market, sat down at the dinner table next to *Cô* Lin. Because he was left-handed, his bare elbow brushed her bare arm every so often as he struggled with his chopsticks. It was the first time he had touched her, and he felt the flesh on his arms tighten. He stole another glance at *Cô* Lin. Goose bumps covered her arms; her face was flushed.

He drank another beer and let his leg drift to the side to touch hers. She did not pull away. He felt the warmth of her soft skin through the silk pants, and he began to become unsteady, but embarrassedly chastised himself and managed to sit politely, at attention, through the rest of the meal.

The opera company departed My Co with less than an hour of daylight remaining. *Cô* Lin waved to the performers and then nodded a farewell to J.W. as she drifted off toward *Bà* Binh's. He felt a surge of need and caught up with her, stood speechless for a moment, then touched her hand. He whispered, "I want to go to sleep with you."

Her face drained of all color, and she stared into J.W.'s eyes for an instant longer than she should have. His hands began to vibrate anxiously as the blood emptied into his legs, and he felt himself rock in anticipation, first warm then hot, and finally in apprehension that what he had dreamed of for so long was about to happen. J.W. started to put his hand out to touch hers again, but *Cô* Lin took a deep breath as her eyes reddened. She answered with a throaty, "I'm sorry," then turned and walked quickly, but unsteadily, toward *Bà* Binh's.

Chapter 20

HE STOOD MOTIONLESS, watching her for a moment, then shook his head at the foolish impulsiveness. He worried that she might report the incident, and that it would find its way to Colonel Sacker. So, he went to his bunker to examine the crate and take his mind off the latest gaff. The wooden box was already water logged, having languished in the torrents of the budding monsoon season on the docks of Saigon. He sent word for *Ông* Khai, who arrived followed by a dozen children. The boys pulled greedily at the box, though the chief laughed, said nothing, and busied himself retrieving each piece of wood, piling the planks neatly, separating the nails and metal packing straps by size. Eventually, a corner of a small, red device, just a bit larger than a four-slice toaster, peeked out of the wrapping paper. With J.W.'s excited whoop, several of the children ran away, though that drew many more who crowded in from the far reaches of the hamlet. The two cohorts passed each other madly without exchanging glances.

Ông Khai turned to the assembly and declared, "Captain Weathersby's Honda generator has arrived!"

Word filtered through the hamlet with the speed of light, luring children and elders. J.W. pontificated to the growing mass of mystified peasants that a generator produced electricity by mobilizing electrons through the interaction of a ferrous based, metallic conductor and a magnetic field. When he began to draw detailed nuclear diagrams in the sand with a stick, *Ông* Khai and his young helpers turned away to study the instruction manual. This time the document was in Japanese, but the pictures were not, and the boys tugged at J.W.'s arms, enjoining him to produce a half-liter of motor oil.

That, however, was an ingredient J.W. had not considered, and the best he could do was drain some of the filthy lubricant from his jeep. The next challenge was to locate the wire and his remaining light bulb. *Ông* Khai thought for a moment and sent a child to retrieve J.W.'s duffel bag. Halfway down the pile of mildewed civilian clothes and unread literary masterpieces, J.W. found the bulb.

The chief dispatched another teenager to *Bà* Binh's to collect the field telephone wire that J.W. had donated for a clothesline. Having neglected to obtain a light fixture into which he could screw the bulb, J.W. attached the light bulb to the wires with scotch tape. Gasoline splashed onto the bulb as they filled the tank, and the tape dissolved. The bulb tumbled from the top of the generator, its path magnetically propelled toward a rock. The panicky silence degenerated into deep breaths as it pinged off the stone's edge to its final bounce.

But the globe endured, and one of the children rushed home, brought a spool of his mother's sewing thread, and fashioned a series of loops to hold the wires in place. J.W. asked the little boy, "Have you ever seen electricity before?"

The child cocked his head and murmured, "What?"

Ông Khai examined the wiring, nodded in approval, and cleared a two-meter circle around the generator. The wherewithal to drag the village of My Co from the dark ages was spread before them, and the congregation came to a hushed silence. To celebrate *Ông* Khai's day, J.W. insisted he execute the first tug on the generator's starting lanyard. The passionate yank begot a cough, a puff of raw gas from the virgin muffler, another cough, and finally silence. He smiled with the faith of a lifetime facing engines that never started on the first try, or seldom on the last.

While Khai hunkered to check the parameters, J.W.'s mind drifted in the haze of his last beer. He lost himself, recognizing that soon all that surrounded him, the meager generator, the desire to make love to *Cô* Lin, to eat pizza, all of it would fade into a dream. He would be home in the real world, warm in winter, cool on the hottest days of summer, with more savings in a bank than all the citizens of My Co put together. There would be peace, and he would walk the streets of his land, even at night, with no fear of ambush or capture. He saw the people of My Co going on with nothing, and it would be forever, regardless of which side won the war.

Even with his cursory understanding of the physics of electron flow and his capacity to control million-dollar flying machines, he had no inkling what would befall these people in the weeks and months after his retreat. For the first time in his stay in Viet Nam, the thought of leaving the village left him deflated. He stared off into the dusk, not quite sure what was stirring inside him.

Ông Khai pulled the lanyard once again. An oily, smoky cacophony brought J.W. back to the hamlet, and to the flickering of a sixty-watt bulb, the first electricity the villagers of My Co had ever beheld. As the engine RPM stabilized, the light glowed evenly, turning a small circle of the NDP into a playground for the children, one a bit brighter than a neighborhood park in the Bronx. Some of the kids dropped to the ground to initiate marble contests with their rounded stones; others grabbed sticks and fought as swordsmen. A few kicked off the World Series of luminescent bug fights. The elders gathered closer and rolled extra fat cigarettes by the man-made light while they kicked at the local dogs, which had sprinted into the gathering to play.

My Co had light. The old men laughed, contemplating the hours they would luxuriate in the radiance brought by the mustachioed foreigner. They would play cards after dark, smoke, talk—a few would read the classics. Several women, seeing the magical glow, rushed into the NDP and concocted strategies by which they would trick their husbands each night that they had gone to sleep, but sneak out and gather by the wizard's light to chew betel nut and revile the menfolk, who, for their own part, had already begun to laugh lasciviously in anticipation of the wonders of electricity. Surely something of a sexual nature could be generated from the foreign devil's astonishing machinery.

For fifteen minutes, villagers streamed out of their huts to witness the nighttime radiance. The level of delighted excitement grew, and with it, there was a peculiar melding of spirits. Arch enemies nodded to each other, sharing toasts from the bottles of *rượu đế* being passed about. The women didn't even glare at them.

One of the men stood and brought a glass of spirits to J.W. Weathersby, who hesitated, sighed, and reached forward, hoping the poison would do the trick. It was at the moment the liquor touched his lips that the first mortar shells rained down upon the outskirts of town. After a few rounds, the attack ceased, and the villagers, who had thrown themselves to the ground quaking, came to their knees, crawling and scratching their way out of the NDP. *Ông* Khai ran to J.W. "Are okay? Please go inside your bunker. You'll be safe there. These are small mortar rounds. I have to go home to care for family."

J.W. held up his hand, motioning *Ông* Khai to wait. "Let me turn off the generator, and I'll go with you," but the next volley began. The VC, acutely aware that the villagers would rush to their homes, waited a carefully calculated period before touching off the next barrage. No matter where the poorly aimed rounds landed, they were sure to cull at least a handful of casualties to reinforce their message that cooperation with the other side was deadly, even if that meant their own brothers and sisters and parents were caught in a capricious life and death crap shoot. Some nights, the hiatus between attacks was minutes, sometimes an hour. Occasionally, the enemy would not indulge themselves in a second and third salvo at all.

This night, the rounds of the second sortie came in less than a minute. They were guided by forward observers using the flickering generator light as their aiming point. Both J.W. and *Ông* Khai dove into Weathersby's bunker head first. The Viet Cong 60 millimeter gun tubes slowly walked their artillery in a straight line, past the remaining barbed wire of Happy Valley NDP, past the former site of the headquarters tents, and into the abandoned GI slit latrine, raising a gush of aged feces. The next shells exploded progressively closer to J.W.'s covered foxhole, and though he considered running, he realized the VC had closed off the routes of escape.

Inside the earthen bunker, J.W. and *Ông* Khai stood without movement, counting in Vietnamese as the shells detonated. With each, the ground shook more violently, causing the light bulb to flicker to the beat of the explosive waves. J.W. stuck his arm out of the bunker to reach for the generator, but a round landed nearby and showered him with hot sand. He dropped back inside, rubbing furiously at his burning skin, though his pain eased in seconds as he realized the insignificance of his wounds. He fixed himself next to *Ông* Khai, the two continuing the count, calling out louder with each blast in an ever-deepening false bravado.

When the tally reached eighteen, both men realized that they were now at the center of the crack and koosh of the erupting rounds. The VC had neatly zeroed in on the light bulb, and were about to fire for effect. J.W. reached out again toward the generator, but he flew back into the bunker, landing on his back. He sucked on his fingers, cursing, "Shit, I've been fuckin' electrocuted. Bare fuckin' wires. I've never seen a fuckin' country where you can't get a fuckin' light socket."

J.W. needn't have suffered such angst over the technologic paucity of life in My Co, for the physical phenomenon of electricity he'd granted proved to be incredibly short-lived. The next round fell directly onto the generator, instantaneously snuffing the light of the Twentieth Century. He mumbled to Khai, "At least they don't have an aiming point anymore."

He was, however, premature in his assessment, for the demise of the generator was followed closely by a fireball of exploding gasoline and thick, dark flames of burning engine oil, which dribbled into the bunker. As he and Khai beat the flames out with J.W.'s mattress, Weathersby. growled, "So much for rural fuckin' electrification."

J.W. was bothered less by the loss of his toy than the realization that the enemy was watching him through the sites of very deadly guns. Perhaps it was a villager with a radio hidden in the buffalo pen, or maybe a Viet Cong lying on the berm with a signal flashlight, who had inched the rounds closer and closer to the opening in his bunker. No matter the source, it was someone very close. He had been targeted, personally. They wanted to kill J.W Weathersby more than they wanted anything else in the world that night. And if they didn't drop a round inside the bunker, he understood very clearly that when he emerged from the dugout, he would likely be a sniper's target.

He spoke harshly to the chief, "When we leave here, I go first."

"This is my village, my country. I go first."

They had little time, however, to consider who was to slither from the bunker and martyr himself, for a round boomed into the layered sandbag roof. The thunder-burst slammed J.W. into *Ông* Khai, knocking both to the floor. They groped in the dark, untangling from each other, clambering in the wet sand of the trench until *Ông* Khai stood impatiently and told J.W., "I must go family."

He started up the dirt steps, but the next explosion blew him back. Weathersby crawled to him, and Khai looked up at J.W. He grimaced, "Captain bleeding."

J.W. lifted a hand to his face and felt the blood trickling along his cheek. He followed the thick, warm fluid back to his ear canal. "It's nothing. *Ông* Khai, look, your family is here, a half-kilometer away, and mine is ten thousand kilometers away, but they are as close as we are. If you leave the bunker, I go with you. No argument."

Ông Khai smiled. He spoke very softly in Vietnamese. "Will you come back after the war to see us, my family? Please don't forget us."

"I promise," J.W.'s voice went on tremulously. "Please take my watch. I want you to have it so you won't forget *me*."

"Captain, I will never forget you."

"*Ông* Khai, if we make it out of this bunker, I'm going to name my first child after you. And that way, my family will never forget you."

"Captain, I am not worthy."

After round twenty-four, there was a lull. *Ông* Khai bolted from the bunker and ran north toward his home. J.W. followed at a sprint. Near *Bà* Binh's, they tripped over a bleeding pig, its front legs clawing desperately at the mud, the hindquarters shredded, a victim of a 60 millimeter Viet Cong mortar round.

At the chief's house, Ba Khai's expression remained flat as her husband rushed through the door. J.W. noticed, however, her pupils widen dramatically as she watched him count his children. *Bà* Khai had just lifted herself form their tiny bunker and limped silently to the single-burner kerosene stove to boil water for tea. In the silence, though, the tea glass in *Ông* Khai's mother's trembling hand dropped to the pounded dirt floor, sending fragments of glass skidding across the room. The youngest of the children cried out in a screeching appeal for *Bà* Khai to pick her up, but the Chief's wife snapped, "Be quiet," then barked at her daughter, Bao Ngoc, "Clean that up." The chief gently motioned Bao Ngoc to sit in a chair while he gathered the shards himself. He touched his wife's shoulder, poured tea, and took a seat at the table. He laughed and recounted the tale of his collision with J.W. It was the first time *Ông* Khai's face had thawed in weeks.

J.W. glowed in response to the change in *Ông* Khai's equanimity, and he, too, began to relax. A moment later though, the exhilaration of having survived another contest of jeopardy spread over him, and a brilliant sense of potency welled in his chest. He and his teammate, his brother, had prevailed under a shower of warheads; they had beaten the weaponry that steadily snuffed the lives of mere humans. His irrelevance and obscurity as a child, the lack of potential in school, his marginalization as a soldier, and the meaninglessness of those years of disquiet crystallized in his heart. He had not cowered; he had not sniveled in fear. He stood and counted the enemy's feeble attempt to destroy him. The melancholy came to an end, replaced with a sense of immortality; God had finally reached out and touched him.

The jasmine tea was fragrant, the communion with Khai's family intoxicating, but J.W. abruptly remembered the wretched sow and excused himself. The report of his pistol shot was replaced by the growing drone of a DC-3, and J.W. searched the skies until he saw Puff the Magic Dragon coming on station from the south. How, he pondered, had the account of a Viet Cong attack already reached the highest American echelons, where only they had the power to mobilize exotic weaponry like Puff? It had been but minutes since the first projectile, and those lumbering ships had to be flying and on their way to My Co long before the VC mortar assault had begun.

Within seconds of the pop of the first flare from the aircraft's belly, the village glowed as if dawn, and J.W. found himself standing in the center of the sunrise, .45 pistol still in his hand. While he waited for the sky to go dark, J.W. searched the paddies and squinted to see a black-clad column of armed figures crash to the ground. With the flare nearing the ground, the silhouettes intensified, as did the outline of parked tanks and armored personnel carriers on the other side of the hamlet, in the southern paddies. He was, he reckoned, at the center of a bull's eye, of what was about to become another dimly-lit Armageddon.

Still, though, on the crest of his transcendent immortality, he became furious, not over the coming strife, but over the fact that the brass had been there that very day, had toasted him, yet not informed him of their tactical plans. He spit on the ground, aware he was as much fodder for his side as he was for the other. The new CO was playing schoolyard pay back with J.W. as the bait.

The flare from the airplane burned out in a final pop, and My Co was again coal black, but not quiet. The armor cranked up in unison and proceeded through the paddies and gardens, over trees and hootches, onto the main road. They fanned into a defensive circle, the .50 caliber machine guns trained inward on the huts, the 90-millimeter tank cannons aimed out at the paddies.

Seconds passed before another flare detonated, and J.W. slammed himself to the ground. He heard a GI call in a southern drawl, "Hey, Martin, they'is one on the ground at y'all's fou' clock. Take the mutha fucka out."

J.W. heard rifle safeties click to the firing position. He pictured the face of a clock and asked himself what was the opposite of four o'clock, and if there was a tank there. There was, and with that, his recent sense of immortality evaporated. He raised his hands and cupped them around his mouth, screaming over the thunder of the engines, "Hey, man, it's me, a fuckin' American. It's me, hold your goddamn fire!"

The GI hollered, "What the fuck? Martin, hold yo fire."

"You sure, Sergeant?"

"Just fo one secont."

J.W. came to a crawling position, waving his hand, exclaiming over and over, "I'm Captain Weathersby, man, I'm an American"

As J.W. approached the platoon of infantry on his hands and knees, the sergeant declared, "Y'all 'bout got yo clock cleant, sir. Y'all need to clear yo'self out this area, sir. We 'bout to be doin' some terrible fightin'. They's Charley all around."

When the glow of the second flare faded, and the Viet Cong mortar barrage started anew, J.W. dove into a culvert as a blue-white flash of deadly radiance flamed from the vicinity of the chief's house. As he turned toward the light, a starburst of burning splinters and chunks of roofing tile roiled up through the palms. With the next flare, the village glowed, and J.W. could see from his slime-filled ditch an oily smoke and a growing fire fed by the tinder of what was left of *Ông* Khai's house.

J.W followed behind the armored personnel carriers as they moved forward toward the chief's house. A surge in the clamor caused him to look to his sides. Two of the M-48 battle tanks were grinding along the main road, approaching the center of the village. They were, though, coming from opposite directions. Was it possible, J.W. wondered, that they were unaware of the other's presence. It had not been long since an identical scenario had been played out on that road in My Co, and J.W. ran off in a sprint to hide.

The track commanders on the M-113 APCs, aware that tanks draw rocket fire like a water buffalo's rear end collects flies, gave orders for their drivers to creep farther and farther away from the forty-seven-ton behemoths. The 113s inched through gardens and beside hootches, often catching a corner of a hut, dragging it along, walls falling away in chunks on the death march. By the point they had retreated to the outer reaches of the hamlet, to hide near the berm, they were tactically useless. That left the tanks to do the fighting, but the drivers of the M-48s sat very close to the ground, sealed away in a tiny cockpit, the turret just inches above the tops of their helmets. They could barely navigate in daylight, and at night, the drivers were basically blind, compelled to rely on verbal instructions from the tank commanders, "Johnson, go left fifty meters, no left, you moron!"

On the other hand, the tank commanders stood so high in the turret, they had poor vision for what was directly below their horizontal line of sight. When the aircraft flares burned out, and night was restored, the tank commanders had no near vision at all unless they switched on their xenon searchlights, which they abhorred using as it made the tank an easy target for B-40 RPGs, the VC's lethal, anti-tank, rocket propelled grenades.

From a muddy culvert, J.W. watched the perfect storm brew. A column of American infantrymen was running up the road toward the sound of Viet Cong AK-47 light assault rifles near *Bà* Binh's. The platoon of tanks had been ordered up the road to support the grunts, unaware that another platoon of M-48s was thundering into town at full speed to make up for the delay when its lead vehicle had thrown a track and blocked the road. The column of infantry was in the middle—it always was.

With everyone night-blind as the next flare petered out, there were five-hundred tons of armor grinding about sightlessly and thirty infantrymen desperate to get off the road. Some of the men went left, some right—a single GI tripped in a pothole and, as he stood to run, was pinned between the two lead tanks as they collided, their knife-blade bows striking head on. One tank commander, knocked unconscious by the violence of the collision, was hanging out of his turret hatch. The other TC screamed at his driver to back up. As the track lurched into reverse, the trapped soldier fell to the ground, his torso held to his legs but by the material of his jungle fatigues.

J.W., who had flown out of his trench, knelt by the soldier, a teenager who wept softly, "I'm dying, sir, ain't I?"

J.W. tried to speak, but before he could tell the man he was going to be fine, there was a gurgle, and the soldier was gone. A medic ran over, then the platoon leader, then a cluster fuck of GIs gagging and cursing. J.W., wedged to the outside of the circle, walked off toward the night defensive position, leaving the angry mob of tankers be.

One of the drivers who had hit the man crawled out of his compartment screaming at the top of his lungs, "Fuck me, fuck me!" He pounded his fists against the front end of his tank until the skin ripped. He saw his blood mix with that of his victim's, and he sprang into the mass of GIs, tore an M-16 from one of the grunts, jammed the barrel into his own mouth, and reached desperately for the trigger. A troop snatched the rifle out of the maddened soldier's hands and a third tackled him, holding him on the ground until the devastated warrior crawled into a fetal ball.

J.W. faced away from the crowd as his vision blurred, and he became light-headed. He dropped to one knee, overwhelmed by waves of worsening nausea. Though he knew there was little point in fighting the need to vomit, he growled to himself, "Fuckin' Ranger, you piece of shit, get off your ass and do your job, you piece of weak crap. You can cry later."

He managed to rise to his feet and shake his head to clear it. He sucked in the deepest breath he ever had, turned toward the west end of the hamlet, and ran to *Ông* Khai's. A hundred yards from the house, a barrage of incoming mortar rounds were being walked methodically along the road, forcing him to withdraw east toward the abandoned NDP. As he retreated, he saw a column of frantic, black-dressed men collapsing in two's and three's as U.S. Army red M-16 tracers whacked into them. J.W. skirted the throng of screaming enemy soldiers and headed for the outlying paths of the west village, but had to reverse course, with no choice but seek cover in Happy Valley. He dropped into the bunker past the rubble of the charred, twisted generator, burned packing material, and beer cans. The sixty-watt light bulb had dropped into the bunker and was unharmed until J.W.'s boot crushed it. He popped his head out to watch the enemy's green tracers ricochet off the bellies of the tanks only to tear into the straw huts. Several burst into flames from the burning daub of phosphorous that gave the tracers their radiance.

In the glare of those fires, J.W. spotted a column of GIs approaching the splinters where Khai's house had stood. J.W. left the bunker to move up the road again toward the chief's house, though he came first upon a diminutive teenager in black pajamas curled on the ground. A pink liquid foamed from his limp mouth as he whimpered, and J.W. knelt to listen. As he turned his head to put his ear next to the boy's lips, he saw the M-16 hole in the child's abdomen squirting blood in a geyser. As J.W. brought his finger forward to halt the bleeding, the flow faded, as did the child's life. The half-full rice bag the youngster had picked up in the village and sought to carry to his compatriots in the jungle was slowly being swallowed by the mud.

J.W. moved on and found the dead pig. When an old villager saw J.W. stop to look, he ran out of his house and asked the captain to help him pull the carcass inside, but the mortars began again and J.W. was forced back toward the NDP. A tank carrying wounded GIs clinging to its sides chewed its way to the NDP. Over the din, J.W. heard the track commander screaming on the radio for medevac helicopters. Weathersby asked the track commander if he had seen a tall Vietnamese man up the road, but the sergeant peered down and spat, "I got no time to be caring for nobody but my hurt men, sir."

One of the wounded men called quietly to J.W. "Sir, you looking for a tall guy with a bunch of kids up the vill?"

"That's right, troop. You see 'im?"

"Yeah. I think the man's dead, sir. He got blasted. Don't know which side got 'im, but he was carrying a kid when a round went off. Made me sad, sir, the kid and all."

But a second wounded GI interrupted weakly, "No, sir, I don't think he was dead, sir, but next thing to it. He was talking to this lady who must 'a got hit too 'cause she was limpin'."

J.W. touched the hands of the men and whispered, "You're gonna do just fine gents. You'll live long healthy lives back in the world because you guys are heroes. You did your duty. I'm proud of you, men. God bless you."

Both men smiled weakly. They let their heads fall back to rest, faces placid with relief that a captain had reassured they were genuine soldiers—the power of words and the potency of human touch.

Several medevac choppers made their approach during a lull in the fighting, one into the NDP just yards from J.W., and one to the north of the village near *Ông* Khai's. As they touched down, volleys of green enemy tracers again arose from all angles. A barrage of mortars, suddenly joined with RPG rockets, followed in less than a minute. The two ships jumped off the ground, becoming airborne with the wounded barely aboard, bleeding men grasping skids and seats. When one of the injured men lost his grip, he fell five feet out of the ship and landed next to J.W. The chopper dropped heavily to the ground, bending the skids, and the crew chief jumped clear, threw the man over his shoulder, and carried him aboard before J.W. could squat to help.

One of the track commanders looked down at J.W. from his turret and smiled, "Man, that pilot was great! You see that shit, sir?"

When J.W. turned to answer him, the sergeant saw the wings embroidered on J.W.'s fatigues and added, "You're a pilot, too, sir! I didn't mean to be nasty before, sir. It's just that I gotta take care of my men first, if you know what I mean, sir. Let's see what we can do to help your friend."

The twelve hours since the market dedication had witnessed a lifting of J.W.'s depression. He envisioned a future as a leader, one of the contributing members of his generation. He would go to graduate school at the Sorbonne, maybe

Cambridge or Oxford, and return to the United States to enter politics. For an instant, he believed even the presidency was within his grasp. He'd become the leader of his nation and never again allow the travesty of that night to happen again anywhere on Earth, at least not at the hands of his countrymen.

He asked the tank commander for the medevac frequency and borrowed a radio to call the rescue helicopter. "That was a hell of an evac," J.W. spoke into the microphone. "Some troop," he went on, "owes his life to you and your crew chief."

A tremulous voice replied, "Send your checks and money orders to Bravo Company, 36th Assault Helicopter Company. No stamps, please. All in a day's work. Glad we could help."

J.W. asked, "Can you come back in here and pick up my counterpart? He's been wounded. Best man there is. We need him."

"He a local?" the pilot asked.

"That's affirm."

"I'll try to get back, but I need to get my cargo to the hospital, get 'em tucked in. We'll do what we can, but don't wait up."

J.W. ran through the village, convinced the Viet Cong were finally out of ordinance, that the war might even be over after the expenditure of munitions the communists had invested in My Co that night. The firing, though, soon recommenced, and J.W. had to crawl east with American red and enemy green tracers snapping inches over his helmetless head. He arrived back at the NDP and radioed the GIs at the west end of the village. *Ông* Khai was so badly wounded, he was breathing only in fits and starts. They agreed to load him on a litter and put him aboard the next medevac helicopter, if he was still alive, if they were still there, and if the chopper ever made it back to My Co. "Big war going on out here," were the final words of one of the GIs tending *Ông* Khai's nearly lifeless remains.

An hour later, a lone HUEY skimmed into the hamlet, drawing fire from the four corners of the compass. It hovered briefly then climbed out of My Co carrying Vu Van Khai into the darkness. Parabolas of green tracers chased the ship, but it was soon out of rifle range, flying east toward Saigon at redline. J.W. radioed the pilot, who reported, "My crew can't tell how much longer he's gonna be alive. But we'll take him to the Binh Ray Hospital in Saigon. They're the only ones with room left to accept patients tonight."

At midnight, the fighting ceased, and an hour later the tanks and infantry were withdrawn, leaving in their wake only tormented sobbing. J.W. crawled up the road toward the elegy of death. The women surrounding the vestiges of the Khais' house opened a passage for him. *Bà* Khai lay on the wooden plank bed, a dingy, threadbare wet cloth on her forehead. *Ông* Khai's mother stood over her, barely turning to greet J.W. when he kneeled next to her. She took the rag off her daughter-in-law's head, dipped it in water, wiped the tears from *Bà* Khai's face and then from her own.

"He'll be okay," J.W. offered hollowly. Neither the chief's mother nor *Bà* Khai acknowledged, and J.W. whispered loudly enough for the gathering to hear, "Don't worry, we'll go to the hospital tomorrow. We'll find him and bring him home. Don't worry." *Bà* Khai squeezed her eyes shut and turned her head away.

At his bunker in the abandoned NDP, J.W. kicked the shredded, burned hulk of the generator from the doorway and sat trembling on the damp sand. He took a Salem from the pile the kids had tossed into the bunker that afternoon and placed himself prostrate on his cot, shaking his head that the euphoria of the early evening could have been so abruptly swept away by the same wind that had begotten such anguish.

When he tried to close his eyes, he felt himself a tiny figure at the end of a great, black cavern, imagining he was becoming smaller and smaller while the surrounding cone of black swelled. He soon envisioned himself outside his body, peering down on a contemptible, burned crust of a once-human figure. When a buzzing vibration filled his head with wailing and screaming, he pictured children mumbling incoherently as they died, and pigs squealing in their death throes. He had been cast into a Hieronymus Bosch triptych to drown in the hellish depths of the third panel.

Chapter 21

J.W. WAS NOT granted a long night to wallow in his despondency. *Bà* Khai and the chief's mother arrived several hours later and hunkered to stare in from the mouth of the bunker. The silence of their mourning eyes penetrated him. *Bà* Khai held a kerosene lamp in one hand and a shiny, tin cylinder with a frail wire handle, a Vietnamese lunch pail, in the other. J.W. glared at them, believing this scene just another in the nightmare that had repeated itself so many times over the past hours. But when he heard his own voice lecturing the women in English that he, too, had a family, and that he was going to be with them in a few weeks, if he could eke out his survival until July 3rd, he understood it was all very real.

J.W.'s growling, though, had apparently meant nothing more to the women than a clearing of the throat, for *Bà* Khai asked in Vietnamese through her sobs, "Yes, yes. Are we going to see my husband now?"

J.W. shook his head, barking again in English, sure they could not understand. "I can't chance another trip on these shitty roads. Kien Tuong Province belongs to the Viet Cong. This whole fuckin' country belongs to the Viet Cong. I don't want to see one more fuckin' twisted, distorted, fuckin' dead body. Why is that so hard to understand?"

But *Bà* Khai and her mother-in-law remained squatted, now silent, and J.W. was relieved that while he had yelped at them crudely, it was in words that could not be understood. He dropped back down on his cot, numb, the pretension of the past night fully beaten out of him.

As neither of the women budged or changed expression, J.W. scowled harder. When that failed to send them home, or to what was left of it, he simply turned away, the most unambiguous refusal he could muster. Again, not a flicker, so he curled up in a ball on his cot and tried to sleep, but the harder he tried, the more rancid became the taste in his mouth, a symptom of the blight he had witnessed the night before, and the three-hundred nights before it. He cursed aloud and rolled off his makeshift bed to brush his teeth then climbed one step out of the bunker to spit, but the elder *Bà* Khai's eyes widened, and she gasped at the dried blood on his cheek. She leaned forward to touch the wound and pulled a piece of tattered rag from her bundle, wet it with spittle, and wiped at the blood. J.W. thought of pulling away from her ministrations, but a cloud of helplessness enveloped him, and he climbed out fully to stand at the entry to his bunker, obediently numb, eyes cast down in submission and shame for his most recent eruption. He could not help, though, think about how frequent the loss of control assaults had become. Yeah, but it would all change the moment he got home. Just a little bit longer to hold on.

It crossed his mind, though, that he had begun to worry about himself even before his arrival in Viet Nam, as he saw the slow change in his personality as his months in the army had passed. Yes, he'd had angry outbursts as a kid, but his temper had been manageable, little different than that of his pals. His wrath, though, had escalated as the days in the military passed, morphing into a fury that did not distinguish between the harmless and the guilty. It made him think of Khai's words, that he could not tolerate those who harmed the innocent, and he thought back to the observations of a 33rd Mech platoon sergeant who had warned, "Sir, whatever you come here with, you leave with the same thing, but to the tenth power."

J.W. hissed aloud, "I can't go home like this."

Bà Khai had still not spoken, but the words poured from her eyes. In deep embarrassment, J.W. pulled enough gas from his buried 55-gallon fuel drum to fill the jeep and a couple of jerry cans. He took the elder *Bà* Khai's hand and helped her into the back seat then patted the front for the chief's wife. They motored without lights through the east gate of the NDP into the village, Weathersby hoping to be just a detached, rasping sound in the night, not an illuminated, glowing target. As they started on the dark journey to Saigon, J.W. turned on his transistor radio and tuned it to the Armed Forces Network's overnight rock and roll station. *Brother Love's Traveling Salvation Show* crackled through the diminutive speaker as they putted along at two or three miles per hour, desperate to avoid the potholes.

J.W. understood it was unlikely he would ever return to My Co, for the chances of surviving until morning were slight. Driving those roads at night in an American jeep was so suicidal, he wondered if it was simply the continuation of the nightmare, and he'd soon awake, safe, on *Bà* Binh's mahogany bed.

J.W. stopped at a crowd of old men and women who had gathered around the house in which J.W. had dined on his first day in My Co. Each time he had passed the hut over the months, he had thought back to the meal of scaly-tailed rats he'd found so luscious. He recalled the people he had met that day in the village, *Ông* Long, *Em* Huong, the old ladies, and *Cô* Lin.

But that was a lifetime before, and though he had not seen *Em* Huong recently, when he did, the child was respectful, bright, and forever engaged in entrepreneurial activities. His most recent effort, J.W. laughed, was a scheme to gather the village's manure and sell it back to the farmers whose cattle had produced it in the first place. As in the American medical field, there was a handsome profit to be made in shit. Huong's only material investment in the venture was a sheet of cardboard from the mimeograph machine packing, and the wisp of string he had won in a bug fight. He tied the twine to the rectangle of cardboard, lashed a couple of sticks on the bottom as runners, having learned that engineering technique from studying the helicopters that dropped into and out of Happy Valley, and set out to make a profit. He dragged the assembly around town, scraping animal scat from the ground, the fields, and from the floors of huts of villagers who kept their cattle indoors for protection. He could often be seen about town, heaping the steaming brown gold aboard the lorry, his smile widening with each biscuit.

That night, however, J.W.'s attention was drawn back to the crowd for which he had stopped the jeep. The wispy-bearded *Ông* Long was barely able to speak through his tears, but grasped the captain's wrist and pulled him almost viciously out of the jeep to the center of the circle. The old man mumbled on and on, but J.W. was not that evening able to think in Vietnamese. Finally, Long took J.W.'s head and physically pointed it toward the ground.

A child lay on a primal litter of sticks and vines, his rolled up left pant leg exposing a mangled calf. Blood spurted from parts of the wound and oozed from others, the different velocities forming a black eddy, a sanguine whorl that momentarily captured J.W.'s awareness, reminding him of the cone of darkness in which he had finally fallen asleep hours before. A shaft of splintered, pearly bone stuck through yet another section of the child's leg, but that didn't bleed, and J.W. fixed his gaze there, afraid he would lose consciousness if he had to watch another creature exsanguinate that night.

The old man, still grasping J.W.'s wrist, asked, "Please spare his life. Please, sir. You are from America. Please spare his life."

J.W. finally screwed up the courage to look at the child's face, aware it could only be one soul, for this was Viet Nam.

J.W. pulled a towel from under the driver's seat and placed it over the boy's wound then wrapped jumper cables around the leg, tightening the coil by degrees until the bleeding ceased. He carried the nearly comatose child to the vehicle. Old man Long climbed aboard into the back next to *Ông* Khai's mother. As J.W. put the jeep into gear, a father carrying another child came up to J.W. pleading, "Please bring my son back to life. Please, sir!"

This child's eyes, however, were riveted open, unblinking, a patina of dust already clouding the lifeless corneas. The boy seemed to be looking up at the father, who sobbed, "They were playing, these two, with a bomb from last night. I told them not to. I always told them not to. Please bring him back to me. He is my only heir, foreign devil. Please, bring him back to life."

On the transistor radio, Simon and Garfunkel's *The Boxer* now played over the cheap mini-speaker, and J.W. thought selfishly of his childhood in New York City, and of his own story that had not been told. Though there were tears in the man's eyes, J.W.'s heart could not see them.

As the seconds passed and he contemplated the suicidal journey ahead, the man's agony could not break through the dread and fury that boiled within J.W. Finally, Weathersby sucked in a deep breath and looked away from the man. He mumbled in broken Vietnamese, "He's dead. I can't do anything." He turned to *Bà* Khai and snapped, "I told you I didn't want to see any more dead bodies. I've seen enough, goddamnit."

The father's expression remained unaltered as he drifted off silently through the crowd, carrying his burden tightly. J.W. restarted the jeep and sped away from the village of My Co along the muddy road, crying as he had not since he was a little boy.

A few miles from the hamlet, the pathos of the past ten hours, of the past ten months, lost its dominion, and he slowed the vehicle to a crawl, turned, and looked back at *Ông* Long and *Em* Huong, touching the boy's pale face gently, offering, "He'll be okay."

J.W. crept east slowly, without lights, stopping every hundred yards to scan for columns of black-clad men. With less than four miles covered in the first hour, he gave up and just drove, ignoring that he was in command of an overloaded sarcophagus wandering in the middle of the night on communist-controlled roads without an escort, a single, rusty, never fired, .45 their lone protection.

Bà Khai took up security. She stared vigilantly into the darkness, occasionally placing her hand gently on J.W.'s arm, mumbling in a whisper that he should stop. She'd point into the paddies at dark objects, and J.W. would pull over long enough to convince himself the shadows were changeless.

At one point, *Bà* Khai directed J.W.'s attention to a hazy shadow far down the road, and he turned off the ignition and let the jeep coast silently to stop against a stand of bamboo, hoping to conceal their silhouette. Staring at the distant roadway, he became sure, this time, there was movement, and he peeked at *Bà* Khai, who nodded almost imperceptibly. He watched the column redeploy into the paddies and take up defensive positions. After a moment, a circle of shapes rose out of the muck and began moving cautiously toward the jeep. J.W. considered abandoning the vehicle to run into the thickets of bamboo and hardwood, reasoning that if discovered, the Vietnamese passengers would not be harmed, and only the jeep with its radio would be taken. But he also thought of the hassle of reporting the loss of yet another vehicle and decided to turn the jeep back toward My Co.

As his hand moved forward to grasp the starter switch, he heard the main rotors of a Sikorski S-64 Flying Crane and a Cobra gunship escort. He made out the nav lights, beacons, and load lights as the ships lumbered northeast toward Long Binh. Against the Asian moon, he distinguished the twisted carcass of a HUEY slung under the mammoth helicopter. The load had begun to swing so violently in a pendular arch, the colossal S-64's crew was losing control. The pilot slowed and maneuvered toward an unpopulated area while the gunship shined its powerful landing lights toward a patch of countryside a hundred meters in front of J.W.'s jeep. And there the crane's pilot quickly released the damaged HUEY.

J.W. could not see the falling payload, but he saw and heard it crash onto the road. It rolled over and over toward the column of shadowy soldiers, the former million-dollar aircraft gyrating as pieces of the hull flew like rockets into the paddies and woods. Near the end of its journey, a flash of exploding JP-4 helicopter fuel blasted into the air, lighting the night twice as brightly as the flares from Puff. In the brilliance of the oily, orange flames, *Bà* Khai pointed to a platoon of rifle-toting silhouettes sprinting helter-skelter in a dozen directions as the shrapnel of the disintegrating helicopter rained down. Two of the wildly scattering enemy soldiers passed within a couple of dozen yards of the jeep, though they were running with such abandon, they never saw J.W.'s rusty pistol aimed at them.

Weathersby assumed the ships would land, and he could get *Em* Huong aboard for a ride to the Australian children's hospital in Saigon, but the choppers climbed together, leaving the burning HUEY to a private demise. J.W. held his breath and peeled out, speeding past the fiery remains.

An hour later, the sun began inching over the emerald eastern paddies, and the jeep crept into the suburbs north of My Tho. Here there were muddy villages and earthen dikes crisscrossing glistening patches of flooded paddy, pearls punctuating miles of deep green forest. Farmers, legions of them, were already at their toil, stooped under conical hats, alive for another day to pull weeds and place delicate, infant rice shoots in the mud. There was little else those laborers would ever do besides remain bent at the waist from dawn to dusk every day of their lives, save the two turns of the sun at the lunar new year, *Tet*, that ephemeral respite *Bà* Binh had told him about.

J.W. shook his head, for this was the manner in which the overwhelming majority of humans had passed their lives since the beginning of time. He was not surprised when nary a peasant expended the energy to glance up from the watery fields as the laden jeep curled deliberately around puddles and potholes.

J.W. pulled off the road outside the main gate of the army base near My Tho. Ignoring the order to stop and identify himself, he marched past the guard toward the mess hall, where he enjoined the cook to pack a breakfast for his "troops." Though J.W.'s passengers had never before envisaged Wonder Bread, Planter's Creamy Peanut Butter, or Welch's Grape Jelly, they accepted their fare without expression.

Em Huong revived a bit as the sun warmed the air thirty miles east of My Co. He whispered, "Grandfather, we must be very far from home. These people here, they look so different." But at the outskirts of Tan An, *Em* Huong's head was limp again and soon lay against his grandfather's chest. As the sun rose relentlessly, *Em* Huong further withered. Though J.W. had planned to be in Saigon by dawn to place the child on the pediatric ward of the Australian Hospital, the finest facility in Viet Nam, he realized *Em* Huong would soon be gone, regardless of where he was admitted. He couldn't, though, bear to let it happen in his jeep.

J.W. pulled into the courtyard of the first hospital they came to. An orderly emerged, looked into the jeep, clucked his tongue sadly, called several supervisors out to examine the boy, and stood there stoically while a great discussion ensued. Finally, the panel of inspectors spoke to the orderly, who gathered the near-corpse in his arms and carried the child toward the building. *Bà* Khai pushed *Ông* Long gently, urging him to follow.

J.W. called to the old man and handed him a few dollars of funny money. *Ông* Long took the bills without counting, crushing them into his fist and disappearing into the hospital. J.W. quickly pulled back onto the road before the hospital administrators could reconsider and expel the boy. As they escaped onto the semi-highway toward Saigon, J.W. told himself it was better for the child to die in the arms of his countrymen than in those of foreigners.

⁂

The suburbs of Saigon swelled with endless, crumbling refugee encampments, the walls of the shanties mosaics of U.S. ammunition crates and C-ration box cardboard. Roofs were fashioned from beer cans slit open lengthwise and tack-welded into sheets, the names Budweiser and Miller and Beer 33 repeating seventy or eighty times on the five-foot lengths. Expressionless refugees squatted in precious corners of shade as peasants in conical hats and faded, threadbare, black pajamas hawked morsels of pineapple, shreds of coconut, and glasses of warm tea. There were no customers, only kids in baseball caps who squinted against the furious sun to glimpse the spectacle of a U.S. Army vehicle, driven by a heavily mustachioed captain, carting Vietnamese passengers.

At 1 o'clock, the jeep puffed across a rusting railroad bridge over the Dong Nai River into Saigon proper. They edged along the exhaust-choked, refugee-crammed, semi-paved streets, the busier crossings unregulated despite the vintage-Thirties traffic lights. As J.W. pushed toward the hospital, the jeep spent the majority of time stalled in massive traffic jams, the police helpless to direct the in-and-out flux of archaic busses; decrepit French cars; scooters enveloped in black-smoke; bicycles with wheels but no tires; pedicabs; horse, donkey, and ox carts; and the mob of pedestrians who weaved through the intersections as if immune to the smack of a bus. This was a technology that bewildered the two women, having last seen a traffic signal in Hanoi in the early '50s, before they'd fled the Communists. *Bà* Khai held a handkerchief to her mouth and nose against the blue fumes gushing from the swarms of ailing vehicles.

The Saigon Hospital, where the pilot of the medevac chopper had reported he'd transported *Ông* Khai, sat on Le Loi Street, not far from the huge Ben Thanh Market in the center of the city. The crumbling sanatorium was surrounded by cardboard hovels. Family members not allowed to squeeze inside and sleep on the floor next to their dying kin paid extortionate rents in the form of wedding rings, gold earrings, and jade bracelets, just to wait for the inevitable. A patchwork of frayed telephone and bare electric wires, none of which carried current, formed a drooping spider's web of black threads around the hospital, a barrier through which no helicopter J.W. had ever encountered could execute an approach.

He asked himself aloud, "How'd that guy get in here? And in the middle of the night. And there's no landing lights? And how the hell did he find the hospital in the first place?" J.W. shook his head. No one, not even the extraordinary flight instructors at Fort Rucker, even the ones who had piloted helicopters through the Korean War and had already spent two tours in Viet Nam, could ease a chopper through the maze of lethal cables netting that hospital.

He searched the area for a landing pad, but soon realized there was not a single square inch of land anywhere near the hospital that wasn't packed with refugee shanties. And if the chopper had really come in there the night before, all those cardboard hovels would have been blown to pieces. As the jeep rolled to a stop outside the main doors, J.W. tasted an early fury in his mid-section, for it was more than likely that *Ông* Khai had never been delivered to this hospital.

Bà Khai stared at J.W., shocked by his sudden pallor. She stammered, "Are you feeling well, Captain?" He did not answer but parked sullenly next to the market, where he paid an old man twenty-cents to guard the jeep. He took not only the distributor cap but the distributor itself off the engine, scratching timing marks into the metal of the block with a rock he kicked from the earth. J.W. stuffed the entire grease-caked device into his pocket and snaked along skinny paths between hovels, leading his two dazed companions toward the hospital.

Inside the massive iron gates was a courtyard filled with squatting refugees. There were no doors, only a considerable open area with a little desk at the center. A nurse with vacuous eyes sat guard at the small table, her crisp white uniform in stark contrast to the hospital's sweating green walls. J.W. ignored the tawny, fungal plaques that trimmed the ceiling, and the gecko lizards that clung motionlessly to the dirt-opaqued windows. Both the fungus and the lizards appeared more alive than the Vietnamese soldiers awaiting surgery, dozens of whom lie crammed together upon stretchers lining the filthy floor. Those strong enough looked up, eyes pleading, but when they understood the interlopers were not there for them, they withered and stared back at the walls.

Ông Khai's mother pushed her daughter-in-law toward the desk. Timidly, she asked for her husband. The nurse consulted a schoolchild's notebook in which the hospital census was recorded. Vu Van Khai had not been admitted. *Bà* Khai turned to J.W., who surmised the chief had been so weak on admission, he had not been able to give his name, if he had ever been delivered there at all.

As *Bà* Khai nodded and stepped back, accepting the pronouncement as fate, J.W. marched forward but soon slowed to a docile shuffle. He smiled weakly and began. "Miss, a helicopter brought *Ông* Vu Van Khai here last night. Could you look in the book to see if he was brought in? He was very wounded, and we need to find him right away."

She gave her head an indifferent shake and turned away, not looking back down at the book. J.W.'s lips pursed, and *Bà* Khai took another hesitant step backwards, her conical hat clutched submissively, though in rigidly tensed hands. It reminded J.W. of the pictures of the Jews in Nazi Germany standing hat in hand before the *Waffen SS*, pleading for the lives of their children. J.W. shook his head angrily, whispering, "Never again," then hissed audibly in English, more to himself than *Bà* Khai, "No, lady, you're supposed to take a step forward. Don't let this little *pishiker* push you around. We're not running this time."

He turned to the nurse. "Miss, an American helicopter pilot told me he brought *Ông* Khai here, to this hospital. I want to speak to a doctor or your supervisor."

"That is not possible," the nurse answered sans expression.

"Look, goddamnit," J.W. snapped, "I want to know where *Ông* Khai is. Do you understand?"

Bà Khai and her mother-in-law backpedaled to the entrance, their faces devoid of color. J.W., though, turned to them determinedly and motioned with his head for them to follow. To this point, the nurse had simply ignored J.W.'s blustering, but when he marched through a set of swinging doors into the hospital proper, *Bà* Khai and the chief's mother in tow, she clucked angrily and left her post.

The three stepped over and around litters packed on the floor even more densely than in the reception area. The wounded lolled, some on stretchers, some on the concrete floor, rows of them lining dingy halls, moaning, desperately reaching for the strangers. But there wasn't a moment to spare on compassion that afternoon, and when J.W. saw his companions set their jaws to endure the wretchedness, he pushed on harder, marching the halls as might a livid surgeon.

They searched overflowing, post-operative wards and crumbling verandahs crammed with threadbare cots, each supporting two, and sometimes three, near-cadavers. J.W. hastily ducked in and examined the sewer-like squat toilets that some of the patients still used. He gagged and ran, coming to an exit which opened into an alley behind the hospital. Several workers sat and smoked beside half-covered barrels of the day's surgical remains.

It was there that J.W. weakened, accepting he had probably burrowed too deeply into the underbelly of a society so deeply ravaged, the unequivocal obligation for a being to do the right thing, no matter the cost, had become as alien as his behavior. He understood that a jury of his peers, had there ever been such a notion in that forsaken land, would convict him of antisocial crimes and jail him for years. He grasped a rusted iron railing to steady himself, but the ghastly odor of the surgical vestiges, and the sight of a pale, diminutive forearm poking from an uncovered garbage can drove him back into the hospital.

The bravado of pushing past a ninety-pound, nineteen-year-old nursing student had fully ebbed, and when the orderlies caught up with him, he stopped and stood silently, awaiting arrest. The three slight men, however, just stood obsequiously, heads sagging.

J.W. mumbled, "I hope you will understand that the Vietnamese man I am looking for is my best friend." He offered Salems and a book of GI matches. The orderlies thanked him warmly. They walked J.W. to the entrance, where he rejoined *Bà* Khai and her mother-in-law. There were apologies on both sides, handshakes, more proffered Salems, and the three intruders walked away silently into the severe afternoon.

On the trip back to My Co, they stopped at the hospital south of Saigon to retrieve *Em* Huong's body, to carry it home for burial. J.W. walked casually past the front desk, smiling at the young nurse. She smiled back. He looked in the three wards—no Huong. He made his way out to the rickety wooden morgue, where an old man in stained hospital whites listened patiently to J.W.'s saga. He shook his head. "Captain, you are in the wrong hospital. Come with me."

The man led J.W. to the steaming pediatric ward across the dirt road. *Ông* Long hunkered beside a piece of canvas suspended a few inches off the ground. It was more hammock than bed, and two youngsters were squashed together on it, both staring at the dripping ceiling. *Em* Huong smiled weakly at J.W. and tried to pull himself closer to his bedmate to give J.W. a place to sit, but the other patient, a bulky mummy thoroughly wrapped in blood-stained gauze, took up much too much room. *Em* Huong sighed.

J.W. shooed flies from the red-soaked bandages covering Huong's leg. The bindings on the other child's head, arms, and left leg were also enveloped, and J.W. excused himself to dash into the streets of Tan An looking for insect spray. He came to a black-market stall with a disheveled pyramid of olive drab, pilfered, GI bug repellent. J.W. growled about the ten American dollars demanded by the proprietor but glanced at the setting sun and dropped two bucks into the mendicant's lap. The man looked down at the bill, a good week's pay, but did not change expression. J.W. threw another dollar down, snatched the top can, and disappeared. He also got a bag of fruit, three *chả giò* egg rolls, and two pairs of kids' sunglasses before sprinting back to the hospital. Long bowed slightly and touched J.W.'s arm.

Before driving out of town, J.W. bought tea for his passengers. They sipped the lukewarm liquid without a word then sat silently during the last miles to My Co. When they arrived in the village, Bao Ngoc rushed out expectantly as the jeep pulled up to the shell of their home, though her expression deteriorated when she saw the emptiness in her mother's eyes. *Bà* Khai and the chief's mother trudged stiffly into the ruins, and J.W. drove off to his bunker.

Chapter 22

AT DAWN THE next morning, a sense of being watched startled J.W. out of sleep. He rubbed his eyes, sure he was dreaming that *Bà* Khai and the chief's mother were hunkered beside the mouth of the bunker. *Bà* Khai again held the small pot of fried noodles with goose in the little cylindrical tin lunch pail. J.W. sent them home, but before the women reached the barbed wire, he had brushed his teeth, shaved, and yelled for them to come back.

As they climbed aboard, J.W. asked the women where it might be best to search, but they did not answer, so he told them to go back into the rubble and pack their things for a night away. They drove east to My Tho, then hours and hours north, through Saigon, coming finally to Lai Khe, where the helicopter pilot who had transported *Ông* Khai was stationed. It, too, was a perilous town, like My Co, also just miles from the Cambodian border and the Ho Chi Minh trail, a mortar round's range away from regiments of North Vietnamese regulars.

J.W. set his jaw and told Khai's wife he would query the pilot, eye-to-eye, and pry the truth from him.

The journey was quiet once again, the two women staring at the golden sunlight dancing off the flooded paddies. J.W. thought of the stories *Bà* Binh had told him about traveling that very road to Lai Khe at the turn of the century, of the orchid-canopied pilgrimage with her new husband. But in 1969, the roads had become dusty, muddy, treacherous bare paths devoid of flowers, trees, or hope. Unable to imagine Viet Nam a fragrant, shaded kingdom, J.W. had to wonder how the ancient woman had come up with those treasured memories, and go on to embrace them for over sixty years, as if they had been real.

They found the pilot and his crew asleep inside, under, and on top of their helicopter, snatching minutes of precious rest between the constant, day and night, dust-off missions. J.W. shook the pilot awake and asked impatiently, "Hey, Chief, sorry to bother you, but where'd you take that Vietnamese guy the other night? I can't find him anywhere."

"What guy? Excuse me, sir, but who are you?"

"You're the dust-off that flew into My Co two nights ago for the 90th..Yes?"

"What's My Co, Captain? I'm sorry, sir, I don't know what you're talking about."

"Two nights ago—the village of My Co? I called you and asked you to medevac my counterpart—33rd Mech. The tall Vietnamese guy who was wounded at the west end of the vill. Hey, I'm not trying to bust your balls, Chief. Thank you for coming in, but I need to find him. You said you took him to the Sai Gon Hospital."

"Oh yeah, I remember now. Yeah, we took 'im down there. He was fucked up. Crew chief said he didn't have a chance."

"Yeah, but I went down there yesterday, and they never heard of him."

The pilot called up to a man sunning himself with a reflector on the roof of the helicopter. "Hey, Crew Chief, where'd we drop that local two nights ago?"

A small man with a bristling Mohawk hairdo, red bandana, and a heavy Bronx accent piped up, "The usual, sir, wasn't it? Yeah, yeah, that's it. I remember for sure. The Mayo Clinic. The one down by the big market."

The pilot smiled acerbically. "See, I told you, Captain. I promise, we didn't keep him. Take a look in the back of the ship if you don't believe me."

J.W. snapped, "Chief, listen to me. I searched every ward of that shithole hospital, every goddamn bed, every face. The lady at the front said there was no helicopter that night."

"I'm sorry, sir, I got no reason to bullshit you. That's where we dropped 'im. I don't know what to tell you."

J.W. stared out at the red mud of the helicopter base and finally sighed, "Okay, Chief, I believe you."

"Why, thank you, sir," the warrant officer added sarcastically.

"I'm sorry, Chief. I didn't come here to piss you off. Look, the guy was my best friend here. At the least, I need to find his body." J.W. started to walk off but turned back and added with a smile, "Hey, I gotta ask you one question, Chief. How the *hell* did you get into that place, and at night? There's wires everywhere."

"I don't know, sir. Been flying an hour or two since I got here. You know, you just put it down where you gotta put it down. Hope they don't send you back enough times so that you learn how. I'm sorry you lost that guy, sir."

J.W. walked back to the pilot and shook his hand, adding, "Hey, man, I'm sorry. Thanks. You were great the other night. You're a good man, but this whole fuckin' place sucks. I'm never fuckin' comin' back. Watch me now."

The pilot eye's reddened. "A fuckin' men, sir."

⟞ ⟝

The two women were hunkered at their duty stations outside J.W.'s bunker the next morning, but the road to Saigon was closed east of Moc Hoa to clean up after a 526th Engineers' gasoline tanker hit a mine. The MP's didn't bother to roll down the windows of their air-conditioned Chevy sedans when J.W. and his passengers pulled up to the blockade. They just waved from behind the glass with the backs of their hands, sending J.W. into a U-turn and home to My Co. The next day, the trio made it back to the Sai Gon Hospital, but the nurse recognized J.W. and fled from her desk to return with a platoon of orderlies.

When J.W.'s conversation with the nurse escalated by several tens of decibels, the orderlies positioned themselves in a phalanx by the swinging doors. On the other hand, by virtue of his ranting, J.W. was eventually granted an audience with the hospital director, who ceremoniously consulted the nurse's census book and assured his visitors no Vu Van Khai had ever been admitted or died there. The director invited J.W. to search for himself, though after half-an-hour on the wards, J.W. became miserably despondent, grumbled madly, and finally gave up with a poorly hidden expletive.

⟞ ⟝

For fifteen days, the trio motored to hospitals deep within South Viet Nam, going over the same territory so often, the kids at the sides of the roads recognized them; a few waved. Most of the peasants, though, had become so used to the curious sideshow, they hardly looked up when J.W. and the ladies bumped by. The expeditions took them so far afield, it was often dusk by the time they pulled into My Co. As the women climbed stiffly from the jeep, J.W. bid them return in the morning. "We'll find him," he promised, "we'll find him."

But as the list of hospitals dwindled, J.W. failed to heed his own council, and he became daily more angered at the two women, for they sat unceasingly erect, without expression, never revealing their passion or their sadness. Scrutinizing the unbending stoicism, J.W.'s frustration grew exponentially until he could no longer contain himself, and one scorching afternoon, he stopped the jeep in the middle of a road, miles from the nearest settlement. He sat for a moment quietly. He was hungry, tired, hot, and finally depressed to a level below any plane he had ever imagined a human could sink. But at the same time, he also seethed with an anger so profound, he knew he would not be able to restrain himself.

On that broiling afternoon on Highway 29, he begged himself to keep his mouth closed, but the bitter fire within him won the battle, and he turned to his passengers to bellow in English, "Don't you Vietnamese ever cry? Have you lost so much you can't care anymore? Why the hell am I doing this? Why, goddamnit? I fuckin' hate it here!"

The women sat politely through the tirade, hearing words they could not possibly understand, but unquestioningly did. While their faces remained blank, J.W. screamed a curse into the heavens as he jammed the vehicle into gear and sped back to My Co, his fury growing deeper with each pellet of red gravel that stung his face. The faster he drove, the tighter the two women held hands, though their mien stayed even more non-committal.

Ignoring his comportment, *Bà* Khai and her mother-in-law continued to emerge from the darkness each morning to hunker at the mouth of J.W.'s cave, invariably armed with the packed lunch for *Ông* Khai. J.W. finally muttered, "If we don't find him soon, there ain't goin' to be any geese left in Viet Nam."

⟞ ⟝

By mid-June, the three sojourners had penetrated the defensive perimeter of sylph-like nurses in twenty-six III Corps surgical centers, each hospital stuffed with a slaughter of war worse than the carnage they had stepped over and around the day before. On the Sunday that marked only two weeks left in his tour, J.W. sped through Moc Hoa without offering to stop for tea. The next dawn, though *Bà* Khai arrived on schedule, she was without the tiny pot or her mother-in-law. She started to thank J.W., but her voice trailed off, and she limped away quietly to join the chief's mother, who had been watching surreptitiously from behind a hut near the village restaurant.

The two women disappeared together into the hamlet, and J.W. crawled back into the bunker to rest on his cot, ruminating about the past weeks, wondering what more he could have done, worrying if *Bà* Khai believed J.W. had abandoned her family as he had the heartbroken man carrying the dead son so many weeks before. Yet, as J.W. thought more about the past month, he began to understand that *Bà* Khai had come each morning for his sake, for she believed it was J.W.'s promise to continue the search. She had known by the second day, perhaps even the first, that he was gone; that they would never find her husband's grave, that his mortal remains and their lives had fallen victim, like everyone else's, to the butchery of Viet Nam. *Bà* Khai had too much self-respect and, he suspected, fondness for him, to share her torment and sadness.

J.W. made plans to hide in the bunker for his remaining time in country, ignoring the thought of regret he would someday suffer for not spending those last days with *Bà* Binh and her neighbors. He wondered if *Cô* Lin would come back to the village before he left, and if she would let him stay for just one night. He was afraid that if he didn't sleep with her, he would never be able to put her out of his mind. On the other hand, if he did make love to her, and she was as gentle as he imagined, he would not be able to bridle his need to return to Viet Nam and find her.

After a couple of sweltering hours in his foxhole, he climbed out and decided to go to *Bà* Binh's for a glass of tea. As he walked the paths, villagers popped out of huts to say hello, pigs attacked his boots, and water buffalo snorted stinking sewage onto his worn-out uniform. His chest tightened as he saw the old lady's hootch. Maybe he would take some time to say good-by to the faces, houses, and gardens he would soon lose forever. He turned back to the NDP and rooted through his duffel bag until he came to Hemingway. The autumn leaves his wife had sent were mildewed and faded, and while they still held his place, the paper had begun to rot. He fanned the pages, letting the fragments fall to the ground.

At *Bà* Binh's, J.W. called sheepishly from the doorway. She hobbled out, staring as if she had never before laid eyes on him, and J.W. worried that her memory had at last deserted her. Or, perhaps, she knew he had abandoned *Bà* Khai. J.W.'s embarrassed silence must have told of his pain, for she reached up and pinched his cheek, asking over and over why he had not visited in so long. Her abbreviated revenge complete, she laughed and tugged him inside, forcing him to the table. He savored the sweet tea and told her of the odyssey, the hospitals and villages, and the Buddhist temples and saffron-robed monks in the beautiful hills to the west on the Cambodian border. Her coal black eyes, though, sparkled most brilliantly when J.W. whispered, "Lai Khe."

She dropped into her hammock, rocking, asking if he had stopped at the grand *Cáo Dài* Temple shrines in that city of her youth. "Oh, yes," he affirmed, seeking in his heart to fulfill the spirit of a once fetching, quiet, young Vietnamese woman. "They were so impressive. Better than anything you would ever see in America or China." She asked if the orchids still hung over the road but was asleep before he had to lie again.

J.W. rested on the hard bed, waiting for *Bà* Binh to wake, to ask if *Cô* Lin might be coming to the house for dinner, but the sound of a lone HUEY on approach to the village broke through the whir of insects, a plague that had begun sweeping across the humid tracts of Kien Tuong Province. J.W. ran from the hut to greet the chopper, drooling in anticipation of this final replenishment of C-rations and cigarettes, and the usual stack of letters that had been posted months before. But instead of landing in the NDP, the chopper floated slowly over the hamlet, sucking clothes, straw, rice, and baby chicks into mini-cyclones, blowing the stew of offal into the paddies. The ship finally settled like a bird of prey into a nearby garden.

Through the mud and trash churning about the helicopter, J.W. recognized the outline of Major Trott emerging brusquely from the rear hatch. He commenced a ram-rod straight march toward J.W., who was surprised the man was still in country. Surely, Trott had been there over a year, but as the major drew near, J.W. understood. Trott was now wearing the silver leaves of a lieutenant colonel, a promotion apparently granted on the prerequisite he extend his tour. The freshly-anointed colonel had also allowed his facial hair to grow beyond military guidelines, further even than the span of J.W.'s blooming upper lip, until the handlebars of Trott's blond mustache curled like the horns on *Bà* Xuan's water buffalo.

J.W. moved forward to congratulate him, but the brutal earnestness in the fresh colonel's blue eyes was so benumbing, J.W. stood at attention in silence. Trott, though almost striding past J.W., thought better of his disdain, and turned angrily to J.W., snarling, "I want to talk to some of the villagers, Captain."

He turned away from J.W., nearly sprinting toward *Bà* Binh's hut. He jackknifed through the squat portal without invitation, swooping inside to halt a foot from the ancient soul's hammock. He allowed the old woman to lift herself creakily and start toward the teapot, though after half-a-step, he jigged to his left, blocking her path. *Bà* Binh stopped in mid-stride, expression unchanged, eyes fixed horizontally ahead at the "U.S. ARMY" embroidered above Trott's breast pocket.

"You VC?" the colonel demanded, wagging a finger in her face. No answer. The solitary discourse became slower, but louder, Colonel Trott supposing that if he eeee-nun-see-ay-ted each word syllable by syllable, she would understand. "You like Prezz-eeee-dent Thieu?" No answer. "Translate, Captain."

Trott walked to a raw, narrow wooden shelf over the religious alter at the front of the hut, pointing to the yellowed photographs as he boomed, "Are these your grandchildren? Are they out there with the VC?"

Bà Binh's eyes shot to the pictures and saddened. No answer.

Trott snapped at J.W., "I told you to translate."

"Sir," J.W. hissed, "I'm not translatin' shit for you."

J.W.'s breathing deepened as the colonel slammed his fist onto the delicate alter, pieces of thin bamboo and joss flying across the hut. He took two giant steps to the front of *Bà* Binh. Trott's face relaxed. Surely, he was about to apologize. J.W. sighed. The calm, however, vanished as abruptly as it had surfaced, broken by the thud of Lieutenant Colonel Douglas Trott's palm smashing *Bà* Binh's face. Her left cheek reddened where the thump of his college ring had landed, and she began to crumble but drew a breath so deep, it took seconds to finish. She straightened her miniature frame, waiting sullenly for the next blow. This time his fist clenched, but her eyes raked back into the cold, blue eyes so viciously, Trott faltered and wheeled suddenly, ducking through the doorway.

J.W. followed him toward the chopper, screaming, "Hey, you bastard, get back here. I'm gonna kick your ass, prick! You come out here just to slap an old lady in the face? The assholes in Saigon pushin' you that hard?" But as J.W. steamed past the empty marketplace, he thought back to his last day with *Ông* Khai, and he stopped in his tracks, dazed, caring for no one or no thing, holding only one ever-present, hedonistic, obsessive thought—to be allowed to leave My Co, to exit Viet Nam in one physical piece, and go home. Time would deal with the wounds in his soul and his heart over whatever years the Lord would grant him—just as long as it was in America. He sat by the banyan tree, trembling too hard to smoke, as Trott's chopper lifted.

An hour later, J.W. returned to *Bà* Binh's and bowed tentatively under the thatch and stepped up submissively to the old lady. Slowly, he lifted two fingers to stroke the red mark on her face, but she pushed his hand away and walked to a corner shelf to prepare a wad of betel nut. Soon, pink-green spit drizzled from her swollen mouth onto the floor. She glanced at J.W. before squatting to pick up the scattered pieces of the altar. When he dropped to his knees to help, though, she waved him away.

She did not understand, nor did J.W. at that moment. It wasn't until years later he realized the colonel had wrested from the incident everything he had come to appropriate. Word would spread; the story would be embellished with each family that discussed it around the evening fire, and the next time the blond, blue-eyed, mustachioed American officer swooped into town, some of the villagers would run or hide. Those he caught would talk.

Sipping tea, J.W. sought to lose himself in Hemingway, to forget that he would, in short order, answer for his insubordination. He fidgeted, fearing the newly-promoted colonel would wait a few days to report the incident, then wait a few more before having J.W. brought back to Long Binh for discipline. Next, he'd apply for an in-country R&R to delay the hearing for seventy-two additional hours. If Colonel Trott was willing to spend a few minutes on the arithmetic, he could engineer the postponement of J.W.'s DEROS for many days beyond the fourteen officially left in his tour.

J.W. could not concentrate on his book, or on the image of *Cô* Lin brought by the presence of her things on the table. He lay on the hardwood bed, seeking solace in sleep, a respite from the nauseating thought that he might have to remain in Viet Nam for even a millisecond beyond the scheduled end of his tour. But the monsoon abruptly hammered the thatch of *Bà* Binh's hut with a thunder so deafening, it thwarted his escape. When the rains subsided, he drifted off for a few moments but soon jumped awake, aware that he was being watched. In the dim light, he focused on a diminutive, smiling figure sitting at the table facing him.

"Captain, I have not seen you in a long time. Grandmother says you are going home soon. A lot of people in My Co will miss you."

"Thank you, but I may have to stay longer. I'm sorry our colonel hurt your grandmother. Not all Americans are like him."

"Yes, I know. You have told me that before."

J.W. whispered, "Are you staying here tonight?"

Cô Lin did not answer, but she glanced instinctively toward her grandmother, who was still asleep in the hammock. "Captain, have you eaten?"

"No, but I'm not hungry. We had a bad day." He paused to gather courage then went on. "*Cô* Lin, would you sit here?" He touched the edge of the bed. "Maybe just for one minute?"

She hesitated but stood, walked to the doorway, peered left and right, slid the tin sheet closed, and walked around the table toward him. When she sat on the edge of the planks, J.W.'s fingers brushed hers delicately, and he expected her to recoil, but she smiled hesitantly down at him, and he saw in the fading light of that unhappy day a flushing of *Cô* Lin's skin and a darkening of her lips. Soon they were breathing in symmetry.

A clap of thunder boomed in the distance, and *Bà* Binh stirred in her hammock. *Cô* Lin flew from the bed and returned to the table.

"Will you be here tonight?" J.W. asked again.

She whispered, "Yes," but she jumped up and dashed from the hut.

Chapter 23

THOUGH J.W. PUT his head down and tried to sleep, the rumble of a helicopter passing over My Co brought him back to the retribution he would soon face. A moment later, he heard another chopper and stepped outside *Bà* Binh's to watch villagers pour from their huts, poised to flee, clutching children and meager belongings. They were pointing up at two elephantine Chinooks on a coordinated approach into My Co. J.W.'s worst fear was coming true—Colonel Trott had gathered the ships and troops to arrest him, along with as many villagers-prisoners he could squeeze into the bellies of the gargantuan aircraft.

Fifteen feet off the deck, the helicopters settled into a hover that sent the 120 mile-per-hour-rotor wash off their flanks into gales of mud and feathers—chicken, geese, and small dogs lifted a hundred feet in the air, only to succumb to gravity's punch, flung back down onto the roofs and into gardens. Thatch from the nearby houses soon joined the fog that engulfed My Co, and it was not long before the battered Coca Cola ice chest became a victim as well, whipped so hard, the hinges twisted to freeze the lid upright, as if it were flipping off the whole world.

The ships did not touch down but came close enough to allow thirty or forty GIs to jump off, men dragging combat gear, cartons of paper, tactical radios, pots, and old stoves, all of which capitulated to the rotor wash as the ship lifted off. The soldiers assembled comfortably, smoking and bitching, ignoring the equipment they had off-loaded, which had joined a bicultural corpus of debris that scattered over several hectares. The empty Chinooks rose, and now so much lighter, they splattered only a meager barrage of mud and trash into the remnants of the hootches and the suddenly roofless restaurant.

As the air settled, a smaller command helicopter landed near J.W.'s bunker. From it sprang another in the endless procession of colonels and sergeants major who had come to pass a day or two in My Co.

While the colonel scrutinized his battalion settling into a new battle zone, the sergeant major dismissed the men to dig foxholes, bunkers, latrine slit-trenches, and garbage pits. Several of the larger troops rushed over to claim J.W.'s bunker; the most heavily built of those troops dropped his duffel bag into the portal then turned to brandish threatening looks and muscular poses to those of lesser bulk. Satisfied he had again established himself as the alpha male of Second Platoon, he climbed down into the bunker, tossing away the rusted, charred remnant of the Honda generator J.W. had procrastinated on throwing into the slit latrine of the last battalion of interlopers.

The other men walked off muttering and gesturing with their middle fingers but soon found the leftovers of abandoned bunkers and settled in. The sergeant major bellowed at the first sergeants, who bellowed at the platoon sergeants, who bellowed at the squad leaders to start digging in.

J.W. bristled as he marched down the road toward the colonel, though he slowed as he approached the battalion commander, admitting, not all that grudgingly, he was relieved to see them. Thirteen days and change left in Viet Nam was far too short for verbal heroics or ideals; it was, however, just time enough to process the villagers' claims for the property and cattle destroyed by the Americans over the past month. That was a safe pursuit, one that could be accomplished two feet outside the NDP beneath an umbrella, but, most importantly, under the watchful eyes of this latest infantry unit. J.W. tried not to admit that his spiritual attachment to Khai's dream of peace and prosperity was buried somewhere with the man in an unknown, unmarked, untended grave, if providence had granted him interment in something other than a garbage can behind a hospital.

J.W. wanted the VC to know a whole battalion, perhaps a division, had taken up residence in the hamlet, and for the enemy forces to steer clear of My Co for just a fortnight. He would spend his hours with *Cô* Lin, protected by the infantry of the United States Army, another of the bizarre gifts he had been offered in the war. His pace slowed, and he assumed a weak smile as he took his position in front of the colonel and saluted.

"Sir, Captain J.W. Weathersby, S-5, 2nd Battalion, 33rd Mechanized Infantry Brigade, reporting, sir!"

The colonel was a large, beefy man with ham-like paws. His right hand lifted a few inches until J.W.'s eyes locked on the massive, blue-stoned West Point ring. J.W. cursed under his breath, "Shit, another nose picker."

J.W., entranced with the flapping of the ring, was silent for a moment, at least until the colonel delivered a deeply resonant, controlled, "Who the hell are you?"

J.W. recognized those words. They had been the foundation for the overwhelming majority of conversations he'd had with superiors over the months in the hamlet. He answered perfunctorily, bearing the usual smile that accompanied his well-rehearsed explanation. "I'm the S-5 for the Mech, sir, 33rd Mech, sir. Colonel Bierlein assigned me out here. He said I was the Mayor of My Co."

"What's My Co?"

"This is My Co, sir." J.W. spread his arms and pointed into the distance on both sides of the NDP.

"Bierlein went home months ago. Who knows you're here?"

Unfortunately, J.W. had to pause for an instant before answering. As far as he knew, only Colonel Trott was really sure. "Well, sir, I guess my unit knows, but they don't do a whole lot to get my mail or food out very often." His mind fogged, and he found his anger swelling. "That's a real problem, sir" he went on, "and I'm stuck out here and..."

The colonel cut off the burgeoning diatribe with a wave of the ring. "Where do you stay at night?"

J.W. hesitated, but the contortion on the colonel's face loosened his tongue. "Well, sir, it's in the village. Most nights recently, I've been staying at *Bà* Binh's house. It's right up the road, sir."

"You sleep with the Vietnamese? You live here? And who the hell is *Bà* Binh?"

"She's an old lady, sir. Maybe eighty."

"Uh huh. Tell you what, Captain, you stay here in the NDP with us until I can get this thing straightened out."

"Sir, I can't do that. I have my orders to stay in the village."

"Let's see 'em."

"Hold on, sir, they're in my duffel bag." J.W. pointed toward his underground home but saw his worldly goods tossed about, floating in mud-choked puddles outside the bunker. "Goddamn son of a bitch," he spit, only inches from the colonel, before stomping off toward the bunker. He stopped when he saw cigarette smoke wafting up through the muddy portal. "Who the hell's in there? Get out, troop! You're in my bunker. Take a walk, pal."

A thick-necked, shaved-headed man with angry eyes peered from the opening. He looked at J.W. curiously then ducked back inside. The sergeant major bristled over. "Sir, how can I help you?"

"Sergeant Major, I been in this hole for nine months. I want him outta there, and I want my gear picked up, dried off, and placed neatly back inside."

The sergeant major called down into the darkness. "Petroski, outta the bunker. Move in with someone else. And then get behind that 60 on the perimeter."

"Sergeant Major," Petroski rumbled as he ducked low to negotiate the bunker opening, "I was on the 60 last night and also two nights ago. I need a break."

The colonel glanced over at the rising voices and drifted toward the disturbance. The growing crowd of spectators parted to let him pass. He spoke without emotion, "Sergeant Petroski, get yourself on perimeter, and Captain, into the bunker. You stay there until I find out what the hell you're doing here. And that's a direct order. Consider yourself under house arrest."

J.W. laughed haughtily, "That's no big deal, sir. It's not the first time."

"I'm sure it's not. Sergeant Major, get the 33rd Mech on the horn."

At dusk, driven by the thought of *Cô* Lin's acquiescence, J.W. emerged from his bunker and walked casually toward the latrine the infantry had dug on the perimeter, a virtual shooting gallery for a VC sniper. He pretended to lower his pants then squatted over the slit trench, waiting a full thirty seconds before weaving through a longstanding gap the in the rusted apron of barbed wire. He knew it well—the kids had fashioned the gash to hawk sodas, beer, and joints to the GIs. Though the trip wires for the perimeter flares had surely long since rusted away, he managed to find the one that had survived. After a pop, light flooded the area between the concentric rolls of concertina wire. J.W. threw his arms into the air screeching, "It's me. Don't shoot, goddamnit, it's me!"

When J.W. heard the clank of an M-60 being charged, he bellowed again that he was an American officer and dropped to the ground, a maneuver that detonated another flare. A torrent of red tracers streamed over his head, and he dug his fingers into the soaking earth, hollowing a one-man trench. The sergeant major called out, "Captain, sir, get your ass outta that wire and into headquarters."

J.W. marched to the GP Medium tent at the center of the NDP. "Sir, I'm caught in the middle here. My orders are to remain *in* the village when our troops are present until relieved by my CO. If I disobey those orders, I'm accountable."

"Captain, *I* am your CO. Your responsibility is to remain in your bunker until I tell you you can leave. Don't try that again."

J.W. sat on his cot devising tactic after tactic to escape the NDP. The thought of touching *Cô* Lin blinded him, and he was crawling out of the bunker just as the sergeant major walked up and grumbled, "Sir, the old man needs you to translate. Follow me." J.W. saw a dozen villagers hunkered at the west gate. They were holding sticks, the ends swathed in oil-soaked scraps of burning cloth. They had approached the NDP, torches ablaze, a rag-tag delegation of old men and women howling their presence. Nonetheless, the Americans surrounded them as if confronted with a platoon of Viet Cong, M-16s on full automatic, safeties off.

"Captain Weathersby," the colonel muttered from behind him, "these people asked for you by name. What are they saying?"

"Sir, they say a woman is bleeding to death in the village. They want us to save her life. Is there a medic in your unit, sir?"

"We have one. You can have him for a few minutes. Sergeant Major, get one of the company commanders to put together an escort patrol. But I want this whole thing over quickly. I don't want my troops out in the village if we need to move."

J.W. left Happy Valley NDP at the center of two heavily armed squads of infantry. As they passed *Bà* Binh's, he saw *Cô* Lin sitting by candlelight at the table, staring out the open door, and in the corner, *Bà* Binh asleep in her hammock. He tried to signal *Cô* Lin, but she could not see into the darkness.

The patrol proceeded further into the village past *Ông* Khai's house, and it struck J.W. that he had spent very little time recently mourning his friend, his life more consumed with the tally of hours and minutes left in country than in the fabric of what would haunt him for years. There was no light in the ruins of the house, and J.W. wondered if the Khais had left My Co for good.

At the far end of the road, the villagers pointed to the hut in which the prostitute had died. Her sister now lived there and was prostrate on the very bed on which *Cô* Thi had bled to death. She was desperately pale in the flickering of a kerosene lamp, and the medic, without asking questions, dropped to his knees to start an IV. The wooden planks were awash in bright red blood, and more was dripping from her black silk pants. It dawned on J.W. that she was bleeding vaginally.

The medic cursed aloud, "Shit, spontaneous abortion." He turned to J.W. and declared, "This lady's in shit up to her neck. Sir, they got a hospital around here? This lady needs blood, and quick."

"No. The closest real one is in My Tho, a lot of miles east. The only way we get people outta here is by vehicle. Medevacs don't usually come in unless it's for one of our troops."

"Yeah, well, say good-by, sir, 'cause she's dead in an hour without blood. This IV's only good for a little while."

J.W. returned alone to the NDP and asked the colonel if he could use his helicopter to take the woman to the hospital at My Tho, and if he could borrow the medic for the trip. The colonel woke his pilot, who asked J.W. if he knew a route to the hospital, if he knew if there was a helipad at the hospital, if he knew if there were landing lights at the hospital, if he knew if there were wires surrounding the hospital, if he knew if there was fuel at the hospital, and if he knew how long the woman was going to live. When J.W. answered no to all the above, the pilot turned without another word and went back to sleep.

The sergeant major asked for volunteers to go along as shotgun with J.W. in the jeep. Petroski stepped forward. The sergeant major conferred with the battalion commander, who wagged a plantain-sized finger in the man's face, ordering him not to assassinate Captain Weathersby on the journey.

J.W. drove to My Tho faster than he had ever moved on a Vietnamese road. The hospital lay in a heap of rubble. They drove north to Tan An. He could not tell if the woman was still alive when she was wheeled through the moldy, green doors to surgery. At the reception desk, he gathered his courage and asked if a child named Huong from the village of My Co had survived the wounds to his leg, but the attendant looked in the book and shook her head, reporting that his name had been inscribed in the book on the day he was brought it, but there was no record of his disposition. J.W. nodded without comment.

On the road back to My Co, J.W. asked Petroski why he had agreed to go along. "A few hours ago, you were trying to kill me with a machine-gun, and now you volunteer to guard my life. I don't get it."

"Sir," he drawled, "I wasn't shooting at you. We were two feet above your head. I saw you got a Ranger tab on your shoulder. That shit doesn't bother you guys. We were just having some fun. I know you got a hard job out here."

Unconvinced and waiting for the other shoe to drop, J.W. asked sarcastically, "How do you know what I do in the village?"

Petroski thought for a moment. "You think I'm stupid because I'm big and got a shaved head and because I'm an enlisted man, don't you, sir?"

J.W. started to answer, but Petroski went on. "I'm no troglodyte, sir. I play that game to get my way. Works, too. But I got plans for the future. I could've had my degree by now for the time I pissed away in the army. A man doesn't throw away few years of his life for nothing, but that's what I'm doing here."

J.W. tried to answer matter-of-factly. "Well, supposedly we're doing a job in Viet Nam. Making the world safer for your kids. You should be proud of yourself. You got a CIB pinned to your shirt, troop. Lotta people look up to grunts. I'm not lyin'."

"Well, they're fools, sir. All we ever do is walk. I haven't done a damn thing positive since I got here. Six months and I haven't seen a gook. I been shot at one time, in a bar fight, by some crazy, fuckin' G.I. Shit, I don't even drink."

"You want to get shot at?" J.W. laughed, warming to the big man, "I can arrange it for you. Stick around My Co for a while."

"No, sir. I don't want to get hurt. I'm not crazy. I just hate it here. I'm gonna give up my life to make sure a bunch of rich fuckers at home keep making money? Sitting on the 60 tonight isn't going to enhance my future. At least now I can write home and tell them that I did something in Viet Nam. Maybe I'll take a writing course in college and do a book about it someday. Yeah, a book about the night I did something in the war."

They arrived back in My Co at 5:30 A.M., in time for a freezing shower and breakfast. The colonel took a seat next to J.W. in the mess tent and advised him the 33rd Mech had corroborated his unlikely story, and that he would be allowed into the hamlet to carry out his duties, particularly the calming of tempers over the loss of the huts near the landing pad. J.W. agreed that fence-mending was in order, again, but warned that the process, with its complicated paperwork and delicate international negotiations, might require weeks to complete. Toward that end, he suggested solemnly that he, and he alone, be allowed access to the hamlet. The colonel agreed to keep his men clear of the village proper but warned that he intended to send them out every night on patrol into the forest and paddies. "And you need to stay in sight of the NDP at all times, Captain. I don't want you hanging around where I can't get a hold of you."

J.W. agreed with a nod and at dawn left for work, erecting the familiar folding table and chairs to interview those who had lost all they owned to the American helicopters. In Pavlovian response to the sight of a uniformed white man at a tiny, olive drab table, the first homeless platoon of victims hobbled over. J.W. explained, with head bowed, that the pilots had just been following orders. Didn't the citizens of My Co understand that the vulnerable, negligibly armed transport aircraft had flown the only approach into the hamlet that would allow them to land without being shot down by the battalions of hateful enemy soldiers lurking in the jungle? He paused for a moment, the string of his thought lost in recalculation of the hours and minutes left in his war. When his head cleared, he stood, astonished by the burgeoning audience coalescing in concentric circles a dozen deep.

"Our soldiers don't want to die," J.W. went on, his eyes hardening as if delivering a new Gettysburg Address, "they're good men, just like *your* sons. Our pilots did not do this to hurt you."

"Screw the colonel," he bellowed as he grabbed the little table, hooked the chairs in his elbows, and dragged the mobile insurance agency to a shaded corner of the unused market. He strung up a poncho to block the dust from the road and eyes inside the NDP then walked into the morass of plaintiffs, pushing them gradually into winding lines of hunkered boredom. J.W. moved to his desk and arranged his papers with such sloth, several men in the queue shouted to their wives, "Go home and fetch rice and tea." When J.W.'s cigarettes were exhausted, they sent the women back for tobacco.

From Weathersby's perspective, his mission that day, and for every day and hour and second left in Viet Nam, was to minimize the scrutiny of the majors and the colonels who could, if they desired, fling him back into a real combat unit for a week or two, just to test his mettle. So, J.W. spoke to each of the villagers very slowly, recording precise notes, intent on not making a single clerical error. In the end, though, all his work amounted to was copying the data from the previous infantry helicopter incursion forms onto the new infantry helicopter incursion forms. A simple task, but one he did with such indolence, the peasants looking over his shoulder were beginning to read English. One man pointed out a misspelled word.

After several hours, the sergeant major marched into the market, searching for J.W. "Old man's been looking for you for half-a-day. He's hot. Wants to know what's taking so long."

Weathersby gathered his papers and left for headquarters, swooping up under the flap of the command and coming to attention inches from the battalion commander. The colonel snatched reading glasses from his fatigues and focused on the dust-enveloped apparition inches from his face. Before the colonel could draw a breath, J.W. slipped an infantry helicopter incursion form from his stack of papers, waved it, and pointed, quite hastily, to several expressions in Vietnamese which he declared impossible to translate into English. "Sir, I'm just trying to avoid another global incident, like the last one out here, which I'm sure you heard about. Look, sir, you'll be gone in two days…"

"I sure as hell hope so. Go on."

Sir, you'll be gone, but the villagers aren't stupid. Some of them can read and write. They keep notes about when their stuff was damaged. Sir, they draw pictures of the infantry unit patches they blame, and the numbers on the helicopters."

The old man's face barely twitched as he waved his finger toward the tent flap and the village of My Co.

As J.W. worked on the forms, he mumbled to the peasants that the actual reparations were in the hands of President Nixon himself, and he declared, "Sadly, you will not see a piaster until the great American leader reviews each and every petition." He waved a stack of forms. "If the president wasn't so busy with the war, your money would already be here. So, I think you should tell the Viet Cong to stop fighting. If you do that, Mr. Nixon will have the time to help you."

Though his audience rejoined with a hundred blank stares, when the paperwork was done, the villagers sidled up to him, urging J.W. to put in a good word with Mr. Nixon about the vigor of deceased Water Buffalo Number Six before it had been used as target practice, or how plump *Bà* Nguyen's rooster had become by the day it was swept away.

While the congress of fiduciary-minded citizens refined their arguments, J.W. suggested the residents gather each morning at the market and shout into Happy Valley NDP a demand that J.W. present himself for an update on the status of their claims. As a general consensus built amongst the villagers regarding J.W.'s plan, he took out his copy of Kafka's short stories and pretended to read. But really, he was just waiting until the folks drifted away so he could sneak to *Bà* Binh's.

The old lady was in her hammock. J.W. entered gently and accepted a glass of tea, not wanting to appear as needy as he was. The first thing he noticed was that *Cô* Lin's books had disappeared, and when he finally screwed up the nerve to ask if she was in My Co, *Bà* Binh shook her head, offering a very quiet, "She's gone again. But this time, she seemed upset. I don't know what happened, or where she is, or when she's coming back. She never tells me."

Chapter 24

J.W. SPENT THE remaining days at the market behind the poncho, reading and sleeping and assuring the citizens of My Co that the Americans were honorable people, and that the reparation payments he had sworn were on the way would get there in due time. There were two highlights during those last days. The first was the ancient Citroen that occasionally blew through My Co. The fair-haired western journalist at the wheel always stopped to give J.W. a cold, German beer, and ask where the VC were operating that week. It wasn't the brew that J.W. waited for, but a peek at the magnificent Vietnamese woman always by the correspondent's side. The two made their rounds of the combat units in III Corps, following the war but never stopping in it.

The second was the arrival of the governor in his helicopter, followed by a platoon of swarthy soldiers in an American truck, and finally a party of civilians on scooters. The latter commandeered J.W.'s table and his stack of reparation papers. They handed out money, though only pennies on the dollar. When a few very old men spoke up, the governor nodded to the platoon leader. The soldiers marched them behind the market and, in plain sight, pushed them around with their M-16s, one troop placing the tip of his rifle in the nostril of an eighty-year-old.

With three days left in Viet Nam, a 33rd Mech helicopter dropped into My Co with orders for J.W. to present both himself and his jeep to regimental headquarters at Normandy Base Camp, where his odyssey had begun a year before. He was to report within twenty-four hours.

The moment had finally come. He sipped tea at the market, trying to accept that while his tour in the village of My Co was finally over, his time in Viet Nam was not. He would repair to the safety of Normandy, but would also be ordered front and center to answer for his insubordination to Lieutenant Colonel Trott. J.W. cursed himself for having gloated over the skirmishes in which he had frustrated Trott, those lesser victories mattering nil now that he was being summoned to stand before the Nuremburg Tribunal.

At his bunker, he made two piles of clothes—one to give away to the villagers, one to take home. Old Dinh Dao, the village idiot, would get the copper antenna from the jeep. The man had asked for it several times, to use it as a walking stick. *Ông* Dinh Dao regaled J.W. with his plans to walk the entire length of Viet Nam, from My Co to Hanoi, a thousand miles he boasted, using the copper antenna as a walking stick he'd swing to ward off dogs, roosters, and angry pot belly pigs. When J.W. asked him about walking around in the midst of the war, and about how he planned to cross over the DMZ into the North, Dinh Dao replied, "American man, I will walk, just as I do here, one foot at a time. This fine antenna, if you'll finally give it to me, I'll use it to steady myself. I'm not a young man anymore, you know."

His foam rubber pillow, the one he'd hand-carried ten thousand miles from the Bronx, would go to *Bà* Binh, who had never slept on one in her whole life, but who wanted it to sit on. J.W. warned that it reeked of the fetor of a year's absorbed sweat, and he offered instead to burn it, but the old lady insisted. *Ông* Long, if he ever came home to My Co from wherever he went after *Em* Huong's death, would get the 5-gallon jerry can on the back of the jeep and *Ông* Tinh, the jeep's tools: a screwdriver, pliers, ball-peen hammer, and useless tire jack.

J.W. sat at the market the next morning building the courage to say goodbye. He agonized over seeing *Bà* Khai. Her problems were profound. The solatium paid by the Saigon government, despite J.W.'s cajoling, demands, and threats, was so small, the family had lost their house in Tuyen Binh, forcing her to remain in the crust of what was left of their shanty in My Co. *Bà* Khai and the children had found cardboard to patch the roof, and had plastered gobs of mud over the shrapnel-peppered walls.

The one time J.W. had passed the hut, rags covered the window frames, and a musty smell wafted from the darkened house. He was not sure if anyone was living there, though he had heard that Bao Ngoc, the eldest daughter, roamed the village at night begging for food. When *Bà* Binh had offered a tiny piece of sugar cane, the little girl glared with bitterness. J.W. wondered how long *Bà* Khai could delay the inevitable poverty and wretchedness to which they were fated. Would she keep her children, or would she wither away, and the children end up in a muddy Saigon alley alongside their generation of war orphans?

A once-yellow, 1950s bus, the stenciled CHICAGO PUBLIC SCHOOLS nearly a phantom, bucked to a stop in front of the market. A collection of bamboo chicken coops, vegetables, and battered cardboard luggage was scarcely lashed to the rusted roof. It was the same vehicle in which J.W. had motored months before, the day he'd returned to My Co after the bunker explosion. The driver, perched on bare springs covered with the same scrap of splintered plywood, nodded to J.W. distantly while drumming his fingers on the steering wheel, waiting for his disembarking passengers to stop gabbing.

Several of the children gathered to gawk at the villagers with sufficient funds for the ten-cent trip to the market in Moc Hoa, fearless adventurers who had stared into the mouth of the dragon and survived. The first passenger to climb off the rickety steps was an old man with a turban and a wispy beard. He waved to J.W. and pointed excitedly back into the bus, where the driver had gone, grumbling, to guide an emaciated child with a bandaged leg up the aisle.

J.W.'s jaw dropped so far, it seemed to touch My Co's ochre earth, but as *Em* Huong limped onto the steps, J.W. sprang forward to lift him to the ground.

The boy laughed. "Your mustache, sir, has grown so long. It points up to the sky like a set of water buffalo horns made of iron! The people are right. You are *Đại Úy Rào*!"

J.W. was struck silent, bewildered, sure he was suffering another of the implausible fantasies that had become the substance of his dreams and, recently, his waking hours. But this one seemed so real—the heat, the odors, the boisterous chattering, the villager's feet actually touching the ground. And there were the families converging from the far reaches of the settlement, throngs assembling to witness the miracle of *Em* Huong.

Suddenly, though, a quiet blanketed My Co—the phenomenon of resurrected life silencing even the children. Eventually, one of the women whispered incredulously, "That boy is indestructible. He must be in contact with the gods. One day he will be very powerful." J.W. nodded his head in concord.

In due course, attention shifted back to *Ông* Long, who held a letter in his hand. He lifted it over his head to wave it at *Ông* Khai's daughter, Bao Ngoc. "Take this to your mother," the old man ordered gently. J.W. sighed in relief that the government had finally given in and accepted his demands to treat the family of such a good man with decency. He nearly fell back into his seat, light headed, realizing that for the first time in his life he had *done* something.

Half the gathering crowd marched along with the child toward the Khais' home, the other half remained behind to pester *Em* Huong, pulling at his skin, pointing at the scarred, mangled remains of his leg.

While J.W. was trying to explain to *Ông* Long that he had been told the child had died that first day in the hospital, a procession of villagers marched back down the road toward the market, *Bà* Khai in the lead, limping at a gallop. Spotting J.W., she hobbled forward, hesitated, composed herself, then thrust before him the wrinkled, stained letter. The retinue that had followed her, now reinforced by those who had remained behind with Huong, surrounded J.W.'s chair. The ring was so tight, he could not lift his elbows to reach forward and take the letter. A few men jammed into the center of the target and pushed the swarm back so that J.W. could stand and accept the note. Assuming the villagers believed his Vietnamese sufficiently polished to read Vietnamese for the illiterate, J.W. studied the document, but the writing was weak, the words ran together, and he looked up to apologize. "I'm sorry, I can't read it for you."

"No, no!" She snatched the letter back and pointed impatiently to the frail signature on the back. "It says Vu Van Khai. He is my husband." She turned the letter over and tapped a nail on the second paragraph. Even J.W. could make out the name of the very first hospital at which they'd searched in Saigon.

J.W. jumped from his chair. He pulled the letter from her, tearing the tissue-thin document. He skimmed through the wavering scribble. "When, when, goddamnit?"

Bà Khai grabbed the letter back. She pointed to scrawled numbers at the top and spoke in English, "Two day ago!"

J.W. stared blankly at her for a moment and then at the letter for another few seconds until *Bà* Khai rolled her eyes in disbelief and snapped loudly, "I am wife of husband Khai. Khai in hospital Saigon. Khai write letter two day ago!" With that declaration, her eyes clouded, her skin blanched, and she collapsed into the arms of the women who pushed J.W. aside to settle her sit in his chair.

Silence once again fell upon the assemblage, all eyes locked on J.W. He thought for a moment that, in theory, he could find roads to detour his trip to Saigon, drop Mrs. Khai off at the hospital, drive back south to My Tho, and take refuge at Normandy Base Camp. But a cold wave of uneasiness seized him, and he allowed that he was simply too scared to drive even one more kilometer on the roads of Cochin China. Khai was alive. That had to be good enough. It mattered not if J.W. resumed his duties as taxi boy. Why not just give her the money for the bus; maybe even some for food, roast goose—if the species had survived her cleaver—and lodging?

He took out his wallet, but before opening it, he spoke to her gently. "*Bà* Khai, I must tell you that I am leaving My Co today for good. I will not be back. I am going home to my country. I am very sorry. I can't take you to Saigon. Here," he whispered sadly, handing her twenty funny-money dollars, a peasant's income for half-a-year. "I hope this is enough for your trip."

She smiled respectfully, barely looking down at the bills, then turned to limp back to what was left of her life. J.W. was thankful she had not spit on the money. Bao Ngoc, who'd remained at the edge of the gathering, stared at J.W., a blank anger clouding her beautiful eyes. In his last glimpse of the preteen, he realized that even a trace of the perpetual, joyful smile was gone. She turned abruptly to run after her mother.

J.W. sat to smoke a Salem. His chest was seized with so much bitterness and confusion, he pushed away the hands of the old men grabbing at his cigarettes. The smoke, though, mitigated his anger enough to accept it was not Bao Ngoc or her mother or the villagers who were the source of hostility, for they had remained kind and gentle despite their suffering. They owed him nothing. He owed them everything.

J.W. called to the chief's wife, "*Bà* Khai, wait. Let me talk to my colonel."

At headquarters, a massive hand motioned him in. The walls were hung with a dozen maps, each covered in plastic smeared with grease pencil markings so dense, J.W. assumed the whereabouts of every VC in the province had been detected. The battalion sergeant major was sketching in an afternoon assault in the forest near the hamlet. J.W. noticed his own name listed on the acetate as the interpreter. The colonel and most of the other men were, though, gathered around one of the eight tactical radios that crackled in every niche of the command tent. They were listening to the terrified screeching of a South Vietnamese soldier yelling the same thing over and over into his transmitter. The colonel asked J.W., "Do you know what he's saying, Captain?"

J.W. closed his eyes, trying to concentrate on the high-pitched screams, nodding finally, "I think he's a platoon leader, sir. He says the Viet Cong are killing his men one by one, cutting their throats. He's hiding in a bunker begging for help. He thinks he's on his company commander's frequency."

The colonel shook his head sadly. "When he stops, see if you can find out where he is, or at least tell him he's on the wrong frequency."

The sergeant major, frustrated, muttered to no one in particular, "Signal's getting weaker. You can't hold the transmit button for that long without running the battery down. The guy hasn't taken a breath in twenty minutes."

The radio hissed a few times before it went silent. The colonel handed the pork chop to J.W., who tried several times to contact the platoon leader. There was, though, no reply. The colonel shook his head. "Maybe he figured it out." He paused and turned to J.W. "What can I do for you, Weathersby?"

"Couple of things, sir. I got my orders to return to Normandy today. But I got a big problem. You remember the Vietnamese village chief I told you about, the one I looked all over III Corps for?" The colonel nodded suspiciously. "Well, he's alive, sir. His wife just got a letter from him. It was dated two days ago, from a hospital in Saigon. I need to go down there, bring his wife and his mother. Sir, we need to do this."

"So, go ahead and 'do this,' Captain."

"Sir, I can't drive down there, find him, drive back here, drop off his family, then make it to Normandy before dark."

"And?"

"Sir, I would like to borrow your helicopter. Just for a little while. And if you could get a message to my CO that I am out on a mission, that I'll be back tomorrow, that would really help, sir. Then I won't bother you ever again, sir. I promise."

The large man considered the request for a moment. "Take my helicopter, Captain, but I want it back by noon, by noon! Is that clear, Captain?"

J.W. convinced the pilot he knew the way like the back of his hand and was allowed to take the controls. *Bà* Khai and her mother-in-law, strapped in the back, clutching each other in death hugs, refused J.W.'s pleas to look down on the very roads they had bounced along weeks before. J.W. turned frequently to smile at the ladies in the back, but the dark visor was down on his helmet, and anyway, their eyes were too tightly shut to see him. The exotic smells, the mud, and boredom could not reach the cool, fragrant air at three thousand feet. Nearing Saigon, the helicopter descended into the stench and scooter fumes of the city's slums. The pilot took the controls and hovered above the courtyard, whipping up dirt and bedding, pots and pans, all of it quickly showering down upon the refugees as they fled into the streets. There was a small gap in the wires through which the man dropped the ship, his body bobbing to *Mony Mony* on Armed Forces Network.

"How the hell did you do that?"

"I donno."

The air remained cool until seconds after touchdown. As the nauseating tropical heat rammed through the open chopper doors, J.W. acknowledged that no one ever escaped Viet Nam for more than a few moments.

The same nurse was at the little desk to greet them, neatly coiffed, uniform bright white. J.W. felt a blast of adrenaline clutch his solar plexus as her head dropped to consult the notebook as if she had never before laid eyes on him. "Yes, he been here. Now he no here." She closed the book and looked away.

J.W. slammed the desk with his fist. "Look, the last time I was here you said, goddamnit, that...Okay, just tell me where the hell he is now, and I will leave you alone."

"He go hospital Vung Tao. Yesterday, go."

"Are you sure? Did you see him go?"

"Yesterday, Vu Van Khai go Vung Tao." She reopened the notebook and pointed indignantly to an entry that verified her statement. "Yesterday, go Vung Tao. You see, Vu Van Khai he go."

The pilot was standing at the door winding his index finger in the air above his head, pointing at his watch. As the foursome lifted off from the courtyard, it was as if the air flow from the helicopter sucked the people in reverse, back into their cardboard hovels. He hovered over the grand Ben Thanh market, leering down at a beautiful Vietnamese woman in an iridescent red *áo dài.* She fought to hold the skirt down as she glowered at the pilot.

J.W. took control of the ship. The man leaned his head back to rest as J.W. skimmed along the roofs of the Caravelle, Continental, and Rex Hotels, pointing the ship west toward the Delta. He was cruising as fast as the helicopter would fly toward My Co. J.W. turned and yelled to *Bà* Khai how sorry he was, and she nodded, her eyes still locked shut. As the ship gained more altitude, J.W. smiled to himself, realizing it was the same route he had flown on his first sortie as pilot in command out of Saigon to My Co, a lifetime before. He also thought of the first schoolyard payback with Colonel Bierlein, and the miserable little man who'd fired on the commander's ship.

Bà Khai and her mother-in-law finally opened their eyes, accepting his apology that Vung Tao was forty miles to the southeast of Saigon, perhaps another half-an-hour, and after that, they'd have to fly all the way across South Viet Nam to get back to My Co.

J.W. was alerted by Saigon Artillery Command that several of the flight lanes to the south, west, and northwest were closed to all low altitude traffic due to heavy American cannon activity. They would have to fly east of Saigon and wait for the firing to cease. The other choice was to fly north forty miles then circle east around the cannon fire, and finally back down south to My Co. J.W. calculated that if they chose the second, meandering course, the flight would go on for hours. It was already eleven-thirty, barely time to return to the village before the colonel's deadline. J.W.'s orders had been clear and reasonable. He would return the helicopter to the colonel before noon. He developed a grand headache glancing back at the two women he would never again see after that day.

He started north toward Bien Hoa Air Base to land and call the colonel in My Co. As the red-and-white-checkered water tower, his old checkpoint, came into view, he sensed the image of Colonel Bierlein's face, and he heard the old man chuckling dryly, "In life, ya pays your nickel and ya takes your chances." Imperceptibly, J.W. eased the stick to the right, guiding the aircraft onto a southeasterly heading toward the South China Sea and Vung Tao.

Nearing Long Thanh, he woke the pilot and told him he was making a short detour toward the coast. The warrant officer muttered, "What the hell, we can't get home anyway, and I could use the rest."

They tried to radio Bien Hoa Tower, but the air traffic controllers were frantically trying to reestablish control over their airfield after a battle-damaged F-105 jet fighter had crashed, jagged pieces hurling into a quonset packed with troops fresh from America. Instead, J.W. tried to raise the infantry battalion at My Co, but the ship was far too low, and he settled instead for Saigon Artillery Command. He asked them to open a narrow corridor to the east of Saigon for five minutes to let the chopper through on a mercy mission, direct to the South China Sea and Vung Tao. When they were cleared through, J.W. thanked them warmly. The controller answered, "No problem, that's why we're here. Good luck to you and your crew."

Emboldened, J.W. requested the Saigon Arty controller to use his powerful radio to call the colonel at My Co and tell him of the delay. The man "rogered" heartily, declaring it was as good as done.

With the cannons of the U.S. Army silenced for the moments, they sailed toward Vung Tao, J.W. regained a safe altitude, and the aircraft's passengers relaxed, even the women. The four silently took in the beauty of the Vietnamese countryside. Twenty miles to the east of Saigon, the terrain became mountainous, and the helicopter flew through craggy gorges, whooshing by the fragile lean-tos of the hermits who'd taken flight from the war in the lowlands. On past sorties,

J.W. had seen these bone-thin, reclusive creatures drinking from the rushing streams that streaked the velvet hills, and eating from dying fruit trees that were succumbing to Agent Orange. J.W. pointed down when he spotted a barely-clad man running through the scrub like a wild animal.

The pilot laughed sadly, "He's trying to hide. Thinks we're gonna hammer 'im. Sometimes you see bunches of 'em sittin' around, and when we pop up, it's like an atom bomb, the way they scatter. Captain, some day, when I'm sixty-somethin', gettin' ready to die, if I make it past twenty-two, I'll think back to these guys, livin' so simple. I'll never forget this. I mean, I hope I never forget, sir."

J.W. nodded but thought for a moment and added, shaking his head, "Yeah, and we shoot by and remind them they're as vulnerable as a rat in a can. In this shithole, you can't escape, Chief. Can't be that great a life." He gave the pilot a tap in the shoulder, and they nodded gently to each other.

As they cleared the last emerald mountain pass, a coral sea spread before them, endless water and the promise of freedom bordered by the filament of Vung Tao's white beach. They could just make out the red-white-and-blue umbrellas J.W. had seen that first day as his 707 descended over the coast. They still dotted the sand, and he was thankful they were there, for he had begun to believe all the world was a muddy, colorless, dirt road.

The controller at Vung Tao tower cleared the light observation helicopter to land behind a flight of Thuds, F105's that had streaked above them so fast and close, and with such a thunderous boom, the two women in the back had begun to howl that they had finally arrived in hell. The ship was ordered to hover-taxi across the vast runway and park on the far side of the field. "That's a long walk to get to the gate, sir," J.W. radioed ground control, adding, "How 'bout we slide over and park next to the tower?"

"That's a neg," the controller snapped, "we got guests scheduled. Everything on this side's off limits. I'll call your unit and ask them to send a ride out. What's the number?"

J.W. didn't answer but set the ship down in the shadow of the wing of a giant C-141 jet transport. The pilot saw one of his buddies in a HUEY parked nearby and told J.W. to go on by himself, but not to be long.

Two aged women and a young soldier zigzagged through the labyrinth of spent, corroding aircraft engines, propellers, and tires, untold tens of millions in his parents' tax dollars lying in mounds. J.W. mumbled to the women, "Look at the shit they're hiding out here. Outta sight, outta mind."

Rather than walk the mile down to the end of the runway and then the mile back up to mid-field and the gate into town, J.W. explained to the women that they would, instead, wait until there were no aircraft landing or taking off and run like hell across the tarmac to the other side. As they neared the point of their crossing, however, *Bà* Khai slowed, dragging her left leg in pain. The chief's mother hung back with her, and the two crouched on the asphalt, breathing so heavily they could not hear J.W.'s plea, "Ladies, come on, we need to haul ass to the tower side." When they realized he was yelling at them, they threw hands over their ears and cried.

An angry voice blasted over the PA system ordering them off the tarmac, but by the time J.W. explained the message to the women and helped *Bà* Khai to her feet, a 707 on final approach had already retracted its gear to abort its landing. As the plane thundered just a few feet over their heads, J.W. was struck by the anger on the pilot's face, and by the crisp, polished, white and sky-blue of the fuselage. It was only after the oddly-hued transport turned cross-wind that J.W. realized that he had managed to disrupt the final approach of Air Force One.

The women listened through their tears to J.W.'s explanation, but there was little time for them to appreciate just who might have been aboard that plane, for a military police sedan pulled up to clear the runway. The sergeant at the wheel stopped J.W.'s exegesis with an outstretched arm, smiling, "I know, I know. There's a great reason why you're on the runway with locals, women no less, who were flying in your helicopter, Captain. I know, I know, there's always a great reason." J.W. started to answer the sergeant, but the man raised his hand and snapped, "Save it for the CO. Now, all three of you get in and..."

J.W., though, was not going to "save it," and by the time the police car reached the gate, the sergeant had radioed for a cab to take them into the city of Vung Tau. He added as they left, "Let me know how it turns out, sir, and give me a call when you get back. I'll take you out to your helicopter."

The cabbie drove along several streets looking for hospitals before he stopped to have a cigarette and ask for directions. J.W. waited but soon called to the driver, "Hey, pal, let's *đi đi mau*. We're running out of time."

The driver pointed at his watch. "It's 2:30. Plenty of time left before sunset."

On Cong Dinh Street they pulled up to the faded brick portico of the American rehabilitation hospital. J.W. expected more of the fungus-stained walls, floors, beds, and patients they had encountered during their two-month odyssey, though here the halls were white, the floors polished, and the corners sparkled. At the oak front desk, an American sergeant looked up from his detective mystery to search a leather-bound census volume. He perused the current admissions, yesterday's admissions, and a section in the back marked "DECEASED." There was no mention of a Vu Van Khai.

As the familiar anger welled within J.W., he reminded himself that he already had a lot on his plate—the infantry colonel, Colonel Trott, both portending obstacles to his escape from Viet Nam on schedule. "It'll all be over in a few days," he whispered to himself several times soothingly then asked the sergeant, "You mind if I take a look myself?"

The sergeant shrugged. "Help yourself, sir," and went back to his Mickey Spillane.

A dozen silver quonset huts radiated from the main building, five reserved for Vietnamese patients. J.W. began the search in the closest indigenous ward, an air-conditioned, immaculate facility, in which the thick-mattressed beds lay three feet apart lining an aisle so long, the cots on the far end looked like doll furniture. *Bà* Khai walked between the beds, examining each contorted face slowly, carefully, stepping back, stepping forward, as if an art critic. A delirious man reached out for her calling a woman's name, and with that, *Bà* Khai became excited, but soon realized the name was not hers and moved, sadly, to the next patient. J.W., having made his evaluation quickly, waited impatiently at the far end of the quonset, his uneasiness boring more deeply with each face *Bà* Binh and her mother-in-law stopped to probe.

The second quonset was identical to the first, only colder. Thin white sheets covered fifty shivering bodies. *Bà* Khai persisted in scrutinizing each desperate face while J.W. squirmed at the far end. The third ward was different only in the increasingly longer shadows cast by a sun that was well into the western sky.

He turned away from the window and yelled, "*Bà* Khai, I'm sorry. We gotta go. There's no more time. Vu Van Khai is not here."

Bà Khai looked up from her quest, oblivious to the stares of the wounded and dying. Most of the men turned away uneasily at J.W.'s display of passion, but one, a sallow skeleton at the far reaches of the ward, raised his arm so feebly, J.W. missed the gesture. J.W. called impatiently again, "*Bà* Khai," for she had resumed poring over a near-cadaver whose head was covered in gauze, save for his benumbed eyes and limp mouth.

The shadow at the end of the ward who had raised his arm now heaved a faint breath, which caught J.W.'s attention. Finally, the man waved his open palm as frantically as his dying spirit would tolerate, so hard that his wrist watch, an olive drab, U.S. Army model, slipped to his elbow. The emaciated figure, with catheters protruding from every orifice, tried to make a sound, but large tears welled in his eyes, and his head fell back to the pillow. In reflex, J.W. touched his own wrist, feeling for a watch he knew was no longer there. Blood drained deeply into his legs, and a vibrating gray mist clouded his senses. He was drifting toward the figure.

For an instant, there were no colonels, no helicopters, and no threats of being kept in that sorrowful land for a second longer than had to be. J.W. Weathersby had been reduced to an automaton approaching a tremulous, skeletal hand. With effort, *Ông* Khai pulled two tissues from a packet on his bed. He handed J.W. the first and brought the second to his own eyes.

J.W. took a deep breath and tried to say in Vietnamese, "Do you know how long we searched for you?" but he wasn't able to choke back his tears. When he finally gained control, he blurted in English, "Wait, wait, there's someone else!"

J.W. waved to *Bà* Khai, who was still halfway down the ward inspecting a row of patients whose faces were hidden under layers and layers of gauze. She finally looked up sheepishly and limped slowly toward J.W., unaware of the light that would, in an instant, emerge from the morass.

As she neared him, *Bà* Khai spoke softly with her eyes cast down. "Captain, you are right. We must go. We will find him another day. I am sorry for having made you late."

"No, no, *Bà* Khai," J.W. nearly screamed in English, "look, look!"

But *Bà* Khai looked only into J.W.'s eyes, and seeing the foreigner's tears, became even more saddened. J.W. finally took her by the wrist to the bedside and verily pointed her head down. *Ông* Khai, however, gasped and gathered what was left in him, curling into a semi-sit-up, nearly striking his wife's head. *Bà* Khai fell to her knees at the bedside, silently touching her husband's face as he wheezed with exhausted, labored breaths. J.W. left them for half-an-hour, spending much of the time trying to call the infantry colonel in My Co. Though he failed to reach Happy Valley, and he knew that meant certain court-marshal, he felt clean, almost whole, a very thin sliver of affection for life wedging into the mire.

When he returned for *Bà* Khai, he and the chief held hands. "When do you leave?" *Ông* Khai whispered.

"A few days, but I'm not sure."

Ông Khai squeezed J.W.'s hand and whispered, "Remember that night? The mortar rounds, the fire. You promised you'd return someday."

It was past four o'clock when they lifted off. Though J.W. returned *Bà* Khai's smile, thoughts of colonels and misappropriated helicopters had long since overtaken his conscience, wrenching from him the one tolerable moment of his tour. He radioed My Co from miles out that they were approaching, and the sergeant major stood by the helipad. He stomped up to the ship and informed J.W. sternly that the old man was waiting in the command bunker.

The two women crawled out of the ship and thanked J.W. for his strength, but he was too frightened of the coming fusillade to pay attention. As they turned away, he might have nodded to them, perhaps he had not; he couldn't remember as he caught a glimpse of *Bà* Khai and her mother-in-law walking briskly into the village.

Chapter 25

THE INFANTRY COLONEL placed him under genuine arrest. The large man's face grew scarlet, his voice high. "Did you know, Captain, that your regimental commander was out here looking for you? Do you have any idea how much JP-4 we burned in the search? Your pay is going to be docked for that fuel!"

J.W. had been staring at the pulsating West Point ring during the harangue, letting the harsh words float by until the colonel mentioned taking his money. Suddenly, J.W. was overwhelmed with the freedom his troubles had bought him. For the first time in his life, there was nothing to lose. "Sir," he snapped, "You've got to sit down and listen. Just sit down, goddamnit, and listen for one damn minute…sir."

The colonel's jaw dropped, and his eyes widened. J.W. braced for a retort that would surely land him in the military prison, back down to LBJ, or perhaps a punch in the jaw like the one he had received from his commanding officer back in Ranger School, and then prison for 20 years. But the old man only nodded, took a seat, looked up, and pointed to a chair for J.W.

Weathersby drew a deep breath and recounted the history of *Ông* Khai's life, beginning with the escape from North Viet Nam in 1954 as a refugee, of caring for Buddhist orphans, of putting himself through several schools, and of laboring as the lord of the shit burners for months until he was awarded, by President Thieu himself, the position of village chief he had worked so hard to earn.

When J.W. recited the saga of searching hospital after hospital, the colonel grimaced with each failure. J.W. had hit his stride, and was not sure if the colonel's eyes had reddened, for the man had turned his head slightly to let his good ear take in the rest of the story. He chuckled when J.W. told him how *Bà* Khai was still halfway down the ward when the chief saw him. J.W. continued without a breath, swearing he had called Saigon command to tell them he would be late, and that he and the pilot had tried over and over to call from Vung Tao.

Since the colonel appeared to be listening, J.W. went on about *Bà* Binh, and that he was past due to answer for that indiscretion with Colonel Trott.

The colonel heard J.W. out to the end. He ordered calmly, "Wait in your bunker, son." As J.W. about-faced, the colonel roared to his radio operator, "Get Saigon Artillery Command on the horn. Did they call here and somebody didn't tell me, damn it?"

J.W. sat in his bunker calculating the cost of jet fuel for two search choppers flying for five hours at, say, forty-five cents per gallon. He wondered if the bastards could take his money. Worse, could they really keep him there? Would this sentence be added to the one Trott would extract? Would he stay or go AWOL? How would he get back to the States? Where would he get the money to pay for the ticket on an old steamer? Maybe he could work off his passage cleaning latrines and washing pots and pans. Envisioning a life on the run was less painful than contemplating paying back the cost of the fuel.

J.W.'s figures filled several pages of his olive drab notebook before his arithmetic was interrupted by the sergeant major. He announced brashly, "The colonel's ready for round two...sir."

The battalion commander loomed larger than before, and J.W. braced for the blade, but the old man mumbled something that J.W. heard as, "That's the first time that helicopter's done a damn thing worthwhile in this war." The colonel looked up from his desk and handed J.W. a 3rd Battalion shoulder patch, presenting it with a slight flourish. "I hope you will remember us."

J.W. turned to leave. "By the way," the colonel boomed, "Trott is an ass, and your CO knows it. The old lady okay?"

"Yes, sir. Just pissed off."

"Good. So be smart. Forget about the incident. You don't need to report back to him. Trott won't be back in My Co—ever. Stay here until the end and then go home as fast as you can. What you don't want to forget is that you did a job here, Captain." With that, the colonel stood and saluted J.W.

⟞ ⟝

The colonel and his men helicoptered out of the village the next morning as J.W. was arising. He left his cot and watched through the bunker opening as the Chinooks approached and departed over the paddies, hovering far from the huts. J.W. did not see the 3rd Battalion's commanding officer again.

Nor did J.W. see *Bà* Khai again. According to *Bà* Binh, she and her mother-in-law had boarded the bus for Vung Tau at dawn with the kids, to sit squashed amongst three dozen passengers for the two-and-a-half-day overland journey. J.W. asked if she had left a message, but *Bà* Binh whispered she couldn't remember.

As he left her hut, several elders came to him and asked if he would give a speech at the market. The men had come up with dozens of cans of beer which sat to the front of each squatting man. The women crowded the periphery of the market.

"Ladies and Gentlemen, you taught me much about a world I did not know. You treated me with kindness and respect, though you could have thought of me as the enemy. I promise I will come back, I hope as a doctor, and repay the debt I owe you. I will never forget you."

J.W. was gone a day later. An hour before he left My Co, he went to *Bà* Binh's to say good-by, secretly praying to steal a last glimpse of *Cô* Lin. *Bà* Binh offered sadly that the willowy peasant girl had been very depressed for the past days and had gone out into the paddies to work. J.W. hugged *Bà* Binh, and while he had never encountered such emaciated frailty, the old lady, for her part, had never before experienced an act of such daring, and she stood bolt upright, though as he left the hut, he made the error of turning back to see a tear run down the ancient woman's cheek.

He drove out of town staring at *Bà* Binh's hut, but a sparkle from the berm caught his attention. *Cô* Lin waved gently to him, and he saw in the sunlight the reflection of the earrings. He thought of stopping and touching her hand one last time, but didn't. All he could do was picture her face that day and that night, and again the next day and into the next night, even as his freedom bird climbed into the darkness.

⟞ ⟝

When the wheels lifted off, a half-hearted cheer rose from his one hundred and fifty fellow travelers. It was the ecstasy he had waited a year to savor, though it was far more muted than he had dreamed, and all he could wonder was what the rest of his compatriots had left behind.

He pressed his face to the window as the aircraft turned over Saigon, and he searched for the dirt road that led to My Co. He was, however, distracted by the flash of artillery rounds and flares in the night sky. They seemed now merely weak, harmless sparks dotting a black land. By the time he looked again for the road to My Co, the plane pounded into the clouds that would fuel tomorrow's monsoon.

Book II

Chapter 26

The South China Sea
Approaching the Coast of South Viet Nam
6 July 2012

CATHAY PACIFIC FLIGHT 2249 entered a steep descent over the pristine beaches of Vung Tau, the land dotted not with the red, white, and blue umbrellas of armchair commandos, but with the tiny forms of children splashing in the surf of the South China Sea. At first glance, one could not distinguish the rows of dazzling hotels lining the seaside for they blended perfectly with the bone-white sand. Dr. J.W. Weathersby's face remained glued to the window of the Boeing 777 in a frenzied search for the dirt road that led to My Co, but he was distracted by a land carpeted, not with the fury of battle, but by a lush green passivity.

His attention shot to the Mekong Delta, where he probed for a single artillery battle to point out to his wife, to prove his decades of stories and frightened dreams were not just the memories of an aging man. But there was no fire and smoke, not even from the massive, high-tech industrial complexes that dotted the land both north and south of Saigon. Here and there, he could make out peasants stooped in the verdant paddies, many of whose parents, he gulped, had not yet been born the last time he had set eyes upon Indochina.

The plane was buffeted gently as it settled through cloud layers. The co-pilot pushed buttons to repressurize the 777's cabin, sucking in air from the whirling, daily, pre-monsoon fog of southern Viet Nam. Driven aboard the plane were scents and odors that culled from J.W. misted memories of his last weeks in Viet Nam, forty-three years before, a twenty-four-year-old frantic to escape the war.

The sudden musk of humid air stifled the excitement and bravado that had swept him this far. J.W. thought of his kids, both proud marines, and he hoped they would never have to taste the dread that was building in him. But he also remembered both had gone off, this time to the Middle East, heads held high, as if to prove they were what they supposed their pop had dreamed they would become.

As they approached the city, J.W. looked to the north, toward Long Binh Post, and his eye caught the checkered water tank near the Bien Hoa Air Base. It was barely grey on grey, and it stood alone, surrounded by fields of scrub and shanties. A few trees dotted a patch of flat ground that held the ghost of the two ten-thousand-foot runways. Long Binh Post was gone.

The aircraft taxied past decaying, half-cylinder, aircraft revetments, their thick cement walls twenty feet high, open ended garages in which U.S. Air Force jets had been parked and sheltered nearly half-a-century before. But the cement was green now with an overgrowth of tropical weeds and vines; many of the walls had crumbled, victims of neglect. J.W. stared at the meaningless chunks of American concrete lying where they had fallen, not touched in decades, ignored, inconsequential. He thought of his long-gone parents, and how hard they'd worked, dragging themselves up from the poverty of the Depression, their taxes, their sweat, now rotting on the dirt of a forgotten scrap of Asian soil. He also thought back to the vicious F-105 jet fighters that had been protected within those cement bunkers during the war, and to the helicopters that had been allowed to sit exposed next to them. He pointed excitedly, telling his wife that he had actually flown from that very patch of earth eons before. She patted his hand calmly, warmly. “Oh, wow, sweetheart.”

At the door, flight attendants handed each passenger a tiny packet of clear plastic, but by the time J.W. figured out it was a folded raincoat, the travelers were already down the stairs, making the rainy dash to the air-conditioned coach that would carry them to the terminal. Though J.W. had been warned by pals who had returned to Viet Nam that AK-47-brandishing Vietnamese soldiers, dressed identically to the North Vietnamese troops of the 1960s, would herd them around the airport, there was but a rare, unarmed airport policeman watching lazily from a Colonel Sanders, far fewer officials than in the most relaxed of Western airports.

The bus took them to the ultra-modern, eleven-plus-million-passenger-per-year International Terminal, now perched on the very spot J.W. had spent his last few hours in Viet Nam, at the officers' bar, eating tiny pizzas and drinking 33 Beer, anesthetizing himself, killing precious moments of his life, anticipating nervously the arrival of his Freedom Bird. But his former watering hole, with its moldy wooden chairs, peeling linoleum, and sullen barkeep had been replaced with overstocked shops—Burberry, Borsalini, Gucci, Cartier, and Hermes.

An immigration officer in a crisp green uniform and blue surgical mask broke J.W.'s open-mouthed reverie, calling out, "Next please," waving J.W. politely over to the desk. He asked softly, "What is your business in Viet Nam, sir?"

"I've come back to see my friends."

"Friends?" The official pulled from below his computer terminal a thin governmental form and handed it to J.W. "Please you write name and address of friends."

"I don't know their names. They're in a village in Kien Tuong Province. It's called My Co."

The young immigration officer screwed up his face in question. "Kien Tuong Province? This is not a province in Viet Nam."

"Kien Tuong Province? Of course it is. It's just west of Saigon."

"There is no Saigon. You have landed in Ho Chi Minh City."

"I'm sorry, of course you're right, but I spent a year in Kien Tuong Province. Sixty-eight and sixty-nine."

"Ah. You American soldier. Come back. You are welcome come back, but you know many changes in countryside. Viet Nam very different now. Not little America now. You must talk police."

J.W. asked sheepishly, "Do you know if they let foreigners into the countryside?"

"You talk police."

There was nothing further from the officer except the immigration stamp pounded on J.W.'s passport and the man's call for the next client. At customs, an official eyed the suitcase chock-a-block with donated medicine dragged by J.W.'s wife, but when J.W. uttered in long-practiced Vietnamese, "This is medicine for the children of Kien Tuong Province," the agent nodded and allowed him through but quipped to a pal, "Where's Kien Tuong?"

Outside baggage claim, J.W. and his wife hailed a cab. It inched from the parking garage to meld into the thousands of motor scooters and cars exiting the facility. As the cab crossed in front of the terminal, J.W. noticed the grand sign that read Ton Son Nh*a*t Airport, rather than the Tan Son Nh*u*t he remembered, but he shook his head and laughed at how his memory of everything in life was fading.

As the cab picked up speed, J.W. looked for a handle or switch to open the window, to draw in and share with his wife the scents of Viet Nam he had so long missed. The cabbie, however, grunted that the windows did not go down because the van was air-conditioned and, "Environment inside computer control."

The brutal potholes that had pocked Truong Son Boulevard leading away from the airport forty years before were gone, as was Truong Son Boulevard. It had been replaced by a six-lane highway with neatly marked lanes and traffic lights, the latter electronically tied to giant LED screens that counted down the seconds until the light was programmed to change.

In the city of Saigon itself, J.W. was prepared for legions of armed North Vietnamese soldiers patrolling every corner, the ones he had been forewarned would glower at him and tighten fists around trigger housings. But the rain was now falling in torrents, the sky having darkened to the point of foreboding. J.W. assumed the deluge had driven the soldiers, grandchildren of those he had faced in battle, indoors to take refuge within the jewelry and fine clothing shops. It bothered him that he could not see them, for he knew they were there watching, waiting for him to make the slightest wrong move, for a less than submissive twist of his lips. He looked harder along the litter-free streets. Where were they?

For a moment, his mind clouded, and he plunged into that deep tunnel of despair that had so permanently and darkly stained his spirit since the day he first entered that tortured land. With the smells and the peculiar darkness of the sky, it all began to drift back, the sense of gnawing fear that had clutched and corrupted his early twenties, and, if he was honest with himself, so many of the years of his later life. But it was neither the thought of pith-helmeted North Vietnamese infantrymen, nor of their Kalashnikov assault rifles, that fed his apprehension. He suddenly realized it was, instead, an awareness of the scent of wet pavement commingled with the reek of the graying, mildewed tropical buildings, and the diesel exhaust from nearly defunct engines that was dragging him backward in time. He had learned in medical school the power of olfactory stimulation to activate memories, and he was distressed to revisit, not only the foreboding of mortal danger, but also the emotional fear, the uncertainties, and profound self-doubt he'd harbored as a young man. He had not been aware the two sentiments had been so umbilically joined.

As the taxi rolled to stop in front of the Huong Dong Hotel, J.W. was shocked how quickly a few simple odors had plucked from him the bravado he had worked so hard to secure during the four decades since he'd left Viet Nam. He helped his wife out of the taxi, his head hung, a sign not lost on her.

Though she had been excited to travel to Asia, to witness the land that had so defined her husband of twenty-some years, she'd never been to a non-English speaking culture. Nonetheless, she whispered, "Sweetheart, I think I like it here. It's mysterious. I've never felt this before." She took his hand and secretly kissed it, for J.W. had warned her that public displays of affection in Viet Nam were verboten.

Their passports and airline tickets were tendered to a young Vietnamese desk clerk, who also denied the existence of a province by the name of Kien Tuong. "There have been many changes in the countryside," he admonished. "It is difficult for our guests to leave Ho Chi Minh City without permission. You must understand, there have been many changes in the countryside."

"Yes, I've heard that before," J.W. answered with a plastic smile, mimicking the one growing on the face of the adolescent clerk. "But *you* must understand something." J.W. went on, "My wife and I have traveled very far, and have spent almost ten thousand dollars to get here. I want to talk to someone about going to My Co."

An older man in a Western shirt and tie drifted over. "Sir, why you not spend time in beautiful Ho Chi Minh City? You will see great communist government build just and prosperous society. We have no problem of America. Viet Nam, everyone free, everyone prosperous, everyone safe. Police not kill people with too brown skin. Viet Nam children not shoot other student. Viet Nam people not live in tent city like Occupy America. You safe here.

"And there many site for visitor. You see imperialist building, old America Embassy, and war museum. It really interesting. Our city beautiful." The smile widened.

"I'm sure it is, and I already know that communism has made Viet Nam a worker's paradise—everyone knows that except my foolish countrymen. Maybe that is why we live so poorly in the United States." J.W. grinned. "But I came here to find a man who is very important to me. If I have to, I will walk the fifty miles to My Co."

The manager's smile sank into a wary grin, and J.W.'s wife tugged at her husband's sleeve. "Sweetheart, the man is going to help us. I'm sure he will look into letting us go to My Co."

"Yes, I help, but you must polite. You no threaten. I speak with superior. We contact you. Please you not leave city without paper."

J.W. grabbed his luggage to depart for their room but added over his shoulder, "That man is very important to me. He is my family. This land is important to me. I bled here too, you know, before you were born."

J.W. and his wife spent the next days traipsing the steaming streets of Saigon, killing time in myriad shops, J.W. drawn to those few that still hawked tarnished G.I. dog tags, U.S. Army compasses, pocket knives, and mildewed, faded, army web belts. Meanwhile, his wife drifted in and out of the well-stocked jewelry stores, punctuating her stroll at the Liz Claiborne and Lancôme kiosks. They walked the miles to Cho Lon, the great Chinese market, stopping frequently at the massive, new hotels for iced tea. They sat in air-conditioned lounges along the way, surrounded by young lovers holding each other tightly, oblivious to the foreigners. Returning to central Saigon, J.W. noticed that the great majority of the populace was young and quite well fed, many of the teenaged girls nearing his height.

Though the Weathersbys weaved through the streets unobtrusively, ducking into hotel lobbies at the slightest sign that their presence was noticed, they seemed to attract beggars and street children, a retinue that grew with each block. From the no longer so numerous alleyways and rare crumbling buildings, pickpockets wormed their way into the entourage, boys and men so inept at their art, J.W. caught each of them as they tried to pinch a cheap ballpoint pen or the room key from his pockets. J.W. sermonized to the hapless criminals in a patois of rusty Vietnamese, long-forgotten Chinese, and GI English, pontificating about moral propriety and the need to build the nation of Viet Nam on a bedrock of honesty and hard work.

His wife, however, moved by the starving faces of the creatures, whispered, “Sweetheart, I think they need food, not sermons.” She handed each an American dollar bill, worth twenty times more than at home, and shooed them off to buy dinner. But the crowds grew and demanded more and more.

After lunch each day, J.W. insisted they make a stop at the police station, for it was during the midday respite that a quiet equanimity seemed to fall over the city, though one that lasted for only an hour. While the young police officers always greeted them courteously and offered tea, they reiterated that much had changed in the countryside, and that there really was no need to venture away from the comforts of their grand city. One officer in a particularly majestic uniform, an older man who looked much like the manager of their hotel, also reassured them that the authorities were in the complicated process of examining J.W.’s request for a travel permit. “These things take time. There is always a chance of success.”

“We’re down to three days left,” J.W. reminded. “This cost us so much to come here.”

The officer smiled and reminded, “Much has changed in the countryside.”

Toward the end of each afternoon, with the darkening of the monsoon sky, J.W.’s corps of beggars slowly retired to doorways and the underside of bridges, allowing J.W. and his wife to walk alone, the only time during their days in Viet Nam they were granted that decadence.

Nearing the hotel, a very tiny older man, perhaps fifty inches, with a shock of jet black hair, and a young man with one leg and no forearms sat chattering in a covered doorway. They were facing away from the street, at first oblivious to the presence of the rain-soaked foreigners, but J.W. wasn’t surprised when the two vagrants, through a sixth sense enjoyed by the scoundrels who plied the streets of Saigon, cut short their conversation and jumped up. The little soul shuffled up to J.W., stuck out his hand to shake J.W.'s, and said in perfect English, "I am Nguyen Lan Qui. You can call me Qui."

The one-legged man hopped to Weathersby's wife and bowed his head but did not speak. Qui asked politely for the usual, money and food, but J.W. was hungry, wet, hot, cold, and weary of the constant presence of beggars, and of the fruitlessness of the journey that was rapidly degenerating into one of his grandest mistakes. In a mini-fury, he grasped his wife's arm, guided her into the hotel, and growled over his shoulder, "Why can't you leave us be? I came back here to find what I lost. I am not Viet Nam's father."

Though the words were mouthed in English, the sentiment was not lost on the two soaked outcasts or on the uniformed doorman, who perfunctorily shooed the two men away. The excitement of the confrontation, however, brought several other of the dispossessed from cracks in the buildings, and soon a convention of unfortunates was contemplating the incident, pointing variously at the foreigners, the doorman, Qui, and the armless, one-legged man.

J.W.'s wife offered, "You'll feel better after we get you something to eat, Sweetheart," but J.W. grumbled that he wasn't hungry.

At six, they tried to sneak out of the hotel for the Metropolitan Best French Restaurant at the corner, but Qui intercepted them at the next doorway. "What do you need, pal?" J.W. cracked, safe in having used English.

"Oh, sir," the miniature creature replied in perfect English, "I know you want to be left alone, to go to a restaurant to eat, because you are hungry. But I am hungry, too."

J.W. answered in Vietnamese, "Look, if I give you a cigarette, will you leave us alone?"

"I don't smoke, sir. It is very dirty. I have enough problems without that. I am just hungry."

J.W. cracked in Vietnamese, "Yeah, well, I'm hungry too, and everyone's hungry, and I can't feed the whole country of Viet Nam."

J.W.'s wife tugged at his arm and whispered, "Sweetheart, he's speaking to you in English."

J.W. looked down. There was no anger in the man's eyes, only famine in the face of plenty. But in those eyes there was also a spark that J.W. had not permitted himself to see in anyone's face. The moment in the bunker with *Ông* Khai, under withering mortar fire on their last night together, when all seemed lost, J.W. had sworn he'd never forget. He'd promised to return someday and do something positive for Viet Nam, the country that Khai so loved. In that heartbeat, all of his oaths boiled to the surface.

J.W.'s eyes reddened and he sat down in the doorway of a tiny tailor shop. For a few moments, he did not speak, his eyes cast downward, darts of guilt piercing his chest. With a deep breath, he looked up and reached into his pocket for a dollar bill, adding, "I'm sorry I was rude to you, sir. That wasn't right. I'm just very, very upset with the police here. I am truly sorry." J.W. proffered the bill then took his wife by the hand and walked to the restaurant.

The conference was not lost on the legions of street dwellers who joined a procession and chattered in an ever-growing volume as Qui followed the two foreigners. At the Metropolitan French Best Restaurant, J.W. opened the door for his wife and slipped in quickly behind her in, but she stopped, whispered to him, and he stepped back outside. With a tug at Qui's sleeve, he smiled, "Hey, come on in. The little missus requests the pleasure of your company for dinner."

The man began to turn away but stopped to stare up at J.W., his posture slowly straightening as he considered the proposal. J.W. held the door, and the man stepped through into the air-conditioned dining room. The trio was met by the tuxedoed maître d' who had sprinted over to greet the affluent Westerners and, more importantly, rescue them from the diminutive rascal. J.W. smiled and whispered, "This gentleman is with us."

After a paragraph of grumbles, the maître d' swept them to seats beside the kitchen's swinging door. J.W. was going to comment about being hidden, for Caucasians were invariably placed at the windows to entice prosperous Vietnamese and foreigners into eating establishments, but his wife reminded him that it was cooler in the back, and more exclusive away from the windows, on the other side of which she noticed an accumulation of the curious. J.W., his wife, the maître d', the waiters, and other patrons fidgeted, for word had gone out, and a growing flock of the dispossessed coalesced at the window, pointing and hooting toward the back of the small establishment. Only Qui ignored them. He opened a menu and studied the French selections carefully. He chose the *Côq au vin*.

"Do you know a village called My Co?" J.W. finally asked over a second round of 333 Beer. "It's in Kien Tuong Province."

"Sir," Qui lowered his head, "there is no Kien Tuong Province." The man looked around warily, particularly at the maître d', then added in a whisper, "Yes, there *was* a Kien Tuong Province. That name's been changed. It's Long An now. You can't keep up with the changes. Nothing is for sure anymore. It is just like after the war was over, everyday something new to alter your life forever. It's happening again. How many times are they going to do this to us? Look at this. Look at the beer. This communist regime, always stirring things up, changing one letter just to make everyone crazy. When I was a kid, it was 33 Beer; now it's 333 Beer. And did you see the airport? It was called Ton San Nhut when my father was in the Vietnamese Air Force. Now it's Tan San Nhat. The pigs in the politburo in Hanoi, always rubbing our noses in their great victory. It is not enough that they control our lives; now it's even the beer."

J.W. mentioned, "Yeah, but all the high-def TVs and digital cameras in the shops. Everyone's got a cell phone, even the kids." He shook his head and asked, "My friend, if things are so good, why are you here, in the street? Why is that man without arms or a leg like that? Is there medical care, or is it all just show?"

Qui opened a third beer and continued. "There have been many changes. At first, in '75, when the communists came, everything stayed the same, except that the foreigners were gone, and the fighting finally stopped. But soon, in '78 or '79, maybe '80, I can't remember now, they took the men and a lot of the women off for reeducation."

He stopped to guzzle the rest of his beer, paused for a bit, and allowed his eyes to close pleasantly as the alcohol seeped into his veins. When he went on, the equanimity drained from his eyes, and he hissed, "If you had been a soldier on the government side, or if you had a job with the Americans, or if you had a job selling to people who liked the Americans, or if you were a child of these groups, you were labeled an 'enemy of the people,' and they kicked you out of school if you were a kid, and if you were an adult, they sent you to a concentration camp out in the jungles. They put my father and my brother in separate dirt rooms next to each other, to *reeducate* them, but the cells were half the size of this restaurant and had sixty people in them—each. They were there for five years, and they didn't even know they were only a few feet apart. They were given a small piece of sweet potato or a few grains of spoiled rice every day. Once a week, they threw in a piece of rancid animal fat crawling with maggots—our compassionate Communist Party comrades.

"And all my father and brother did was sit in the room. There was no education or reeducation. No books, no paper, no pens. They sat for years, my father and my brother. Now my father is dead. He was a professor of literature before he joined the Air Force. He knew Nhat Linh! The greatest writer of Viet Nam in the last century. And my brother, a professor of literature at Saigon University, he fixes shoes on the street now. He was a writer before reeducation, too. Now he is afraid to write his name. There are ten thousand stories like that. No family was spared."

J.W.'s wife asked, "Why weren't you taken away?"

"Take a look. Even *they* didn't want me. Would you?"

"So how did you learn such wonderful English? You are an amazing man," J.W.'s wife beamed.

Qui's eyes swam under the sway of the beer. He explained that he had waylaid every English-speaking visitor he had encountered over the past two decades, demanding that they teach him three words before he would leave them alone. Without his ability to act as an unofficial, non-government approved interpreter, he would have long since died of starvation in a country where there was no such thing as social security, and no future for those who couldn't carry out as much labor as the man in the hovel next door.

He popped a fourth beer, sipped, and laughed a bit at himself but stopped abruptly, grimaced, and whispered, "There is still time to leave Viet Nam. I know I can do it. It is not too late for me." He halted unexpectedly again, realizing that his slurred declaration had been far louder than intended. The maître d', who had claimed to speak no English on the previous days when J.W. and his wife had dined there, shot a glance toward the table.

With the meal delivered, Qui ate slowly, occasionally sipping his fourth beer, head bowed, savoring the moment, sampling the fare and ambiance he would certainly never again relish. But he was also ill at ease, realizing he had, under the influence of the ethanol, allowed his tongue to slip, a transgression he supposed would cost him dearly. He spoke occasionally, but from that point on, only about the sauce or the vegetables.

At the conclusion of the meal, in his own near-inebriated predicament, J.W. nervously slipped four folded American bills into the maître d's palm. The man could not help himself and stole a glance at a corner of the notes, his eyes widening into almond crescents when he realized it was nearly a half-year's salary.

J.W. stared into the man's eyes for a moment, hoping the bequest would quickly end the maître d's furtive interest in Qui, but the head waiter moved a step or two away from the table, his stoic face unchanged, still cold and hard as he took a position facing the front door. His lips and eyes contorted painfully, as if he was considering the future of the Democratic Republic of Viet Nam while he walked to the bar stiffly, snatched the telephone receiver, and began to dial. J.W. whispered to his wife that they needed to run for the door and escape before the police came and arrested them for bribery and desecration of the communist ideal, but the maître d sucked in a deep breath and dropped the phone into its cradle. He glanced over surreptitiously toward his foreign patron, nodding almost imperceptibly. When J.W. returned the sign with the barest flicker of his eyes, the man retired quietly to the other corner of the restaurant, hands clasped behind his back, staring off into space.

When J.W. and his wife came down for breakfast the next morning, an official letter typed on tissue paper sat waiting for them at the hotel desk. Their presence was requested at the police station. They ran the five blocks to the dilapidated structure, J.W. making loud plans the whole way for the rental of a car and driver, and where they would stop on the way to buy gifts for the citizens of My Co, who would undoubtedly remember and welcome him with tears in their eyes. The young police officer saw them enter, jumped out of his seat, and nodded at two other officers, who took positions behind him.

"Please sit."

The first policeman remained standing. J.W. was not concerned until the man began speaking without having first offered the bitter green tea of previous visits. "There have been many changes in the countryside. We are sorry, but the farmers will not remember you. You will not remember them, so you see, there is no reason to go there. You have two days remaining in our country. Perhaps there are sites you have not visited in Ho Chi Minh City. Have you seen the Cu Chi Tunnels? Kilometer after kilometer of underground passages, some with three levels, hospitals, kitchens, meeting rooms. It is a wonder of the world built with the sweat of our Communist Party brothers during your war here. We will take you there. If you don't like that, we can arrange many great tours for you."

J.W. considered the dictum slowly, and as he understood that he would never again lay eyes on My Co, his face flushed a stroke-like scarlet. He stood and lowered his voice. "I will tell every GI in the United States what happened here. You took our money, and now you tell us to go home. All I can do is go to every single veterans' group. Let them know what's going to happen to them. That's going to cost you a lot of fuckin' GI money."

The officer was smiling, but one of his helpers grimaced, "You no say fuck. This Viet Nam. This our country. This not you country! You no say fuck!"

J.W.'s wife pulled J.W.'s tremulous body, 110 pounds versus 210 pounds, into the street. There, waiting patiently, mouths agape, was the usual panoply of beggars and pickpockets. J.W. blew angrily past the crowd. Only Qui, who was standing silently at the edge of the gathering, was not laughing in mortification over the foreigner's embarrassing public display of wrath. "Fuck this place," J.W. hissed to no one in particular as he strode toward the hotel.

J.W. closed the curtains in their room, and lay brooding on the bed. His wife kissed him on the forehead and announced she would be in the silk and jewelry shops next to the hotel, but would be back before dinner. She kissed him gently again and whispered, "Sweetheart, millions of people died here. Theirs and ours—mostly theirs. Maybe one of our bombs killed that policeman's grandmother. Maybe his grandfather was a soldier like you, but on the other side. Our feelings? How can they care about some rich foreigner's feelings? They don't know what you did here. They don't know who you are, or what's in your heart. We'll come back. We'll see My Co. Soon. I love you. At least we have each other." J.W. rose and kissed her gently, content to know she was, as ever, sailing right behind.

By late afternoon, the monsoon rains pounded the hotel window, water squirting through the rotted seal as if the glass was not there. The grimy liquid cascaded onto the floor, further staining the worn carpet. The crash of the wind-whipped, grape-sized rain drops became so loud, J.W. almost missed the rapping on his door. He awoke groggily from an uneasy, sweat-drenched sleep and made his way through the darkened room. As the banging intensified, he opened the door a crack and snapped, "What 'a you want?"

He peered straight ahead. Seeing nothing but the dank green walls of the hallway, he angrily pushed the door further open to give it a good slam, but his eyes dropped to see Qui.

"Doctor, you must go back to the police. Please go now. They want to talk to you."

"Fuck the police," he spat, but Qui peered up at him.

"Please. It is important. And please don't say 'fuck' when you get there." J.W. searched the room for a pen and paper to leave a note for his wife, but Qui urged, "You must hurry. They want you now."

The crowd of regulars shadowed them to the police building. Most waited outside, but a squad of eight and nine-year-old street kids, all sucking on Western cigarettes nearly as long as they were tall, stood in the doorway, shoving to get a better view. The officer greeted J.W. with a sanguine smile and asked him to sit. Not plain green, but jasmine, tea was served, and the officer shook J.W.'s hand. "We welcome you to the interesting and just communist nation of Viet..."

The policeman's attention, however, shifted abruptly away from J.W. to a man in civilian clothes pushing his way past the vagrant children. He carried a burlap bag over his shoulder. Shuffling behind him was a pair of magnificent Saigonese women in exquisite, pure white *áo dài.* Without waiting for an invitation, the man took a seat behind a battered, corner desk of the stationhouse. He wagged his fingers for the ladies to sit to his sides.

The precinct's police officers gathered in a lazy queue, and the man nodded for the women to open their ledger books. They filled antique fountain pens from a bottle of ink and stared blankly into the future while the civilian untied the string around the burlap sack. He extracted thick stacks of paper currency which he assembled on his desk, compulsively straightening the bills and the piles. He looked up cheerlessly. With another nod, the women took up their pens.

Each policeman recited his name and number obsequiously and pretended not to be watching the cash-counting machine. After the bills were put through a second reckoning, each man took a pen and signed a slip of paper handed him by the first woman. She took it back, put a checkmark in the left corner, jammed a silver-dollar-sized red stamp on the chit, and passed it behind the paymaster's back to the other woman. She recorded the name in her journal, checked off the right corner, and handed it to the man in the middle. The paymaster examined the chit, stared at the officer, and nodded to the first woman, who placed the chit on top of the bills and pushed the stack forward. The cop bent forward in a near-kowtow to gather the pound of money, his sixty-dollar monthly salary, and trotted off to the corner of the stationhouse to count it.

The hordes of vagabond children who had coalesced at the stationhouse, tired of the matter of J.W. Weathersby v. the Democratic Republic of Viet Nam. They drifted out onto Tu Do Street to get in a half-hour's work pestering foreign visitors before the next swipe of the monsoon.

J.W. stood to leave, furious for having allowed himself be bullied yet again.

As he turned to exit the stationhouse for the final time, Qui appeared at the door, dipping his diminutive body in J.W.'s path as if a fearless running back blocking a marauding defensive lineman. Qui shook his head, adding, "No. You must stay."

The officer rushed over to J.W. "Doctor, you should have told us you were a friend of Nguyen Van Thu. We could have helped you sooner."

He muttered, "Who? I don't know Nguyen Van Thu. Who is he? And is this the way all public servants are paid in Viet Nam?"

"Oh, yes. We are the police. We are trusted. In other departments, they must send many of us police to guard the man with the bag. Yes, yes, we are the police. Yes. Now, Nguyen Van Thu, perhaps you remember? He is your friend, the head waiter of the Metropolitan French Best Restaurant."

A wave of heated air washed over J.W. His legs wobbled as he searched the room for a place to sit. Instead, he leaned against the wall to steady himself, wondering if the handcuffs would be placed in front or behind his back. His shoulder still ached from a fall in Viet Nam, and he was about to ask the irons be to his front, but he understood he had besmirched the purity of the communist movement by having offered so obvious and offensive a bribe the evening before. There would be no mercy for a scoundrel who had so defiled Marxism.

His wife's words echoed in his skull: "Sweetheart, this is not America." She had not given J.W. a chance to answer before she added, "I love you so much, but we're not at home. Leave these people alone. They've suffered enough. You can't change the world."

J.W.'s reverie was broken by the grinning police officer who added, "Nguyen Van Thu, he neighborhood Communist Party committee leader, too important. He say you too kind Viet Nam people. So, now we invite you go village My Co. It not far. Of course, you must hire car. And you must have interpreter and driver. It is law. You must pay. Of course, you must pay American dollars only. It is law."

J.W. looked up blankly. "How much?"

The policeman took a deep breath. "Oh, not very money. Maybe three or five hundred dollar."

"Five hundred dollars? My Co's only forty or fifty miles away. I think I'll just find a cab. I could take the bus for thirty cents."

"Oh, we must not go My Co taxi bus. You see, Doctor, it much more money if far in countryside. Of course, you not have to go if'n you no want."

"Well then, I'll drive myself. Don't worry, I'll find a car. I know the roads."

The officer gasped. "Doctor, that not good plan. May I recommend we drive car? Our road too dangerous. If you have accident, you have pay so much."

"What if it's the other guy's fault?"

"Doctor, we try help you. It always you fault. Let us drive for you."

J.W. looked away from the officer toward the window that faced the street. Qui had hoisted himself precariously onto the sill and called quietly to J.W. "He is right. It is not good for a foreigner to drive in Viet Nam. There are many problems on the road. There have been many changes."

"Yes, many change," the officer added.

J.W. grunted, "Okay, okay. When can we go?"

"You must go tomorrow morning."

"That's fine. May we stay in the village overnight? The farmers will let us sleep in their huts. We will bring our own food and water. I used to sleep in the huts all the time. With *Bà* Binh, *Ông* Long..."

"I am sorry, Doctor. You must back before dark. And you must leave Viet Nam next day. Not change visa. We hope you tell all GI come our beautiful country."

Chapter 27

AT 5 A.M. the next morning, Qui was hunkered in front of the hotel dressed in a spotless, pressed, white shirt. When J.W. and his wife exited the hotel, the small man stood and nonchalantly recommended the Weathersbys consider bringing several platefuls of *chả giò* to the village as a gift. "I can show you where to buy this Viet Nam traditional food." Qui asked nervously, "Have you ever tried them?"

J.W. laughed, "Of course."

"Well, good. I can take you to the best *chả giò* in all of Saigon, maybe in all of Viet Nam."

J.W. nodded. losing himself in the memories of the steaming afternoon he, the chief, and the egg roll man had rested under the banyan tree in My Co. He could not remember if it was three or four decades ago, or all of time. His lips pursed in private embarrassment for having allowed himself to have taken even ten cents from the chief that day, but his chest quivered thinking he would soon be in My Co. He would repay *Ông* Khai a thousand-fold for his kindness and show him he'd never forgotten. He had become a doctor. He had graduated from the Sorbonne and sat in the very same lecture halls as Khai's father. He would regale Khai and his children with stories of an ignorant American in France. He'd show them photos of the Sorbonne, even the very room in which his father had lodged a century before. He would try not to cry when he gave *Ông* Khai the framed picture of the wall on which his father's name had been chiseled in stone for the scholarship J.W. had endowed in the Vu surname. In just a few hours, *Ông* Khai would see he had kept his promise to return, that he had never forgotten.

A long, green, brightly shined Honda limousine rolled to a stop in front of the hotel. The white-shirted passenger in the front seat opened the door and placed his foot on the ground, but J.W. was standing over him so quickly, the man could not exit the car. "Are you from the police, from the travel agency? You looking for Weathersby?"

"We Da By. You We Da By?"

"Yes. We are. When are we leaving? We don't have much time."

"Time. Time five-and-one-five."

"No, no. What time are we leaving?"

Though the man answered calmly, trying to form the words perfectly, the only sounds J.W. understood of the broken English was that his name was Ngo, and that he was to be their interpreter. Ngo apologized that he had gone to university in Moscow, and that while his Russian was strong, he spoke little English. "I have been told," the interpreter went on in Vietnamese, "that you speak our language, but just barely."

"Yes, a little." J.W. chuckled.

J.W. called over the car, "Sweetheart, I feel like a puddle of water-buffalo diarrhea. I can't speak Vietnamese, not today. I'm too nervous, and this guy's no help. What do you think?" Without hesitating, she motioned with her eyes toward Qui.

The first stop was the egg roll shop. J.W. fidgeted as Qui woke the owner, but his hands soon trembled as he watched the proprietor-turned-cook ever so slowly prepare bits of pork and shrimp. J.W. nearly lost consciousness when the man woke his children and sent them out to buy vegetables. Qui, the interpreter, and the driver were content to watch, explaining to J.W.'s wife the preparation of Viet Nam's national food. She, though, was distracted by her husband's pacing.

"Doctor, the farmers will love the *chả giò*," Qui nodded. "They will thank you as a friend."

"If we ever get there."

"Doctor, the village of My Co has been there for many centuries. It will still be there in an hour."

"No," J.W. answered, "it is hours and hours from here. It'll take an hour just to get to the bridge out of Sai…I mean Ho Chi Minh City."

But once the *chả giò* were loaded in the trunk, and the limousine turned west, J.W. became disoriented. Lush vegetation overhung the road. Gone were the wide stretches of open fields that had bordered the primitive highways, the foliage in those days having been devastated by Agent Orange. Gone were the ubiquitous forty and fifty-vehicle convoys of deuce-and-a-half and five-ton U.S. Army trucks plying the roads between Saigon and the provincial towns. There was, he shook his head, a rare, generations-old, captured, clap-trap American Army deuce-and-a-half wobbling along the neatly paved highway, its faded olive drab more rust-gray than army-green. Most of the vehicles they passed were late model 4 X 4s, Hondas, Mercedes, and thousands upon thousands, if not millions, of modern motor bikes.

As they crossed a new bridge over the Saigon River, the road opened up into a broad highway with macadam surfacing and white lines separating the lanes. Every few miles a set of stoplights appeared, the broad, digital screen counting down the seconds until the green flashed. J.W. tried to tell his wife that the road had once been mud and potholes, but it came out as a ramble, so he leaned back and held her hand silently.

At the My Tho signpost, J.W. asked the driver to stop to show his wife the 33rd Mech's field headquarters. But the young man looked to the interpreter and shrugged in quandary, adding indifferently in local dialect, "There's no army post in My Tho. This guy is nuts."

J.W. pointed and the driver complied, driving on muddy tracks through empty fields, finally stopping in a graveyard. There were a few water buffalo grazing where J.W. was confident the helipad had been. There was another expanse of brush and trees. They came to a flat, skinny swath in the scrub, which J.W. recognized as the residue of the main runway, and he got out to pace off several hundred yards until he came to the plot upon which Major Trott's trailer had caught fire, several times. He kicked at the dirt and came to one of the whitewashed rocks that had been the perimeter past which enlisted men and junior officers were not to venture. His eyes reddened. He was about to get his wife and show her, but all he could picture were the millions of dollars that had vaporized on that irrelevant, shadowy patch of weeds. He tried to avoid the memory of the countless helicopters that had launched from that sacred ribbon of earth and never returned.

He kicked dirt over the rock, returned to the car, and smiled weakly as he pointed the driver back to the main road. He asked his wife, "Why did they lie and say there was no base here? They could've just told us it was gone."

"I think they're too young to remember, maybe their parents, too"

Driving back toward the highway, J.W. spotted the carcass of a "D" model HUEY lying on its side in the garden of a tiny house. Gutted of engine and avionics, it served as a playhouse for a band of local children who chased each other around the faded remains. They ran when J.W. walked up to take pictures, but an even greater mass of older children took their place, gathering to watch J.W. climb through the wreckage, and soon peasants in conical hats and faded, threadbare, black pajamas arrived to hawk morsels of pineapple shreds, chunks of coconut, and glasses of warm tea. "What'd I tell ya, sweetheart"

The crowd followed as the car lurched and bumped back toward the highway and the crowded suburbs. A young girl on a bicycle several dozen sizes too large for her miniature frame wobbled along the road, and J.W. marveled at the continuity of life, remembering his own daughter bobbing and weaving, learning to ride a two-wheeler.

The child suddenly swerved hard toward the barely moving limousine, colliding with the back door on his wife's side. A few milliseconds prior to impact, though, the child lifted slowly off the bike and settled softly to the pavement. Once the girl was comfortable the ground, and sure the occupants of car were watching, her father began screaming from the sidewalk. The girl's arms and legs began flailing, and when the diver approached, she began to shake violently in a grand mal seizure, the features of which were new to Dr. Weathersby. J.W. threw open the door and ran to the child's side.

A crowd gathered immediately, soon doubling and quickly tripling. The rumpus intensified until Qui leapt from the limousine. "Comrades, this man is an American doctor. He will treat the young lady who foolishly rode her bicycle into this car." He turned to J.W. and groaned, "Tell them she is fine, and let's get back in the car and get out of here."

J.W. evaluated his patient, realized she had not so much as scraped a knee, and spoke to the throng in his finest Vietnamese. "Nah, she's okay," he reassured, raising his outstretched thumb skyward to the crowd and then to his wife, who had remained in the car, her face ashen.

J.W. started back to the car but stopped, turned to the child, and reached into his pocket. This tightened the crowd and elevated the volume of patter. J.W. pulled out a twenty and handed it to the girl. Before she could curl her fingers around the money, though, Qui snatched the bill away, pulled J.W. by a pant leg to the car, and shouted at the crowd. "Go home, there's nothing to see here."

"Doctor, we did not hit that girl; she hit us. This is why I respectfully advised you not to drive yourself to the village of My Co. If you do not cause an accident in my country, one will be arranged for you. You must not forget that you are the foreigner, and you have money, and you will be separated from that money, one way or the other, as fast as it can be taken from you. Please do not make it so easy."

The driver continued west, making turns, nodding confidently as the miles passed. After another hour, the chauffeur spoke to the interpreter, who turned to J.W. and asked in Vietnamese, "You know where is village My Co?"

"Wait a minute. I thought *you* knew."

"Police talk drive west. We drive west. They say you say you know."

"Well, shit. All I remember is that it's in Kien Tuong Province, but everybody tells me there is no Kien Tuong Province. Where are we now?"

"Long An Province."

"Can you find the town of Moc Hoa? My Co is a few miles west of there on Highway 29." J.W. turned to his wife. "Sweetheart, Moc Hoa, that's where I ran the night I escaped from the VC. I told you, didn't I?"

She nodded and spoke in a whisper. "Maybe we can stop and ask for directions. The old-timers might remember," but when J.W. translated for the driver, he shook his head obstinately and pushed harder on the gas pedal.

Another half-an-hour slid away, and though J.W. assumed Qui had not been able to see out of the car from his post scrunched between the driver and the interpreter, the little man counseled, "Oh, I think I know where we are, but first

I need to go to the toilet. Stop the car." He disappeared behind a row of shanties, and when he emerged less than a minute later, he spoke to the driver. "I do know where we are. If you go up this road maybe eight kilometers, that's Moc Hoa."

And three or so miles later, in fact, they came to the provincial town. J.W. ordered the driver to slow down so he could search the road for the American base at which he had been arrested. "It was right here. I'm sure; it was right along this road."

But they could not even find the empty field where the army post had once stood. J.W.'s wife squeezed his hand. She laughed, "I do remember. That was the night you peed your way out of captivity. And the Americans wouldn't feed you."

As they rolled through Moc Hoa, J.W. mumbled, "It's hard to believe that everything's gone. It all seemed so strong and secure. It was the United States Army. It was tough sergeants and angry troops, and majors and colonels chewing my ass every hour on the hour. They always threatened to send my sorry butt to jail or the DMZ, up with the marines. They had my life in their hands. I guess none of it mattered, did it?

"But it's in my head—concrete and steel. It really happened, but when you get here, all of a sudden, the memories aren't so sharp. Maybe none of it is." He paused and laughed sadly. "Sweetheart, I guess it's time to tell you the truth. I was never in Viet Nam. Wasn't even in the army. It was all a lie."

She answered, "Apparently!" When J.W.'s heart skipped, she took his hand. "Sweetheart, look, whether there's a base here or not half-a-century later, you escaped that night, and that made you a hero. Hardly anybody else did. Right? You know what happened here. You don't have to prove it to me or to any of these guys. It's okay. I know who you are. And you know what's better, you finally know who you are. That's got to be enough."

"Maybe, Sweetheart, but I'm not so sure of anything, 'cept that I cherish you."

J.W.'s memory of the distance he had traversed the night he escaped from the Viet Cong was as clouded as his other memories of Viet Nam, for within minutes of driving out of Moc Hoa, the limousine pulled into a luxuriant stand of trees. Hanging from the branches was succulent fruit, bright greens, reds, and purples. Some were star-shaped, some oval. He leaned out to photograph the foliage, happy to see the driver had learned to stop for pictures, but the driver also switched off the ignition, pushed his seat back, and spoke to the interpreter, who turned triumphantly to J.W. "*THIS* MY CO."

J.W. looked at his wife questioningly. "Sweetheart, they're screwing with us. This isn't My Co. There's no fruit trees, hey, no trees at all growing in My Co. It's all flat rice paddies and tobacco fields." He turned back to the interpreter. "Mr. Ngo, this is not My Co. I know My Co. I lived there a long time."

"Doctor," the interpreter spoke seriously to J.W. in Vietnamese, "look at the sign over the door there. It says, 'Communist Party Headquarters of the Village of My Co.'"

Indeed, a faded, hand-painted, red sign inscribed with those very words was tacked over the door of a wooden shed fifty feet off the road. It was at that moment the truth about his time in Viet Nam crystallized for the first time. Though he had seen the North Vietnamese soldiers riding tanks in the streets of Saigon on the newsreels in 1975, though he had studied the modern history of Viet Nam at the most prestigious universities in the Western world, though he knew from his poly sci textbooks that Viet Nam was ruled by a staunch communist regime, though he had seen, with his own eyes, the communist red flag of the Democratic Republic of Viet Nam waving over the airport in Saigon a week before, this was the first moment it became real that he had lost the war.

For a few minutes, J.W. sat mutely in the car. He finally glanced at his wife and at the men in the limousine, their shoulders taut, eyes twitching. J.W. forced himself back to the moment and smiled remotely. "Sweetheart, maybe this is My Co, but it's like a jungle now. It was all flat, for miles. You couldn't get a chopper in here now. No way. I don't care how good you are."

The car's occupants exhaled. The two Americans exited the car cautiously, J.W. taking a few steps, calling his wife forward with a tenuous hand signal, as if he sensed an ambush. They trouped in file through the dense foliage toward the shanty with the Communist Party Headquarters sign. "Look at those houses.

They're fancy brick," he whispered. "Look. There's glass in the windows! Do you see rice paddies anywhere?"

J.W.'s wife, her eyes staring from one unexpected vision to the next, laughed, "This is not what your slides look like at all. It's hard to believe." She pointed. "Look J.W., power poles. My Co has electricity. And did you notice, Sweetheart, the road's paved?"

J.W. took a deep breath to answer, but a group of children drifted over to the car and the peculiar visitors. The girls went to J.W.'s wife and stared at her bright blue, silk pant suit. The boys surrounded J.W. and pulled at the hair on his arms. A few children scrutinized Qui, until several older men arrived and shooed them away.

J.W. walked back to the car to retrieve his pictures of the village and *Ông* Khai. When he returned, what had been a tiny gathering had multiplied exponentially. Several generations of peasants gawked. The tranquility, however, lasted only until J.W. pulled pallid photographs from a manila folder. An echo swept through the assembly as the men and women of My Co realized the foreigner held images of them as children. They pointed to the pictures and picked out individuals in the crowd.

J.W. spoke to the interpreter. "Ask them if they know what happened to Vu Van Khai. He's the tall one standing next to me in this picture."

The interpreter turned to the mounting crowd of western-dressed citizens and repeated Weathersby's question. A handsome, middle-aged man in pressed pants and button-down-shirt stepped forward and took the picture with both hands, studying the image of the two figures in the peeling, brown and white Polaroid. A dozen younger villagers gathered to peruse the photo, though most drifted toward the car, more interested in the limousine's GPS system and internal television than in the foreigner.

The small man spoke briefly, and the interpreter turned back to the graying visitor. "He want to know who you are. I tell him you American. He say..."

The little man interrupted, his lips tightening as he wagged an index finger in the Caucasian stranger's face. He snatched the picture back, tapping hard with the nail of his index finger, *"Ông có biết Đại úy Weh Da By, không?"*

The interpreter translated perfunctorily. "He want to ask if you know Captain Wehdabee in America."

The American stepped closer, pointed to his own chest, and choked, "*Tôi là Weathersby.* I *am* Captain Weathersby."

The villager turned to the growing crowd. "*Trời đất ơi, Trời đất ơi! Đại úy Rào.*"

The interpreter laughed nervously. "He say, 'Oh, my God. Oh, my God!' Then he say you, 'Captain Iron Mustache, moustache like barb wire.'"

As the interpreter translated, the little man's eyes grew as large as the jack-fruit hanging in the lush gardens of the hamlet. He yanked up one leg of his trousers and, facing Weathersby, pointed to a mangled ankle. "Don't you remember me? I am Huong, *Em* Huong. The night I was in the explosion. You took me to the hospital. *Trời ơi* I was scared. Don't you remember? You drove the whole night to Tan An. My grandfather, the one with the wispy beard and the white turban? *Ông* Long? He's dead now. I was twelve. You saved my life. Don't you remember?"

"Yes," Weathersby answered slowly in tear-soaked Vietnamese, "of course I remember. Yes, I remember."

Ông Huong pulled J.W. by the hand into the wooden shack then sent several children to fetch coffee. J.W.'s wife followed closely, surreptitiously handing him a pack of Salems from her purse, a gift for *Ông* Khai, who J.W. assumed still loved the strong menthol.

Inside the shack, J.W. and his wife were placed at the head of a rough-hewn picnic table as a council of old men took seats around it. J.W. offered the pack of cigarettes to *Ông* Huong with two hands. Huong proffered them to the elders. The ancient men smiled as if J.W. had presented them with the finest of Cuban cigars. When Huong realized J.W. hadn't taken a cigarette for himself, he apologized and placed one respectfully in J.W.'s hands.

Ông Huong took out a lighter and leaned forward toward J.W., who drew in a first puff but put the cigarette into an ashtray and again showed Huong the picture of *Ông* Khai. "Do you remember this man? He was the village chief in 1969."

Ông Huong glanced momentarily at the picture. He spoke dispassionately. "He is dead."

"Dead? When?"

"I think 1970. Right after you returned to your country. He was sitting at the market early in the morning drinking a cup of coffee. Yes, I remember the day. He was shot."

"Who did it?" J.W. whispered, choking, his eyes reddening.

The surrounding elders were silent—rigidly so. A young boy at the window made a comment, and one of the old men lifted his hand threatening a slap.

J.W. calmed himself and asked, "What about his family? Where is his wife?"

Huong shrugged. "I don't know, Captain. It has been many, many years. Who knows?"

J.W., having spoken in Vietnamese, realized his wife was unaware of the fate of the man they had traveled so far to find. But she saw by his tears that *Ông* Khai was gone. She became riveted by his pallor and took his hand.

Huong relit J.W.'s Salem then his own. The other men lit up, and soon the tiny room was thick with yellow smoke.

J.W. was quiet for a bit. He turned to his wife and whispered, "Sweetheart, I'm not feeling so good. Gimme a minute." She put her hand on his arm, and he tried to smile. "I'll be okay."

He stood abruptly, excused himself, and left the shack to drift about. Nearly half-a-century had not intervened. The Sorbonne, medical school, and a daughter named Khai were a fantasy. Suddenly, he was in My Co, a captive again of the Viet Cong, standing outside a hut waiting to be executed.

In the thick bushes behind the Communist Party Headquarters, J.W. retched. He screamed at himself, "You will die like a man," but he vomited again violently, tears clouding his vision, the roar in his ears isolating him from the world. When his wife heard him cry out again, "I will die like a fuckin' man!" she ran to his side. She hugged him so tightly, he sobbed harder, but soon her warmth comforted him, and he looked out from his black tunnel at the well-fed children, at Qui, the interpreter, and the sleeping limousine driver.

Slowly, J.W. calmed, grasping that he had suffered a break with reality, a simple anxiety attack. He was not to be executed, those memories simply an artifact of a potent toxin locked for so long, so deeply within him, he had had no idea it existed.

His wife held him even more tightly and asked quietly through her own tears, "Sweetheart, how have you managed to live with this for so long? You never said a word."

While J.W. had encountered such melancholy in the souls of thousands of his patients over the years, he had always believed the miasma that surrounded them to be of their own doing, a matter of dementia, of insanity, diagnoses he would never entertain or tolerate in himself. "I really am out of my fucking mind, huh?"

"How have you managed?"

Chapter 28

J.W. REFUSED ANOTHER cigarette, or coffee, or tea. He sat silently with the men in the shed and tried to smile. *Ông* Huong presided over the makeshift ceremony.

Qui asked J.W., "Did you know that Mr. Huong is the village chief now? He said that if it wasn't for you, he wouldn't have lived to be here now. He says if it wasn't for you, many of the children you knew would not have grown up."

Huong spoke, though J.W. did not understand.

Qui translated. "He asks if you remember the time you were captured?"

"Tell him I have a hard time forgetting. Sticks in me craw, if you take my meaning."

Qui cocked his head but turned to Huong. "Yes, I think he said he remembers."

The chief continued, laughing. "We knew everything you were doing. The VC knew everything. When you escaped, we let you go. If they had killed you, My Co would have been destroyed by the Americans, and if that happened, there would have been no way to get rice and supplies to the freedom fighters in the jungle. They didn't want to release you, but we villagers convinced them. We knew you would come back."

J.W. laughed uneasily and asked Qui in Vietnamese, "Please don't translate that into English. My wife thinks I'm a great hero."

Qui smiled, "Okay, that's our secret."

"Nah, I'm kidding. Go ahead. She'll laugh, too."

But when Qui rendered the translated story, he hemmed and hawed with a patter that was more pigeon than English. "The chief say you capture and rice for VC and after capture, rice for VC and no bombs for My Co."

Before J.W.'s wife had a chance to decipher the message, Qui hopped onto his feet and asked the village chief to invite J.W. and the entourage for a stroll through the hamlet. Huong nodded and took J.W. by the hand.

J.W. touched his wife's face softly, the women gasped in envy, and the men smiled, perhaps happy that the old captain had found a measure of comfort in his life. He spoke softly to her. "I'll tell you what he said later."

The growing congregation walked along the paved road for a few yards toward a clearing. The chief asked, "Do you remember the school you built? It was right here, but it has been rebuilt by our government."

Coming around a stand of jackfruit and banana trees, J.W. stopped, astounded. On the patch of sand where he'd helped build the one, and then two-room, schoolhouse, sat a modern, three-story building. "The My Co School" read a sign emblazoned in proud, red letters on the roof.

On wobbly legs, J.W. walked toward the building and tried the door to one of the classrooms, but the chief told him the building was locked for summer vacation. Looking through a window of a first-floor classroom, J.W. spied a computer on the teacher's desk next to an LCD monitor, one larger than on the desk of his wife's classroom.

Huong turned to one of the men and asked him to find the principal and get the keys. The man asked around and was told the principal had driven up to Tuyen Binh to visit her in-laws.

J.W. stuttered, "What part of the village are we in now, Mr. Huong? Where was the army post where the American soldiers lived? Happy Valley Defensive Position?"

The chief smiled and answered, "You are standing in the middle of it right now, Captain." He gestured across the road to a thicket of tropical growth fifty yards away and added, "That is the market you and the old chief built."

J.W. raised his eyes toward the small structure. Huong pulled his guest's shirtsleeve and guided J.W. around a slight bend in the road toward the market. J.W. stopped abruptly, his face flushing. In front of the market, tacked to the old flagpole, was a sign: "My Co BP Station." There were two gasoline pumps and one diesel nozzle. The market's walls were now cinderblock, and the front was glassed in. He peered inside at the sodas, beer, cigarettes, toothbrushes, and lottery tickets.

All that was left of *Ông* Khai's dream was the bare cement floor and the roof. J.W. broke away from the crowd and marched through the door, stopping at the northeast corner. A display of chips and crackers stood there, but he slid the wire stand aside. The handprint he had secretly embossed forty-three years before had not been erased. He considered calling out to his wife to show her, but as the pressure in his chest built, he glided the shelves back into place and whispered, "Excuse me," as he returned to the gaggle of silent onlookers.

Farther up the road, they came to a brick house. J.W. drifted toward the door and peeked into the large room, noting a dirty tile floor dotted with several wooden tables and a dozen plastic chairs. In the corner stood a bar, behind which a man was busily repairing a video tape deck. The technician looked up, a generous, hand-rolled cigarette hanging from the corner of his mouth. The scent drew J.W. back to the harsh, Vietnamese tobacco he had at first been forced to inhale, and soon craved. The man looked up, spoke to the village chief, and sprang to his feet to greet J.W. "Do you remember me? I was a kid, *Em* Lan. I hit you in the eggs one day when you told me to go back to school and promise the teacher that I wouldn't fight or steal anymore. Don't you remember? I was a bad kid then. Come in, come in. Have some beer. I'll sell it to you cheap."

But the village chief took J.W. by the hand and led him out. "That's the karaoke bar. He runs it. He's still a bad kid."

As the entourage trekked north along the road, old ladies emerged from their homes to see the visitors, and when the village chief told the women who it was, many rushed over laughing wildly, "You were the one who was supposed to marry me! Yeah, but you liked *Bà* Lin instead. Don't you remember? Hey, do you want to see *Bà* Lin?"

J.W. gasped, but the chief smiled and pulled him along. "Ninety percent of the people remember you. All the old ladies think you are handsome. They want to know if you remember *Bà* Lin, and if you came back to find her."

"I remember her, but I'm married." J.W. paused a moment longer than he should have and finally asked, "Ah, is she here?"

"Not today. Oh, she is the school principal. She's the one who's in Tuyen Binh visiting her in-laws."

J.W. asked softly, "Is she married?"

"Oh, yes. Many children. Her husband is the district police chief."

"And *Bà* Binh?"

"*Bà* Binh? Of course, *Bà* Binh, *Bà* Lin's aunt. She is the oldest of the citizens of My Co. She is ninety-one years, maybe more. She lives with *Bà* Lin and her family. Right there, just up the road. How do you remember her, Captain?" *Ông* Huong pointed toward a copse of exotic, tropical growth a couple of hundred yards up the road.

J.W. asked with a wavering voice, "I do. I did. She's alive? Is she there now. I mean today, now. Is *Bà* Binh there?"

Ông Huong held up his hand to stop the procession. He pulled a smart phone from his pocket, pushed a few buttons, and placed it to his ear. In a second, he was screeching into the tiny device, and after several unintelligible phrases, he pushed a button and dropped it without thought into his pocket. He turned to J.W. and nodded, "*Bà* Binh is at home. She is napping, but a neighbor is over there and is going to wake her."

As they began the short walk, J.W. began to shiver and sweat as if he had just run the miles the night of his getaway. The nausea rebuilt. He ran from the minions that had now built to several hundred souls, the children still more interested in the hair on J.W.'s arms than visiting the most ancient of the hamlet's souls.

J.W. loped toward one of the new homes, around the side, and behind the structure. He retched for a minute, but quickly stood straight up, slapped himself in the face twice, then walked, head held rigidly aloft, back to the silent mass.

From inside a profoundly deep crevice in his mind, J.W. felt the direction he must walk to get there and nearly took the lead in his impatience, but grasped his wife's hand and let the elders steer the way. Whispering in her ear, J.W. weakly apologized for his behavior, but she squeezed his hand and drew him as close as she could. After another thirty yards, he whispered again, "Wait 'till you see this hootch. Remember I told you about the little fire in the corner. Bet'cha she'll make tea. And we need to drink it. Not to worry—the water's been boiled."

Ông Huong mentioned as they walked that *Bà* Lin had had the old house torn down decades before, and that her family had rebuilt three times since; first a modest wood structure, then a small brick home, and when the family's fortunes and those of the village and country had blossomed, they tore down all remnants of the past and built a brick and stucco home that spanned nearly twelve-hundred square feet. At the thick patch of trees, the procession walked up a neat gravel driveway, past a pair of nicely painted, decorative wrought iron gates securing a carport at the far end. A Honda 4X4 sat in the enclosure. The house itself was surrounded by a stand of fruit trees and flowering bushes.

Village Chief Huong nodded toward the Honda and mentioned casually, "Ah, *Bà* Lin's car is back. Maybe she's home."

One of the ladies called out, "She is back, but she went running out of the house a few minutes ago. Look like she'd seen a ghost."

J.W.'s gut clenched, and he turned off the road, afraid he'd be sick again, but he caught movement from inside the wide doorway as an ancient creature hobbled toward the portal. J.W.'s eyes exploded open, but there were shrieks from the entourage as several of the women rushed forward to grab the old lady and steer her back into the house. Even Huong gasped as he realized the woman had emerged from her bedroom without pants. An instant later, she reappeared fully clothed, limping out to stare at J.W. for a moment until *Ông* Huong told her the mustachioed captain had returned to My Co just to see her. She chortled, became very quiet, and J.W. sighed that the ancient being was totally demented, incapable of recognizing even her own children. He was suddenly saddened that he had come to the village, fearful he had made the grandest mistake of his life. As his head drooped, the woman virtually lunged at J.W., breaking into a howl of tears. She pinched his cheek as passionately, perhaps harder, than she had during the war.

J.W. asked Huong how old *Bà* Binh really was, and he reiterated, "Ninety-one."

J.W. laughed to his wife, "You married a moron. If *Bà* Binh is ninety-one now, she was only fifty, if that, when I met her. I swear I thought she was ninety-one back then. And I thought she was *Cô* Lin's grandmother. Wonder how much else I got wrong."

Before J.W.'s wife could answer, *Bà* Binh was dragging J.W. through the door into the living room, where she pushed him into a mahogany rocking chair.

J.W.'s wife was shown a seat on a wicker couch across from the flat screen, HD TV, which was tuned to a daytime quiz show, the Bob Barker of Saigon cackling about the grand prize of five million Vietnamese Dong, two-hundred-and-seventy-five dollars. *Bà* Binh asked one of the kids to turn on the air-conditioner, and another young lady to bring tea, unless the captain wanted a cold beer from the fridge in the kitchen. Several young people moved into and out of the house, wiping feet carefully before stepping onto the ornate tile floor.

A lovely woman, perhaps in her in her early twenties, rushed into the house and stopped breathlessly in front of *Bà* Binh. J.W. became lightheaded. She was even more beautiful than he had remembered. The woman carried in her arms a tiny baby girl dressed in a pristine pink top and matching pants. *Bà* Binh and the young woman whispered for a moment, then *Bà* Binh pointed toward the strange visitor and waved the back of her hand at the girl, motioning for her to twist around and greet their guests. When the young woman turned shyly toward J.W., she bowed slightly and smiled with a warmth that stopped J.W.'s heart.

Bà Binh creaked, pointing to the young woman, "This is *Bà* Lin's granddaughter, and the little one is her great-granddaughter." The infant burst into tears when she focused on the foreign apparition, so J.W. began to look away. His heart stopped and he turned back abruptly. Unable to stop himself, he moved closer to the child and reached forward softly to brush his fingers along the baby's earrings.

J.W. took his wife's hand and kissed her cheek. He whispered, "It's time to go home."

As they motored out of the village, J.W. stared at the neat houses and the cars. Toward the end of town, they passed an attractive brick home from which a delicately thin woman with long grey hair peered intently through a glass window. Their eyes locked, and he stared at her for a second longer than was comfortable. J.W. turned away but gasped and snapped his head back. The woman, though, had vanished.

Other Titles by William S. Gould, MD

At Yonah Mountain

BRAND NEW SECOND Lieutenant J.W. Weathersby is on orders to depart for a combat tour in Viet Nam. At a West Point wedding, though, he commits a very public faux pas and is thrust as punishment into a class of 160 select young officers who sweat and freeze through months of brutal training at the United States Army Ranger School. J.W. joins an African American PhD candidate and a Rose Bud Sioux Harvard graduate, the three pushed together to trudge the mountains, forests, and deserts as Ranger buddies. As half the class is weeded out, they share their disparate lives and dreams. J.W. struggles to be cut from the program, and at the same time fights desperately to remain. At Yonah Mountain is a coming of age adventure, an examination of race relations in the military, and an authentic tale of Army Ranger training.

In Black Granite

In Black Granite is set in the decade after J.W. Weathersby returns from the war in Viet Nam. He eventually accepts the assessment of family, friends, and medical school deans that he will never become a doctor. He drifts without focus until the miracle of his first child's birth rekindles the craving to study medicine. This is a narrative of his dogged struggle to beat the overwhelming odds against a man in his mid-thirties gaining admission to an American college of medicine. In Black Granite scrutinizes the ruthless battle for places in medical school, and how the psyches of the chosen are sieved as they are herded through the decade as students and residents. The strain of endless days and nights away from family, of sleepless months, and of pervasive arrogance, distort the souls of even the strongest. Some find the path more treacherous than surviving a war.

C.O.L.A.

THE DAY HIS father died, Dr. Solomon Forte promised his mother he would honor the man's memory by dedicating his years as a doctor to the treatment of injured workers. It seemed so clear a decision—his patients would be like his dad, stoic, honest, working class stiffs who sought nothing more from a doctor than an arm around the shoulder, a word of reassurance, and an ally in dealing with the state industrial insurance system. His life at the Whitaker Hospital and Medical Center is, though, the antithesis of his dream. He can't tell which of the roadblocks is most daunting: that posed by his medical colleagues, the threats of S.M.A.C., the State Medical Abuse Commission, the bureaucracy at C.O.L.A., the state's Commission on Labor Affairs, or the duplicitous patients, some of whom spend every waking moment trying to dupe him out of drugs and government benefits. Occasionally, a case is obvious–the worker really was devastated by an industrial accident. It seems to Sol, though, that those are the very patients C.O.L.A. torments. On the other hand, claimants skilled at ripping off the Commission run free for decades. C.O.L.A. also examines the specter of serious medical errors, and how they are so much easier to make on patients whose care is mired in the aggravation of government-sponsored insurance plans. Questions are also raised about the state-appointed morality commissions that determine which doctors relinquish their licenses for treating pain. Finally, it is a disturbing look behind the scenes of a modern, multi-specialty medical clinic.

A Heart Wind from the Desert

Dr. Solomon Forte has lost everything. There is little left but to offer himself to the wretched in war-torn Sudan. Arriving in the desert, heart brimming with hope, it does not take long to recognize that the social and political beliefs that have spawned the war and famine are the very forces that prevent him from carrying out his dream of caring for the dispossessed. At first, despite the warnings of the tiny European medical team left at the refugee camp in Darfur Province, he fights back with typical, strident, American resolve to save the entire population of refugees. The obstacles of central African life, however, soon draw the spirit from him, and he turns his efforts to preserving the lives of his Western companions. He falls deeply for a gorgeous, but outwardly hardened, British nurse. When she disappears from camp, he spends what strength is left searching for her. A Heart Wind from the Desert examines the need in all of us to accomplish something meaningful in the tiny fragment of time we are allotted, and the impossible hurdles faced when trying to change the way people have thought and behaved for the millennia. It is a tale of beautiful, warm children, but also of the stark life in the sub-Saharan Sahel.

Raphael's Blanket

RAPHAEL BLUMENKOPF IS born clandestinely at the Bergen Belsen Nazi death camp on the 14th of April, 1945. His birth is an unprecedented miracle, as is the liberation of the camp by British forces that very afternoon. He has only his mother and a few surviving villagers from their home in Checzonovska, Poland. While the majority of the refugees leave Central Europe for Israel and the West, his band travels across Russia to China. A relative has promised jobs in Shang Hai's old Jewish settlement. The journey is fraught with threats from starving Russians, barbaric border guards, and destitute Chinese peasants. Just as the lives of the immigrants begin to normalize in China, the victory of Mao Zedong's communist army forces them to flee, this time to Hanoi. Five years later, the communist movement in North Viet Nam topples the French government, and the Jews run again. They settle in Saigon until the unrest there compels them to emigrate to America. Raphael's years in the U.S. are colored indelibly by the poison that follows him from the Holocaust, and he formulates a plan to extract revenge from a Federal judge with ties to the Nazis. Who could have envisaged the price he'd pay?

Lincoln Friday

LINCOLN FRIDAY IS born into nothing, an obscure, dirt farmer's son, destined to live dominated by the jagged edges of two wars. His early years are an endless series of losses, yet he struggles back after each blow, and slowly, a strongbox of dreams emerges from the fog of his hopelessness.

The harshest test of Lincoln's life, though, comes when the effects of his exposure to Agent Orange devastate both his and his daughter's lives. While the Fridays fight back passionately, the courts, Congress, and the VA turn their backs on them.

In the end, his deeds were neither profound nor dazzling, but he left his mark on disparate people in disparate lands. The world he touched chafed less for his quiet dignity.

www.ingramcontent.com/pod-product-compliance
Lightning Source LLC
Chambersburg PA
CBHW060346260626
47160CB00006B/2217
* 9 7 8 0 9 9 1 2 2 3 7 5 6 *